Praise for the books of
Carole Cummings

———◆———

"*Blue on Black* is a fresh new take on the Steampunk genre, combining imaginative technology with mind twisting mystery and adventure. A character driven story, there's plenty here for readers to enjoy.

Amazing Stories

———◆———

Sonata Form is "a sweet standalone romantic fantasy that's richly imagined"

Publishers Weekly

———◆———

More books by Carole Cummings

NOW AVAILABLE

Sonata Form

Blue on Black

The Aisling Trilogy
Guardian
Dream
Beloved Son

Don't Fear the (Not Really Grim) Reaper

COMING SOON

The Queen's Librarian

The *Wolf's-Own* Series

Carole Cummings

Copyright Information

SONATA FORM
Published by
FOREST PATH BOOKS

P. O. Box 847 – Stanwood, WA – USA
info@forestpathbooks.com

SONATA FORM Copyright © 2020 by Carole Cummings. All rights reserved.

This is a work of fiction. All characters in the publication are fictitious, or are historical figures whose words and actions are fictitious. Any other resemblance to names, incidents, or real persons, living or dead, is purely coincidental.

Forest Path Books supports writers and copyright. This book is licensed for your personal enjoyment only. Thank you for helping us to defend our authors' rights and livelihood by acquiring an authorized edition of this book, and by complying with copyright laws by not using, reproducing, transmitting, or distributing any part of this book without permission.

Forest Path Books publications may be purchased for educational, business, or sales/promotional use.
For information, please email the publishers at:
info@forestpathbooks.com
or address:
Forest Path Books, LLC
P. O. Box 847, Stanwood, WA 98292 USA

Front cover art © 2020 by Zaya Feli
https://zayafeli.com
Cover content is for illustrative purposes only, and any person depicted on the cover is a model.
Kymbrygh map © OllieR
https://www.instagram.com/fartingimp/

Stay informed on Forest Path Books releases & news.
Join the reading group/newsletter at:
https://forestpathbooks.com/into-the-forest

Library of Congress Control Number: 2020918337
ISBN: 978-1-951293-18-5 (trade paper)
ISBN: 978-1-951293-17-8 (e-book)

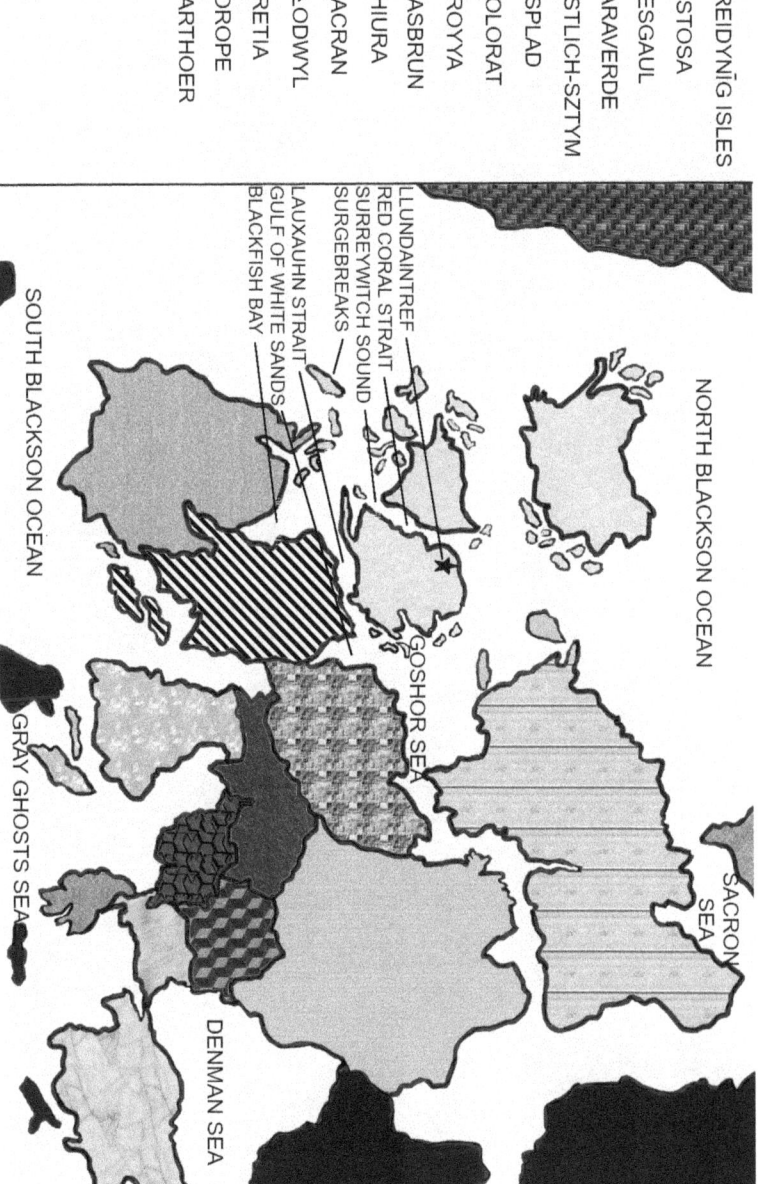

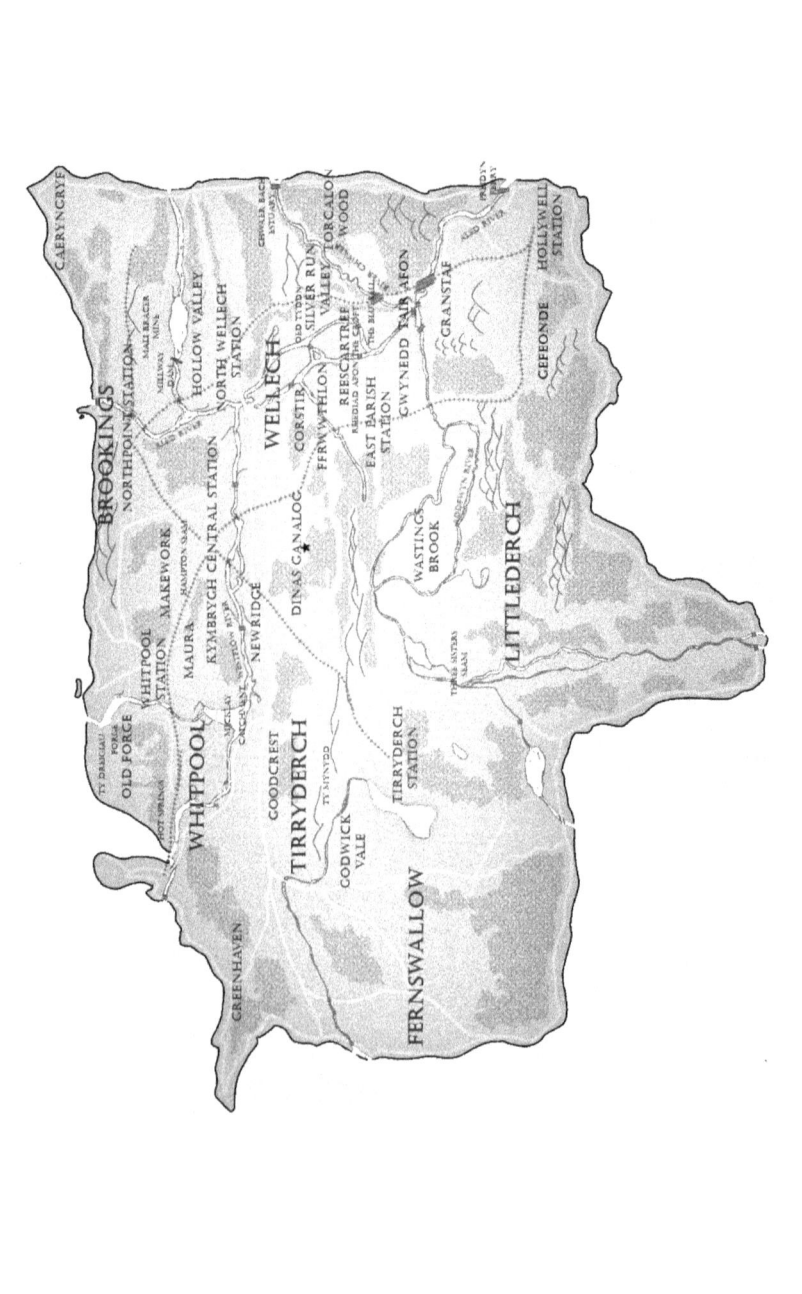

For Pam

BOOK ONE:
TIMBRE

Chapter 1—Exposition

: the opening section of a Classic sonata form in which the two opposing key centers are exposed to the listener for the first time

Getting punched in the face, Milo was abruptly forced to admit, hurt just as much now as it had back in primary school. More, since this was no pudge-knuckled fist swung with all the strength of a nine-year-old. Though, Milo's brain took an inconvenient moment to reflect, there was exactly as much surprise involved now as there had been back when Freddy Jenkins dy Moss had decided "by-blow" rolled more easily from his obnoxious tongue than "Milo" did.

Milo had taken exception.

"This is assault, you know." Milo straightened, fingers tapping lightly at his throbbing bottom lip and coming away unquestionably bloody.

"More like serving and protecting," was the bored response from the Warden, nothing more than a too-tall, too-broad shape blocking Milo's way in the fog-drenched pitch.

It was dark, too dark, which was what had started all of... *this*. No moon, no stars, the indigo of twilight long since fettered to murky black opaqued by river fog. And these idiots had dropped their lamp. Milo had been trying to be *helpful*.

The one in Milo's blindspot had yet to let go of Milo's shoulder. The grip was rapidly becoming as much of a problem as the unfurling thump in his jaw. Tendons probably weren't supposed to grind into bone like that.

"Protecting from what, exactly?" Milo leaned against the hold to spit the taste of metal from his mouth, dabbing at his lip with the back of his hand. "It was a bloody *magelight*, you great, spineless ogre."

Indignation was quickly overriding surprise as Milo tried again to shrug away the hand on his shoulder and couldn't. Fighting harder would only make his jaw throb. He could swear the emergent ache pulsed in time to the rippling tempo of the river beneath the bridge—upon which he'd just been *assaulted*.

He prodded his lip some more. "I swear, if you've loosened teeth I'll have your guts."

Milo had good teeth. And he'd like to keep them.

"And that's a threat to a Warden of Wellech." This voice was female and sounded more irate than the man who'd done the punching. The grip on Milo's shoulder shifted to the back of his neck. *Squeezed*. "What d'you say, Andras? That's enough to charge him with—"

"Hoy, what's the trouble there?"

It came from across the bridge, loud and deep and somehow arrogant, and Milo could swear he heard amusement beneath it. He couldn't see for the wide shape of the brute—Andras, apparently—in front of him, but he could hear the hollow clop of hoofbeats on the boards of the bridge as the man approached. Dim light came with him, haloing Andras, so at least this new arrival carried a lamp, unlike these other two halfwits.

Damn, now it was three against one. If Milo wasn't growing so patently *furious* about the injustice of being accosted then assaulted while minding his own damned business, he might take a moment to cultivate a bit of concern over being so obviously outnumbered.

Rather than loosening the grip on Milo, the woman who had hold of him tightened it, making Milo wince and curl his shoulders up as she said, "Suspicious person caught trying to cross the Outpost, sir."

"*Suspicious*!" This time Milo didn't hold back—he shot a warding hex at the woman to make her let go, and when she did with a yelp, he ignored the heavy-looking truncheon Andras brandished nearly in front of Milo's nose.

"I was nothing of the sort!" Milo directed his ire at the man who'd paused in the middle of the bridge to dismount and lead his horse toward them. "I was merely *existing—which,* last I checked, I'm permitted to do—when these two accosted me and demanded my papers, and when I tried to hand them over, I was *assaulted*!" He held his bloody fingers out as proof, though he had no hope anyone could actually see them. "Is this how the Wardens of Wellech always behave? No wonder the rest of Kymbrygh think you lot are a pack of inbred—"

"Yeah, you might want to pin that," the man drawled as he hooked his shaded lamp to a sling across the horse's withers. Slow-stepping closer, he nudged aside Andras and handed him the horse's reins. "I've a feeling you've already made a couple enemies, and...." Gingerly, he set a finger to the tip of Andras's truncheon and pushed it aside. "Wouldn't want to make one of me as well, I'm thinking."

It was pleasant, almost jovial, but threat ran through it as obviously as light through clear glass. He looked like he'd have no problem carrying it out too. His glimmer-limned silhouette was tall and broad, and he held himself with the calm authority of one who knew his strengths and how to use them. A truncheon twin to Andras's hung at the man's belt, the skirt of his long coat pulled aside to expose it—subtle menace no doubt. A wide-brimmed hat made it impossible to see anything but a meager gleam of eyes in the dark.

"*I've* made no enemies." Milo said it evenly but didn't try to dampen the undercurrent of fury to it. "*These two*, on the other hand, will be reported directly to the Kymbrygh MP's office once I've concluded my business here in Wellech."

"Reported for what?"

"Reported for—?" Milo gaped. "Didn't I *already say* for assault?"

Proper tamping now, he threw his hands out, refusing to flinch or even acknowledge it when Andras's truncheon came up again. The horse blew with a shift of hoofs on the boards, clearly picking up on the tension. The man in front of Milo, however, the one obviously in charge, didn't so much as twitch.

"Is everyone here ignorant as well as asinine?" Milo demanded. "I admit I haven't been to Wellech in years, but I don't recall it being an actual *crime* to enter, and I'm *quite* certain getting punched in the face for trying to comply with a request is not considered serving *or* protecting by people who are actually *sane*!"

"Y' got punched in the face for attempting to use magic for harm," Andras put in, clearly piqued.

"It. Was. A. *Magelight!*"

The woman sidled out to stand shoulder-to-shoulder with Andras. "It was magic out of the dark with no warning and without permission. You deliberately—"

"*Permission?* Since when do I need—since when does *anyone* need—?" The mix of outrage and exasperation was making it difficult for Milo to form sentences. "And anyway, it was magic *because* it was dark! I was trying to be *nice*!"

"By threatening—"

"Wait, wait, wait, wait, wait." The man in charge held up a hand. He waited until all heads turned his way before he said, "Rhywun Andras. Rhywun Bethan." Calm. Flat. "Where is your lamp?"

Andras and Bethan were silent for a moment, before Bethan cleared her throat. "Fell in the river, sir."

"...Ah-ha. I see."

"It was an accident."

"Yes. No doubt."

"Because they were too busy chatting to each other when I approached," Milo put in, unapologetically bitter. "I said 'pardon me,' and *this one*"—he pointed an accusing finger at Andras—"yipped like I'd just goosed him, and there went the lantern."

"Syr." This from Andras, loud and fairly indignant, and said directly to the new arrival. "He's wearing... and he's got...." Andras waved his great hand at Milo. "He's clearly Dewin Sect."

It shook Milo rigid. He was used to people knowing what he was just by looking at him. He'd never once had such in-his-face cause to view it as a possible drawback. Not until now. The sigil-etched gold earring was a right he'd earned through years of study and practice, and he wore it proudly. In retrospect, perhaps *too* proudly, considering he was in Wellech. Prejudice had been an infrequent thing in Milo's admittedly rarified practical experience thus far, but it wasn't like he wasn't aware of its existence. It would be rather difficult to remain ignorant considering what was going on only half a continent away, and with the Purity Party twaddle getting louder every day. Only, he hadn't actually run into it facefirst before. And the powerless disbelief and newness of it *stung*.

"I am." Milo squared his shoulders. "Dewin Sect, that is." He addressed the man who was clearly a superior to Andras and Bethan, and so far the only one who was actually *listening* to Milo. "Funny, though. That's never been cause for anyone to treat me like a criminal before." He lifted his chin. "Has Wellech taken to outlawing orthodoxies they don't like?"

The man sighed as though this was all just too trying for him. *For him*! "Now let's not get carried away. This is not—"

"*Carried away!*"

"It was magic in the dark!" Bethan burst out, overloud and offended. As though she had the *right*.

It silenced everyone for a moment. The River Aled bustled beneath their feet, all cheerful and minding its own busy affairs. The fog, by contrast, seemed to gain oppressive weight, sinking into lung and bone with a chill that stoppered breath and shuddered right down Milo's spine.

The man broke the uncomfortable hush with a weary-sounding "Uh... *huh*." He dipped his head, rubbed at his chin. "So." He blew out what sounded like an exasperated sigh. "Am I to understand, then, that this"—he waved to encompass all of them—"came about because this man tried to supply a magelight by which to see the papers you asked him to produce upon broaching the Outpost and attempting to cross the bridge?"

Milo huffed and rolled his eyes to the heavens. "*Finally!*"

"Hush, you," said the man and turned back to the other two. "Rhywun Bethan?"

Bethan lifted her chin. "Syr, we were given instructions to be extra vigilant tonight in light of the coven assembling. Your tad wanted no trouble, and said we were to—"

"Bethan." The man hadn't raised his voice, hadn't moved, but it cut Bethan off clean. "Tell me—who is the First Warden of Wellech? Would that be my tad?"

Bethan's silhouette slumped. "No, syr. That would be you, of course."

...Wait.

"Your... tad," said Milo. "First Warden." He tried to squint through the dark, but he still couldn't see anything but shapes. "Is that... is that Elly?"

The man twitched. "It's *Ellis*, yes. Ellis Morgan dy Rees." He paused. "Do I know you?"

"Well, it's been years, but I should hope you wouldn't have forgot entirely. And if you'll permit me to produce a magelight without getting punched in the face for it, I reckon we can find out."

Another pause, this one shorter, after which the man waved a hand and said, "By all means."

Smiling now, perhaps a bit smug, Milo flicked his fingers until a soft little globe flared at the tips, a wash of yellow-blue skimming the faces of Bethan, Andras, and... well. Magelight was always chancy, cutting out shapes in monochrome blues and skewing them with shadows that didn't belong. But Milo's memory was already busy filling in blanks that seemed to have shifted beyond it, melding it to *here* and *now*, and the result was... interesting.

Ellis had changed. *A lot*. Taller, of course, and broader—*so much broader*—and the podge of youth in the brown cheeks had honed to bold angles, nose straight with a slight upturn, and a wide, firm jaw that looked like it could bite through leather. His hair was longer, a crimp-curled sweep across wide shoulders, lighter now than the bark-brown sunstreaked with auburn Milo remembered. The eyes, though... well, Milo couldn't see them in the dark, really, but he'd wager they were that same fathomless slate, uptilted at the corners so Ellis always looked like he was enjoying a private joke, possibly at your expense.

"Duwies and all the goddesses." Ellis rubbed at his mouth; Milo suspected it was to hide a grin. Shaking his head, Ellis kept his eyes on Milo but said to Bethan and Andras, "You've no idea who this is, have you?"

Andras scowled. "That's what we were trying to find out." Petulant.

There were so many retorts Milo could give to that. He kept his mouth shut, and merely shrugged at Ellis.

Ellis rolled his eyes but finally dragged his gaze from Milo to turn it on Bethan and Andras. He opened a hand toward Milo.

"If this man had wanted to attack you with magic, rest assured, you'd be nothing more than a couple of greasy streaks of ash right now. And while I appreciate your extra vigilance this evening to keep any threat away from the coven while they meet, you might want to consider the fact that the only reason this man is not sitting Second Chair in said coven is because he's yet to sit the rites. Also, Meistr Eluned refuses to die, but that's another matter and not the point. The point *is* that the only reason he's not sitting First Chair"—Ellis paused with a grin and dropped his hand—"is because his mam is."

So, that... was not the way Milo would have liked Ellis to handle this.

Firstly, it was mostly inflammatory, vicarious boasting. Milo was still newyddian, after all; he wouldn't receive the adept—arbenigwr—rank until after he'd sat the rites this evening. And he had a long way to go to even get within touching-distance of a meistr rank, let alone lead a coven.

And secondly, the instant and shocked regard from Bethan and Andras was already heating Milo's cheeks and making him want to sink through the boards of the bridge. Fused so abruptly with the lingering wrath, it was all coming together to make his stomach roil.

"Your mam is *the* Black Dog?" Bethan's voice was again overloud but her tone this time was eager.

"The Black Dog Corp is a myth," Milo said, reflex, because it was how his mam always answered any hint of that question—instant denial; instant scorn. He shrugged. "But yes, my mam is C—"

"Ceri Priddy." Andras was apparently so awed he'd forgot his truncheon entirely; it hung limp at his side now, his grip loose enough Milo could probably snag it and whack him with it if he wanted to. He sort of wanted to. Almost breathless, Andras said, "The Witch of the Namurs Front, and Angel of Marnet."

Milo scowled. "She's Dewin too, since that seems to matter to you, and so prefers the term 'mage' over 'witch.' And I'd like to see someone try to call the Offeiriad of the Kymbrygh Coven an angel to her face. It's not even the same sect!"

No one was even listening to him. Bethan and Andras, it appeared, had forgot entirely that Milo was even there, too busy talking over each other with tales of courage and intrigue involving a woman who Milo knew had trouble remembering where she'd left her spectacles, and who'd cried romantically maudlin tears when Milo had confessed to having experienced his first kiss while away at school. This "witch" and "angel" was not someone Milo knew, even if he'd heard the stories as much as—probably more than—anyone else.

Ellis, though, was smirking quite blatantly, eyes sparking mischief right at Milo. Amused satisfaction was all over his familiar-unfamiliar face as he listened to his apparent minions wax rhapsodic about epic battles in a war they only knew through history lessons, and possibly a few sozzled veteran's tales at the local pub. Ellis let them run on long enough for Milo to start shifting uncomfortably then held up a finger. Only that, a small, silent gesture, outwardly unobtrusive and benign, but it shut Bethan and Andras up in seconds and had them both straightening their backs. And Ellis wasn't even looking at them, eyes on Milo the whole time.

When there was no sound left but the quiet rush of the river, Ellis lifted his eyebrows at Milo, and... there. *That* was Elly. *That* was the boy who was a little too confident and more annoying for it because his charm, combined with his undeniable cleverness, meant he was good at everything he tried—and the arrogance was infuriatingly justified.

As though privy to every single thought currently hogtying Milo's wits, Ellis grinned, though it only stayed long enough for him to turn to Bethan and Andras. Ellis's whole demeanor slid immediately into disappointment and mild irritation as he stuck his hand in his pocket, and jerked his head toward his horse.

"Bethan, please take Calannog to the stable at West Spring and tell them I'll pick him up on my way back to the Croft. Andras, I've got Dilys on her way to relieve you. Please remain at your post until she does. I'll see you both in the morning to discuss"—Ellis waved a hand—"this."

"But, syr," Bethan objected, even as she reached to take the horse's lead from Andras. "Dillie's only still training, and she's only just—"

"She is, at the moment, more prepared for this post than you." Ellis flicked his gaze to encompass Andras too. "Than either of you. Wellech has not had the honor of hosting a coven for longer than I've been alive, and I won't have reports of inhospitality preventing us from hosting another."

With an absent pat to the horse's neck, he unhooked the lamp from its sling and shoved it at Andras. "Don't drop this one, yeah?" He turned to Milo. "I see no luggage."

"No, I..." It took a second for Milo's brain to adjust to the jag in conversation. "Your mam sent a hire car to the station for us. I felt like a walk, so I sent my bag along with Mam and told her I'd meet her at the Bluebell."

"Ah!" Ellis grinned. "So you'll both be staying at Rhediad Afon with Mam, then? She didn't say. I'd been wondering why she's had the kitchens in a dither, but she wouldn't tell me." Before Milo could answer, Ellis gave Bethan a brisk "Off with you, then, quit your gawking" then took hold of Milo's elbow and tugged. "C'mon, I'll walk you to the Bluebell."

"You shouldn't have told them what you did. That 'greasy ash' thing you said." Though there was mild censure in Milo's remark, he suspected the grin behind it was audible. "They were clearly keyed up about the prospect of magic in general, and just the word 'Dewin' seemed to scare them spitless. Feeding the worry will only make them more—"

"Hidebound?" Ellis cut in. "Narrow-minded? I've been trying to nip that kind of twaddle where I can, especially in my own ranks, but it's getting more and louder, and it just… well, it pisses me off." It was angry, but the touch to Milo's arm was gentle and the tone more placid when Ellis said, "Lift that light a bit, would you? I can't see ten paces ahead."

Milo gave the magelight a bump; it rose, its glow enhanced to burn more brightly against the fog as they reached the end of the Reescartref Bridge and stepped onto the path eastward.

What memories it brought back, being here with Ellis beside him. The weather was all wrong, nothing like to the summer nights spent traipsing like puerile sharpers askulk, jubilant and bug-bitten, with the whole of the world laid down at their grubby bare feet. The mood was off too, uncomfortably charged and unfamiliar now, when everything Milo remembered about his summers here was sundrenched and silt-scented.

"So, what I've heard is true, then," Milo ventured carefully. "You've taken the Wardenship from your tad."

And knowing Folant Rees, it must have been quite a show.

Ellis sighed, breath curling out in a long plume to melt into the fog. "It wasn't a matter of *taking*, really. More like just… stepping into the gaps, I guess, and daring him to stop me." He paused, thoughtful, then said, "There were a lot of gaps." A shrug bumped his arm into Milo's. "Things sort of went on, and the title shifted along with them."

That wasn't even close to what Milo's mam had told him, and she'd got it from Ellis's. Obstacles thrown viciously across every path Ellis took for the first few months, trainee contracts deliberately breached, low-ranked novices sacked for following orders, and high-ranking old hands demoted based on nothing more than whim and spite. Until Ellis began to plan around the interferences, thinking around his tad's corners and cutting him off before he got to them.

Ellis had moved out of Oed Tyddyn—the sprawling estate that was the only thing Folant had really proffered his contract bed besides his contribution to the making of his son—and taken the Croft for his own. It had been, according to Milo's mam, a quietly violent struggle, carried out through procedure changes and training methods and patrol schedules, and Folant was as unapologetically and publicly bitter about losing it as he was about his once-almost-cariad having no use for him once she'd quickened with Ellis.

"And Pennaeth?" Milo asked. "Will you ta—fill in those gaps too?"

Ellis's smile was grim. "I guess we'll see, should the need become more needful."

He should, really. From what Milo had heard, Folant remained chief of Clan Rees, and thereby the parish head of Wellech, only because Ellis had pointedly allowed him to keep the title. Ellis was the one fulfilling the responsibilities of it—which, Milo now suspected, was the only reason the coven had been extended the invitation to meet here after what could most kindly be called a decades-long snub.

Milo had been a bit dubious when his mam had relayed the gossip, to be honest. He'd known Ellis as a callow, somewhat overconfident boy—eager to shirk a day's chores for a swim in the river; unabashedly brandishing his family names to avoid all manner of consequences. Ellis never suffered so much as a willow-wand to the bum nor cross word from the locals for any of his boyhood mischiefs. His mam was a different story, but still.

Milo spent a great deal of the summers of his youth wondering why he wasn't resentful and jealous of Ellis, because *Milo* would certainly never get away with any of their more questionable adventures on his own. In truth, he hadn't minded much. He'd benefitted from Ellis's overconfidence countless times just by being in the same adolescent orbit.

And, every goddess in the pantheon, it had been *fun*.

Seeing Ellis now, the man he'd become... well. It had only been a small fistful of time, no more than a few furlongs' walk yet, but there was something about him—the set of his shoulders; the careful expressions; the jut of his jaw—that told Milo he'd missed an awful lot of growing up when it came to Ellis Morgan dy Rees.

"Needs, by definition, are always needful, I think," Milo said then changed the subject. "Did I hear you say you've got someone called Dilys training with the Wardens? That's not little Dillie Moss dy Rydderch, is it?"

"Ha!" That brought a grin to Ellis's face, the sternness wiped clean and replaced by open fondness. "She's not so little anymore. Well, I mean, she is, but you wouldn't know it by the way she handles herself. Flipped me three times the last time we sparred."

"Dillie did. *Dillie* did?"

"And I was trying!" Ellis shook his head. "I admit I was dubious when her application came in. And even more dubious when Dillie showed up." He turned to Milo with a smirk that looked downright doting. "But she hadn't been idle, our Dillie. Still a little dab, but stout with it, and balanced out just so. I haven't set her to train with a rifle yet, but she's already worked her way through just about everyone in hand-to-hand, and her archery skills are probably the best *I've* ever seen. Even without magicked arrows, she'll nail the bullseye more than not."

"She's always been crackerjack with a bow," Milo agreed. They'd certainly had their turns at the targets, but they'd never hunted together as children, and they'd only dared the smallest, most benign magics in Folant Rees's jurisdiction. "Your mam's training her, then?"

"Well, Mam says it's more a matter of taking Dillie through the tests and handing over the 'adept' marks when they're through. Apparently, no child of Terrwyn Rydderch will be caught short and without the proper training, so he's been putting Dillie through her paces since she hit twelve."

"And yet he still won't have anything to do with a coven."

"Well." Ellis snorted. "A Rydderch admitting anyone has authority over them besides the Queen? Please. Terrwyn barely acknowledges that much."

Milo laughed. "True, I suppose. Still, though. I wish I'd at least had Dillie at Llundaintref with me. If not for the comfort of familiar company, I could've used her on my rounders team."

"I dunno," Ellis said lightly, "if she'd been in Llundaintref with you, I wouldn't've got to see her for ten years either."

Deliberately lightly, if Milo was hearing what Ellis wasn't saying.

"I wrote you. I wrote you lots." Milo kept his own tone as peaceable as he could. "And you never wrote back."

"I did so!"

"Twice."

"Twice is more than never."

"*Twice.* Once for my eleventh birthday, which I'm pretty sure your mam made you do, and one Highwinter card a couple of years later."

"...It still counts."

"Two posts over ten years does not a correspondence make, Elly."

Nor a friendship wafted faintly at the back of Milo's mind.

"You couldn't have been *too* broken up about it." Ellis's voice was low, night sounds and the damp of the fog nearly swallowing it. "You never came back, after all."

"I hardly ever even got to go *home*, Elly, let alone have a holiday."

"You went home every Reaping and Sowing, at least that's what—"

"Yes, because it's migration season, and even before Nain died, there were maybe ten other people in the whole of Màstira who know how to care for old, sick, or crippled dragons besides me and Mam and Howell, and they're not dragonkin."

"I... ehm." Ellis was quiet for a moment before he said, "I was sorry to hear about your nain."

Milo looked away. All he could manage for a moment was a gruff "Ta, Elly" because it hadn't been much more than a year yet and it still felt fresh. The loss had only been made more difficult by knowing that through it all—the wake and the funeral and the burial—there'd been a polite yet vicious fight going on behind the scenes between Kymbrygh's MP and Ceri's solicitors over whether or not Milo would be allowed to go back to school when it was over and leave Old Forge with no dragonkin. As it was, he'd still been wearing his mourning band when he'd had to sit his final exams.

"I would've come," Ellis said. "It's only... things were a bit, ehm. Well, everything was very unsettled then, and I couldn't—"

"I know. It's all right."

"You'd've come if it'd been my bamps. So I think it's not, really."

Milo didn't argue, though it really was all right. He'd barely made it home in time himself, missing the first days of vigil entirely and only showing up after the wake had already started.

"How is your bamps?"

Ellis huffed something that might've been a snort but didn't sound amused. "Sometimes he actually remembers me."

Sundown sickness they called it. Old and frail before one's time, and it might not be quite so heartbreaking if it didn't start with one's mind. Ellis's bamps had been a force back in the day; he'd already been a more-often-dotty-than-not scarecrow of an old man in a bath chair by the time Milo started spending summers in Wellech.

All Milo could offer was, "I'm sorry."

"Ta," Ellis said, short and clipped. "You were saying?" Which meant he was done talking about it.

Milo would like to oblige, but—"I forget what we were talking about."

Ellis laughed then, a quick bark of it, genuine and deep. "You were telling me why my best friend abandoned me for a posh exclusive school miles and miles away on a whole other island, and then never came to visit."

Best friend. *Abandoned.*

Milo tamped down the tiny bit of brittle indignation that flared at the accusation. Because it wasn't *actually* an accusation, though Milo wasn't entirely sure what it was. A bid for reassurance, maybe, from someone who'd never admit, even to himself, he might need it.

"...Right. Anyway." Milo pulled in a rough breath. "There's no other dragonkin in Kymbrygh now, let alone anywhere close to Old Forge. Mam *and* the Kymbrygh MP demanded a leave at Sowing and Reaping be in the contract when I started at the school. I had no say in any of it."

You, on the other hand, Milo only just stopped himself from saying. Instead he scowled and watched his boots tromp the muddy path to hide it, deliberately kicking at a clump of rotted leaf-fall so his sigh wasn't too obvious. Everything was abruptly entirely too serious, and it was *stupid.*

It shouldn't still sting the way it did. They'd been children. Back then, three months of summer once a year was the only worthy sum of a too-young life. Concentrated companionship made a best friend before they'd been old enough to even know what "friend" meant, let alone "best." Children were capricious and callous, trading companions for convenience. Memories became fine, gossamer things with age. Precious, too-malleable treasures to take out and dote on once the adult had finally arrogated the child, abandoning him to his jacks and conkers at the twilit edge of grownup reminiscence.

Still.

It *did* sting. As though some part of Milo was still that ten-year-old, all alone in a new school, a new city, a new *life*—no friends, nothing familiar—and waiting to hear his name called every Midsday when the post from home came. Waiting for a letter from someone other than his mam or his nain. Waiting for *something* from the boy who'd been hardest to leave, and wondering why it never came.

It took a moment for Milo to realize Ellis had stopped, head down, thoughtful. The magelight was bright, beating back the fog for a good thirty paces around them now, but Milo couldn't see Ellis's face beneath the brim of his hat. Not until Ellis huffed and looked up, a smile that was several parts embarrassment tilting at one cheek.

"I suppose I was... angry." Ellis shrugged when Milo frowned at him. "I didn't understand why you went away to school. I'd thought you'd come live here, actually. Or at Rhediad Afon, I mean. Have my mam teach you the magic." He rubbed at the back of his neck. Grimaced. "And then, after I wasn't angry anymore, it just...." He rolled his hand. "I didn't know how to... pick it back up, I guess."

"Elly." Milo took a step closer. "You know I had to go, right? I wasn't leaving *you*, or even—"

"I know. I do." Ellis rolled his eyes, seemingly at himself. "Llundaintref is the only place someone like you *could* go. I know that. I *knew* that. It's only...." He shrugged again, halfhearted. "It didn't help. The knowing. Not back then." He spread his hands. "I missed you."

You had a funny way of showing it, Milo couldn't help thinking, that ten-year-old still biding somewhere at the back of his heart, looking for a letter that would never come. But Milo *wasn't* that ten-year-old anymore, and neither was Ellis.

Maybe it was the almost forgotten scent of river silt that lifted Milo's heart just a touch and made him smile. Maybe it was the memory-sound of splashing river water and laughter and hoots of approval for a particularly impressive dive. Maybe it was Ellis—

taller, stronger, changed and grown into something... well, proper *lush*, if Milo was honest, but still *Elly* beneath it all—standing there with a rueful grin he wouldn't let quirk and an apology in his eyes he'd never voice.

It had been years ago. They'd been children.

Milo stepped in, slung his arms around Ellis's wide—great Goddess, the *muscles*—shoulders, said, "I've missed you too," and waited, abruptly warm and content, until Ellis hugged him back.

It only took a second or two.

Chapter 2—Theme

: *the main self-contained melody of a musical composition*

"... Being very forthcoming just now. It's not *quite* worrisome yet, but it could be soon enough."

"Then I don't see why we're discussing it now. Our agenda has been planned and approved, and is too full for—"

"It's our *job* to discuss it, Arbenigwr Idwal, regardless of your agenda."

"It's our *job* to discuss a lot of things, Meistr Eluned, most of which we won't have time for if we don't stick to the agenda!"

Milo just sort of watched the byplay around him and tried not to gawk too much. And also tried not to look at his mam, who'd been trying to catch his eye for a while now. Milo knew if he let her, he wouldn't be able to keep from laughing. And he really didn't want to get kicked out of the first coven he'd ever sat as a full member.

...Well. Full member once they finally got to the rites, but that wasn't until the end, for no good reason Milo could discern except to keep him quiet one last time while they still could. Newyddian—novice—status meant he wasn't allowed to speak unless addressed directly.

They were talking over each other now, Idwal getting red-faced and irate, Eluned calm but clearly getting more annoyed, and now Saeth was chiming in acerbically, but Milo thought that was only because she had too much fun watching Idwal get riled into near-apoplexy. To be fair, it wasn't terribly hard to do. And watching the color climb up Idwal's wattled neck, over his pale cragged face, and then basically consume the whole of his shiny bald head *was* kind of entertaining.

The volume was rising, though the warding charm around the table had been set by Milo's mam, so there was no danger of any of it leaking out to the ears of the other patrons of the Bluebell's common room.

You wouldn't know it by Ellis. Two of his mam's sleek little herding dogs had basically mauled him with happy yips and slobbery kisses when he and Milo entered the inn. Ellis had been so involved in greeting them he hadn't even noticed when Milo stepped back to allow some space, then, feeling a bit superfluous, skulked away and took his seat at the coven's table. The dogs now lay at Ellis's feet, begging the occasional scrap from a random patron, but mostly content to snooze and enjoy the fire.

Ellis, though.... This old-new Ellis was difficult to read. He'd commandeered the snug but left the doors open, holding casual court from a sturdy chair tipped back against the wall, muddy boots propped on the arm of another, and a jar of the inn's bitter summer ale in his hand. He'd been ostensibly socializing with some boyos but really keeping an eye on the coven's table since he'd sat down. Smirking, of course. Milo would find it annoying, maybe a little insulting—covens were *Serious Business*, after all—but he himself had been keeping in sighs and dutifully not rolling his eyes for some time now. He supposed he couldn't give Ellis the stink-eye he really wanted to without being a flaming hypocrite.

Milo had been wrong, back at the bridge. Well, really the magelight had tricked his eye into seeing memory more than reality, but it came to the same thing—he'd been off in his assessment of Ellis and all his changes. Ellis's hair was more gold now than auburn-on-ochre, brighter in the firelight that rosed his brown skin. His grin as he relayed some story that seemed to require a lot of expansive hand gestures to his mates was more wry and knowing than puckish. The way he sprawled in his seat was relaxed and confident, rather than the cocky pose Milo remembered.

Milo wasn't sure why any of it mattered, but somehow it did.

He was staring, probably sort of wistfully, since he was busy wishing he was over there in the snug with Ellis, rather than slumping at the coven's table, waiting for Idwal to claim chest pains so everyone else would let him have his way. So when Lilibet—Ellis's *mam*—caught Milo at it, turned to follow where his gaze had been then turned back with a too-familiar smirk and a lift of her eyebrow, Milo sat up straight so fast he knocked the table.

Wenda's ale tottered; she caught it before it tipped. With a chiding look at Milo, she skimmed an exasperated glance all around the table, before letting it land and stay on Milo's mam.

"Offeiriad Ceri." Wenda raised her voice to be heard above the nattering still pinging between all three points of an invisible triangle across the table and back again. At her formal address, it stopped. When she had quiet, Wenda went on, "Perhaps you'd care to settle the matter of changes to the evening's planned agenda?"

Milo's mam was peering closely at Milo, brow drawn, corner of her mouth turned slightly up, and dark blue eyes squinting like she'd forgot her glasses, though they sat prim on the bridge of her nose. Or maybe like she was trying to figure something out. Milo reckoned she was wondering why his lip was getting fatter by the second. Or, possibly, how he'd managed to nearly upend the whole table for apparently no reason. Neither of which he really wanted to explain, so he tried to look as clueless as possible. Eventually, Ceri shared an indiscernible glance with Lilibet before she folded her hands atop the table and cleared her throat.

"Thank you, Meistr Wenda." Ceri gave Wenda one of her kind smiles then gave Idwal one that was a bit more indulgent. "And thank you, Arbenigwr Idwal, for attempting to keep us on course. These things do tend to drag on when we don't." The chuckles around the table, Milo thought, were probably a bonus; what Ceri was really waiting for, he decided, was the conciliatory smile and shrug from Idwal, because she smiled back with a wink and turned to Bowen. "But I think we all need to hear this news. Newyddian Bowen?"

Bowen's thin shoulders seemed to wilt a bit once everyone turned their gazes his way, but he shifted them straight then tipped Ceri a respectful nod. "It's less news and more rumor just now." He waved a willowy hand. "Or conjecture, I guess."

"Then why," said Arbenigwr Gildas, his southeastern accent thick with an implied harrumph, "must we spend the coven's time on it now?" His dark eyes, canted down at the crowsfeet corners, strafed the assembly with a look that was somehow both bored and indignant at the same time. "Shouldn't this issue be tabled until there's something to actually report?"

Lilibet sighed. "Thank you, Arbenigwr Gildas, for your input."

Her remarkable ability to shut even the most vocal and vociferous antagonist up—witness Gildas's sour roll of eyes but decidedly closed mouth—with nothing more than a soft word or pointed glance hadn't changed since Milo was small. Still just as beautiful as he remembered, too, her sable-dark skin gaining a roseate radiance in the flux-and-flow light of the gas lamps that lit the inn's common room. And yet it was her kindness that Milo remembered most from his youth.

Lilibet reached across the table to set a soft pat to Bowen's subtly shaking hand before pulling back and then, with a contrasting look of firm expectation, said, "Your report with as much confirmation as you can give us, please, Newyddian Bowen."

The mild dustup had clearly thrown Bowen. His mouth was flapping, and the color had drained a bit from his narrow face. Milo tried not to squirm uncomfortably on Bowen's behalf. Young and newyddian for only a little under two years now, Bowen hadn't been inducted into the coven at an early age like Milo had. Bowen and Undeg, Bowen's twin sister, had come into their magic suddenly and painfully, one right after the other, when they were fifteen, having had no indication prior that they were even sensitive, let alone the middling-powerful natural elemental sorcerers they were. Eluned had taken pity on the twins' decidedly unmagical parents and presented them to Lilibet for instruction and, because the coven hadn't been a true thirteen for too many years, sponsored them for induction. The pickings had been worryingly slim since before Milo was born, and they'd needed the numbers.

Bowen only kept staring at Lilibet like a stoat beneath a cat's eye until Undeg gave him a nudge to the ribs and a look that said "today would be nice." It seemed to bolster Bowen. His anxious frown drew into firm resolve and he sat up straight, tossing thick brown hair out of his green, impossibly wide eyes.

"Apologies, Meistr Lilibet, but I haven't had confirmation because no one will give it to me." Bowen undoubtedly caught the flat look Gildas gave him but resolutely looked only at Lilibet. He cleared his throat. "But with Taraverde claiming annex over Colorat, communication has become... unreliable."

Milo frowned, paying attention now and no longer amused by the preceding bickering. Colorat was an ally of the United Preidynīg Isles, of which Kymbrygh was a part, and Preidyn's Queen was reportedly not taking this hostile move by Taraverde lightly. Talks, still ongoing, had already broken down more than once.

Bowen put out a hand, palm up. "I wasn't surprised when the posts stopped coming. But the last one said leadership of the Colorat Coven had changed, that all Dewin had been expelled and their offeiriad—pardon me, their *magie*—would now be chosen by Taraverde's chancellery. They said they'd contact us once the transition was settled. They never did. And now Magie Nis—*former* Magie Nistor*"—it was clear the correction tasted bad in Bowen's mouth—"doesn't answer cables or even scrys. Not even personal ones. Not even 'are you all right?' ones."

"Magie Nistor is also a minor government official, yes?" asked Fflur.

Bowen nodded. "Governor of...." He shuffled through a small pile of notes. "I'm sorry, I can't remember the name of the city, and I don't have it with me. But." Bowen paused, expression pained. "He's Dewin." He shot a nervous look at Ceri, and then Milo. "And he was somewhat... outspoken in his opposition to a new government under Taraverde's rule. Bravely so."

"Or foolishly," Fflur muttered.

Bowen bristled, as though he couldn't help himself. "He led protests in defense of his country and its people. He spoke out for what was right. How is that foolish?"

Fflur sighed and gave Bowen a look of jaded sympathy. "He saw what happened in Ostlich-Sztym. We all did." Protests that turned into riots when Ostlich-Sztym invited Taraverde's Elite Constabulary to move in and "help quell the unrest." And then the constables started shooting. "Call it foolishly brave, if you will, but he couldn't have expected it to end any other way."

Lilibet narrowed her eyes at Milo's mam, but other than that, no one immediately spoke. The implications were plain enough that no one really had to.

Finally, Heledd broke the silence with a murmured "Interesting." Her wide mouth was pursed down to a thoughtful line. "And... very troubling, if it's what it looks like." She was a pop of color in the common room's fickle light, the considerable bulk of her swathed in kerchiefs and kirtles in reds and golds, and her long, black twistrows shot through with startling white. Her dark gaze was soft on Bowen, but sharp when it shifted around the table. "But still only conjecture based on rumor."

Perl huffed out a derisive snort. "What Meistr Heledd doesn't say is that we all know what's going on in Colorat, and that—"

"What Meistr Heledd doesn't say," Heledd put in, "is what Meistr Heledd doesn't *know*. And what Arbenigwr Perl forgets is her place."

Milo sank down in his seat, a bit wide-eyed, and exchanged an uncomfortable look with Bowen. Both Lilibet and Ceri remained blank-faced, watching, though Eluned, usually impossible to surprise or ruffle, had gone thin-lipped and tense.

Perl's round, tanned cheeks went nearly as red as the parts of her hair that hadn't already grayed. Her jaw set. "A sister coven has gone dark. We all know what it means." She waved a plump, freckled hand around the table, clearly agitated. "Three of us here are veterans of at least two wars, and every one of us knows there isn't a government in existence that doesn't either fear or covet—or both—every sect on the planet, and Dewin right at the top of that list, *especially* on the main continent right now. When they fear us, the covens are the first against the wall. When they covet us, we're the first to be recruited. Even our own queen recruits from—"

"Enough!" Idwal shot up and slammed his hand on the table so hard it made Milo jump. "I will hear no slander of our good Queen Rhiannon, and especially not within the bounds of a formal coven!"

Out the corner of his eye, Milo caught the movement of Ellis sitting up straight, leaning forward. Elbow on knee, he was blatantly staring right at Milo when Milo carefully slid his glance over. Ellis lifted an eyebrow, inquiring. All Milo could do was shift a shrug as subtly as possible. Even if he knew what was going on, he wouldn't be able to tell Ellis. Or anyone, really. One of the first things he'd learned when he'd first been inducted at age eight was that coven business stayed in the coven. The coven's secretary—Bowen now, since Milo's nain had passed—reported directly to the offeiriad and Kymbrygh's MP and no one else.

Idwal strafed a glance over the table, breathing hard, to meet the eyes of the abruptly silent gathering, then said, through his teeth, "Offeiriad Ceri, your humble arbenigwr begs forgiveness for addressing the coven so. But I remind us all that Rhiannon is

Offeiriad herself, in the World Court, no less. She's not here to defend the honor she's earned from us through unfailing good will toward every coven under her purview and even those that are not." The blurred consonants and rolling diphthongs unique to his Fernswallow accent usually made him difficult to understand, but not now. He set a glare on Perl. "There are *four* of us here, Arbenigwr Perl, who've served in Her Majesty's forces and fought her wars—no draft, no conscription, but by *choice*—and I'll not have any forgetting why we did it!"

"All too easy to forget," Perl said evenly, "when so many of us never came back, and so cannot remind us."

Before Idwal could fire a retort, Ceri said, "Idwal, Arbenigwr, please take your seat." She waited, dark blue gaze level on Idwal, not unkind but not exactly kind either, until Idwal huffed, sent one last glare at Perl, then sat. Ceri nodded, satisfied. "Thank you, Arbenigwr Idwal, Arbenigwr Perl, for giving the coven something to consider for our next gathering. But, as Newyddian Bowen took care to point out, we currently have nothing more than rumor and conjecture." She raised a hand, her glance warning, when Perl opened her mouth. "We do, however, recognize that our positions demand we take these intimations seriously. I move we form an investigatory committee, the directive of which will be to ferret out what it can and report back to us at the next gathering. All in favor?"

All hands went up, including Milo's.

"Very well." Ceri nodded. "Newyddian Bowen, please record that the motion has carried unanimously. Meistr Eluned and I will discuss committee nominations in private. Now." She smiled and folded her hands atop the table. "Next order of business?"

The rites, Milo decided, were just as boring when enduring them as they'd been the two times he'd watched others sit them. A big circle, a bunch of magelights in the branches of the ancient oak to light the Bluebell's yard, and an awful lot of "Do you?" and "Will you?" from each meistr in the coven, to which the expected answer from the newyddian-cum-arbenigwr was always, of course, a confident "Yes."

Unlike the formal coven, this was an open affair. Those interested ambled out from the inn's common room to witness and lend their good will to the circle. Milo could feel it like the fog that still clung, though this was warm and embracing, rather than chill and oppressive. Lilibet's dogs still hung at each of Ellis's hips, but even they gave off a friendly air.

When the final promise to uphold the coven's principles was extracted from Milo, all the onlookers were invited to join the circle around him. Milo couldn't help the unexpected warmth that moved through him when Ellis shifted deliberately to stand directly behind Milo, joining hands with Gildas and someone Milo didn't know, dogs again positioning themselves to either side of him.

Prayers in Milo's name went up to every goddess, everyone in the circle reciting them carefully. Milo could swear he felt every good thing in them rise with their voices to skim along the unified resonance and slick back between his ribs to hum with the echoes. Like a symphony, the prayers coalesced, melody and harmony tangling into one voice, rising, ringing, building in volume and tucking in close around Milo, stilling him, shrouding though not stifling. The cadence shifted, the volume rose, until Milo was *sure* he felt a swish and clatter inside him, power manifest in the faint ethereal strings he could feel connecting each in the circle with the next. 'Round and 'round the ring it flowed, until it surged in like spokes on a wheel and straight into Milo.

His mam would kill him if she knew what he was thinking, but it was abruptly imperative that Milo see it. He wanted to *See*, as he usually only did with the dragons, but it was different with them—a necessary risk when it was only him and creatures who needed him to know what they were thinking, how they were feeling, what ailed them, where it hurt, and could never tell anyone what Milo could do anyway.

This... he needed to See this because it was *his*.

He shut his eyes, tugged at that place inside him where sight and knowledge curled together like sleepy dragons, a thing instinctive and bone-deep, yet also something that spent so much time buried and repressed inside him it had become almost as instinctive to keep it there. It was risky doing it here, out in the open and in front of so many witches and sorcerers, but it wasn't like anyone could tell just by looking at him. And when would he get a chance to See something like it again?

Quietly defiant, Milo let it flood through him, pulled in a soft, slow breath and... opened his eyes. Blinked.

It didn't so much flare at him as slide across his vision in smeary whorls, bright and brimful with cordial sentiments he could all at once See and feel and taste. The Seeing, when he set it loose like this, never failed to dazzle him. As though he spent most of his time colorblind and now suddenly wasn't.

He didn't cry out or anything dramatic, though he gasped, his mam's gaze skipping to him sharply, startled, *knowing* because she could See Milo as well as he could See her. Lilibet, too, was watching him shrewdly, and Eluned, both of them staring before catching each other's glances then frowning slightly, as though bemused. Milo's mam, though....

Watching. Glint-eyed, and.... Yes. Red and sharp and all but shooting off sparks. *Angry*. Because she never stopped warning him.

Milo couldn't care, because the wishes and the songs and the colors and the knowing all pitched up and welled out through him. It was all he could do to stand straight and not let his knees buckle at the shocking beauty of the twisting aurora-bursts winding out from everyone around him.

It wasn't power, Milo decided, not really. Potential, perhaps. A promise borne on the chanted prayers, rising from them in bright scattershot prisms, and the echo of an answer in the strange soft rapture trickling into his veins like warm water. Awash in the magic offered by every sorcerer and witch in the circle, and the goodwill of everyone else, motes of it clinging to the fine hairs on his skin—he could *See* them—burrowing in and down like it belonged to him. And then, somehow, it did, slender streams of light and color slipping from the nimbi of every living thing and into his own like he was sipping at them with a straw.

Not a theft, but the acceptance of a gift. Not a reduction of power for those who offered, but an increase of his own nonetheless. It filled Milo so completely it seeped from his skin like soft misted light. He knew almost no one else could see it, yet was still somehow shocked they couldn't.

He peered at his mam—only another in the circle, no Offeiriad set apart here—asking he wasn't sure what. She gave him nothing but jagged colors and an exasperated stare.

Milo knew better than to smirk. He almost did anyway. He was going to catch proper misery for it, no doubt, but how could he *not* want to See this? Natur magic from Saeth blooming up from the ground, spangling all over her, then sending shoots of opaline out to Milo. Elfennol magic gathering in the air around Idwal and pushing out in a soft-blushed brume.

There was magic in every blade of grass; Milo had learned that at his mam's knee, his nain's, Lilibet's, and then studied it deeper in his years at school. Now, like this, when he opened himself wide, he *Saw* it, pulsing like blood through veins. More defined than it was with the dragons; maybe because that was more observation than participation. Here, now, the small gifts of power from everyone around him coalesced into something bigger, sharpening his Sight, deepening the colors and pulling wispy strands into richer focus. The oak above him was almost too bright to look at, the magic of every rite ever performed beneath its gnarled limbs still beating like a heart beneath bark and branch. Streamers like the tails of tiny comets skirled on the breeze and worried at the edges of the sparkling fog still clinging to grass lying low for the coming winter, breathing the magic in slowly, storing it up for its approaching long sleep.

Faint shades in muted hues wore the shapes of those who had stood here before and those who stood here now, colorful ambient *bwci bos*—abstruse ghosts that came and went in the steps their physical bodies once walked. Milo knew, if he concentrated, looked at them properly, he could determine who'd been here before and what they'd been doing. If he touched those not-quite-wraiths, saw their colors, felt their edges, he could See yet more, could....

He caught his mam's eye, saw her mouth pursed in an angry line, then followed her pointed glance down to his own hand. He'd been reaching out, wanting to touch and know.

He jerked his head and pulled his hand back.

There was no blast of magic to signal the rite's completion, no flash of bright light, no chorus of otherworldly voices. Instead a soft new power swelled to lap at his core, so serene and intimate it felt almost unseemly to greet it here in company. A gentle burst like nothing he'd ever felt before striated out through every limb, every fingertip, as though he were touching the fine, fragile hem of the gossamer robes of Duwies herself.

It was beautiful and forever, though it was only a moment or two. When Milo started paying attention again, the prayers were only just tailing off into completion and everyone around him was still calmly watching him as though nothing extraordinary had just happened. Milo stood in the center of the circle, trying not to vibrate, surrounded by men and women he'd never met before tonight, as well as witches and sorcerers he'd known all his life but had never dared to See before. And yes, his mam knew what Milo was doing, she was going to *kill* him, but *this*... this made it worth it. Nimbi flared with colors and feelings and intentions Milo had no need to interpret; the benevolence and generosity were ingenuous and plain.

It was too big and beautiful to just put away again, bury so deep no one could ever suspect, so Milo decided not to. At least for now. He pulled his gaze from its contemplation of the prismed smudges of color and blinked at the circle of people now grinning at him with genuine delight and perhaps even some pride.

The chanting had stopped while Milo had been too deep in his own head to notice, prayers complete and rite finished. He was arbenigwr now, a full member of the Kymbrygh Coven.

It wasn't long before the circle began to break up, hands separating to slap Milo on the back, congratulations gusting over him like warm summer wind. Milo was still somewhat drunk on it all, so he only stood there and nodded when it felt like he should, smiling and trying not to stare at everyone, make it obvious he was Seeing them with eyes he shouldn't have, power he could never admit.

His mam's glare was burning holes between Milo's shoulder

blades, he could feel it, but he refused to feel guilty. This night was special, a rite of passage he'd only ever experience once—he *deserved* this, damn it—so he let himself have it while it lasted.

Which wasn't for very long, because when Milo finally chanced a look over at his mam... all right, wow, did she look *tamping*. Sharp violet fractals twisted in silent detonations all around her, burnt garnet erupting jagged through orange stained with a murk as dingy blue-gray as rot on an apricot. All of it was barbed rough with tawny metallic fragments that somehow seemed violent, like bursts of shrapnel, and actually made Milo's teeth hurt.

Before Milo could break free of all the well-wishers, his mam was stalking toward him, her nimbus whipping in a smear behind her as she took hold of Milo's arm in a grip that hurt, and leaned up and in.

"Put it away," Ceri said, low and fierce. "You hear me? *Now.*" She pulled back, gave Milo... it wasn't a glare, not as such, but it was definitely angry, teeth clenched and face set, and everything about her was now drenched in indigo and crimson.

"Mam, it's not like anyone can even tell what it—"

"*I* can tell."

"You don't count."

She knew, she knew *him*, she could *See*, and she knew what to look for. It wasn't like anyone else did.

"Just *do as I say*, Milo Priddy, then put on your party face. You've a long night to get through."

She didn't give Milo a chance to ask what that meant. She let go of his arm, backed one pace, two, still glowering at him, then turned and pushed her way out of the circle, and disappeared around the back of the inn.

Milo would have followed her, maybe even apologized, but when he stepped to the side, Lilibet was there, shining a grin at him like she was proud. "All are welcome at Rhediad Afon to celebrate our newest arbenigwr!" she called to the crowd, her hand snug on Milo's arm. "Come along, everyone! The cider is warm and the tables overflowing!"

A cheer went up. Lilibet beamed and started leading Milo away.

Still a bit dazed, still a bit confounded by his mam's overreaction, Milo let Lilibet pull him out of the Bluebell's yard. He knew he shouldn't, his mam was already furious with him, but he was too happy, too curious—one last time, Milo let himself See.

He hadn't been aware there were so many shades of green. Lilibet was soaked in every one of them. The sunny clarity of new apples washed seamless into the cool tranquility of timeworn seaglass. Calm, staid evergreen slipped gentle and slow into burgeoning moss then swirled with the jade iridescence of a peacock feather.

He couldn't help wondering if Ellis would look the same, how much of his mam Ellis had grown into, how much of his cocky golds and obstinate violets had matured and mellowed into more settled shades of prudence. And Milo would really like to find out. But when he scanned the faces around him, searching, Ellis was nowhere to be found.

The disappointment was weirdly embarrassing. Milo kept his smile, thanked the stragglers still wishing him well as they all followed the path to Rhediad Afon, but when the colors began to leak away, Milo let them.

Chapter 3—Instrumentation

: the combination of instruments that a composition is written for

"No, it doesn't mean I'm actually *related* to dragons. I mean...." Milo flailed a little. "How would that even work?"

The man—Milo couldn't remember his name, only that he claimed close relation to someone in the Peerage, and had clearly taken on the more obnoxious behaviors he apparently thought befitting someone of his dubious "station"—the man blinked at Milo as though Milo were the one who'd just implied someone in his more-respectable-than-yours family tree had somehow had intimate relations with a creature as big as a house.

"But." The man gave Milo a suspicious frown. "Dragonkin. Kin. *Kindred.*"

Milo looked helplessly at the man's daughter, standing off to the side looking bored and annoyed. Milo couldn't tell if it was at him or her tad.

"Kindred doesn't necessarily mean related," Milo said slowly. "And in the 'dragonkin' sense it only means they tolerate me better than most. I can get close to them without them trying to eat me or roast me." When the man only continued to stare blankly, Milo gave him a bemused squint. "You *did* say you hail from Werrdig, didn't you?"

He was wearing a formal kilt, so clearly he *was* from Werrdig. There was, therefore and at least as far as Milo was concerned, no excuse. Werrdig, though not on any of the migration paths, was still one of the Preidynīg Isles, and the dragon was the *national* bloody symbol of the Preidynīg Isles. Surely they taught children about dragons in the schools in Werrdig like they did in Kymbrygh?

For pity's sake, there were dragons on the *money*!

"Yes, well." The man harrumphed and took his daughter by the elbow. "All very interesting, I'm sure." His expression said he found it all more distasteful than interesting, and that he still wasn't convinced Milo wasn't hiding scales and a tail beneath his clothes. "Come along," the man said to his daughter. "I'd like to see if I can find Folant before the dancing starts."

Good luck with that, Milo didn't say. There was no way Lilibet would allow Folant anywhere near Rhediad Afon even if it were underwater and Folant owned the only boat in the world, let alone at a party she'd clearly worked very hard to make pleasant and enjoyable. Folant had a way of souring any atmosphere he happened to enter.

The girl shot Milo an apologetic look as her tad led her away. Milo gave her a shrug and a wave, then resolutely turned and made his way to the edges of the party. The huge windows of Rhediad Afon's main dining hall, turned ballroom for the occasion, had nice thick curtains; though they were pulled back and wouldn't hide him entirely, angling behind them as much as he could would at least make him harder to find.

It was payback, Milo knew it was. Why else would his mam not tell him Lilibet had planned a party in his honor, and then disappear and leave Milo to... this? Come to think of it, Lilibet was also suspiciously absent. And where the deuce had Ellis got off to anyway?

"Milo, dear!"

He pretended not to hear it, ostensibly absorbed in the view out the windows. Too many conversations this evening had started exactly like that—*Milo, dear!* and *Priddy, dear boy!* Not friends or distant family or acquaintances congratulating him on sitting the rites, but apparent potential contract partners or their representatives. And all of them looking him over as though they were one personal question away from asking to see his teeth or possibly something more intimate.

Milo'd had enough. More than enough.

The fog was still too dense to see much beyond the edge of the manor's yard, but Milo put on his thoughtful face and stared hard enough to melt the thick glass. Even his mam left him alone when he had his thoughtful face on.

"Milo?"

Milo changed it to a scowl. It was nothing personal. He was just off balance and already exhausted by the talk of possible offers and negotiations, and being sized up by everyone of contract age, or even near it, like a prized sheep at the fair.

He was tired of the crowd. He was tired of the noise. He was tired of being asked for demonstrations of his magical skill. Of assessing looks. Of people trying to touch his earring. And he was *bloody* tired of the insulted looks he got when he referred all negotiations to his mam, who very obviously was doing a better job of hiding than he was.

He hadn't been expecting this. Any of it. He'd *just* sat the rites!

If only he could see the river from this window. The landscape here was so very different from the rocks and cliffs and salt-seasoned air of Whitpool. On a clear day, Milo could watch the sea from almost any window of his mam's rambling old tower house, could walk and walk and walk to almost any point of the preserve and never lose sight of restless gray waves capped with foamy silver. And when he couldn't see it, it was still a live thing all around him, a constant thick hum that was so present, so gently relentless and *there*, he sometimes forgot to hear it.

Here, with the trees grown full and dense and only just starting to drop their bright autumn foliage, the broad expanse of the Aled narrowed to wine-dark flickers glimpsed through trunk and leaf. That was, if one could see past the fog.

"*Milo!*"

Damn it. Whoever was calling him wasn't giving up.

Milo sighed, turned from the window and blinked wearily at—

"Oh! *Haia*, Nia." Relieved beyond sense, Milo smiled, genuine and pleased, as he stepped in for a quick hug. He hadn't seen Nia for... well, since Nain's funeral at least.

She'd barely changed at all since Milo was a boy, her bronze skin still youthfully plump, and her smile brilliant and lovely beneath eyes that sparked like emeralds. Her blue shawl set them off even more in the bright electric light. Layered silk kirtles had been gathered up at the hip to expose colorful wool leggings and tucked amongst the handkerchiefs at her belt. Clearly ready for dancing. And that wasn't even counting the ornately tooled clogs on her small feet.

"Look at you, all grown." Nia gave Milo's arm a squeeze then stepped back, and set her hand to the shoulder of a young woman waiting impatiently at her elbow. "You remember—"

That was as far as Nia got before the young woman shoved her tankard at Nia then unceremoniously launched herself at Milo, landed smack against his chest, and wrapped around him like a starfish.

Milo buried the *Oof!* of surprise in a breathless laugh and wheezed out, "Dillie!" while he adjusted his grip and refound his balance so they didn't both go through the huge window behind him. Ellis had been right—Dilys was still a tiny thing, a proper *dwt*, in fact, but she was solid. And *strong*. Her arms around Milo's neck were like steel bands.

"We've been looking for you for an hour." The rolling consonants and hard dip of the vowels of Nia's Tirrydderch accent made the mild rebuke songlike and pleasant. "We're so sorry to have missed your rites. Dilys and her Warden business, you know." She rolled her eyes at her daughter, though fondly, and took a sip from the tankard. "Of course Ellis is no better, putting her on duty tonight of all nights, and don't think I won't have words with that boy once he—here now, Dilys, let the lad *breathe!*"

Laughing, Milo helped Nia pry Dilys off him, settling her as gently as he could on her feet before pushing her back to have a good look. He didn't think he would've recognized her had she not been with her mam and so very *Dillie* about her greeting.

Taller now, certainly, but still not tall. Compact and thick-boned, with curves melded to muscle beneath a richly embroidered waistcoat and trousers cut to accentuate a shape fit and healthy. Gone was the wild mop of frizzed black hair that looked like it spent most of its time in a tail that had been let down only minutes before. Now she was primped and slicked and kohled, green eyes like her mam's sharp and still full of mischief.

"You got so *tall*!" Dilys grinned with slightly crooked white teeth, squeezing Milo's arms as she pulled back. "And handsome!" She reached up to slide a finger over Milo's earring; it wasn't nearly as annoying as it was when strangers did it. "By the Nine, you're going to be *swimming* in contracts by the end of the night."

Milo couldn't help the wince. "Yes, well." He rubbed the back of his neck. "I hadn't really realized that's what all this was about."

"Oh?" Dilys blinked, all innocence. "Like a proper calf, you are."

"*Dilys*, for pity's *sake*!" Nia huffed then gave Milo a sympathetic smile. "To be fair—"

"I know, I know." Milo waved it away. "It's my own fault. I should've at least suspected. Only, I've been... I dunno, I guess I was only—"

"Up your own arse, as usual, we know." Dilys nodded sagely and patted at Milo's arm. "'Tis good to know you've not changed *that* much."

Nia sighed. "Dilys, honestly."

Milo's grin was rueful, though his pinch to Dilys's ear was sincere and sharp enough to make her yip and swat where she'd just patted.

He *had* been kind of up his own arse lately, still trying to reacquaint himself with life in Whitpool, so glad to be home but also finding he didn't quite fit anymore, and unsettled about it. He'd just been sort of drifting along for weeks, allowing his mam to direct him because he hadn't had a direction of his own. And with his dubious heritage... well. It wasn't as though most people knew he'd been born without the benefit of a contract, but enough did, and without his nain there to glare them into silence anymore...

Anyway.

He hadn't really thought he'd be what might be considered a good option. This was Wellech, after all. He'd been conveniently ignoring the fact that, to the sort of people Lilibet would invite as guests at least, a young mage, dragonkin and heir to an established estate, son of a respected veteran, and now of age and a full member of a coven, would get offers.

Although, it never even occurred to him that his mam and Lilibet would actually throw a party to accommodate the blatant "Assessment of the Prospect" so everyone could look him over like a horse at auction. And he *certainly* hadn't suspected his mam would abandon him to navigate the quasi humiliation on his own.

Punishment. He knew it.

Milo scanned the crowd. "I don't see Terrwyn or Steffan."

The other two-thirds of Nia's cariad trio. Milo remembered Terrwyn as a gruff but fond and permissive sort, more apt to play with any urchins who came within his orbit than scold them, but Steffan was the one Milo remembered more warmly. Steffan and Nia had grown up together; their cariad contract once they came of age had not been unexpected, though the addition of Terrwyn had been. While not quite as bright and spirited as his partners, Steffan was somehow the axis upon which they all turned, and a wonderfully doting "uncle" when Milo was wee and probably a bit more obnoxious than he had a right to be.

"They're home with the boys." Nia smirked, clearly pleased with herself for having managed an extended outing alone.

From what Milo knew of Dilys's rambunctious little half brothers, Nia had every right.

A few honeyed notes from a triple harp wove through the ambient noise of partygoers' chatter. Diffident hollow beats followed, and sweet-toned ripples, as someone warmed up on a pipe and tabor.

A small orchestra was setting up across the hall. The dancing would start soon.

"*Well.*" Nia, still smirking, pushed her cup at Milo then took hold of Dilys's hand and set it to Milo's elbow. "Since neither of you seem eager to pursue a contract"—she gave Dilys a stern and quite blatant *and you'd better not be* glower—"you can look out for each other, yes? I've been sinking for a dance, and possibly a chance to pry some of Lilibet's plum wine from her stingy clutching fingers. I can't do either standing about." She dropped a quick kiss to Dilys's forehead. "Behave yourself. Your tad's poor heart can't take another offer just now.

"And *you.*" She dragged Milo down by his lapel and set a smacking kiss to his cheek. "Congratulations, dear heart. We're so proud of you. Only, remember—this is *your* celebration. Don't let anyone turn it into something more"—she wrinkled her nose—"permanent."

With a last pat to Milo's chest, Nia swirled away with a bright grin, the bells in the lace of her kirtles' hems chiming cheerfully with every clop of her clogs.

Milo watched her go, then turned to Dilys. "Offer?"

Dilys rolled her eyes. "Oh, the Glasscocks from down Fernswallow are still trying to buy their way into a magical lineage, and they apparently thought I might've gone blind as well as hopelessly dense because they offered Bryn." She made a face. "Nothing the Sisters would approve anyway, but it did send Tad to growling like a bear and shutting himself in his study for over a week."

She had to nearly shout that last as the music swelled and lines began to form on the dancefloor.

The mention of the Sisters made Milo brighten up a bit. A council of nine priestesses, one to represent each goddess, every contract offer went through them to ensure there were no crossed family lines, and no concentrations of power enriching one clan over another. They'd been extraordinarily stingy with their approval of offers when his mam had come of age, and extraordinarily indignant when she'd come home from war with Milo in her belly. According to his mam, they only finally agreed, five years after the fact, to issue him the proper papers so he could inherit because Lilibet had done... something—something neither she nor Milo's mam ever actually confessed. Whatever it was, it had done the job. That and the fact that Nain had made it clear by then that Milo had been claimed as dragonkin, and Ceri was not only no such thing but had told the Sisters in no uncertain terms she had no intention of expanding her brood beyond Milo. The Sisters could either accept Milo as the heir to Old Forge, or fight it out with all the parish councils as well as Kymbrygh's parliament over why they wouldn't.

Surely the Sisters could be counted on to be as choosy with any offers Milo might get as they'd been with his mam. In fact, they might be even choosier just out of petty, bureaucratic spite.

"I'm surprised anyone would have the brass to make an offer at all just yet." Milo took a good gulp from the cup that used to be Dilys's, hoping she wouldn't notice and snag it back. It was metheglin, mead brewed in the traditional Kymbrygh style, and very good. "You're too young."

"I'm perfectly eligible to entertain offers, as long as nothing is signed until I come of age next year. I'm not *that* much younger than you, y'know, O wise one." Dilys gave Milo a soft elbow to the ribs. "But you'll be pleased to know I'm as unprepared to start considering contracts as you are." She paused to watch a pretty girl swoop in to set her jug on the floor as the distinctive notes of the Broom and Bottle kicked up. "Although...."

Milo snorted. "Didn't your mam *just* say—?"

"Oh hush, you. As long she's not of age yet either, we won't have to worry about contracts just yet."

"Well, what if she is, though?" Milo only said it be contrary; the girl, in fact, looked to be right about Dilys's age.

Dilys gave Milo a sly wink. "Eh, people tend to look away as long as there's no chance of an accidental crotch-goblin."

Milo nearly choked on his mead. He shook his head, trying to stifle the laugh and maintain his annoyance with his current life in general as he muttered, "Maybe in Tirrydderch," into his cup.

Tirrydderch might as well be its own little independent realm, for all they adhered to the mores and traditions of the rest of Kymbrygh. They certainly didn't look away in Whitpool. Wellech... maybe. It had been too long since Milo had been here, and it wasn't exactly something that might enter a ten-year-old's awareness—at least it hadn't entered Milo's back when he'd been a seasonal fixture.

Ugh, this wasn't something Milo'd found a need to contemplate much at school. Kymbrygh, Werrdig, and Preidyn, not to mention all the minor islands, were all so very different from one another, for all they rallied under the same flag and loved their queen fiercely. Llundaintref—not only the capitol of Preidyn but of the entire United Preidynīg Isles—was like a microcosm of Preidyn's generally repressed population, and that attitude leaked into the codes of conduct imposed on, and apparently absorbed by, Milo in his years at school. Even group study sessions had been chaperoned. It had made the occasional breathless stolen moment that much more precious and intense, but it had also delayed Milo in having to deal with... well. This.

Dilys dragged her gaze from the girl to give Milo a lift of her eyebrow. "Boys or girls?"

"Either, I guess." Milo shrugged. "It's all just skin in the end."

"Then I'll take the girls, you take the boys. Problem solved."

"Except for the part where it isn't, because I'm of age. I *do* have to worry about contracts now, apparently."

It still kept smacking him in the face. Shouldn't he feel more... grown up? Something? Shouldn't all of this have occurred to him before? Like when he'd *actually come of age* last month?

"Aw, bless." Dilys's tone was more mocking than sympathetic, and the way she stuck out her bottom lip was flat insulting. "If you're going to be a stuffy stick about it, you can just live vicariously through me, then."

"Meaning you're getting set to abandon me already."

"Well." Dilys was still eyeing the dancefloor. No one had yet succeeded in sweeping the girl's bottle out from under her. "Call me superficial, but right now, skin is what—"

"Nope, not listening to you grinding on about your sex life." Milo took a calming sip of mead.

"Your loss, then, but since I'm the generous sort and have no wish to explode your too-genteel-for-your-own-good head, I guess you needn't take on so, you great prude."

"Anyway, you haven't worn your clogs. And you've no broom."

Dilys grinned, wide and wicked. "Clogs, I don't need." She gave Milo a smug look, said, "And a broom?" as she snagged one from the hands of a passing dancer fast enough that it took him several steps of the dance before he realized he'd been disarmed. It didn't matter; Dilys was already gone, calling "Wish me luck!" to Milo over her shoulder as she charged the girl and her bottle, purposeful grin on her face and stolen broom in her hands.

Milo only sighed, raised the tankard in a toast Dilys didn't even see, then emptied it in two hearty swallows. If he was going to make it through this with no one to run interference, he was going to do it from within a relatively painless haze of alcoholic torpor. He eyed the table laden with casks and jugs, calculating how he might get across the great heaving room and begin his descent into drunken debauchery without running into anyone else who might want to not-so-subtly question him using clumsy euphemisms for stamina and size, and oh by the way, could he *actually* breathe fire?

"Milo! *There* you are!"

Milo's shoulders went up around his ears as he tried to sink into his coat and disappear.

...Now there was a thought. Some mages could cast an illusion of invisibility. Milo didn't happen to be one of them, but he was a fast learner.

"I've been looking all over for you!"

Oh! *Oh*! He hadn't recognized the voice through all the noise, but now he whipped around, smile bright and genuine.

"*Elly*!" He took hold of Ellis's arm and clamped down tight. "Thank every goddess. Where have you *been*? Did you know about this?"

Ellis blinked. "About what?" He looked around. "I told you Mam's been going spare with preparations for some kind of party, but she wouldn't tell me—"

"This isn't a *party*, it's a damned bloody *auction*! D'you know how many times I've had to say, 'sorry, I have no representative to entertain negotiations this evening' because your mam and my mam have conveniently disappeared, and *no one* told me about *any* of this, they just *left* me here, I've never had a contract offer in my *life* and now I think I have *nine* of them, and I don't even know who most of these people *are*!"

Milo was panting.

Ellis looked bemused. "*Haia*, Milo. How's your evening been?"

"Augh!" Milo slumped. "I'm sorry. Only, I'm really glad you're here."

He drew back, self-consciously loosening his grip on Ellis's arm. The thick velvet of Ellis's coat was crinkled where Milo's fingers had been clenching it, so Milo brushed at it, trying to smooth it out. It was dark, midnight-blue, and worn over a tailored brocade waistcoat done in red with the shapes of dragons woven subtly through in muted silver thread. Ellis's hair was pulled back into a neat tail at the base of his neck, clean and shining, and his brown cheeks and jaw looked freshly shaved. And he smelled... just. Really good. And. Well. *And.*

Save him, with all the talk of contracts, Milo was abruptly wondering if Ellis already had one. Or at least offers. He would've come of age this past summer. Plenty of time, really. And for pity's sake, *look* at him, of *course* he had offers. Which made Milo a little sad, actually, like he'd missed out on something before he even realized it existed.

"Sorry," Milo said again, abruptly awkward and a little bit tongue-tied as he made himself stop fussing at the velvet and take a step back. "I'm only." He shrugged. "Mam's angry with me, which would explain...."

He waved his hand around, though truthfully no one had really approached him since Nia had commandeered him. Which wasn't surprising, really—Nia was Pennaeth in Tirryderch, which meant she was a force in Kymbrygh in general. Maybe people thought she'd staked a claim for Dilys. Milo didn't even want to think about how that might go over with Dilys. Who, when Milo chanced a look at the dancefloor, had roundly captured the bottle, and appeared to be in the process of capturing the girl who went with it.

Ellis was still smiling, but now there was a touch of curiosity. "Why would Ceri be angry with you?"

"Oh, I—" Milo looked around to see if anyone might hear, but there were too many people to risk saying it out loud. "Nothing, only. You know. Mams." He rolled his eyes and gave Ellis a grin.

Ellis lifted his eyebrows, curious, but only said, "Want to get out of here?"

Milo didn't even pause. "I really, really do."

Rhediad Afon wasn't nearly as old as Ty Dreigiau, Milo's mam's ancient house that sat at the sea-edge of the Old Forge preserve. It was old enough, though, and infinitely better built, timber cruck framing melded seamlessly to stone-built integrity in a breathlessly beautiful mishmash of long hall building and tower house. When they were boys, all Milo cared about was that the undercroft stayed dry and cool all summer, and made for comfortable sleeping when the slick, fresh breeze from the Aled didn't quite make it past the open windows of the upper floors. Now, knowing all about what went into the constant upkeep of his mam's house, he noted the tight seams of the stonework as Ellis led the way up the stairs, the smooth dry gloss of the sturdy timbers that supported the vaulted ceilings.

Milo followed Ellis to the wing that housed the private apartments—maybe to Milo's guest room, which, now that Milo thought about it, would be nice, since no one had bothered to show him yet where he'd be sleeping or where his bag had got off to. The thick rugs beneath their feet muted the noise downstairs as well as their footsteps. It left a hush between them, something thick and… not unbreachable, exactly, but full and pleasant enough Milo didn't necessarily *want* to breach it.

"Here we are," Ellis said, quiet, as though he felt it too, and eased open a door, gesturing for Milo to go ahead.

The fire was going nicely, gold-red pitching flickers from the hearth and into the small sitting room that appeared to adjoin a well-appointed bedroom, if the glimpse of walnut posts and rich blue duvet through the half-open door were any indication. The massive electrolier that hung from the ceiling was dark; two small gas lamps were lit instead, one on a table set between two fat, squashy-looking chairs. Everything about the room was warm and welcoming, drenched in soft amber light.

It was all too fine and lived-in to be a guest room.

"Whose room is this?" Milo finally asked.

"Ehm. Mine?" Ellis said it with an amused lilt as he moved to the sideboard and took up a carved clay decanter, grinning like he had a secret, and poured its contents into two fine crystal glasses. "Why? Something wrong?"

"Well, no. I mean, of course not, but." Milo shook his head. "You've moved from your old one. This one's so…."

Grown up.

"It suits me," Ellis said simply and offered a glass to Milo.

Milo took it absently. "It does. But I thought you'd taken the Croft?"

Ellis shrugged. "When I was a boy, I split my time between here and Oed Tyddyn. Now I split it between here and the Croft." He gestured to the chairs. "Sit."

Milo did, waiting until Ellis took the other chair before he ventured, "So. You and your tad, then. Is it really—?"

"However you meant to finish that question," Ellis cut in, "the answer is yes. It is. Really. And I'd prefer to not talk about it now, if you please." It wasn't terse or angry, but it was clear and unbending.

"Fair." Milo sat back in the incredibly comfortable chair, lifting his glass for a good sniff before venturing a taste, as a childhood spent with Ellis and his endless pranks demanded. This wasn't anything of the sort. This was—

Milo grinned at Ellis in delight, abruptly and wholly diverted. "This can't be."

"Oh, can't it, though." Ellis was unapologetically smug as he clinked his glass against Milo's. "Lilibet's finest plum wine. Sought after by all, enjoyed by few."

"Don't I know it." Milo took a good taste, sighing as dozens of different flavors—sweet and bitter, fruity and floral and woody—washed together into incongruous harmony and burst like fireworks over his tongue.

He'd only had it a few times in his life, Highwinter presents from Lilibet to Ceri, and Ceri was shamelessly stingy about sharing. Lilibet's orchard was small and she had no interest in expanding it. The few bottles it produced each year, therefore, were for friends. Lilibet didn't sell her plum wine—she gifted it to those she deemed worthy, a very short list as opposed to the very long one consisting of those who wished they were on the short one.

They'd tried to steal a bottle once, Milo and Ellis, and it was possible Dilys had been with them, but if she had been, Milo didn't remember. All he really remembered was getting chased—for *hours*—by whatever kitchen minion had caught them, escaping and thinking themselves quite clever, and then getting a good hiding from Lilibet anyway when they'd shown up later for supper. They hadn't even cared much about the wine or getting drunk; they'd only cared that it was coveted, guarded, and therefore a challenge.

Milo grinned at the memory. "Your mam's going to kill you."

"Not if she wants her roof fixed before winter." Ellis grinned back. "Anyway, it was her idea."

Milo narrowed his eyes. "Your mam *gave* you plum wine. *Gave* it to you. Your mam."

"Think of it as an apology."

"I *knew* it!" Milo jolted so hard he almost sloshed some of the precious wine out of his glass. "They *did* leave me alone down there on purpose!"

Blood and rot, his mam must be *really* angry with him.

"I don't know what you did"—Ellis tipped his glass at Milo in a pseudo toast—"but I approve."

Ten minutes ago, Milo hadn't approved of any of it, even a tiny bit. Now, coveted wine in his hand and Ellis smiling at him with his white teeth and soft eyes... well.

"You know what?" Milo emptied his glass then held it out for Ellis to refill. "So do I."

✺

"Show me."

Milo squinted up from where he sat on the floor. "What?" He'd slid down to stoke the fire a while ago and then just sort of stayed there.

Ellis sat down beside him and cracked open the second bottle of wine. "*Show* me."

Milo held out his glass, grinning, because yes, he remembered this—staying up far too late, considering they habitually rose with the dawn, and grinding on like pepper mills about anything, everything, until Lilibet invariably came by to shush them and threaten to separate them. And once they'd quieted, settled down, Ellis would say "Show me." And Milo would.

He waited until Ellis had refilled both glasses then asked, "What would you like to see?"

Ellis set the bottle aside, propping back on one arm and stretching out his legs. "I dunno." He waved his glass around. "Something with fire."

"Fire," Milo hummed, thinking, then narrowed his eyes.

Shapes first—a dragon, because it was the first thing Milo thought of, wings dripping dainty beads of flame like dewdrops onto the hearthstone, then a horse in full gallop, and a cat because it was easy. Faces next—Dilys because Milo'd been so pleased to see her, then Bethan from the bridge because Milo still wasn't over his pique. Conjuring Ellis's face out of fire was nearly effortless; Ellis had always been so fierce and bright, it seemed as though the flames *wanted* to take the shape.

"You've got better at this." Quiet. Gaze following every flicker and flash.

Milo shrugged. "I took art classes at school. Learned to draw. It helps."

"Clearly."

Milo let the portrait linger for a moment, staring when he shouldn't, before he let the fire slip then shift and take on the contours of the sea. Rolling swells and crashing breakers rippled across the small fireplace, fierce enough Milo could almost taste the salt.

"Now," Ellis said, tone soft like spring rain, "show me what it Looks like."

Even having been expecting it, part of that long-ago ritual, it still made something bloom inside Milo, warm as a kitchen hearth. Secrets shared, and the intensity of the friendship upon which the secrecy depended, the trust inherent to such a massive confidence, and how Milo had never, not once, thought Ellis might betray it. Milo's mam'd had a right fit back when a tiny Milo thoughtlessly blurted his secret at an equally tiny Ellis, but this—this slotting back into place, this ease and... *relief* after so many years—this made any risk taken on by the unfledged boy he'd been worth it.

So Milo only tilted his head, concentrated, and showed Ellis as near as he could what Milo Saw: the pearly wisps that gathered in like a fingers to a fist, curling and coalescing to a great swath of might that drove the surf made of fire; the prismatic whorls that roiled into undercurrents that could swallow ships; the legion of colors that twisted beneath the swells and surged up to cap silver to their churning tips.

Ellis dropped back on his elbow, smiled, soft and dear, and said, "Beautiful."

Milo peered at Ellis, drenched in firelight, and thought... *Yes.*

And then he blinked and thought... *Oh. Crap.*

―――

"So. Did you have a nice time at the party?"

Milo slitted open bloodshot eyes to scowl at his mam. His head felt too huge to be cradled in his hand the way it was, and tender, like a bruised fruit, and Ceri's voice was very much too loud. And still with that thread of anger all through it.

The constant clatter and sway of the train wasn't helping. It was far too early to even be up, let alone hungover and slumped in the nearly empty dining car across from his mam while she was clearly still stewing over Milo's transgressions the evening before.

He poked at the plain porridge in front of him, muttered, "Lilibet outdid herself," and thought about reaching across the table for the honey. But then he'd have to actually move, and he'd just got the pounding behind his eyes to thump a little less harshly. "Not that you'd know, since you abandoned me without even *telling* me what—"

"You can't be that naïve, Milo. You knew exactly—"

She stoppered it when a porter waddled past their table and down the aisle, linens in his hand and a determined look on his face. Ceri instead sipped at her tea and looked out the window.

Still bleary-eyed and fog-brained when he'd been more or less dumped from his guest bed by his mam's terse demands, Milo had been immediately bustled into packing the small bag he hadn't really unpacked, then shoved into a hire car before even Rhediad Afon's cooks were up. He hadn't shaved. He hadn't put on a tie. He hadn't even really woken up properly before he found himself at the East Parish Station, saying, "But I thought we were staying another two days," and realizing he wasn't going to get to say goodbye to Ellis.

It was that small cask of brandy Ellis had dug from the depths of the sideboard and tapped after they'd finished both bottles of wine. Probably. Or the jug of... something eye-wateringly strong he'd pulled out later for shots. Maybe. Milo couldn't remember if anything came after that, but considering that Ellis had kept pulling potables out of that cupboard like a mage pulling scarves from his sleeve....

Ceri took a deep breath as though looking for calm. "Last night was only a taste. And after what you pulled at the rites..." She shook her head, mouth tight. "If anyone knew, if it got out, it wouldn't only be potential suitors waving contracts at you, Milo. Don't you understand?"

"I understand you wanted to teach me a lesson. Ta very much, I've learnt it quite well—don't piss off Ceri Priddy or she'll throw you to the wolves." Milo made the mistake of rolling his eyes, and then found it necessary to very carefully massage them until the knives behind them dulled some. "*Gah.*" He blinked, squinted. "Can we do this another time? My head feels like—"

"We could've done it last night, if you hadn't shown up legless."

Milo vaguely recalled that she'd been waiting up for him in the guest suite, throwing the door open before Ellis could even drag Milo all the way down the hall. To be fair, they'd been pretty loud, though Milo couldn't remember what it was they'd been laughing about when they'd stumbled their way from Ellis's rooms. He did remember, though, that Ellis had taken one look at Ceri's face and abandoned Milo with a meek little "Well. Ehm. Cheers, then."

Coward.

"It was supposed to be a *celebration*." Milo sighed and dropped his spoon. The porridge had gone cold by now, and it wasn't like he'd been intending to eat it anyway. His stomach had been roiling when he'd been pressganged out of bed the way it was. His mam wasn't helping. At all. "If you'd wanted to talk last night, you shouldn't have stormed off the way you—"

"I did not *storm*."

"—did, and if you'd wanted me sober, you should've...." Milo huffed and shoved his bowl away. "I didn't do anything wrong! I can't help the things I can do—"

"Lower your voice!"

"—and sometimes it just happens."

Damn it all, he'd had such a nice time with Ellis last night. Granted, he'd got much drunker than he should've, and some of it was a bit smeary and vague. But they'd talked for hours, getting to know one another again, and Milo'd enjoyed it so much it had mostly blotted out the preceding events of the evening. Now, just like she'd done last night, his mam was yanking the rug out from under what should have been a happy event and leaving Milo flailing for balance.

Ceri was still strung tight, napkin clenched in her lap and back rigid. At Milo's—granted, rather petulant—complaint, she seemed to deflate some.

"Then you clearly need to practice controlling it more. Perhaps you should go back to the private car and go through the exercises that outrageously expensive school taught you."

Expensive because it was a Dewin school, private and parochial, and one of the best in the country. *Outrageously* expensive because it was known for its discretion, else Ceri never would've allowed Milo out from beneath her careful eye to attend it in the first place.

"Shan't." Milo glowered, stubborn. "Can't. Headache."

Ceri leaned in, frowning. "What has that to do with anything?"

"My head hurts? Not really conducive to doing mental exercises that already give me headaches? Would rather not make it worse?"

"You... what?" Ceri sat back in the cushioned seat, bemused. "Your exercises hurt you? You've never mentioned that before."

"I don't...." Milo hesitated, trying to choose his words more carefully, because conversations like these never seemed to go well. His mam was always more concerned that Milo hide the fact he had this particular talent at all, so it was generally more "never speak of it" than any kind of concerned "aw, poor baby."

Still, Ceri's tone was gentler than Milo expected when she said, "Tell me."

"Sometimes it's like holding your breath." Milo chanced a look at his mam's face. "Like... lungs want to pull air in and let air out—it's what they do, what they're meant for—and when you hold a breath in for longer than you should, your muscles cramp up and your head starts pounding." He shrugged. It was the closest he could come to explaining how it was to constantly keep something that was a natural function from functioning at all. "Most of the time I don't feel it. But when you're deliberately not breathing, when you're concentrating all your will on it...." He reached for his teacup; the tea had gone cold too. He grimaced and set it aside. "Sometimes it hurts, is all."

Ceri studied him for a moment, sharp, before her expression softened. "You never said."

"Maybe I wouldn't have to if *you'd* ever had to do it, but you don't have to *bury* yours, do you?" He didn't try to hide the resentment, though he was too tired and headachy to maintain it. He huffed and looked away. "And anyway, it's not as though you've ever once wanted to hear anything about it except that I was keeping it secret and under control. Why would I tell you this?"

"It's only because—"

"I *know* why. I've known why all my life. What I *don't* know is why letting it slip—*once*, when no one but you and I even knew what it was—required you to cut me loose in the middle of the entirety of Wellech like a steak bone thrown into a dog pit. It was unfair and uncalled for, and if it hadn't been for Ellis—"

"An overwhelming choice of possible contract partners is nothing at all compared to what you'll face if others find out, Milo. Count on it. You think it was some sort of desperate trial to have people look at you and want something from you as simple as a pleasant night or maybe a courtship? Ask me what it's like to have generals looking you over, assessing where the things you can do will hit the most targets, kill the right people, and whether the chance of accomplishing those things will be worth it if they lose you in the bargain. Or worse still"—she leaned in over the table, her voice a low hiss—"befriend someone who in another life you could've loved, get them to trust you while you're looking for the right place to slide the blade in." She sat back, gaze hard. "Spies aren't only for wartime, you know. And don't think for a second you're not already being watched to see what you might have inherited from the Bl—"

She cut it off, but Milo heard it anyway. *The Black Dog.*

The fact that Ceri had almost said it was shocking. Milo could do nothing but stare in the wake of such an uncharacteristic outburst. His mam stared back, belatedly throwing a hasty ward around them that fizzed at Milo's skin like static.

The history books barely spoke of Captain Ceri Priddy, but when they did, it was in terms both respectful and pragmatic. Old Whitpool stock, her matrilineal line—sparse though it may have been with few children born to each generation—nonetheless went back to before Old Forge was Old Forge. Powerful, a Seer, though showing no sign whatsoever of being dragonkin, Ceri Priddy nonetheless emerged early in life as a scholar. Her proficiency in magic grew along with her education, and she reached her meistr rank at an unprecedented age of twenty-three.

Like most in her generation, she was inducted into the Royal Forces at twenty-seven when the United Preidynīg Isles joined their allies in the Green Coast War. She was assigned to the 1st Kymbrygh Battalion as a lieutenant under Eastern Regional Command, and after that... well. After that, her military career seemed to get... murky. There were the usual notations of promotions in rank, commendations, pertinent participation in maneuvers. But after her involvement in the Battle of Namurs and her commendation for distinguishing herself on the fields of Marnet, Ceri Priddy herself seemed to disappear between the lines of written history. All that was left were rumors and wide-eyed speculation.

The Black Dog Corp were myth, that much was true, but only because there was no official acknowledgment of their existence. That didn't stop them from reputedly being home to two magical divisions dreaded by any enemy unlucky enough to witness myth become reality. Spies, it was said, but not only moles and scouts and agents. Saboteurs. Guerillas. Demolitionists. Assassins.

The people of Preidyn followed the news of the war across the continent like everyone else did. But the covens took special notice of every mysterious factory explosion behind enemy lines. Every unexplained death of an opposing champion, every lost battle turned to victory when what the combatants on both sides swore were wraiths emerged, fierce and cloaked in red-eyed shadows, charging from conjured mists. Breathless tales of vicious black dogs rose from the smoking ruins of battlefields, and the people of Kymbrygh, where the Black Dog legend had been born centuries before, knew. It didn't take them long to connect it all with the too-powerful-for-anyone's-good Whitpool girl who'd disappeared into Her Majesty's ranks just as the stories of the Black Dogs emerged. They didn't need their government to confirm the existence of the corps; in fact, the consistent denial merely lent life and veracity to rumor and myth.

So it was disconcerting for Milo to sit across the table from this same woman, who'd supposedly struck terror into the hearts of enemies, and watch everything about her just sort of... shrink. All his life, Milo had existed in a queer stasis, both scorning as improbable the tales that made of his mam equal parts war hero and brutal specter, while simultaneously believing every word. Now, he had no idea what to think. And wasn't entirely sure he wanted clarity either way.

"Oh, sweet." Ceri looked older, careworn and weary, as the dawn grew into sunrise and thin gray streaks washed through the dining car's window and slashed the table in halves of shade and light. The silver at her temples somehow stood out more against the black bound at her nape in an untidy bun. She'd taken her glasses off to rub at her eyes and never put them back on again; without them her blue eyes looked huge and bloodshot. "I want you to be safe. That's all."

Milo knew that. He did. It was only... he'd forgot how constricting it was to live beneath her critical eye while he'd been away living an entirely different life. He'd got used to being just another student, watched for nothing more than the expression on his face that told his instructors whether or not he'd absorbed the information they were imparting. His trips home had been necessarily short and overwhelmingly focused on the dragons, and therefore full of nothing more than happy reacquainting, favorite meals, and avoiding anything that could result in bad feelings that might spoil the visit.

Now that he was back for good, without Nain as a buffer, he was finding his mam's attention sometimes reassuring as he tried to fit back into life in Whitpool, and sometimes all but smothering. The low-grade choking discomfort of it only flared all the hotter when his mam went on,

"Which is why I want you to withdraw your application to join the Home Guard."

"...What?" Milo's stomach dropped. "Mam, no. *No*. We talked about this. We *agreed* it would be—"

"And we also agreed you wouldn't do what you did last night. And the fact that you *did* do it—right out in the open, surrounded by witches and sorcerers—makes me wonder how many other times it 'just happened.'"

"That isn't—Mam...."

Milo sucked in a tight breath and looked away.

It was only the Home Guard. Marching in formation. Fake rifles at the shoulder. Wooden swords at the hip. "Yes, sir!" and "No, sir!" on demand. Once-a-month bivouacs on someone's backfield that were more camping out than learning to live on a battlefield.

Pretending, really.

Still.

He'd watched the Whitpool Regiment since he was a boy, loving the sharp look of the uniforms with their shiny buttons and spit-polished boots, and envying wildly every step they marched in the White Day parades behind the Kymbrygh Reserves Regiment. Certainly less bloodthirsty and glorybound now than he'd been as a child—as every child, really—but the appeal was still there.

"Everyone does their service in the Home Guard." Milo set his jaw and looked back at his mam. "*Everyone*. It would be more noticeable if I *didn't* do my part. It would—"

"Ellis won't be joining. And Dilys—"

"Elly is a Warden. And Dillie will be once she's done with the training. The Home Guard *wishes* they were as competent and prepared for trouble as the Wardens. It's not the same, and you know it."

"Your work with the dragons is just as valuable to the Crown as any Warden, or anything you might do in the Home Guard. More. Dragonkin have a right to exemption. A duty, actually. There are only so many who can do what you do."

"I don't *want* exemption. I want...."

It wouldn't come, lodged up in Milo's throat hot and tight, because he wasn't sure he could put it into coherent thought, let alone words. To belong, maybe. To figure out how to fit back in with neighbors who looked at him funny now when he waved to them at the village shops, a vaguely familiar stranger who'd been one of them once, but had gone away and sort of wasn't anymore. To find a skin he could fit into, one they would accept.

"Darling boy." Ceri sighed and reached across the table to set her hand lightly atop Milo's. "Sometimes it doesn't matter what we want." She squeezed. "I'm sorry. It's done."

"...You." Milo swallowed. "You don't need me to withdraw." He pulled his hand away. "You've already spoken to the Colonel-in-Chief."

"I have." Plain, and entirely unapologetic.

It really shouldn't have hit Milo in the solar plexus the way it did. He didn't think there was a military, or former military, person in the whole of Kymbrygh his mam didn't know personally. And as the Holder of Old Forge, it wasn't as though she needed to—she could have knocked the legs out from under Milo's intentions just as easily with a simple word to Whitpool's council, or even the Sisters, if she'd wanted to make bloody sure.

"Well." Milo's voice was humiliatingly gruff. He cleared his throat and stood. "There's my life sorted, I reckon."

"Milo, don't—"

"If you'll excuse me, Captain Priddy, I believe your orders were to retire and practice my exercises." Refusing to shake or let his voice quaver, Milo straightened his back and shifted a deliberately over-the-top salute. "By your leave."

He didn't wait for her to give it, merely executed a smart about-face and stomped down the aisle of the dining car like the thwarted child he apparently was, thinking miserably that the already long train ride home had just got infinitely longer.

Chapter 4—Tonality

: *music centered around a "home" key*

"Listen, you." Milo stood from his crouch, hands held out so he didn't smear plaster all over his good work coat. He strode around from where he'd been working on the dragon's foreclaw and stood far enough back it could see him with both eyes. "I can't repack it unless you *stay still*. You're getting mud all in the plaster, and it'll never set."

The dragon blinked moss-green eyes twice the size of Milo's head, unimpressed. Her snout quivered, a burgeoning snarl, and smoke puffed from her nostrils as her frill flared out, but since Milo knew it was only for show, he stood his ground. Yellow-tailed spitters packed venom that could stick to their prey like tar, and eat right through skin and bone while paralyzing the nervous system. This one, for all her snarly attitude, was still a calf and had lived on the Old Forge preserve for all of her short life, and would likely remain for the rest of her days whether she liked it or not. And while she'd never allowed anyone else—even Glynn—to get close enough to so much as throw her a haunch of venison, her show of annoyance with Milo was *only* a show. The drugged meat he'd fed her to calm her down and coax her out into the open couldn't be hurting, either. The sleep charms he'd been layering over her for the past hour *might* be helping, though magic on dragons was iffy, and mostly useless. But her nimbus was cool and sedate, gray-streaked indigo shot through with playful coral, though all of it was edged in small jags of muddy red pain Milo could absolutely take care of. *If* she'd only sit still and let him finish.

"See that?" Milo pointed a hand dripping with gooey plaster to where his violin sat in its case on the back of the sturdy old cart hooked to Poppy, Milo's grumpy little dappled mare. His mam's mongrel, Lleu, kept a bored eye on them from the cart's bed, desultorily gnawing on a deer antler, his reward for helping Milo track the spitter across the preserve and lure her out of the thicket where she'd gone to ground when her wound hobbled her.

The spitter swiveled her head to where Milo was pointing, indifferent gaze sharpening for the briefest of seconds before she looked away, a very clear *pfffft*, or at least that's what Milo read into it. He smirked. Drunk dragons were always fun.

"You let me finish without being a great child about it, and I'll play for you. If you *don't* let me finish, that claw is going to get more infected, and you'll not only be sore, you won't get any music, because it's already getting dark and I'm cold and hungry. Understood?"

Intelligent creatures, dragons, though the prevailing wisdom was they didn't understand words so much as tone and nuance like any other animal. Milo privately thought it was a bit more than that. He was pretty sure the dragons Saw the same way he did. Either way, the spitter clearly understood Milo's offer of a bargain—her colors flared, slate-blue indignation, before a roseate prickle of unease flickered right down the middle. She swung her head away so only one great eye was glaring at Milo. Deliberately, or at least it seemed so, the nictitating membrane slid over, blatant dismissal, though the dragon did plant herself more firmly in the mud and make a great show of going still. All of it done with a low, rumbling growl, but still.

Milo snorted with a fond shake of his head and went back to work. Once he didn't have to contend with careless claws waving about at unexpected moments, or getting whacked in the head with her stunted wing, it was easy. The plaster he'd managed to apply before had started to solidify, and there was indeed dirt and mud now mixed with the herbs and medicines he'd packed into the wound an hour ago. Removing, recleaning, then repacking took only a few minutes, and once again Milo began applying the plaster from his bucket around the claw bed, working it between the small scales on the toes and on up to the carpal joint.

He smoothed it as much as he could, leaving it thickest over the ragged mess of the torn claw, and crouched with his knees in the mud to have a good look. The raw throb of red was still sliding over and around the wound, though that was to be expected until it was allowed to heal some more, and it was a clean scarlet, rather than a sickly brick. Milo was pleased to see only a few prickly jags of swampy green winding through, and hoped that meant he'd caught the infection before it could take hold—provided the dragon didn't chew off the cast just to be difficult.

She was too cold, though. Normally being this close to a dragon was like standing next to an open fire. But this one hadn't shown up at the forge for her rations in days, which was why Milo had come looking for her, and why he'd have to keep a good eye on her. The sulfur-on-petrol pong that was sometimes enough to make his eyes water was too faint.

She'd been born here three years ago, her egg damaged and discarded by the migrating clan when it failed to hatch. It was pure chance Nain had found her, weeks later, a pitiful hatchling mewling on the edge of the hot spring nursery on the southwest part of the preserve, trying to use her malformed wings for balance as she tripped and blundered through deadfall and overgrowth. She'd never fly, and with her foot the way it was, she was going to have a hard time hobbling all the way to the forge. If she didn't manage it in another couple days, Milo was going to have to haul out the winch and tractor and get her there himself.

He blew out a weary huff, already thinking ahead to the ordeal and hoping it didn't come to that.

"Don't move," he told the spitter, standing and making his way over to his cart to clean himself up before the plaster on his hands hardened. "Eh-eh, hold it up," he snapped, not even having to look to know the dragon was in the process of plopping the unset cast right back into the mud again.

Intelligent creatures, sure, but dragons were also smartarses, at least in Milo's experience. Like cats, they were equally likely to give you a swat of a spiked tail for no reason as they were to show their bellies to let you scratch a hard to reach spot between their scales. And, like cats, they liked to believe they could get along nicely without you, ta very much, and only deigned to suffer your existence because you could sometimes be helpful and entertaining.

Plaster-free, though freezing now, Milo dried his numb fingers then curled them into fists and blew into them. Once he could move them again without breaking them off, he dug some bits of apple out of his pocket for Poppy then tossed her some hay. It had been a long day, making the rounds of the preserve, and though she huffed her displeasure every time they'd had to stop for a while to tend to wounds or illnesses, or for Lleu to snuffle the undergrowth of a thicket looking for the spitter, she'd been more of a sport about it than usual. Bred from a strain specifically developed to tolerate the dragons, the pony quite frankly typically tolerated them better than she did Milo. Any other day, she'd be surreptitiously trying to turn them for home and stable every chance she got, just to see if she could get away with it. Today, as though she'd known Milo had been worried, she'd moseyed along after Lleu without once trying to nudge Milo toward warm hay and a waiting bucket of oats.

With a good scrub at the mare's neck, Milo turned back to the dragon, amused to see her still standing ostentatiously motionless and with her head turned, deliberately not looking at Milo. Since she was also still standing with her foreleg off the ground and the new cast out of the mud, Milo took it for a win. Smirking, he nudged aside his rifle—dragons might be the biggest predators out here, but they weren't the only ones—and unclipped the latches on the violin case. The dragon perked at the sound, no longer pretending to ignore Milo as he slid the violin out of its case and took up the bow. The drug must have been wearing off; her gaze was sharper, and her colors more vibrant.

"All right, you can put your foot down now," Milo said with a grin, and then he began to play.

It wasn't only for the dragon, honestly, though sure, Milo loved that something so simple could bring such calm and ease to beasts that came to this place because they'd been hurt or were sick and had few other places to go. And he loved that once the first notes left the strings, grappling with the eddy and toss of chill sea air then sliding along it, winding through it, other dragons would come and settle in around him in sleepy piles. Some even now and then softly blew their own calls to furl just beneath the harmonics and vibratos of the concerto or sonata or jig, or whatever Milo chose to play.

Three of them were winging in now, stark shapes against the darkening sky, looping wide and slow like hawks. Two of them were blackhorns, bellies pulsing like winking stars with a soft orange glow, fresh from their rations from Howell at the forge. The other had the slick javelin-with-wings shape of a whip-tailed wrangler, iridescent scales catching the flagging light of the gloaming and sparking warm. One at a time they skimmed into a soft glide and circled to ground far enough away so the bursts of wind from their backwing landings didn't blow Milo over. The ground only shook somewhat as they plodded toward the little spitter, allowing her the space she'd already claimed, though still moving in close to warm her. Even that display of care didn't prevent the occasional snap or snarl or nip at a neck as they poked and bumped each other for dominance and position.

More came as Milo slipped his bow across the strings and let his spirit coast away into the glissandos and modulations with this growing pile of dragons that welcomed him with their strange antagonistic affections. They'd mourned his nain when she'd died. He'd seen the colors sodden with grief. They missed Milo while he was gone, he could tell, yellows and greens flaring bright every time he came back, nuzzles unasked for from snouts bigger than he was, and sonorous calls they usually reserved for each other. Howell just wouldn't do, and Milo's mam had never had a rapport with them. As far as Milo knew, she'd never really cared to have one. She didn't even like the smell of them on Milo when he came home from a day of caring for them, and they barely acknowledged her presence on the rare occasions she ventured out to one of the pastures. She and Howell had only just managed that last half year after Nain died and Milo was finishing school.

Milo thought it really all came down to the fact that neither Ceri nor Howell *loved* the dragons, not like Milo did.

It had been difficult these past few months, trying so hard to fit himself back into spaces he didn't really know anymore, or had maybe outgrown. Realizing he was a stranger in his own village, his own home.

She was just standing there. *Grinning*. Wicked. Because she was a brat. Always had been. And, Milo couldn't help noticing, *not* getting a reprimand from Ceri about the open door.

"So, I'm gonna...." Milo gave Glynn the *go away* look he'd been giving her since she was wee and wobbly.

She heeded it just as well as she'd always done.

Milo knew better than to try to wait her out, so he merely rolled his eyes. "You know what? Fine. Here." He tugged the remaining leg free and shoved the trousers at Glynn. "Be helpful if you're only going to stand there. And shut that door."

Glynn creased up with a giggle, and finally stepped out onto the small porch to pull the door shut. "Give me the boots or you'll ruin your coat." She grimaced as she snagged the boots out of Milo's hand and took hold of his coat sleeve. "Pull."

"You'll get plaster all over your—"

"*Pull.*"

Milo pulled.

"And where's your light?"

Milo huffed as he let Glynn help him get the thick coat off. "I doused it when I came up the walk, since I had no idea I'd be turned away at my own backdoor like an urchin." When he was free of the coat, he pulled up another magelight. And paused. He frowned. "What happened to your eye?"

Glynn's mouth pinched in disapproval. "The mud's gone all the way through to your longs. Did you want to take those—?"

"I am *not* stripping to skin in the cold on my own back porch, and with you here to heckle me." Milo waved it away. "Seriously, Glynn—you look like you got punched." And Milo would know, seeing as how the last of the bruise he'd got in Wellech had still been a light yellow-green ghost only last week. Milo took a step in. "*Did* you get punched?"

Glynn sighed the sigh of the very much put-upon. "You're as bad as my tad." She rolled her eyes. "No, I didn't get punched, I got hit. There's a difference. But I promise you, Cennydd came away much worse."

"*Cennydd*? Cennydd Driscoll dy Lloyd?" Milo took the coat back, and then the boots, dropping them into a muddy pile by the washing barrel. "For pity's sake, he's got *at least* a stone or two on you! What were you thinking? What was *he* thinking?"

"He doesn't think at all, innit? At least not like a normal person." Glynn lifted her chin. "That's his problem." When Milo merely stared at her, lost, she huffed and said, "You know how he is about the dragons."

"Yes, chopsy as a crow and a sincere pain in the arse because I won't let him past the wards to wander about the preserve unsupervised."

Glynn wrinkled her nose. "And I can. So he's decided he hates me now." She shrugged, unconcerned. "I get to come to work with Tad when I'm not in school. I get to see dragons." She paused with a speaking look. "And I get to see you."

She kept *looking* at Milo, as though expecting... something. Milo had no idea what.

He shook his head with a frown, rubbing briskly at his arms. He'd been cold when he'd got home, and now he was standing out here in nothing but his long underwear and a tatty, ancient cable jumper.

"Are you telling me you got in a fight with Cennydd because he's jealous?"

"No, I'm telling you Cennydd 'accidentally' hit me in the face with his cricket bat because he's jealous. I got in a fight with him because he's a worm who hit me with a cricket bat, and I was that tamping."

Well. Milo reckoned getting whacked with a bat would get anyone proper cross.

"Oh, bloody.... Fine." Milo sighed as he retrieved the rifle from where he'd propped it and waved Glynn away from the door. "I'll talk to him."

Glynn followed Milo into the mudroom, and shut the door behind her, eyebrows squinched in mild outrage. "Oh, *will* you, then." Huffing, she chucked Milo's muddy trousers into the corner beneath the coatrack. "I don't need you to—"

"I know you don't." Milo set the rifle in its rack, lobbed his hat at the hooks on the wall—missed, of course—and sighed a blessing under his breath for the basin of warm water waiting for him on the bench, more evidence his mam was done being angry with him. He pushed up his sleeves and dipped his arms in up to the elbows, swished them around as his fingertips burned and goosebumps blossomed to race over every inch of him, before he bent to wash his face. "You very clearly can handle your own affairs, Glynn, I'm not saying otherwise." He reached for the cloth she handed him to dry his face. "It's more for his benefit than yours. He's perhaps a bit odd, but he—"

"He's a proper minging sheephead." Glynn held up her hands when Milo gave her an impatient look. "Fine. Have your talk. But I'm telling you"—she snagged the cloth and reached up to rub roughly at a spot of dried mud in Milo's hair; it felt more like a diffident assault—"there's something not right about him. Something... off."

"There isn't. He's not. Only, he's a bit awkward, and a little too...." Milo trailed off, unable to find the right word for what Cennydd was. Odd, certainly, and angry about it, but—

"Exactly." Glynn shoved the cloth at Milo's chest. "Talk all you like. Only, don't show him your back." She turned for the hallway that led to the kitchen. "Rhywun Ceri ran you a bath. You'll have just enough time before supper."

Milo watched her go, not really any more informed than he'd been a minute ago. But the smells from the kitchen were stronger now and doing alarming things to his empty stomach, and the siren song of a hot bath was just as convincing to him now as to a sailor called to rocky ruin.

And anyway, Glynn really could handle herself just fine. Cynnedd and his cricket bat had more reason to worry than she did.

"...And Rhywun Collins says she's some books that might help, and she'll let me borrow them if I want." Glynn's eager smile implied she very much wanted. "I mean, I love working at the forge with Tad," she hastened to put in at Howell's sigh. She sent a pleading look at Milo. "But Rhywun Collins says I'm a natural with the livestock already." Rhywun Collins was the local veterinarian, and her word was not a thing to be dismissed. "And it can't be that different to set a broken leg for a dragon, can it?"

"Ehm. Well. Yes? It sort of can." Milo set his beer aside. "Some of them have legs as big as tree trunks. There are winches involved. And sometimes a lot of magic. That's if they even let you—"

"But not always! And I'd study *so hard*, you'd never—"

"Glynn, it's not that easy." Milo tried to be gentle, but it would hurt less in the long run if he was as plain as possible. He hadn't known Glynn had been tagging after Rhywun Collins, and he certainly hadn't known Glynn had set her sights on the profession herself, but—"Rhywun Collins is the best there is when it comes to animals, and she was a huge help when Lleu ate that rope and almost killed himself with his own stupidity." Milo ignored his mam's indignant noise. "But she's never got within two furlongs of a dragon. Dragons aren't like other animals. And you're not dragonkin."

"Well, I know *that*." Glynn rolled her eyes and toyed with the fish on her plate. Fried brown trout, her favorite, with potato cakes and a cabbage and bacon casserole on the side, because it was her birthday and Ceri adored her like a daughter. From the way Glynn had been pleading her case and ignoring her supper, it was effort wasted. "But Tad's knees are getting bad, and he's getting on—sorry, Tad. I mean, not that you're *old*." She looked suitably contrite for the seemingly unintended slur, but it didn't stop her from pointing another piteous look at Milo. "It's true, though. You know he can't even walk the fences anymore."

"Speaking of," Ceri interjected smoothly, "you'll have to handle refreshing the wards on the outer fences next week, Milo."

"Why?" Milo titled his head. "Are you going somewhere?"

She didn't get a chance to answer because Glynn barreled on, "All dragonkin have at least one apprentice. I looked it up." She leaned over the table, her fork abandoned so she could clasp her hands in front of her chest like the supplicant she apparently was. "What if something happened to you, Milo? Who would take care of the dragons?"

Milo made an effort not to snort. "Ta for the touching show of concern."

"Are we still here?" Howell wondered with an amused look of incredulity aimed at Ceri. He gave his daughter a lift of his slick brown eyebrow. "Pardon me for interjecting a bit of reality into your ambitions, but Rhywun Ceri and I have been taking care of the—"

"Yes, the dozen or so that stay on." Glynn was clearly trying very hard to keep her tone reasonable. "But they don't let you near them."

"They don't let you either."

"Some of them do! I'm in the pastures all the time, and none of them have ever—"

"By *yourself?*" Howell looked alarmed.

Milo had to agree.

"Nain used to take me all the time! I mean...." Glynn looked down, abruptly all-over red. "Milo's nain. Rhywun Ysbain. She used to take me."

She looked... guilty. And sad. As though she thought Milo might mind her using the endearment, when in fact Milo knew his nain had encouraged it. Maybe Milo would have to have a talk with Glynn, too. Let her know that, just because he was back now, it didn't mean she'd been displaced in her found family. He'd been so caught up in feeling like he didn't quite fit anymore, he hadn't even thought to consider that his presence might have disrupted someone else's equilibrium.

"And if I was around them more," Glynn plowed on, "they'd probably get used to me. At least maybe they'd let me get close enough to look so I could tell Milo what to do." She breezed right by the fact that Milo didn't really need anyone to tell him what to do, and gave her tad a stubborn look. "You *know* you couldn't do migration yourself if Milo hadn't been coming home all along, not even with Rhywun Ceri's help, and Na—Rhywun Ysbain wasn't... well, I helped her a lot the last few years when she couldn't...." She looked away, blinking, before she set her jaw and turned back to Howell. "And I saw you, Tad, just from helping Milo this past season and keeping up with the forge. You could barely walk!"

For the first time, Glynn seemed genuinely concerned, rather than trying to implore her way into a new vocation. And Milo couldn't help but notice that Howell didn't deny it, merely pursed his lips and sighed again.

Milo frowned. "Howell, is that true? Have you been having trouble walking?"

Howell sat back with a put-upon air. "I'm not young. And neither are my knees." He shrugged and reached for another potato cake. "*But*," he said with a stern look at Glynn, "I'll thank you not to start building my cairn just yet."

"I don't mean it like that, Tad." Glynn gave the appearance of a daughter suitably chastened, her head down and her shoulders slumped. But she was still giving Milo a calculating look from the corner of her eye.

"Well." Ceri reached over to pat Howell's hand, her gaze soft, her hint of a smile tender. "I don't suppose there's harm in having help when it's around to be had."

Howell rolled his eyes, but gave Ceri's fingers a quick squeeze before he pulled his hand away and went back to his supper.

They had an odd relationship, Howell and Milo's mam, and not one Milo had any interest in dissecting in minute detail. Milo had gone away to school, and had come back on his first holiday to find that Nain had hired Howell to help run Old Forge, and that Howell's daughter Glynn was adorable and insufferable by turns. Milo had liked Howell right away, and suffered Glynn like any eleven-year-old would suffer a child who was too precocious by half, and just sweet enough to prevent the occasional hiding.

The next time he'd come home, Milo found that his mam and Howell had signed a courtship contract, much to Nain's told-you-so glee. The time after that, Howell and Glynn had taken up residence in what used to be a gatehouse, back when Old Forge served double duty as dragon refuge as well as a minor fortress and lookout against invaders and pirates. Milo supposed they'd probably moved on to a conjugal contract, but had absolutely no interest in confirming the suspicion. So perhaps it wasn't so much that the relationship was odd, but that Milo hadn't really been around to see it develop into whatever it was now. Not a partnership, really, and certainly not anything defined by any legal contract terms Milo knew of, but....

Anyway.

They seemed to have no interest in calling the banns for a cariad contract, which... well, Milo had no idea how he felt about that. But since it was none of his business, he reserved the right not to think about it until he had to.

"Right, then." Milo shoved a forkful of fish into his mouth to cover for his other hand surreptitiously feeding some of his casserole to Lleu under the table. The cabbage in it would no doubt have Ceri howling murder at Lleu later, which was always funny, if one didn't have to be in the same room with him. "I wish someone would've said something before now. Howell, I had no idea the load was getting difficult for you. I would've—"

"Nine save me, I'm not that old!" Howell was indignant, but not angry. "I've plenty of good years left in me."

"Of course," Ceri agreed. "But I think we'd all prefer it if those years weren't spent crippled up and useless." She gave Howell a sly wink that Milo was just going to pretend he didn't see. "Glynn's right—dragonkin should have an apprentice." She lifted her eyebrow when Glynn sat up straight, face full of hope. Ceri's tone was very stern when she went on, "Perhaps Milo might consent to hearing the case of an aspiring applicant"—she shot a speaking look at Milo—"on her birthday."

Milo looked from his mam's expectant face to Glynn's beseeching one. And found himself torn between not wanting to give in to manipulation, and at the same time wanting to lift some of what he hadn't known was getting to be a heavier burden from Howell. It *was* difficult work, after all, and downright exhausting during the migration seasons, especially with the odd bit of blacksmithing mixed in with Howell's more important forge duties. Ceri was edging in on fifty now, and Howell was at least ten years her senior. Not, as he'd pointed out repeatedly, old or decrepit by any means, but time and wear did things to a body. From a purely mercenary point of view, Howell was much more valuable in the forge than he was out in the pastures. It was only smart to keep him where he was most productive, and in good shape for as long as possible.

And Glynn looked so pitiably tragic it was getting harder for Milo not to laugh.

"Ugh, you're making me want to pinch your head off." Milo rolled his eyes at Glynn and chucked his napkin over his plate. "Borrow Rhywun Collins's books. You have one week. And then"—he held up a hand when Glynn started to bounce in her chair—"there will be a test."

He hid his smirk as he rose and took his plate to the sink, Glynn's squeals behind him so loud and piercing that Lleu joined in with a lengthy sonorous yowl of protest from under the table.

<hr>

"That was lovely of you."

Milo shrugged as he took the clean dish from Ceri's hand and set to wiping it dry. "It's her birthday. And." He frowned as he set the dry dish on the small stack and took the next from Ceri. "I hadn't really thought about it before. The apprentice thing. I don't feel old enough or wise enough to have one. But it's the safe thing to do."

It was a strange pseudo confrontation with mortality that didn't feel very real, honestly. Glynn's question—*What if something happened to you, Milo?*—had no doubt been a ploy in her effort to get what she wanted, but it had a weird resonance to it that he hadn't truly considered as actual possibility until now. What if something *did* happen to him? Who *would* take care of the dragons? Howell was not, as he'd strenuously and repeatedly pointed out, old, but he was getting there. Ceri was too, and she wasn't dragonkin. Nain had been the last real dragonkin, and Milo her apprentice since he'd been an obnoxious four-year-old and lolloped up to a spined howler to give its tail an impertinent pat, and didn't get eaten or incinerated.

Instead, the dragon looked him over with eyes four times Milo's size, measured him, as Nain sidled up and set a hand to Milo's shoulder. Nain had been bringing Milo out to the pastures with her since before he could walk. This was the first time he'd felt an impulse to touch, to interact, to make a bid for acknowledgement. He hadn't really expected the dragon to comply.

"What do you See?" Nain's voice was soft but not afraid.

Milo hesitated. He'd never Looked at a dragon before. Mam would have his hide, even though she got to do it all the time, but not Milo, never Milo, Milo had to hide it and never tell. It wasn't fair. But because this was Nain, because it was their secret, Milo obeyed.

It wasn't the first time Milo had seen this dragon. They came and they went; sometimes they stayed for a season or two and let Nain see to them, and Nain would teach Milo which had what markings, why the cows were bigger than the bulls, where the different breeds lived and where they were heading.

"He's so... *pretty*."

He was. Astonishingly so. Not only the dragon's hulking build and majestic expanse of wing, but what the dragon *was*, what Milo could *See*. The colors were manifold, churning in wave upon wave, gentle as the sea on a warm summer day, and twice as deep. Enticing. Welcoming.

Milo reached out to touch them, felt them, telling him stories, letting him See. "He's very old."

"He is." Nain tugged the flaps of Milo's bobble hat more firmly over his ears and squeezed his shoulder. "He's my oldest friend." There was a smile in her voice. "He's been leading his clan since I was a little girl." She gave Milo a tender jostle. "Find me a stone as pretty as my friend, *calon bach*."

Milo didn't think there was one, but he scanned the mud anyway, apologizing in his head to the sluggish worms and bugs, the turn to spring not quite convincing enough yet to coax them completely from their winter sleep. Milo was careful with the mud he squished between his fingers, searching, until he found a stone dark and smooth—a bit of coal, maybe, weathered and worn with edges as iridescent as a dragon's scales.

Nain grinned when Milo handed it up to her, blue eyes crinkled at the corners. "That's a fine one, all right." She nodded approvingly as she handed it back. "Hold it tight. Close your eyes." When Milo did, Nain asked, low and gentle, "How much d'you love the dragons, *cyw*?"

"Lots." Milo almost opened his eyes, but Nain hadn't told him to yet. "Lots and lots." As much as he loved Mam and Nain and crabbing on the pebbled beach on summer nights.

"I know you do." Nain sounded like she was smiling. "Now think about how much you love them, and toss your stone to my friend here."

Milo opened his eyes and frowned up at Nain, clutching the stone that tiny bit tighter. She'd *just* asked him to find it! And it *was* a rather nice stone. Shiny. Milo sort of wanted to keep it.

"Go on, then, little heart. Don't throw it *at* him, though. That would be rude." Nain prodded softly between Milo's shoulder blades. "Toss it right in front of him. He won't mind. C'mon, I'll help."

Milo scowled but let Nain take hold of his hand, going with the movement when she swung their arms gently together and said low into Milo's ear, "Let go, love." Milo did, and Nain told him, "Watch now."

Even as Nain said it, the dragon's colors swirled up and out, wild and fierce, flaring in a stream as though reaching for Milo. Milo reached back, delighted, before all of it narrowed to a dense blaze of white, arresting and beautiful. An orange-silver glow ignited in the dragon's belly, climbed its throat, scales flushing hot and steady as the coals of a furnace in deep winter. Milo smelled petrol and sulfur, the air all at once thick with it as the dragon opened its great jaws, teeth taller than Milo, and drew in a great, rumbling breath. Milo pushed back against Nain, startled, afraid, but the dragon didn't snap him up for a snack or spit venom or flame at him; it sent a surprisingly narrow jet of bright-hot fire to the ground at its clawed feet—blinding, beautiful, terrible, terrifying—and when it stopped, in the small charred crater left in the spring mud sat the stone. The size of a red kite's egg now, black and smooth as glass, a bloodshot smudge like a winking eye at its heart pulsing with a beat Milo suspected no one could see but him. Millennia eddied inside it, sonnets made of starfire, the infinite universes in the liminal spaces between drops of rain, the sharp taste of a pause between notes in accelerando, and all of it strong as worlds yet vulnerable as a naked back.

I am Dragon, it said. *We are Clan.*

"It's a dragonstone now," Nain told Milo, stern, as she crouched to his eye level and plucked the stone up, cooled now, but never cool. She held it out to him in the palm of her hand. "They've claimed you as kin." She reached out and thumbed Milo's cheek, fingers warm from the stone. "I rather thought they would do."

Milo had been small, too young to remember, really, but he nonetheless *did* remember every single thing about that day. The shrill, insistent calls of oystercatchers down on the rocky beach; his nain's gray hair, loose from the habitual tail low on her nape, lofting about her head in the still frost-tipped sea winds; thick-bright spring sunlight splashed over mud and grass but Milo and Nain bent together close like secrets in the dragon's shadow; Nain's eyes, blue and dark like Mam's and Milo's, shining with pride; her face, so loved and loving, creased with age and smiles.

"'Tis no small thing. But then neither is your heart, eh?" Nain looked down at the stone, her mouth turned up soft and pleased. "Their hearts and yours, twined and protected." She set the stone in Milo's hand—warm and smooth and alive—and curled his small fingers around it, safe and dear. "Not to worry, pet. You'll grow into it."

Milo felt the weight now like a new thing in his pocket, so used to it being there he didn't even really remember putting it there every morning and didn't notice the small bulk of it unless he thought about it. Keys and watch and coins, routine and thoughtless, and always the warmth of that stone against his thigh.

"Well." Ceri set a stemmed crystal glass on the drying board, and swatted Milo's hand away when he reached to dry it. "Leave it. Drying will smear it." She took the cloth from Milo and wiped her hands with a thoughtful look. "Anyway, it was still well done of you. I know taking on an apprentice will be more work in the short run, but you could do worse than Glynn. She'll work hard, and I swear the child wants to know *everything*." Her shrug was fond. "If you can keep her focused long enough to not get herself hurt, she'll be a good help to you."

"I won't let her get hurt."

He would, however, set Glynn to helping collect the dragon manure from the pastures, if all went well. Old Forge made a proper penny on it, and Milo had enough to do without shoveling small mountains of shite every week.

"I know. And so does Howell, else he'd have put paid to all her grizzling proper sharpish." Ceri draped the cloth over her shoulder and turned to lean back against the cupboard, arms crossed over her chest. She gave Milo an assessing look. "Anyway, it'll free up your time for other things."

Milo snorted. "What other things?" Besides the truncated trip to Wellech, he'd done little else besides tend the dragons and whatever needed doing around the place since he'd got back. He gave his mam a suspicious squint. "Have you got something in mind? Where are you going next week anyway?"

Ceri only smiled and pushed away from the cupboard. "Merfyn came by with some papers for you."

"The stipend didn't come already, did it?" Merfyn was the preserve's solicitor, and Old Forge's representative for parish council matters. "Wait, they're not trying to reduce it again, are they?"

The last time they'd had to fight with the parish council over how much it cost to feed and take care of dragons, it had lasted three full years. Merfyn had eventually taken the case to the Kymbrygh MP, and the two of them had managed to turn it around and eke out enough of a bump to fund a few more annual head of cattle and half a herd of goats. But the boom in the deer population a few years before—and the reason the government had tried to reduce the stipend in the first place—had weakened their case, even if the dragons had already hunted them back down to their normal numbers by the time Old Forge had got its first notice that their stipend would be cut.

"Nothing like that." Ceri chucked the cloth at Milo's head and wafted toward the door, eyebrows high and a smile Milo didn't trust for a second tipping up one side of her mouth as she left the kitchen. "He left a portfolio for you in the study" came from down the hall.

If Milo wasn't very much mistaken, Ceri was laughing when she said it.

⁕

He hadn't been mistaken. She'd definitely been laughing.

"Contract offers," Milo muttered, blinking down at the small stack of papers in his hands. "*Contract offers?* It's only been three weeks!"

How had anyone got approvals from the Sisters already?

Courtship proposals, mostly, but some of them went right for the conjugal contract, which made Milo curl in defensively for some reason he couldn't fathom. Except it again made him feel like a horse getting an offer to stud a corral full of mares. As though he were anywhere *near* ready to think about siring a child, let alone whether or not he'd want to negotiate a claim to it, and be involved in raising it, and have it throw up on him, and probably one day look him in the eye and tell him how terrible he was at being a tad, and every goddess in the pantheon, he *was not* ready for this!

Maybe courtship. *Maybe.* But it would have to be the right

person, and.... Well. How many of those were there? And what were the chances the right one Milo had in mind would—

He shouldn't even be entertaining that fantasy.

They lived too far apart. They both had very busy lives. A lot of responsibility. People *depended* on them. It would be impossible.

And—*let's be realistic here, Milo*—someone like that could absolutely do better than Milo. He probably already had. Anyway, who knew if he even liked men? It hadn't really come up. And Milo was probably remembering that night through a sentimental haze of too much plum wine and brandy.

It wasn't as if Milo was smitten or—

Anyway, if that was really what Milo wanted, he could very well have filed to make an offer himself by now. And he hadn't. Because....

Well, because he'd been *busy*.

And probably he was a coward afraid of rejection.

...He was definitely a coward afraid of rejection.

Milo huffed as he shoved the thought away and shuffled through the—every goddess save him—*over a dozen* offers, cursing his mam to every fiery pit in every mythology. And Lilibet while he was at it. They thought it was all *funny*.

"Bloody hi-*lar*-ious," Milo gritted out between clenched teeth, fingers curled nearly into claws that were marring the thick vellum with the fancy script, and he just. Didn't. *Care*.

Until he got down to the one at the very bottom—*deliberately* at the very bottom, because Milo knew his mam—and everything went abruptly still.

The crackling of the fire was like gunshots. The soft sea wind was a howling banshee.

This one had a note attached to it. Milo didn't recognize the handwriting, but he nonetheless knew who'd written it. *Knew*.

...Hoped.

His heart kicked hard at his sternum.

Breathing was suddenly something other people could do.

There, said the note. *Now you can't say I don't write you. Do hurry with the legalities, won't you? There's a picture show in Brookings in a fortnight. I've already bought tickets.*

And beneath it... a courtship contract.

Milo sucked in a thin breath.

So typical. So *arrogant*.

And yet Milo's grin was hurting his face.

He couldn't make it *stop*.

Also, his heart might have just gone a bit gooey.

It was... well, it was *embarrassing*.

He was an idiot.

He was an absurd, drippy git.

He was going to overdose on melodramatic mawkishness and die of twee right here in his mam's study.

He was... still grinning.

And he was abso-bloody-*lutely* going to burn the rest of that pile.

Chapter 5—Polyphonic Texture

: when two or more independent melodic lines are sounding at the same time

The Whitpool railway station could be mistaken for a grand old house, if not for the three strips of track at its back door. Four chimneys, banks of leaded glass windows, and a wide front drive crowded with buggies and cars, with smart, polished porters attending to all of it.

Only two trains a day, since Whitpool wasn't a port town, merely a rocky crag on the maps between the coastal ferries north to Werrdig or southwest to the Outer Isles. They got more traffic from the brass and trainees that came and went, seeing as Whitpool was where the Kymbrygh Home Guard's command post resided, and all divisions reported to its Colonel-in-Chief. It meant that most of Whitpool's population were transients who only stayed until they finished their training, or the families of those who served a permanent post. Still, one wouldn't guess at Whitpool's relatively unrefined character by how seriously it took its service to those on their way through. The gravel drive was raked neat and tidy, the wooden steps into the station were smooth and sturdy and appeared freshly painted, and the stone of the building was bright and white—no easy thing considering the fug of coal smoke and steam exhaust that hung in layers for good parts of the day.

Milo stepped from the hire car, already adjusting his scarf against the bite of the wind, and handed his mam out behind him while the driver started unloading the boot. The day was gray and overcast, the constant frigid sea breeze inadequate to moving the strata of damp cloud cover that had made the sun a fond memory for the past week. Winter was slotting in like a suddenly found puzzle piece.

"Here, I'll take that," Ceri said, impatient as she cut off a silent—though apparently quite rancorous—tussle between the driver and an opportunistic porter for her haversack. She snatched it up with a roll of her eyes and slid the strap over her shoulder. "My son will get the other." She ignored the thwarted look of the porter, the way it looked like he was trying very hard not to salute her, and lifted her eyebrow at Milo.

Milo lifted his right back, but dutifully hefted the suitcase and followed Ceri up the station's steps. He gave the porter an apologetic shrug. The driver still had hope of a tip when he took Milo back home; the porter was out of luck, and clearly knew it.

"Set it here and give us a hug." Ceri had stopped out of the way of the entrance and was already holding her arms out.

Milo pulled up short with a frown. "I can take it in for you."

"And I appreciate it, but it's not necessary. You don't want to keep the driver waiting."

"It's kind of his job to wait, Mam." Milo tilted his head. "You really don't want me to know where you're going, do you?"

Ceri dropped her arms and gave Milo a pursed-lipped scowl. "No."

She'd been putting him off all week, changing the subject when he asked, or just not answering. Milo'd reckoned she was entitled to keep her own counsel, and hadn't really pushed her about it. Now it dawned on him that she was so determined he not know where she was going, she wasn't even going to allow him to accompany her inside the station on the chance he might get a look at her ticket when she presented it.

She'd taken mysterious trips before. Infrequently over the years, but often enough and peculiar enough to make Milo suspect she wasn't quite as retired as she said she was. And there was no getting around how everyone at the Home Guard's base knew her, or the deference with which every military person in Whitpool treated her. Even the ones—like that porter—who Milo suspected he wasn't supposed to know were military. He also suspected he wasn't supposed to know Whitpool looked more and more like a training ground for spies, the older and more observant he got.

"I'm not half as dim as you seem to think I am." Milo set the suitcase down. He couldn't help the smirk as he straightened. "I've seen that three times in my life." He waved at the haversack hanging from his mam's shoulder, in which, he knew, her Preidynīg Royal Forces uniform was folded with care, medals already pinned in their places. "And every time it was because you were called to Llundaintref to attend at Court."

Ceri huffed at him. "Well, aren't you a tidy dab."

"I sort of am." Milo grinned. "Or maybe you missed that I earned three firsts at commencement, and they even gave me the papers to prove it."

"I never would." Ceri's tone was soft, expression losing the tight annoyance and sliding into something more indulgent. She reached out and fussed with Milo's scarf, eyes on her hands. "I can't tell you if you're right or wrong." She looked up, gaze locking onto Milo's, hand now stilled and pressed to Milo's lapel. "And I can't tell you why."

"I know that." Milo shrugged and laid his hand over Ceri's. "But I know it's something you're not pleased about. I think you might even be worried." He tightened his hand around his mam's when she *tsked* at him and made to pull away. "I'm not trying to get information. I'm only...."

Milo sighed. He took a step back.

"Something is brewing." He paused, but when Ceri didn't say anything, only gave him an unreadable stare, he said, "Isn't it." Not a question.

She'd been off ever since Wellech. Milo had at first assumed it was merely that she'd been narked with him, and she had been. But even once things had gone somewhat back to normal, there'd been a sort of preoccupation just under the surface—long thoughtful looks across the breakfast table; a weird sadness Milo had never seen before when she looked at him. It was only when the connection between that haversack and Court had clicked that he thought maybe Ceri's oddness had more to do with the coven's discussion before she and Milo had even quarreled in the first place.

Ceri sighed. "Darling boy, something is always brewing." She pulled her hand away but not without a soft pat to Milo's chest and a small but warm smile. "Now, hush and give your mam a proper *cwtch*."

Milo did, pulling her in and squeezing her tight. He was tall enough now that he could almost tuck her head beneath his chin had she not had her hair up in a tight knot at her crown.

"Do put Glynn out of her misery, will you?" Ceri said into Milo's shoulder. "Between school and the forge and that mountain of books, she hasn't come up for air in days."

Milo snorted. "I will, Mam. I've only been—"

"I know what you've been doing, you filthy tease. The way you two nibble at each other all the time, it's a wonder you're not actually siblings." She set a firm kiss to Milo's cheek then pulled back. "But she'll be a good help to you if you let her. So let her." There was a twitch at the corner of her mouth when she picked up her suitcase. "And you have a nice time in Brookings. The current contract has a rider in case you want to change the terms, but Merfyn said if you want to move on to a conj—"

"*Bloody*—" Milo waved his hands around, choking on air and checking to all points to see if anyone might have overheard. His cheeks felt like they were on fire. "Save me, are we *talking* about this? *Here*?"

It was bad enough that, as his representative, she'd had to look over all the offers. She'd even scribbled *notes* on some of them. About *fertility*.

Also, the anticipation had been proper *killing* him. He'd been trying to not even think about next week, even though it was almost all he *could* think about, and this was... well, this was just low.

Ceri chuckled. "In my day, courting meant spending a lot of chaperoned time on uncomfortable couches in someone's best parlor, and proper *swimming* in buckets of tea. Now you young people with your 'dates' and your riders and your—"

"Will you—" Milo tried not to make his "keep it down" gesture too flaily and obvious. It was like she was *trying* to embarrass him. "I can't *believe* you're actually saying this out loud, and *in public*!"

"That school was worth every penny, but Llundaintref's prudish approach to the realities of contracts did you no favors when it comes to talking about sex like a grownup." Ceri ignored Milo's sputtering and said, sly, "Don't worry. I won't want to hear *all* about your trip."

"Well, thank every goddess for *that*!"

"I suppose I'll just find out when I get the paperwork for renegotiations." Her grin was evil as she tapped at Milo's chin, hanging low with the rest of his jaw, then turned and walked away. "Cheers, love! Wish me luck!"

"Shan't," Milo managed to croak, then, louder, "I hope your buttons all pop off, and your hair falls out!"

Ceri didn't look back, only laughed as she pushed through the station's doors and disappeared.

Everyone else looked, though, a host of strangers pausing in their bustle to stare, scandalized and indignant on his mam's behalf. Milo ignored them, only shoved his way down the steps and back to the hire car, not even annoyed when the driver gave him the hairy eyeball and didn't open the door for him.

* * *

The wards on the channel rail were... odd. Thinned, maybe, or... no, more like loose. A weave once tight, but now the threads had been stretched and pulled just slightly out of true.

Milo frowned, slid his fingers around the end post, and shut his eyes. Concentrated. He pulled back, bemused, and moved over to the next section.

Same thing.

"Hmph."

He shook his head. Either Mam was getting sloppy with the wards, or....

Well. Milo supposed it wouldn't be the first time someone tried to get into a preserve without leave. The fences, after all, were not to keep the dragons in—which would be foolish effort wasted anyway—but to keep people who didn't belong there out. Dragons didn't generally go after people, but it wasn't unheard of. And if someone who didn't know what they were doing happened to blunder into a nesting area, even if there were no eggs incubating, it could be deadly.

As it happened, there were no roosting cows this season, so at least there was one less worry.

Poachers were rare, since so few dared to trade in anything that could even be construed as having originated from dragons, at least on the continent. But there were countries—far off and isolated, sure—that viewed dragons as good hunting and coveted trophies. None in the various migration paths, but Milo often wondered if that was purposeful avoidance on the parts of the dragons, or if perhaps there had been clans long ago that had been hunted out of existence. He couldn't imagine what it would take to actually kill a dragon, but they weren't invulnerable. And there was a proven black market for scales and claws and teeth.

A curious goat wandered over from the far side of the pasture where the rest of its flock gruffed and grumbled at each other as they nosed the mud for stray clumps of grass. This one was a stout little nanny, fat and cheeky, and making no bones about eyeing Milo with a look both bold and expectant. Milo blamed Glynn. Treating the goats to crusts of bread and bits of whatever fruit was in season, she insisted, was only fair, considering they existed to idle away their lives, well fed and healthy, until the day they inevitably ended up in a hungry dragon's sights and proved just that much too slow.

"Go on, then," Milo told the goat, feeling around the edges of the ward, trying to find where the weakness was centered. "I haven't anything for you."

It didn't appear to believe him. It bellowed at him, thick and glottal, and somehow chiding.

Milo paused in his assessment of the wards and, careful not to knock the bell on the gate that signaled mealtimes, climbed over the fence to the other side. The side with the dragons. Because it was safer. That goat looked like she was thinking about trying to mug him and investigate his pockets for herself.

"Keep being a rude little barmcake," he told the goat over the pickets. He hooked his thumb over his shoulder. "I've got friends on this side who think you're rather tasty and won't—"

Movement flickered out the corner of his eye, a quick shift and furtive flit. Milo looked over, and jerked so hard he almost brained himself on a fence post. His stomach bottomed out.

Wide hazel eyes peered back at him—caught and well aware of it—before, as though to try to brazen it out, they crinkled at the corners above a quick, surprisingly real-looking grin.

"*Haia*, Milo!"

"*...Cennydd.*"

It came out dazed and breathless, but might as well have had *you idiot* tacked on the end of it.

Because only an idiot would be traipsing across the pasture like the gormless calf Cennydd apparently was. Everyone knew better than this. *Everyone.*

Milo shot a look to the sky—empty but for a small flock of sanderlings, thank every goddess—then back over to where Cennydd was eyeing the little nanny warily, like he *wasn't* eyeing the sky.

"Cennydd," Milo said, low and clear. "Get over here next to me. Leg it. Right now."

Instead, Cennydd paused. He blinked at Milo then... *beamed.* All wide-open and thrilled, as though he'd won a prize. He nearly skipped as he started toward Milo.

"Coming!"

The goat examined Cennydd's bottom as he passed like she was wondering how loud he'd scream if she rammed it.

Milo wouldn't mind finding that out himself. He shook it off, keeping an eye out for any dark shapes in the sky until Cennydd was close enough to grab. When he was, Milo did, by the collar, and hauled a surprised and protesting Cennydd over the fence until he wobbled to an equilibrium sufficient enough to feel it when Milo shook him.

"Oi, what—?"

"How did you get out here?" Milo snapped. "*Why* are you out here?" He pointed toward the other end of the pasture, boiling with either anger or alarm. Probably both. He shook again. "D'you *know* what's beyond those trees, Cennydd? *Do you?*"

"Oi, geroff!" When Milo didn't, wouldn't, Cennydd tried to twist out of Milo's grip, only succeeding in screwing the handful Milo had of the coat into a tighter ball. It took Cennydd a few seconds longer than it should, but eventually he stopped trying. He shot Milo a wounded look. "Of *course* I know! That's why I—"

"That's why you're not supposed to *be here!*" Milo shouted it. He couldn't help it. "Do you understand that you just pranced blithely across a buffet spread specifically for dragons?"

Cennydd scowled. "Dragons don't eat people."

"*Usually. Usually* dragons don't eat people. Because we give them pastures full of other things to eat. A pasture you just toddled through like a tasty little nibblet amongst all the other tasty little nibblets." Milo uncurled his fingers and shoved Cennydd back, seething. "How easy d'you think it would be to tell you apart from the goats from ten furlongs up?"

"They wouldn't." Cennydd's tone was defiant and sure, but his glance kept skimming upward now. *Finally.* "They're smart. They know. You say so all the—"

"They know their boundaries. They know where they're safe. They know dragonkin. They *don't* know *you.* They *don't* know you're not here to try to harm them, or take from them, and if you're in the middle of their hunting grounds, it's quite likely they won't know you're not *food*!"

Cennydd flung a scattershot look toward where the ageless pine coppice broke the flat moor and formed the border of the pasture. Except for a wide expanse pressed flat and treeless by generations of dragons lumbering through it to wait for an easy hunt.

The nanny ambled closer, curious, then fetched up short of the fence and gave them a demanding bleat.

"This," Milo told Cennydd, as calmly as he could, "right here, where we're standing—this is a *feeding pen*, where the dragons who can't fly come to eat." He slapped the gate post. "This is where I push a cow through, or a few sheep, or some goats, for the dragons who can't hunt for themselves. Right now I've got a snarly little spitter who's got a limp but can still outrun you and is as big as a small cottage, and she could not only snap you up like a particularly rubbish snack, she could spit her venom at you first so you'd be paralyzed but awake while she gutted you.

"But sometimes, Cennydd—*sometimes*, a dragon doesn't feel like hunting or working too hard for its supper or waiting for me to shove a cow through the gate. And do you know where they come when that happens?" Milo didn't wait for Cennydd to answer, only waved toward the pasture Cennydd had just lolloped through, and said, "*Right here*, Cennydd. Right to this nice, easy banquet spread out just for them."

Cennydd had slowly gone pale while Milo ranted, and now he was going a bit green.

Good.

"How did you get out here?" Milo pressed. "How did you get past the wards on the outer fences?"

Those wards were there for a reason, after all. To keep curious idiots like Cennydd *out*.

Cennydd opened his mouth. Flapped it. Closed it.

"I need to know." Milo eased his tone, gentled his voice. Until a thought struck him, and he couldn't help the way everything turned sharp again. "Was anyone else with you?"

Because if there was some other bonehead out there roaming the fields....

Milo again scanned the sky, but only saw the shape of one of the wranglers far off over the sea, winging out wide and lazy, so not on the hunt. Nothing in the trees, so far as he could tell.

"It's only me." It broke into a wobbly squeak toward the end, either righteous fright or the remnants of teenaged changes.

"You're sure." Milo took hold of Cennydd's collar again, but in a looser grip, and he didn't shake. "You're *positive*. If you're lying to me, Cennydd, someone could actually die, and you'd be the one who—"

"There's no one else." Glaring now, Cennydd shrugged Milo off. This time Milo let him. "I came alone."

The way "alone" came out *this close* to bitter... Milo believed it.

Cennydd was almost as tall as Milo now, though still lanky and awkward with a growth spurt he hadn't quite negotiated yet. Only a year older than Glynn, he was beginning to grow into himself, but he was still spotty and butterfaced and graceless, and had yet to learn that his tad's wealth and his mam's position on the Whitpool council didn't buy him the respect of those he clearly wished would bow to his adolescent rule. Milo had watched him trying in all the wrong ways since Cennydd was a stroppy little creadur who thought bullying a fine and proper path to the esteem of his peers. For a clever boy, he had yet to figure out why it hadn't as yet gone to plan.

Milo sucked in a calming breath and nodded. "All right. Good. But that doesn't tell me how you're here." He gave Cennydd a level, *I'm not playing* look. "How did you get past the outer fences?" He narrowed his eyes. "Are you the one who's been messing with the wards?"

"*No!*"

"You tried, though, yeah? You've *been* trying, haven't you? All this time you've been grizzling at me to bring you out to see the dragons, you've been skulking the fences and trying to get past them."

Cennydd flushed and looked away. "I didn't do anything! I was only... there was...." He set his jaw, angry now, as though he had a right. "I can't help it if your wards are pants." His shrug was entirely unapologetic, and he'd gone from frightened and semicontrite directly into righteous resentment. "Maybe *you* should be apologizing to *me*. If I tell Mam how easy it was to—"

"Yes, tell your mam what you've done today, Cennydd. Please. It'll save me the trouble of doing it myself." Milo took a step in; it was too clear that Cennydd only barely kept himself from taking one back. "Tell your mam you illegally entered a preserve protected by Her Majesty's laws. I mean, you're not of age yet, and I'm sure your mam will use her connections to keep the Wardens from actually arresting you, so you likely won't—"

"I didn't—!" Cennydd had been in the process of puffing out his chest and squaring his shoulders. Now the building bravado collapsed back down into a teenaged boy who'd been caught failing to use the sense he'd been born with. "I didn't... mean to." He caught Milo's look of disbelief. "I didn't! I mean, I always check the fences. Just in case, you know? But the wards are always so tight and strong, and... I dunno. I stopped hoping to find a weak spot ages ago, but it's... it's habit now, I guess." He frowned down at his expensive shoes, probably ruined now with the mud and goat droppings he'd been tromping through. "And then there was one, so...." He trailed off with another shrug, this one clearly uncomfortable.

Milo was still angry, still anxious and outraged and sixteen different kinds of alarmed, but this... this he believed. Cennydd was no mage, he couldn't possibly have queered even Milo's weakest wards. If he was sensitive enough he could find them, maybe even figure out their patterns. But there was no way he could break them.

"...All right."

Milo sighed and ran a hand through his hair. This was going to take longer than it usually did. With the thinned spot he'd just found, and the one Cennydd had managed to get through, Milo was going to have to thoroughly reinforce every inch of fence, rather than the usual spot-checking and general strengthening. And he was going to have to make a report to the council that someone had been at the wards.

Blood and rot, he was supposed to leave for Brookings the day after next.

"Right, then. Damn it all." Milo took a step back, giving Cennydd room. "I need you to show me where."

"I...." Cennydd's glance went from mortified to calculating to, oddly, hopeful. "I will." He stood up straight. "After you show me a dragon."

Milo gaped. He nearly laughed, incredulous. "Cennydd." Now Milo was the one pushing out his chest and pulling back his shoulders. "Are you trying to blackmail me?"

"Naw, mate." Unbelievably, Cennydd *grinned*. "Fair trade, innit?"

"Trade. *Trade*. For you trespassing on a protected preserve, and nearly getting yourself eaten? I'd say a fair trade for that is saving your life. Which I *just did*."

"Tch." Cennydd waved it away. "It would only be saving my life if there'd been a dragon *to* eat me. Which there *wasn't*." He dropped the grin and turned supplicant. "Please, Milo? Please? I'm already here, and I'm with you, nothing will happen, and I'll never do it again, I promise, I *swear*. Please? *Please*? Milo, c'mon, mate, I only—"

"We're not *mates*, Cennydd, you're a trespassing little gobshite who—"

"—want to see one up close, that's all, and if you show me, I'll even stop checking the wards. Please. Milo, *please*, I'm begging—"

"Ugh, you *are*. Save me, on you go like a minging pepper mill, and it's making me nauseous. *Stop*."

Cennydd did. But he didn't lose the imploring expression nor the sick-making pose of blameless obeisance. Gah, he looked so much like Glynn, right down to the hands clasped in front of his chest, and the gormless pout.

Milo was still angry. And a little bit shaken.

Cennydd was a tit and too bloody arrogant by half. And not the good kind of arrogance, not the kind that was backed by skill and knowledge and practice. Not the *Ellis* kind, since Milo's brain never seemed to stray too far from that particular subject these days.

Cennydd's arrogance was the kind that grew from being excluded a little too often, or included for all the wrong reasons. The kind one put on like a recalcitrant, unlikable mask to hide the hurt of rejection. And Cennydd *was* recalcitrant, and he *was* unlikeable, standing there looking both wronged and hopeful, like he had a right to either.

But he was also a boy who desperately wanted to be liked, and just couldn't seem to ken how to arrange the learned social cues and graces into the proper shapes. A boy to be pitied, really, because if he hadn't got it by now....

Milo glared into the beseeching hazel eyes, the podgy, spotted face, the awkward limbs and flat brown hair.

He growled.

And decided he was altogether too biddable when it came to being on the receiving end of determined begging.

·

"What's *he* doing here?" Glynn's scowl was fierce, and the betrayal behind it was unmistakable.

Milo sighed and pushed Cennydd ahead of him, though he tugged him back by the shoulder of his coat when it looked like he meant to just keep going across the stone floor until he actually fell into the forge. Milo wouldn't put it past him. The firepot was full and hot, the slow feed from the hearth roasting coal into coke, and the chimney of the bloomery was blasting so intensely Milo was already sweating.

"It's a long story," Milo told Glynn, then turned to Howell, who'd paused by the tuyere to stare at first Milo, questioning, then Cennydd, suspicious. "Sorry for the intrusion," Milo said. "But with your permission, I'm going to let Cennydd watch you give the dragons their rations." He turned to Cennydd, said, "*Stay*," before moving in as close as he dared to Howell and lowering his voice. "Just trust me for now, yeah? I'll explain later."

Because if Milo could sate Cennydd's obvious curiosity, and give a bit of a boost to his clearly low self-esteem in the process, maybe he'd stop pulling Glynn's pigtails long enough for the two of them to, if not become friends, exactly, then to at least stop antagonizing each other enough that it came to blows.

Howell gave Cennydd another skeptical look, but nodded at Milo with a very clear *I'll hear that explanation, and it better be good* and went back to work.

The smithy sat at the very edge of the eastern boundary of the preserve, straddling the fence with its entrance on the outside so anyone entering wasn't doing so from within the spaces designated dragon territory. The open back end of it was caged with a thick iron grid, which wouldn't exactly stop a determined dragon, but should slow it down and give whomever it might be after a chance to scarper. Not that it ever happened. The dragons knew who kept their fires burning. It was why the preserves that dotted the migration paths were their favored places, and why—in Milo's considered opinion—the dragons had never been a threat to anyone who respected their claimed spaces.

"...not only feeding them hot coal," Glynn was saying while Cennydd watched, awed, as two dragons drifted to graceful landings in the yard outside the caged opening. "We have to replicate what they get out of the volcanic rock in their habitats, so there's smelting to be done as well." She pointed to the arms of the long iron gutters that formed a "Y" between the belly of the forge and the crucible of the bloomery, then joined to a single runner that flowed out through the only opening in the gridwork and ended over the trough from which the dragons fed. "Iron, aluminum, different ores and alloys—that sort of thing. Tad has to get the mix just right, or they can't digest it properly and their fires will go out." There was a great measure of pride in Glynn's tone. She relayed the information as though imparting a rare and treasured nugget of wisdom, explaining the differences between conduction and convection, what oxidation was and why it was interesting.

It was clearly all lost on Cennydd. Milo wasn't even sure Cennydd heard it, too caught up in watching the dragons snapping at each other with their usual posturing, nipping at haunches or necks as they each vied for the ideal spot at the trough while they waited.

Milo was pleased to see the spitter emerging from the pines to the south, and even more pleased to see she was still keeping company with the razorback. He was too old to offer much protection from the others if the spitter managed to get too bold for her own good, and he walked more than he flew these days. But he was huge and held an unquestioned position of respect within the hierarchy of the makeshift clan, the members of which, for one reason or another, had been unable to complete their migration this season and taken up temporary residence here. Milo was surprised but grateful that the elderly razorback seemed to have the patience to take on a calf as ornery and obnoxious as the spitter. If she could manage not to annoy her apparent mentor too much, she might actually learn how to be a dragon.

Howell was keeping count too, because it wasn't until all fourteen were out in the yard that he picked up the tongs.

"Keep him away from the runner," he said, terse, as he opened the gates and tipped the crucible, decanting it into a pool at the riser before letting it flow along with the ore and slag and coke to a burning slurry that seared its way down the runner and poured out into the trough.

It made the space a hundred times hotter. Milo found it necessary to remove his coat and fan himself with his cap. Cennydd probably should have at least taken off his coat—his skin glistened with sweat, and his lank hair was plastered to his forehead—but he didn't appear to have the thought processes available right now. He stared with an open-mouthed smile, entranced, as the dragons slurped from the trough, the glow of the molten metal and rock slicking against scales and pushing shadows into angles that made them look like something from a painting or a fairytale illustration. Never mind that they never stopped growling at each other, or shoving and jostling at each other like toddlers, or that the sound of the gritty crunch of smoldering chunks of coal between massive teeth was enough to make Milo clench his own with a shudder.

None of it seemed to register with Cennydd, who looked to be in raptures, never losing his awed smile, and taking hold of Glynn's sleeve as though to ground himself. The fact that Glynn didn't shake him off, didn't even scowl, made Milo decide that bringing Cennydd here, letting him see what few could, had been the right thing to do. Even if it had come about through half-arsed blackmail.

"Not everyone thinks we should feed their fires." Glynn's voice was soft, with a hint of disdain.

Cennydd frowned, but he never looked away. "Whyever not?"

"They'd be less dangerous if they didn't have fire, innit?" This time, the disdain all but dripped.

"That's just... stupid. And cruel." Cennydd huffed as though personally insulted. "They wouldn't be dragons without fire. Or half as beautiful."

A corner of Glynn's mouth turned up, satisfied. She didn't say anything, only stood there with Cennydd and watched the dragons eat fire.

Milo absolutely *did not* smirk in satisfaction, though he did give Howell a pointed glance along with a lift of his eyebrow.

Howell glared back. Then he took off a glove for the apparent sole purpose of flipping Milo off as he gave the back of Cennydd's head a sour frown.

It would be very insulting, Milo told himself, to laugh right now.

He wondered if Howell would be pleased or even more annoyed when Milo broke the news to Glynn tomorrow that he'd be filing the paperwork with parish council to formally take her on as his apprentice.

Chapter 6—Idée Fixe

: a transformable melody that recurs in every movement of a multi-movement work

"So then she said, 'Listen, my tad knows where I am, and he'll be looking for me soon.' Like she was afraid I was going to *kidnap* her or something!"

"She—" Ellis was laughing so hard he was nearly bent in half. "Over *crowberries*?"

"Well, to be fair, it was the last pint anywhere in the markets, and I make an epic tart. I might've been a touch... strident." Milo grinned. "I *really wanted* those crowberries."

Ellis had to lean against the railing, weak-kneed, roaring out an open, shameless laugh. Milo chortled along with him for the length of time it took him to wonder if that story was necessarily one he should have told to someone like Ellis. Ellis probably never got into arguments over produce in the markets. And if he did, his challenger would likely hand the item of contention over with a wink and a coy smile, rather than worry he might do untoward things to them without their permission.

So, basically, in one short tale, it had just been pointed out to Ellis that Milo was sort of a git when it came to social interaction, and that his neighbors thought he might be the sort to assault and/or kidnap someone over crowberries. That was sure to impress any suitor.

Milo tugged his gaze away from the addicting display of Ellis laughing and back toward the beach below. He pulled his scarf tighter. It was bloody *freezing* out here.

Brookings in late autumn was much like Whitpool in late autumn, or really any coastal village in northern Kymbrygh—cold and windy and wet. As though to make up for it, or perhaps in stubborn defiance, Brookings took great glee in, and any excuse for, festivals, and so seemed to have one for almost anything once or twice a month. Milo didn't know if the timing was purposeful on Ellis's part, but Milo was beyond pleased to find this trip coincided with the tail end of Seal Whelping and the considerably livelier opening of the Oyster Fest. Livelier because it—not accidentally, Milo was certain—corresponded with the Sparkling Wines Exhibition.

Milo could really use a glass of that right now. Or six.

Ellis, calmer now, leaned over the railing, elbow settling snug against Milo's, and peered down the cliffs at the fat gray seals lounging on Ynys Sêl's rocky beach and the wee pudgy milk-white pups flopping and bouncing and cracking out their sharp little barks. Shags watched, vigilant, from the cliffs just below the observation deck, while gannets and gulls swooped through a sky hung low and gray.

"You don't see the pups in Whitpool, then?" Ellis's eyes were on the beach below, but his arm was a solid strip of warmth alongside Milo's.

Milo dared to lean into it just a bit. "We do. It's only that some of the thermal springs dump into the sea right at the coastline, and it makes the water there too warm for them. Plus the dragons will hunt anything that close to the preserve. The seals out our way whelp at Gard Dafina's, all the way out past Doorway Falls, and...." Milo trailed off, unwilling say that he just really didn't go anywhere, didn't do much at all, honestly, besides tool about his mam's house, fixing what needed fixing, taking care of the preserve, and, occasionally, embarrassing himself at the markets.

It was a new feeling, this, a novel realization that, when faced with Ellis and his apparent worldliness, Milo was sort of a rube, even despite his years at school in "the big city." He had no friends in Whitpool. Those he'd made in Llundaintref had since scattered to their various home quarters at all points of the Preidynīg Isles, and only two thus far had bothered to write Milo back. Whitpool itself hadn't got much better since Milo'd been home, the villagers pleasant enough when he saw them but unmistakably wary of him, determined to stay acquaintances and nothing more.

Apparently, the most remarkable thing about Milo was that he'd gone away to school. Now that he was back, he was only some vaguely recognizable nobody who was as much of an outsider as Cennydd, but for different reasons.

Ellis, on the other hand, seemed to have no end of tales of adventures with his boyos, or places he'd been to on Warden business, or people he'd met through getting the Croft back to respectability and who'd become allies or even friends in the process. He'd always been charming, but now he was *interesting* too, and damnably good-looking. Every time Milo found himself laughing at something Ellis said, or listening, rapt, to one of Ellis's stories, or staring, equally rapt, into Ellis's gray eyes as they sparked or simmered or flared depending on what he was talking about, well.

"I imagine it's difficult to get away from Old Forge." Ellis shifted, still looking down the cliff at the seals on the beach, grinning when a pup splashed tip-over-tail into the water with a surprised little squawk. But his arm wound through Milo's with casual ease, like he did it all the time. "Especially since it's all more or less down to you now."

Milo shrugged. "It was always going to be." He tugged his coat tighter and let himself lean in closer. It was freezing up here with a faceful of cold ocean wind. "It was hard to get used to, with Nain gone, but I think I'm managing all right."

"Of course you are." Ellis turned to give Milo a smile. "Somehow, I'm thinking, the only one who ever doubted that was you." His smile turned to a wicked little grin when Milo's mouth flapped. "I was only asking because I'm wondering how difficult it's going to be to do this again."

Milo's brow crinkled, mouth turning down in bemusement as he peered down the cliffs. "This?"

"Meeting up," Ellis said, looking down at the seals again, but cutting sideways glances at Milo like he couldn't look directly at him. Like he was *nervous*. "I was thinking maybe once a month, you know? Here in Brookings."

"You... what, now?"

"Well, it's rather in the middle for us, yeah? Sort of. And they've always got something going. So I thought maybe—"

"You want to do this again?"

Ellis rolled his eyes. "Well, not *this*." He waved at the seals. "It's only once a year, innit?"

"But. I mean." Milo was tempted to pull back so he could get a good look at Ellis's face. But it was cold and Ellis was warm and pressed against Milo like he belonged there. "We only just got here."

"Yeeeees?" Ellis was grinning again, his tone teasing. "I'm aware we only just got here. But, unfortunately, keeping you here forever or stealing you away to Wellech would be against the law. So I thought we might arrange to meet here on the regular." It only took a moment for the grin to lose its devilish edge and begin to slide into something uncertain when Milo only blinked stupidly. Ellis straightened and cleared his throat. "I mean. That is. We can just... agree to not—"

"*No.*" Milo honestly didn't want to hear how that ended. And he really didn't want that look on Ellis's face one second longer. "I mean *yes.*"

Ellis lifted his eyebrows, cautious. "Care to unpack that a bit?"

Milo's internal flailing was reaching alarming proportions.

Not ten minutes ago, he'd come to the novel conclusion that he was, in fact, incredibly dull. And rather a dolt. Ellis, in no uncertain terms, was absolutely not either of those things. That Ellis could do a lot better than Milo wasn't a new thought, but it had rather hit harder at every *look* Ellis received—at the station, hiring a buggy out to the peninsula to see the seals; here on the soggy decking where people were *supposed* to be watching the seal pups they'd paid to see and *not* staring at Ellis. Except they *were*, and Milo couldn't stop noticing and wondering if they were all thinking the same thing he was—*What the* deuce *is he doing with someone like that?*—as he sank down into a depressing little pool of self-pitying angst that would make Cennydd look like the amateur he was.

And yet here Ellis was, *asking*, like he'd done when he'd sent the contract offer, taking that first step that had been so paralyzingly terrifying for Milo that he hadn't even considered it a real possibility. With anyone, let alone Ellis. And not only had Ellis done it for him—he was taking the next as well.

Milo sighed like a character in a penny romance. "I want to be you when I grow up."

Luckily, he'd only mush-mouthed it, and the wind had kicked up, so when Ellis frowned, leaned in and asked, "What?" Milo merely shook himself and gave Ellis an embarrassed little smile.

"I'd like that. To see you, I mean. Here." Milo rolled his hand and tried to make his mouth behave. "On the regular. Like you said."

Ellis's face lit up, pleased, and he leaned back with a grin. "There's lovely, then. Now that's settled." He dug out his pocket watch and gave it a quick glance. "It's getting on. We'd best go if we want to make the picture show."

⁕

It was... sort of breathtaking, actually.

Honestly, Milo hadn't been expecting much when Ellis had led him to what looked like any other storefront along the Brookings High Street except for the posters and playbills pasted to the windows. And the interior wasn't any more impressive. A screen only as big as a splayed broadsheet was positioned at the front of the narrow room. Rows of hard wooden chairs were set so close together Milo wondered if he was going to have to sit with his knees tucked up to his chin. He was just deciding that being forced to squash up next to Ellis might not be a bad thing when the lights were put out, the music started, and....

Nothing like the Dynamoscopes Milo had seen in Llundaintref. Those only cranked a series of consecutive still pictures like flipping illustrated pages fast enough to make a one-minute slapstick comedy in exchange for a 5p. This was *so much better.* For one, it wasn't a stack of individual pictures stuck on a roll—Milo had watched the reel moving through the projector almost as much as he'd watched the picture itself, fascinated. And the story unfolding on the little screen at the front of the crowded room was... well, on its own, it would likely have been predictable and a little melodramatic;

except watching a story that had been played out hundreds of miles away, told to him through a machine that worked very much like magic, made it all into something rather sublime.

He'd been to the opera once, when his mam came to visit him at school and decided they both could stand to acquire a bit of culture. (They hadn't acquired anything, in the end, except the firm opinion that opera was for other people.) He'd seen a revue show with a group of classmates when there wasn't enough money to pay for the roundtrip ferry to go home for his birthday, but just enough to indulge in a risqué bit of theater. (It wasn't terribly risqué, really; Milo had seen more skin in the team dressing rooms at his rounders games. The music had been wonderfully catchy, though.) The theaters had been plush and sumptuous and lit bright with gigantic electroliers, tea served between acts, and people strutting about in expensive silks and wools.

This—uncomfortable wooden chairs; cramped spaces; cheap beer; eye-popping new technology; Ellis snugged right up close—this was definitely more to Milo's tastes.

"That was...." Ellis was starry-eyed as they tumbled back out into the street, cold, wet wind smacking them in the face and pulling them close without thought.

"It *was*!" Milo flailed, too overwhelmed and excited to even keep his ungloved hands in his pockets. "The dragons were clearly fake and kind of awful, but the *train crash*! And the explosions! They had to have had real magic for that. Maybe the heroine is a real mage and wasn't only playing one. There's no way anyone could live through it otherwise. Did you *see* it? It was *huge*! And the heroine just *walked through it*!"

"*Could* a powerful mage do that?" Ellis peered at Milo with a squint and steered them toward a side street. "Could you?"

"Ha! Well." Milo thought about it. "I mean, the strength of the shield one can conjure depends on how good they are, of course, as well as how strong. Plus, there are different shields for different threats. Shielding fire was one of the first things Nain taught me, and your mam endlessly drilled me on technique, since you never know when you might need one with dragons. They're sort of shirty, rubbish arseholes sometimes, and especially when they know you can defend against them. It's like they test you only for the fun of scaring you witless once in a while."

Ellis blinked. "Wait. Are you saying they've shot *fire* at you before? To test you?" He shook his head, clearly disapproving. "These creatures that you take care of occasionally try to kill you. For... *fun*."

"Oh, sure. Well, not try to *kill*. At least I don't think so. But who knows why they do anything, really? Nain always said spewing at you is their way of showing love, making sure you can defend yourself against one that doesn't have good intentions. Mam maintains it's one of their many ways of being gits."

"And what do you think?"

"I guess...." Milo thought about it some more. "It depends. They spew at each other all the time. It's a way of... keeping in shape, I guess? Staying on their game." Milo paused, trying to find the proper words. "I think they see us almost as part of their clan, only different from them and without the scales that would protect us from their fire, or the fire of a dragon that's not clan. So it's as though they're trying to teach us to be on our guard, you know? And, as far as I know, they've never *actually* incinerated anyone just for fun."

"There've been serious run-ins over the years, though."

"Well, of course. They're still wild animals. But those were people who'd tried to hurt them or steal an egg or something. And I've never heard of a case where they shot fire at someone who wasn't capable of shielding themselves, or someone who wasn't trying to hurt them in some way. And it's not like you can't tell it's coming. Well, as long as you're not completely uneducated. All you have to do is watch for the signs. Fuel drooling out the sides of their mouths and fire moving up their throats are pretty obvious warnings. The growls and ear-splitting roars are sort of giveaways, too, yeah?"

"Sure, but." Ellis looked somewhat dubious, tugging Milo across a small open square where people were setting up temporary stalls, complete with stoves and steamers, for the Oyster Fest. "Not everyone sees them every day, you know? We get a few of them flying over Wellech during migration, but they almost never land, so not many get to see them up close. I suppose not many want to. Or should."

"But you know the warning signs."

"I do."

"There you go, then. Good. I was beginning to wonder what Kymbrygh schools were teaching children these days. Someone at your mam's party actually asked me if 'dragonkin' means I've somehow got dragon blood in me."

Ellis barked a laugh. "You're making that up!"

"I'm not! And he was serious, too. Like he honestly thought it was possible!"

"I'm trying to picture...." Ellis couldn't finish, cackles getting in the way, but he shook his head and took a steadying breath. "I mean. You'd have to have... *hatched*, and... stone the crows, I don't want this in my brain, but... Ceri—*roosting!*"

"Oi!" Milo punched Ellis in the shoulder, though considering the size of it and Milo's frozen fingers, it didn't do much damage. Ellis's laughter was, Milo was finding, highly contagious, and it was deucedly difficult to keep the injured scowl Milo was going for. "It's in *my* brain now, you stonking great git. Ta for that."

"If I have to see it, so do you."

"I'm going to tell her you said that."

It didn't stop Ellis from laughing harder. They'd stopped walking somewhere in there, standing now off to the side, out of the way of people coming and going, arms still locked at the elbow. Ellis was laughing so hard he dropped his forehead down to Milo's shoulder, gently whacking a few times, hot breath puffing through the gaps in Milo's scarf and down his collar. It should've made Milo even colder, but instead it heated him right through.

And that was it. Milo was gone. Though, to be fair—who wouldn't be? So when Ellis made a serious effort to catch his breath, and managed to say, "Save me, I can't stop seeing it," Milo opened his mouth, unthinking, and answered, "I'll take you to see real dragons up close. That'll turn the trick."

"Yeah? Something needs to." Ellis was down to breathless snickers now, but he didn't seem to twig to what Milo was actually saying. Asking.

Which, fair play—Milo hadn't either until it had come out his mouth all by itself. Still, though. It wasn't as though Milo hadn't *wanted* to say it.

And yet, Milo hesitated, abruptly anxious, before plowing on, "Would you...? I mean, it's only that... well, it seems that maybe...augh." He set his jaw. "That is. Would you *like* to see dragons up close?"

"Well, who wouldn't?" Ellis grinned. "But it's not as though there's much chance of... oh." Apparently having caught the import—or maybe just what Milo suspected was a deeply pathetic look on his part—Ellis lifted his eyebrows and broadened his smile, clearly pleased. "I'd really like that. Yeah."

Milo had to look away, though he was smiling too. Something no doubt besotted and highly embarrassing, so it was just as well.

He hadn't realized they'd stopped almost right on top of what must be Brookings's version of Preachers' Row, not until he registered the distinctive wailing cadences of sermonizing coming from the men and women who'd set up podiums and pulpits from which to lecture, each trying to out-shout the other. A deliberate gauntlet, no doubt, one each festival-goer was going to have to endure if they wanted to reach the prize of the actual festival on the other side. Milo caught snippets of "The masses assaulting our borders must be turned back!" and "The Triple Goddess needs no handmaids!" He gave Ellis a look that was probably a bit desperate, because Ellis snorted and unlaced their arms, snagged up Milo's hand and hauled him right down the middle.

It was strange how the next moments skidded by so fast they were almost blurred and yet in retrospect crawled so slowly Milo could almost count his heartbeats slip-thudding in uneven bursts. The thick aroma of steaming oysters blundered into the sweeter haze of sugary cakes fried in oil. Music came from just over the low ridge, something sprightly and made for dancing. Men and women in their fashionable high-hats scuttled past the obstacle course of proselytizers, or paused to listen.

Milo didn't actually see the woman until he was right on top of her and trying to slew sidelong so he didn't bowl her over. Ellis still had hold of Milo's hand, pulling one way while Milo tried to yaw the other, and giving Milo's arm a solid yank in its socket when Milo skip-stomped to an abrupt sliding halt just short of sideswiping a sturdy cenotaph commemorating the Green Coast War. Ellis flailed with a laughing "Oi!" as he turned, so he didn't see the woman's gaze take Milo in, surprised, then move to Milo's earring and twist into... Milo didn't know. Something sour. Outraged. *Hateful.*

"So sorry!" Milo stammered, thrown, confused, but he creased a grin at the woman, as friendly as he could make it, and tapped at the brim of his hat. "My apologies, syr." He took a step back. "My friend and I were only—"

She spat. At Milo. At his feet. *Spat.*

Everything in Milo just sort of seized up and stopped working. He stared.

She glared back. Openly hostile. So many things slid over her face Milo couldn't keep up. Disgust. Anger. Hatred. And underneath, the fixed foundation across which all of it played, a feral little glee at what she'd just done, and a *What are you going to do about it?* challenge.

Ellis said "*Oi!*" again, not nearly as friendly, and tried to put himself between Milo and the woman.

Milo didn't move for a moment, couldn't, but when he finally managed to jerk from his dazed contemplation of the well of ill will in the woman's eyes, it was to the realization that they were attracting a small crowd. They were stood in a bundle in front of a monument to Kymbrygh's war dead, the three of them, Ellis shocked and wanting to know "What the deuce was that for?" and the woman stepping back some, brazenly smug, eyes on Milo. Her gaze slid to Milo's earring again, flaring into something so revolted Milo thought if he opened himself and *Saw* her, she'd be crawling with sickly reds and fulsome browns and pulsating greens the color of vomit.

"It's...." Milo shook his head, took a deep breath. His hand was still locked in Ellis's, so he tugged, backing away and pulling Ellis with him. "Nothing. A misunderstanding."

The woman snorted, disdainful, then merely turned and walked away. Like a normal person. Like what she'd just done hadn't been shocking and uncalled for and... bloody damn, it had been *hurtful*.

"Misunderstanding my arse," Ellis snapped, still watching the woman and trying to pull Milo's hand, no doubt meaning to follow her. "She *spat* at you! What even *was* that?"

The earring. Milo had watched her gaze land on it and turn wrathful. Had *watched* it.

He stared at the memorial—names etched in cold gray marble, dragons on the deep-carved coat of arms. Remembrance of honored dead in a war from which his mam emerged a hero. Milo wondered if that would've made a difference to the woman, had she known. He rather suspected... not.

"Dunno," Milo managed, weirdly humiliated and stricken and wounded, and sixteen other kinds of feelings he had no idea how to parse. "Some people are just naturally unpleasant, I reckon."

Except that wasn't it. Milo knew it wasn't. That Warden in Wellech, and now this.

I'm from bloody Whitpool! Milo wanted to shout, right there in the middle of the walk. *I was born there. So was my mam, and her mam, and her mam. My ancestors were Dewin and dragonkin before yours even knew Preidyn existed!*

"That's one way to put it," Ellis muttered, still fuming.

Milo wished he had the comfort of anger. All he could manage was shock and hurt and a strange lump of shame he couldn't fathom, but there it was, hunkered in a sick little ball in his gut. And all he wanted in the world at that moment was to keep Ellis from knowing why. Milo didn't understand it. He took great pride in everything the earring symbolized, all the years and work that went into earning it. Now all he wanted to do was slip it off and tuck it into his pocket so no one could see it. And Ellis guessing the source of the inexplicable humiliation, even guessing it was there at all, was just more than Milo could stand to consider.

"Right then." Ellis gave Milo's hand a bracing squeeze. He pulled on a grin. It might have been just a touch manic, a touch roguish. "Let's get this out of the way, then."

It wasn't ideal for a first kiss—standing in the middle of a fairly busy walkway, having just been thoroughly insulted and unnerved by some horrible woman who apparently hated Milo for existing—and it was nothing more than a peck, really, a soft press, chaste and simple. It still took a tender swipe at Milo's senses while at the same time reassuring him somehow. It settled his breathing. It took his heart from a rabbiting *thwup-thwup-thwup* to something steadier, gentler. *Almost* composed. *Almost* all right again.

Ellis pulled back, peering at Milo closely, assessing. Whatever he saw, it made him smile.

"The thing is," Ellis said, hand still gripping Milo's like he never meant to let go, "before this, I thought it might be nice to get drunk with you on sparkling wine. Now I think we should both get proper bladdered, scoff a half bushel of oysters each, and then snog until we can't breathe."

"...Oh." Milo's wobbly smile made his eyes water. He didn't care. "That...." He swallowed. "That's the best thing I've heard all day."

Somehow all of a sudden brave, as though he'd borrowed courage from Ellis, Milo leaned back in, hesitant, but when Ellis only gave him a cheering smile, Milo tipped his chin and set a soft, grateful kiss to Ellis's mouth.

Better now, more settled in his skin again, Milo pulled back, only a touch. "Actually," thin and feathery, "it might be the best thing I've ever heard in my life."

⁂

"Listen, I..."

Ellis trailed off, a frycake in one hand and a cup of sparkling wine from the Hollow Valley region of Wellech in the other. He had a dusting of powdered sugar at the corner of his mouth. Milo wanted to lick it off, but Ellis seemed hesitant, a bit uncomfortable, so Milo didn't.

Instead he laid a hand to Ellis's arm. "All right?"

"Yeah, it's only...." Ellis shook his head, mouth pursed. "I know it's stupid, but I feel like I ought to apologize."

"For what?"

They were waiting for a serving of breaded oysters and hugging close to the stall for the warmth from the oil kettle as they cooked. The smell was greasy and heavy and savory and divine, and not incidentally making Milo's stomach grumble impatiently.

Ellis waved his hand around before indicating the direction of the square and Preacher's Row, and presumably what had happened there.

Milo rolled his eyes. "For pity's sake, Elly, you had nothing to do with—"

"No, I know. And I do realize it's sort of absurd." Ellis shrugged. "But I Dreamed it only the other night. Or something very near to it, anyway. And I feel like I should've been able to—"

"I thought your Dreams didn't work like that?" Milo's eyebrows nearly took flight off his forehead. Ellis had spent a great deal of his boyhood vacillating between annoyance that he couldn't Dream "properly" and so wasn't considered a witch or part of a sect, and relief that it was one less bone of contention between him and his tad. "Can you control it now?"

"No. Not really. And what I *can* do, I can't do very well. Nothing like Mam." Ellis shoved half the frycake in his mouth. Now he had *more* sugar Milo wanted to lick off. It was a little disappointing when Ellis did it himself. "I still can't make the Dreams come, and the ones I get are few and far between, and usually quite mundane and useless. But I Dreamed of that woman. I didn't realize until after it happened. I recognized her but I didn't know how. Not until only a moment ago, actually."

He held the frycake out toward Milo, contrite, as though offering recompense for an imagined sin. Milo, rather bold after that kiss, leaned in and took a leisurely bite, careful to keep eye contact, and equally careful to lick his lips slowly as he pulled back. Ellis was watching Milo's mouth with rapt attention, so he saw it clearly when Milo smirked. But he also dipped in for another kiss, so Milo considered it a job well done. Even better, it made Ellis smile, soft and secret.

"If you could've prevented it you would've." Milo took hold of Ellis's hand, deliberate and braver than he actually was, and guided the last bite of frycake into Ellis's mouth. No sugar on Ellis's lip this time, but Milo followed it with a kiss nonetheless. Because he could. "If you don't know that, I'll know it for the both of us. So let's just forget about all of that, shall we? I don't want to think about her."

The girl in the stall was just now scooping their oysters into a little boat made of folded newspaper. She handed it over with a red-cheeked grin.

"I can't *stop* thinking about it," Ellis muttered.

Milo thanked the girl and stepped back from the booth to give the next customer room. He missed the warmth immediately and so pushed in close to Ellis as they ambled in the general direction of the bandstand, burning their mouths on too-hot oysters and looking for beer to go with them. Because yes, sparkling wine might be the done thing with oysters, a perfect palate mix for connoisseurs. But when there was breading and frying involved, Milo was of the firm opinion that the connoisseurs could hang, because that was a job for beer.

"Why are you not more bothered by it?" Ellis blurted, as though it had been pushing at his tongue and he just couldn't hold it back anymore. "After what happened in Wellech, I can't—"

"Look," said Milo as he steered them toward a beer stand that also sold pots to put it in, because he hadn't thought to bring a cup with him. "I don't know. It threw me proper when it happened, and all right, it does bother me. I could stand someone hating me for something I've done, but for existing?"

He stopped just shy of the line for the stand and turned to Ellis, taking him in yet again, because Milo kept getting sideswiped by the fact that random passersby could look all they wanted, but Ellis was here with Milo. On purpose. Because he'd asked.

"I don't know." Milo looked away, uncomfortable even thinking about it all, much less talking about it. "Mam says frightened people are the most terrifying thing in the world, because fear crowds out sense and compassion, and it's contagious and easier to catch than the pox. One person's irrational fear of something harmless can turn into a mob in minutes, and...."

They'd been talking about an editorial in one of the Llundaintref papers that had apparently struck so many nerves—for and against—it had been reprinted in nearly all the local ones a week later. Purity Party rot, really, outrage over the Queen's firm declaration that the United Preidynīg Isles were resolved to stand beside their allies in Colorat, now that the dictator in Taraverde who called himself Premier was massing at the borders of Nasbrun, and apparently eyeing up Błodwyl now too. Preidyn had cut off trade—the banks were scrambling, the unions were crying foul, and the shippers were tamping.

And somehow, it was the fault of the Dewin. At least that's what the Purity Party said. And, apparently, people who didn't know better had started to agree.

"She's warned me to be careful." Milo puffed a laugh, small and not at all amused. He caught Ellis's fretful look and shook his head. "I mean, not at home or anything. At least... well, no one in Whitpool has been awful or looked at me any funnier than they usually do. Only." He huffed and waved back toward where the woman had... done what she'd done. "I reckon she meant things like that. It's only that I didn't really think it would...." He couldn't finish.

"Didn't think it would really happen here." Ellis nodded, a grim set to his mouth. "I've been seeing it more too. In Wellech, I mean. Of course, it's always been there against magic to some degree, but most people seemed to understand that was my tad being an arse because of...." He rolled his hand, then his eyes. "Well. You know. But it didn't really *leak in*, if you know what I mean. And I was changing—*trying* to change it. I'm in the process of changing it. But now all this scapegoating and ignorance turning up in casual conversation is getting worrying, and I haven't been able—"

"Elly, no. *No*. You're doing what you can. It's all you can do. And I rather...." It got caught in Milo's throat, a small lump of emotion that was a bit embarrassing, a bit *too much*, but it was also *important*, so he pushed past it. "I rather, ehm. Kind of really fancy you for it."

Milo really did. Because he knew what Ellis had been doing. Enlisting the fishing boats to watch for refugees in their waters, because some were fleeing up through Eretia, and the tides of the Goshor swept them past Preidyn and to Wellech's doorstep.

Finding them homes and employment, and doing his best to ensure Wellech welcomed them, despite Folant and his loud opposition. Horse-trading with the members of Wellech's council to entice them into the odd vote against their Pennaeth's continued efforts to kneecap his son.

"Really fancy you" wasn't quite adequate to capture the admiration Milo held for Ellis for all that, let alone everything else that made him who he was. Milo wasn't sure there was a phrase that would do.

He tried not to wince when he chanced a look at Ellis, not really *expecting* displeasure or amusement at what he'd said, but still hoping he didn't find either. But Ellis's eyes held the same steely hue as the sky, bright and earnest against his dark skin, something honest and truly concerned in his gaze. Milo, in no uncertain terms, absolutely *had* to smile in the face of such open sentiment.

"That woman. Just now. It was one unpleasant moment in the midst of lots of brilliant ones." Milo shrugged. "I'd rather live in the brilliance for however long it lasts."

Ellis's smile was slow, but when it came, it was pleased and easy and genuinely affectionate, as it had been when he'd greeted Milo at the station.

"As long as I get to live there with you sometimes." Ellis tugged at Milo's arm. "C'mon, let's get you your beer."

※

Somehow, it was easier after that. Maybe it was the beer. Or the wine. More likely it was the fact that something happened worse than even Milo had imagined, and it didn't ruin the trip. It didn't ruin anything. It did change things a bit. Somehow.

The space between them was full of an unnamed intimacy now, where before it had been merely space. Bridgeable but not yet bridged. Except now it had been.

They watched the last leg of the working boat races from the eastern side of the harbor's jetty. The colorful topsails of the gaff-rigged cutters jostled for place in the distance while spectators laid bets on which boat would take the Brass Cup top prize in the end. A culmination, apparently, of a summer-long race that today's leg would finally determine. Which meant the locals had the advantage of knowing which boats were already ahead, and which could be counted out regardless of where they finished today.

That didn't stop Ellis from placing small bets with various fellow watchers based on random things that seemed aimed at nothing more than making Milo laugh.

"That one?" Ellis pointed to a bright yellow sail whipping over the waves to catch the three ahead of it. He shook his head. "It's got to be some youngster only learning. That is *not* how you handle a sail."

Ellis would know. He'd been sailing up and down Wellech's wealth of rivers and waterways since he could walk.

Still, it put Milo in mind of the little spitter, so he confirmed the bet with the woman next to him, and grinned as she shook her head at him with a *It's your money you're throwing away* look.

"I'm taking that one," Ellis said, resolute. "With the blue sail."

The woman gave him an incredulous smirk. "I mean, I'll happily take your money, but you should know that *The Sapphire* has the highest handicap in its class, and has still been sitting at the bottom of the pole all summer." She turned to Milo, grinning. "You should tell your...." She trailed off, looking right into Milo's eyes, before her grin turned wide and knowing. "Ah, I see." She huffed an eloquent snort, snatched Ellis's money out of his hand, and turned back to watch the race.

"What?" Milo frowned and turned to Ellis. "What?"

"Nothing." Ellis gave the woman an affable glare, repeated, "*Nothing*," and shrugged at Milo. "Only, I like the color."

The woman snorted again before shaking her head and sliding a sly glance at Milo. "Your eyes are very blue."

Milo frowned, bemused, and then thought *Oh*, and... well, that was sort of it for a while as it sank in. A grin he couldn't help if his life depended on it split his face. Sliding his arm through Ellis's, he rested his chin on Ellis's shoulder, watching the blue sail bob through the water on its way to dead last in the race.

<hr />

"Show me."

Milo was half-asleep, blissed out and warm as toast. But he opened his eyes at the soft demand. Smiled.

"What would you like to see?"

Ellis turned over onto his back, sleek broad body dark against pale linens, and waved toward the ceiling. "Something... pretty."

"Hmm." Milo squinted around the room. Thinking.

The inn's lighting was electric, which made it a bit more difficult, snagging light from inside a teardrop of glass. The small sconce on the wall still burning would have to do, since he wasn't about to leave the warmth of the bed and turn on a lamp.

Stars, he decided, and eased a gleaming splinter, small as a glow worm, from the filament. Another and another, until a swarm hovered 'round the sconce, bobbling in sleepy waves, and then he sent them to the ceiling. Pushed. Tugged. Tweaked.

The mist he drew from Ellis's breath, stretched it like taffy, wove it into the blooming aurora, then swept it out, thin as silk thread on a spindle. It sank back, fine gossamer, then broadened, an iridescent backdrop to the summer constellations they used to lie beneath as boys.

A nudge from Ellis, warm toes against Milo's shin. "Now show me what it Looks like."

This part was easy. The shimmer of the galaxy opened across the inn's low ceiling, a tapestry made of stardust in vibrant colors become soft and pasteled against the black of the spaces between stars. People supposed there was a lot of emptiness in the great void of the universe, but Milo knew that the colors of the cosmos still swayed to the song of its violent birth in boundless harmonic swaths of opaline incandescence.

He settled back, watched the stars wheel, so content it was almost disconcerting.

Ellis found Milo's hand amidst the sea of linens, set warm fingers around it. Squeezed.

"Beautiful."

But he was looking at Milo.

Chapter 7—Sforzando

: *sudden stress on a note or chord*

Winter slid in soft and quiet. The rain was merely rain, not the sharp icy spicules whipped into shards by the brutal winds that normally battered the coast and made Highwinter into more survival than celebration. The dragons hunkered in their caves at the springs, sleeping more than waking, emerging only once or twice a week for their trips to the forge, rather than the daily visits they made in warmer weather. There'd been no need thus far for Milo to de-ice between scales or build and maintain a trail of bonfires in a pasture to warm a dragon that had stayed out too long and needed help returning to its nest.

Winter at Old Forge was usually a time of battening down and keeping the fires going, trying not to die on the inevitably slippery access road on the rare trips down into the village proper, and playing his violin until his fingers ached only out of sheer, bloody monotony. So it was a pleasant change to be able to make trips to Brookings every few weeks to meet Ellis without the usual concerns about leaving his duties.

Glynn was a help Milo hadn't known he'd wanted. She'd been right—the dragons had got used to her quickly, likely owing to Nain's past permissiveness. If they hadn't acknowledged her as kin thus far, they never would; Glynn had cried for two days when Milo coached her to toss her stone, and the old razorback merely watched it drop and walked away. But they tolerated her well, and never gave her so much as a threatening glance. Milo wasn't sure they'd ever allow her right up close without him near, and she was conscientious about respecting their spaces. Still, she was able to carry out day-to-day care and maintenance with no trouble and no danger, and that was more than Milo had ever expected.

He'd always known what his future would be, and he'd never felt particularly tied down by it. He loved what he did and he loved the dragons. He knew he'd spend his life right here at Old Forge, fighting with the furnace, patching ancient crenellations and merlons, digging birds' nests out of chimneys, as well as everything that came along with running a preserve. He'd known since he was learning at Nain's knee what he was in for and never really wished for something different. But he couldn't deny that having Glynn there to look after things when Milo wasn't was freeing. Milo expressed his gratitude by applying to increase Old Forge's stipend and subsequently increasing Glynn's allowance.

Brookings became something quite special to Milo. The festivals were nice and all, and the people of Brookings did take their food quite seriously. But it was, of course, Ellis who made the place into somewhat of a homecoming every time Milo met him there.

"I've signed an annual lease on the room," Ellis said as he and Milo lingered in the inn's tiny dining room, empty dishes scattered across the tablecloth and the heat of the crackling hearth rosing his cheeks to dusky merlot. It was the first time they'd been able to meet since after the Highwinter fairs. "The holder of the place was quite reasonable, and she even—"

"Wait, you what?" Milo dropped his spoon and nearly upended his dish, which would have been a right shame—it was stewed apples and currants, doused in cinnamon and crowned with cream, and it was proper bliss. "Ellis, I can't pay for a room I'm only in for a few days a month. Even half would be—"

"Which is why *I* signed the lease." Ellis grinned, entirely too pleased with himself, and shrugged. "It was getting difficult to arrange to have the room free on only a week's notice, and I've grown to like the place."

"Well. Yes, but." It wasn't like Milo could disagree, but still. "Ellis, I can't let you—"

"Oi, boyo, you don't *let* me do anything." It came with a softer smile, and so without the sting it might have had otherwise. Ellis leaned over the table and lowered his voice, though it was raining old women and sticks outside, so they were the only ones here. "Milo," he said, easy and intimate, his gray eyes intent as they locked onto Milo's. Milo wasn't sure what to expect—sometimes Ellis dipped down into sop that should be cheesy and melodramatic, but nonetheless made Milo weak-kneed and melty—so when Ellis said, "I'm rich, I do what I want," and his grin edged even more smug, Milo could've cheerfully thumped him.

Instead, Milo picked up his spoon and shot a wad of cream across the table. It landed almost perfectly across Ellis's mouth.

Ellis gaped. Then he sniggered. "You'd best be cleaning that up."

Let no one ever say Milo Priddy was one to waste an opportunity when it was handed to him.

He leaned across the table and obliged. Thoroughly.

<hr />

Spring on the north coast of Kymbrygh wasn't easily discernable from winter but for the creeping warmth beneath the frosted winds.

Frozen mud thawed to knee-deep muck that too often turned a trip across a pasture into a fight to keep one's boots.

Milo kept as much as he could to the road on the way down to the main gate, giving Poppy a chiding chirp every now and then when she tried to pause for a taste of the new spring grasses and crocus popping up along the berm. Last week's rain had washed out the public access road to the forge outside the fences, and the ore delivery couldn't wait. Milo really didn't have time for any of this, but had no choice but to *make* the time to meet the wagon at the main gate and escort it up the private drive. Migration season meant a lot more dragons wandering the pastures, and since the private drive was well within the preserve's perimeter, a chaperone for visitors was needed for obvious reasons.

The wagon was already waiting by the time Milo crested the little knoll that looked down on the gate, though Harri wasn't waving his hat at Milo in greeting as he usually would do. He was standing beside his little mule team as though at attention, and giving Milo a curious look.

Milo saw why immediately. And couldn't help the bit of hope that sprang up in his belly.

The colonel was in full uniform, standing in front of a motorcar with the Home Guard's coat of arms painted in gold on its doors. A lieutenant—also in uniform—waited behind the wheel.

"Milo." The colonel tapped at the bill of his hat.

"Colonel-in-Chief Alton. *Haia*. It's... nice to see you."

No one ever came to the gate unexpected. It was too far from Old Forge for a bell to be of any use, and the wards didn't allow anyone onto the preserve unless Milo or his mam were there to let them through. The view from Ty Dreigiau stretched all the way down to Whitpool, but the trees along the outer fences blocked the road, and even if they didn't, one would have to be looking to know someone was loitering at the gate. Showing up out of the blue would only result in a very long, likely fruitless wait.

Milo dismounted and let Poppy wander toward where the clover was beginning to sprout around the fence posts. He tried not to look too eager, too hopeful. Because service in the Home Guard wasn't required but it *was* expected; maybe the colonel was here because he'd rethought acquiescing to whatever screws Ceri had put to him to hand over that exemption Milo didn't want. There was a new push for enlistment, and no one doubted it was due to the growing unrest on the continent. If war was as inevitable as it was starting to look, perhaps whatever deal Ceri had made with the colonel was off.

The colonel wasn't a particularly imposing man. Tall and fit, smooth olive skin puckered in a tight swirl beneath one down-tilted hazel eye, the scar tissue stretching white from cheekbone to ear. It might have been off-putting in someone else, called to mind war and violence and things best unspoken or forgot. It seemed more to point up the colonel's natural serenity, a contrast between appearance and demeanor that was perhaps subtly but still easily discerned. Milo had only met him a handful of times, but the colonel had always been pleasant—if not exactly friendly and cheerful, then at least amicable; if not entirely unreserved, then at least somewhat approachable.

Today he was expressionless, giving nothing away.

Eventually, Milo remembered his manners and greeted Harri then released the wards on the gate before creaking it open. Harri gave Milo a questioning look as he steered his wagon through. Milo could only shrug. When Harri pulled up to wait for his escort, very obviously looking anywhere but backward, Milo turned to the colonel and lifted his eyebrows.

"I wasn't told to expect you. To what do we owe the pleasure?"

"I'm here to see your mam."

"Oh." Milo hoped his shoulders didn't slump too noticeably. Still, though. Even if the colonel was here to take back the exemption, he'd have to speak with Ceri first. Right? Milo tipped a tight nod. "All right, then. You're in luck. She's home. Although...." He eyed the car and then the road. It would fit, but. "I need to escort Harri to the forge, and we can't go any faster than his mules can haul the wagon. You can follow us, but it's a choice between a very long walk or a very slow drive. Or you can wait here and Mam or I can come back for you."

That would probably be the better choice, actually. Ceri clearly hadn't been expecting any visitors, so it was only polite to alert her before Milo dumped them in the dooryard. And if this *was* about what Milo hoped it was, he'd prefer Ceri be in the best mood possible.

But the colonel said, "We'll follow you," curt, and headed back to the car, so Milo could only give Harri a nod and wait for the car to drive through the gate. Once it did, and once Milo reset the wards and coaxed Poppy away from her late-morning snack, Milo mounted back up, situated himself between Harri's wagon and the colonel's car, and started the little caravan back up the road.

And if he couldn't stop hoping while he kept Poppy on task and scanned for stray dragons overhead, well. There were worse things.

✺

He was a little less optimistic when he left the lieutenant in the car and the colonel and Ceri in the kitchen. The colonel was still laconic and pokerfaced; Ceri was tight-lipped and clearly angry while she politely—though still rather loudly—put the kettle on and pulled out some biscuits Milo knew were at least a week old and would likely have been goat treats already had Glynn not been in school this morning.

Milo had been dismissed, in no uncertain terms and rather rudely, actually. His mam's harsh "*Go*, Milo," still rang in his ears as he made his way back over to the forge to help Howell unload.

He should be out in the pastures. With the transients that migration brought, there was always a hissing match to break up, or a brooding cow to check, or whatever nonsense territorial dragons got up to when left to themselves. And with someone still messing with random wards every now and then, Milo had taken to making the rounds to check them once a week, rather than his mam's customary once a month. He'd even been forced to inform the Wardens of the problem, and now they did regular patrols as well. Clearly it wasn't enough, since the tinkering didn't stop. Milo had no choice but to keep as much of a watch as he could himself. All of it ate into his time, and he found he couldn't spare much lately.

But he couldn't really wander off too far until he'd taken Harri and the colonel back down to the main gate. And he was feeling rather nosy just now. Maybe the colonel had said something to Harri about why he was here while they'd waited at the gate.

"...getting scarce," Harri was saying as Milo stopped to pat one of the mules, searching his pockets for treats but coming up empty; Poppy had been especially recalcitrant on the trip back up from the gate and had needed a lot of coaxing to stop being a git. "The mines are going harder than ever, hiring so many on they had to set up a tent city outside Makework. But most of the ore's going over to Werrdig, and they won't say why."

Howell frowned as he lifted the tarp over the wagon's load to inspect it, but it didn't look like he was unhappy—only thoughtful. "Looks like everything's here."

"O' course it is." Harri was mildly indignant. "I would've told you if I didn't have the full order. I'm saying don't be surprised if that starts changing."

"It better not." Milo let go of Poppy's rein and took a step closer. "They can't short a preserve. The orders come from Parliament itself."

Harri gave Milo a tight once-over. "So do the ones that are sending the bulk of the ore Hampton Seam produces to somewhere in Werrdig." He turned back to Howell. "I haven't said anything to anyone else. I don't want to traffic in rumors. But"—he paused to give Milo another glance, narrow-eyed, assessing—"Cadwyn's on the utility crew at Hampton. She says the guards they've just hired on look an awful lot like soldiers to her eye."

Howell's face blanked then closed down altogether. He shot

Milo a look, as though wondering exactly what Milo had parsed from that.

Milo was afraid he'd got all of it.

Something is always brewing Ceri had said, troubled and restless, and she would know.

An ally had been invaded. Sabers were rattling all up and down the continent. Metal ores were suddenly getting harder to come by.

And with the Colonel-in-Chief showing up like he had....

Spies aren't only for wartime, you know.

This unexpected visit wasn't about Milo. It wasn't about the Home Guard.

Milo waited until Howell and Harri were deep into a debate over whether mines even needed guards in the first place before he quietly sidled Poppy away from the forge, and started back to the house.

The colonel was just stepping out the backdoor when Milo arrived, Ceri standing in the doorway behind him with her arms crossed over her chest and glaring at the colonel's back. The colonel looked... well, Milo still couldn't tell. Although he'd really like to learn the trick of keeping his emotions concealed like that; Ceri always said Milo should never play poker, and Ellis was of the firm opinion that Milo couldn't lie to save his life because everything he was thinking was all over his face.

Three dragons drifted by overhead, coasting along the thermals from the ocean and gliding out over the waves in a loose arrow. Milo squinted up, taking automatic inventory, but it was only the two horned ringtails that had arrived a few days ago, and the white broadwing that had started the fight over a deer carcass the other night. The transients would all be gone in a few weeks, heading toward their summer roosts, and Milo had hope that at least three of his winter charges were recovered and healthy enough to go with them. The preserve had acquired another razorback, apparently having bred well before season, fat and clumsy and looking as though she'd barely made it over Tirryderch; Milo might end up stuck with a brooding cow this summer, and—providing all went well with the hatching—a new calf to look after come winter. Which would really cut into his jaunts to Brookings, so Milo couldn't help hoping the cow managed the rest of her trip. Since Old Forge was the last stop on this path before—

"*Ow!*" Milo was thumped from his meandering by a sharp jab at his shin, just above where the top of his boot would've blocked it had Ansel not had such impeccable aim for a rooster that could barely see anymore. "Ansel, you stroppy little knob." Milo nudged at him with the toe of his muddy boot. "Go on, then, or I'll have you for dinner."

It wasn't as though Ansel was good for much else these days. Though he'd probably be too stringy anyway, just to be the same contrary arsehole in death he'd always been in life.

"Majestic, I've always thought."

"Majestic is absolutely *not* the word I'd use," Milo muttered and looked up from his tiff with Ansel to see the colonel, hands in pockets, ambling toward him. It took a moment to realize the colonel's gaze was pointed at the sky and not Ansel, who'd backed off some but only enough to get Milo to forget about him long enough for another sneak attack. Milo followed the colonel's gaze. "Oh. Dragons. Right."

The three dragons had ventured out farther over the water, circling past the oyster boats and fishing coracles, and tightening their formation. Definitely on the hunt for something big. It was too early for whales, and too close to shore anyway. A stray pod of dolphins, maybe?

"Yeah, I'll give you majestic." Milo gave the colonel a wry smile. "But I feel compelled to add temperamental, cantankerous, and too often patience-wearingly fussy."

The lieutenant had never left the car. His gaze was nailed firmly to the dragons out over the ocean, his hands were knuckle-white on the steering wheel, and the car's door was firmly shut. He must not be from Whitpool.

Ceri watched Milo and the colonel from the doorway, posture still rigid. The wind off the water was getting warmer but still biting, and she wasn't wearing a shawl or even a jumper. Still, she didn't move.

The colonel chuckled. He stopped right next to Milo, eyes still on the sky.

"Ever hear from the dragonkin on the other paths?"

"Sure." Milo shrugged. "I mean, most everything goes through Llundaintref, but when I can't get—"

Milo cut himself off. He probably didn't need to be telling the Colonel-in-Chief of the Home Guard that Milo sometimes made a habit of circumventing protocol in favor of faster answers.

The colonel seemed to know anyway. He pulled his gaze from the hunting dragons—yep, definitely found some dolphins—and over to Milo. He lifted an eyebrow, sardonic.

"Yeah, all right." Milo huffed. What could anyone do, anyway? Sack him? "Sometimes going through channels is too slow, and I can't wait for an answer. So I keep in touch with the dragonkin on the other paths. If a dragon shows up here shedding scales and with its fire sputtering, I need to know what it's been into. If I wait for it to go through channels, the dragon might be dead by the time I get an answer."

"I imagine disposing of a carcass that size would be quite the chore." The colonel said it with a quirk to his lip.

The dragons took care of their own dead, incinerating a corpse as though tending a respectful pyre. Sometimes there were scales or charred bones to see to afterward, and it *was* a bit of a chore, but that was never the point.

Milo bristled. "It would be a massive *waste*. It would be a *dead dragon*, and for what? Because someone in some government cubby somewhere needs to check I'm not telling someone in Vistosa something they already know? It's a stupid rule, and it's impractical, and if—"

"Ho there, lad. No need to set fire to my eyebrows." The colonel held up his hands. "I'm only curious. I get copies of those reports, you know. And sometimes I don't understand what various bits of information might mean."

"Like what?"

"Like." The colonel slipped his hands back into his pockets and leaned against the side of the car. He squinted out over the waves. "You keep track of all the dragons on this path."

"Of course."

"So if one didn't show up before the migration season is done, you'd know it."

"If one didn't show up here at Old Forge, yes. Not every preserve along the way, though."

The colonel peered at Milo from beneath the bill of his smart black cap. "Why is that?"

"Well, at Sowing, Old Forge is the last stop before the North Blackson. It's a long stretch of nothing but water from here to Harthoer, where these clans are heading. If a dragon hasn't rested here for a week or so before moving on, if it hasn't refueled with fresh game or had its fire topped off, it's likely not going to make it. We're the last stop at Sowing and the first at Reaping, so we generally get a full count because they need the rest before or after braving the ocean. But at Reaping, once they get past Vistosa, you've got the whole of upper Drensland before you hit the southern waters. The stronger dragons might skip a preserve if they feel like hunting for themselves, or if they're the ornery type that just prefer to stay away from people."

"But you'd know if a dragon didn't show up at any one preserve?"

"Sure. If they skip one, they'll usually stop at the next, and if not, someone will probably at least spot a flyover. We all do counts and submit them in the reports."

"And?"

Milo rolled his eyes. "*And*, yes, we write to each other if one goes missing. Hopefully it's stopped at another preserve somewhere on the route and hasn't died or disappeared along the way."

"Do many disappear?"

"That's enough, Alton." Ceri had come off the porch and was slowly making her way across the yard, chickens clucking in disapproval as she stepped through an apparently worm-rich smudge of mud.

"I don't think it is." The colonel stood straighter, like he couldn't help himself.

Ceri's teeth set. "Anything you want to know, you can ask—"

"I'm asking dragonkin." The colonel lifted his eyebrows, some kind of silent rebuttal Milo couldn't parse.

Somehow, it shut Ceri up. She winced as though slapped then curled her lip, angry again, and looked away.

Milo had never seen his mam back down like that. *Ever.*

The colonel turned back to Milo. "Have you ever had a dragon disappear?"

Milo frowned between his mam and the colonel, looking for clues, because this had abruptly turned very odd, and he had no idea what the tension in the air might be. The colonel was still as unreadable as he'd been down at the gate. Ceri was clearly seething, but still strangely silent. Wary, though. On the balls of her feet, waiting to step in again.

"Yeeees?" Milo answered slowly. "I mean, not exactly. Not on this path. If one goes missing we can generally track—"

"There have been times when one has disappeared along other paths, though?"

Milo clacked his mouth shut, still trying to figure out what was going on here, and still unable to do it. His mam was staring a hole into the ground, no help at all.

"The central path has had a few instances, yeah." Milo watched them both for reactions, but when Ceri gave him none and the colonel only nodded for him to go on, Milo said, "The preserves in Błodwyl reported two spitters that never showed up last Sowing, and a blackhorn this past Reaping. All cows. I mean, there's always the chance they were pregnant and stayed behind to brood, in which case they'll turn up again in about a year or so."

"But you don't think so."

"The dragonkin in Błodwyl said they'd've noticed. And since *I* would've noticed...."

The colonel stared at Milo, thoughtful, waiting, but when Milo didn't go on, asked, "So what d'you think happened?"

Milo shrugged. "Well, everyone heard about the plane in Ostlich-Sztym last year, for all they tried to keep it a secret. So there's the possibility people are getting bolder, or stupider, when it comes to encroaching on flight paths." The newspaper article had outraged Milo, less mournful about the lost pilot and more furious about anyone taking a chance like that anywhere near a migration path, off season or no. Planes were more at risk than dragons when it came to something like that, which was why no one with any sense ventured into what had been dragon airspace long before people found a way to launch themselves into the skies as well. But if a propeller managed to damage a wing and the dragon landed badly... Milo shook it off. "Honestly, though, with the trouble in Colorat and Ostlich-Sztym, I just figured it was a matter of not getting reports. Like the Colorat Coven going dark."

He paused, ruminating, then went on, "Although, now that I think about it, Kriuces was missing one a few seasons ago. Might've been a horned redcrest, but I'd have to look it up. We had a couple of redcrests stop here, in fact, last Sowing, and a grayback, which was odd since they don't usually venture this far west. But none of those were the one that disappeared, and I think that was before everything started with Colorat. I don't remember anyone ever explaining it, though."

"And Kriuces is the first stop on the central path after the Gray Ghosts Sea going south from Colorat."

"Yeah." Milo frowned at the colonel. "Is someone in Colorat killing dragons?"

It made no sense. Dragons weren't easy to kill, and it was stupidly dangerous to try. Moreover, anything that might be got from some black market somewhere wouldn't be enough to make it worth the risk.

"Not really what I had in mind," the colonel said, low and with another speaking glance at Ceri.

Ceri seemed to understand what it meant, because she tightened her jaw and lifted her chin, scowling.

Milo only wished he could decode whatever silent language they were using. Because something was going on, something to do with missing dragons, and that was absolutely, unquestionably something dragonkin had a right to know about.

"And have any of your dragons been acting... different? Odd?"

That made Milo blink. "I mean, they're all odd in their own ways. Odd how?"

"I don't know. I'm asking you."

"Well then, no. There's nothing I can think of."

"Is there anything you know of that could *make* a dragon act oddly?"

"I don't even understand the question. If you tell me what you mean, maybe I can give you the answer you're looking for."

"I don't really know, Milo. That's why I'm asking dragonkin."

"Then my answer is still that I don't understand the question. Very few things could *make* a dragon do anything. In fact, I'd have to say, in my experience, *nothing* can make a dragon do anything it doesn't want to do. So if you've heard of—"

"Thank you, Milo, that's all I need."

Dismissed. The colonel had just *dismissed* Milo, in his own yard, as though Milo were one of his subordinates. Which he absolutely *wasn't* since the colonel had given Ceri her way and booted Milo out of consideration for the Home Guard.

Before Milo could say as much or demand the answers he definitely deserved, the colonel tipped a firm nod. "This is between us, Milo. Do you understand?"

"*No.*" Milo gave the colonel the dirtiest look he could muster. "If someone's hurting dragons, I've a right to know about it."

"Not when Her Majesty says you don't." The colonel all but snorted at him, condescending, and turned to Ceri. "Think about what I said. It's the best you're going to get." He slid his glance at Milo then back to Ceri. "Better than most."

Before Milo could marshal a response that clearly wasn't welcome anyway, the colonel opened the car's door and slid into the passenger seat. Milo couldn't help a bit of petty satisfaction when it made the lieutenant—still watching the sky like a dragon was going to descend from it and eat him—jump nearly out of his snazzy uniform.

Ceri grabbed hold of the door before the colonel could swing it shut. "Burn in the nether, Alton." Snarled. "You and all the rest of them."

The colonel huffed something that wasn't exactly a laugh. "Last one there buys the drinks." He shut the door when Ceri let go of it then rolled down the window. He lifted an eyebrow. "I assume I'll still need an escort off the preserve."

✺

They had to wait until Harri and Howell were finished unloading the wagon. Howell somehow read Milo's dazed awkwardness, his confused silence, and headed directly up to the house before Harri even got his tarps refastened.

The trip down was forever. The trip back up was even longer. Milo had dragons to check on and wards to test, and Glynn would be back from school this afternoon, expecting to have her excursion with Milo out to the pastures and whatever was waiting for them there.

It was all going to have to wait.

He left Poppy, still saddled, in the little corral off the sideyard and burst through the kitchen door. His mam sat at the table, alone, a fresh loaf of bread on a cooling rack in front of her, cold tea at her elbow, and her usual composure belted up around her like the deflective armor Milo was only recently coming to understand it was. She didn't startle when Milo came charging in. She didn't even look up at him.

She said, "I can't tell you."

And that was all.

Howell was nowhere to be seen. Lleu was curled in his bed beside the hearth, looking as poised and unconcerned as Ceri did.

Milo set his teeth. "You can't just *say* that! Not about... I'm *dragonkin*. If this doesn't concern *me*, then who—you can't just—I have to know what—"

"What you have to know, Milo, is that I love you. Since the day I knew you were growing inside me, everything I've done, everything I will ever do, is for you."

It was so infuriatingly *calm*. And even more infuriatingly *uninformative*.

"Mam." Milo took a step forward. "I know that. I've never, ever questioned it. But this isn't about—"

"You don't *know* what it's about!"

"Because you won't *tell* me!" Milo threw out his hands, frustrated and edging on furious. "He didn't come here for information on dragons. Every question he had, he could've asked me down at the gate. He came here for you."

Ceri huffed with a roll of her eyes. "A word of advice, Milo—never try to decipher Meredith Alton."

"Yeah? Well it'd probably be easier than deciphering you. At least he doesn't lie to me when I ask—"

"I have never *lied* to—"

"You do it all the time! You're doing it now! You look me right in the eye and say 'I can't tell you, Milo,' or 'It doesn't concern you, Milo,' when clearly it does, because even if it didn't concern dragons it concerns *you*, and you're *my mam*!" Milo paused, chest tight. "Something is always brewing. You said that. And now he shows up and you shut down, and I have a *right*—"

"You have *no* right to demand—"

"No, stop! *Stop*! I'm not a boy anymore. You can't just order me to accept 'I can't tell you, don't ask' for an answer." Milo took another step closer, hand gripping the back of a chair to keep himself from... flailing, raging, swooping in and *shaking* her, he didn't know. "He came here for the Black Dog." No reaction, not even a twitch, because Ceri Priddy used to be a spy and knew how to be unreadable when she wanted to be. Milo clenched his teeth. "He came here because something is always brewing, and he wants the Black Dog to find out what. And you're thinking of doing it, aren't you?"

Ceri snorted. "Honestly, I don't know where you come up with—"

"So you won't be leaving on another mysterious trip, then?"

"—these wild ideas. Alton is Colonel-in-Chief of the Kymbrygh Home Guard, not some secret spy organization."

"Except he gets his orders from Llundaintref just like every other commanding officer. The Home Guard ranks in Tirryderch and Wellech are full of locals, commanded by locals. Not Alton's. D'you think no one's ever noticed how many times brass from Parliament pass through here? Or how you and a select few others always have your 'reading group' when they're in town? *I* have. *I've* noticed. I know what a handler is, Mam, and it looks exactly like Alton. I'm not an *idiot*!" Milo slammed his palm on the table so hard the bread jostled off its cooling rack. Lleu sat up with a halfhearted *whuff*. And still, Ceri only sat there, looking exasperated now, as though Milo's concern was a *bother*. It made Milo even more livid. "Blood and rot, Mam, I'm not blind and I'm not nearly as naïve as you seem to think I am! It's not hard to guess—"

"No, you're a stroppy, disrespectful boy who suddenly seems to think he knows more than his mam!"

"Oh, I've never had *that* delusion, since I've never *not* known my mam has been keeping secrets from me all my life!"

"Because there are some things you've no right—"

"I'm your *son*!"

"Which is why you should be trusting your mam and not trying to interrogate her!"

"Does Howell know? D'you tell *him* all these secrets you keep from me?"

"Howell has nothing to do with—"

"Then who does? Who *does* get answers from the Black Dog? Because I'd like to sign up for some lessons!"

"Stop *calling* me that! You've no right! You've no idea what—"

"Because *you won't tell me*!"

It was something between a cry, *asking*, and a roar, *demanding*. It was vehement and borderline desperate, and it shocked them both silent. The resonance of their voices—hanging together, interweaving, sharpness turned to a dull ring, like the aftermath of a struck bell—sat in the still air of the kitchen as thick as fog between them.

A dragon growled in the distance, something annoyed and petulant, likely a row over a sunny slab of rock in the south fields. The bells from the fishing boats trilled, high and bright. Kittiwakes and petrels squabbled on the pebbled beach at the feet of the cliffs. The sea rumbled and crashed.

Background noise Milo had been hearing all his life. Comforting. Welcoming. Loved.

And all he could hear right now was the booming silence that hung between him and his mam. Too full of secrets to be intimate.

Too full of an excruciating love Milo didn't understand to be anything but cruel, however unintentionally.

Ceri broke it when she stood, chair scraping across the scuffed wood of the floor. She pulled in a deep, calm breath, laid her hand to Milo's cheek. "Because I *love* you." Then turned and left the kitchen.

Three weeks of cross words and angry silences later, Ceri left.

Just *left*.

Without even having told Milo she was going.

Howell took her to the station while Milo was out in the pastures. Milo came home that night to a note that more or less said *I know you didn't mean it, but even if you did, I love you, and I know you love me*. And that was all.

"Where?" Milo croaked, head a bit light and his gut a sudden depthless cavern. He was sitting in the same chair Ceri had sat in while they'd torn at each other like angry dragons.

Howell sighed. "You know better than to ask, boy."

"Did she tell *you*?"

"Don't be dense." Howell huffed a mirthless laugh. "*I* know better than to ask."

"For how long?"

Howell was quiet for a long time, squinting into the middle distance, clearly seeing nothing but what might be behind his unquestionably sad eyes. He jerked his head, set his jaw, and laid a hand to Milo's shoulder.

"I know better than to ask."

He left Milo there, sitting blankly in the kitchen, Lleu forlorn and needy but quiet at Milo's knee. Milo sat for quite a long while before he stood, bunged his chair across the kitchen—a burst of fury he couldn't have helped if he'd tried—and went to find his violin.

He stayed out late that night, confused and angry and afraid without quite knowing why, and played for the dragons until the calluses on his fingers were creased and sore.

It... didn't really help.

When he got home, he stalked to Ceri's room, broke the lock on the door with magic, and did what he'd never done before, never dared do before—he Looked. Because if he could touch the nimbus she'd left behind....

She'd wiped it clean. Somehow. Right down to the back corners of her cupboard, the bottoms of her drawers. The whole place was drenched in her magic, obliterating any trace she may have left behind and any chance Milo might have had of understanding what she thought she was doing.

All of it as gone as she was.

Chapter 8—Chord

: a harmonic combination that has three or more pitches sounding simultaneously

"Another Dewin. The place is bloody crawling with them, and all of them lousy with magic they hoard for themselves." Folant turned toward Milo. "I guess you'd know. You and that bloody coven, *all* the bloody covens, tugging at the Queen's skirts and petitioning for aid to the exiles. *Refugees.*" He rolled his eyes.

As though the word itself was a lie. As though people would leave their homes and lives and settle in an entirely different country only to annoy him.

He'd fought against accepting any into Wellech. Especially those who happened to have magic. And while most other communities in Kymbrygh welcomed those who'd managed to flee Colorat and Ostlich-Sztym—or at least didn't blatantly challenge the Crown's recent policies on immigration from the unsettled nations—Folant hadn't even bothered to try to conceal his open bigotry. Or his wrath when both the Crown and his son thwarted his attempts to refuse asylum.

Now Milo understood the hostility from those Wardens when he'd come to Wellech last year. And he was starting to understand the resentment in that woman in Brookings.

It didn't make any of it better. It rather made it a bit terrifying.

"If they're refugees," Folant said, "explain to me how they've so much coin to throw around."

"Because fleeing for one's life doesn't necessarily preclude taking a bit of money with you?"

Folant snorted, derisive. "Fleeing for their lives. Feh. More like trying to manipulate us into fighting a war they'll happily profit from, and making our Preidynīg Isles their janissary, as well as a dumping ground for the scum they don't want. Crime in Llundaintref is already out of control because of them, it's no wonder—"

"For pity's sake, they're either so unfairly wealthy and elite they deserve to be hated, or lowlife criminals who deserve to be hated—pick one!"

"Well, now you're just trying not to see reason." Folant leaned in toward Milo with a confidential air. "C'mon, boy, you're Dewin. You know. You can admit it."

Milo turned his eyes away, refusing to respond, because clearly anything he said was a waste of breath and somehow fuel for Folant's fire. Teeth clenched, Milo did his level best to hold back a growl.

He concentrated instead on the glow of the colored lanterns. When had it got dark, anyway? He peered up at the sky; no stars tonight, only thick cloud cover and the threat of rain in the next day or so, but not tonight. It wouldn't dare spoil Ellis's birthday party.

He'd been trying, Ellis had. Really *trying* to make things between him and his tad less caustic. For the good of Wellech, he'd told Milo. So he'd let Folant throw him a birthday party. And more or less begged Milo to attend.

So here Milo was. Here Folant was. And there Ellis was, dancing with everyone else—*everyone* else—and leaving Milo to... this.

"Ah, now that one's a better fit. Nice local girl. Look how nicely her head fits just beneath his chin."

And look how nicely my foot fits up your arse.

Milo loosened his tie. If he thought he could move without keeling over, he'd just lose the bloody thing, and his coat along with it, but the only part of his body that seemed willing to work was his arm and that had been busy with the chore of getting his drink from the table to his mouth. Which was doing a semi-adequate job of dulling his senses but wasn't helping at all with the fact that it was bloody *hot* and that, in turn, was not very helpful insofar as Milo's temperament. Then again, neither was his "drinking partner."

"Nice and plump, that one." Speaking of whom. "He likes them plump. More to hang onto. But then, I don't suppose that's something he'd discuss with *you*." Folant paused with a self-satisfied chuckle. "Milo-lad, you're looking peaky. Are you quite well?"

The problem, as Milo saw it, was that he wasn't drunk enough yet. "Just... brilliant."

Folant had always been a narrow-minded pill—or, as Glynn would put it, a proper minging sheephead—and Milo was well aware his own insecurities tended to sabotage him. Only, Folant knew a weakness when he saw one, and always had a spanner ready to throw into whatever works he felt like mucking up for his own entertainment. Ellis knew how to shut him up or ignore him, whichever was more effective at any given moment. Milo, not so much.

"How's your mam, by the way? Ohhhh. Sorry."

He was like a shin just waiting to be barked, a toe aching to be stubbed. Milo gritted his teeth and stared straight ahead.

She hadn't come back for the coven in Greenhaven after Sowing migration was over. That was the thing. Ceri Priddy had never missed a coven. At least as far as Milo knew. Certainly not since she'd become Offeiriad. Meistr Eluned had presided, with Lilibet as

Second Chair, and though everyone had carried on as though it was only a small inconvenience, it had thoroughly unnerved Milo. He didn't think he'd really stopped being unnerved since. And considering a great deal of the meeting's business had indeed been dedicated to discussing how they might help their sister covens—how they might even go about finding missing members *to* help them—it didn't exactly do anything to cool Milo's anxieties.

He slouched in his seat, picked up the shot glass and knocked back his fourth shot of grain liquor. Or maybe it was his fifth. Let's see, there was the mead he'd started with, still half-full and looking altogether forlorn, sitting next to the almost empty tankard and the three completely empty shot glas—

Three! Three on the table, one in his hand.... All right, so it *was* his fourth shot. Wait. Hadn't someone come by a while back and collected a few empty glasses? Maybe it was closer to seven. That might explain why Milo was having a difficult time remembering when the wineglass had appeared in his other hand. And that was nearly empty, too. Huh.

"Aye, the girls surely do love him."

Milo clenched his teeth, found his eyes unwillingly following Folant's gaze where they lit upon, and refused to turn from, Ellis. No more than a blur of gold and green at the moment, his colors smearing into the blue and bluer smudge of one Efa Owen dy Pryce, third granddaughter to Jac Pryce, he of *the* Pryces of Littlederch.

"That's my lad." Folant was unbearably smug.

My lad. Fie! As if Folant had anything at all to do with the remarkable way Ellis had turned out. As if Folant hadn't done everything in the world possible to try to turn the gloriousness that was Ellis into a pale shade of Folant's own ignoble self.

A sharp jab to Milo's ribs and this he *couldn't* ignore. Because *ow*.

"Why settle for one or three when you can have 'em all, eh?" Folant leered.

This as Ellis swung away from Efa and straight into the bosom of—

Well. Damn. Alys Hughes dy Evans, she of the too-gorgeous-to-be-real eyes of deep-shot amber, and chestnut curls swinging down to her pert—bloody *pert*!—bottom, and a waistcoat that never seemed strong enough or big enough to effectively hold the bounty in its charge.

"Good Wellech stock, that one. No magic hiding in her family tree. And no Dewin taint, which is—"

"No, sorry, *what*?" There wasn't enough liquor in the world for Milo to let that one go. "*Taint*? Are you out of your blinkered *mind*? You sound like those nutters in the Purity Party."

"Those 'nutters' make an awful lot of sense if you—"

"You *really* think you're somehow better than—"

"Oh, quit your righteous grizzling, boy. I don't mean *you*, of course." Folant held up his hands, all blameless virtue. "You were born in Kymbrygh, can't argue that, even if it *was* on the wrong side of a contract. Have some bloody pride in that, yeah?"

"Pride in what, exactly? Being born somewhere isn't an *achievement*, Folant. You think being born here makes you special? Makes you *better*? You didn't *do* anything, you didn't *earn* anything. You were lucky enough to be birthed in the right place. You did nothing but not die or kill your mam when you slithered your way out. You had no control over any of it. If that's all you've got to be proud of, p'raps you'd best start looking hard at your life."

Which would really help everyone in Wellech quite a lot, and especially Ellis.

"And yet that earring of yours..." Folant grinned, wicked, when Milo narrowed his eyes, but he held up a hand. "Peace, lad, we're not talking about me, or you, or even all Dewin, comes to it. Only, it's the gutless vermin from down-continent crashing our borders and giving you all a bad name."

"If you mean the refugees accepting our Queen's offer of asylum because their countrymen have turned on them, perhaps you'd best check your definition of 'vermin' and apply it to those who'd see their neighbors, sometimes their own families, turned out of their homes, arrested, attacked, spat on"—Milo couldn't help how his teeth clenched—"and all because they were born into a sect you happen to—"

"See, that's what I'm *saying*, lad! A person can't help how they were born. I ken it proper. Only, that doesn't mean they should be mixing with their betters." Folant's expression turned to ostentatious sympathy. "I mean, you do know, lad, that this *courtship*"—he said it with a roll of his eyes—"is only a bit of cotting, yeah? You're not setting your heart on him, I hope." He stuck his lip out, moving like he meant to set a hand to Milo's shoulder; Milo ducked away, jaw clamped so hard it was aching. "Aw, you are." Folant sighed dramatically, then waved at Ellis, still dancing with Alys. "Poor lad. Here you are, gambling above your class, and there he is, laying in better bets."

And that was it, just *it*.

"Something you know quite a lot about." Milo kept his tone aloof and casual. "Or maybe I should say you know very little about it. Tell me, Folant: was it a pair of threes or three deuces you held when you lost Lilibet's plum orchard? Or, well, tried to, I guess. Not like she'd ever allow you to co-own anything. I heard the to-do over your attempt to forge the contract was almost as impressive as your decades-long strop when she turned down your cariad contract. All eight times. That I know of. Although, the gossip about the orchard was only all over the Whitpool pubs for weeks, as opposed to years, so not to worry. It was hilarious, though. Oh, sorry, I meant distressing. It was all horribly... distressing."

Milo's smile was thin and careful as he took a slow sip from his wine.

Perhaps it was cruel. Ignorance should be pitied. Perhaps Folant didn't deserve so much pent-up malice simply for his endless stream of sarcastic jabs at Milo tonight—*all* night—and his very plain insinuations that Ellis would be better off without Milo hanging on his too-good-for-the-likes-of-you coattails. But he definitely deserved it for putting Ellis through such a scandal. And for his awful, gut-turning bigotry.

"Ah, there it is." Folant raised his glass in an ironic toast. "That's one of the few things I like about you Dewin. You always go for the throat when you're cornered. Like the treacherous, nasty little sneaks you are."

It just... didn't stop. Milo had forgot just how dreadful Folant could be, the years since Milo had spent time in Wellech softening the memories into something less vicious, less deliberate. Now all the sneers, all the jibes, all the small-minded, petty little cruelties rammed about in Milo's brain, took a dip into the liquor already sloshing about in there, and came dripping from his tongue like so much acid.

"You know, I've often wondered how low you could sink, and I suppose now I know. Then again, I can't say I'm surprised. I mean, for pity's sake, Folant, anyone else would be proud to have a son like Ellis, but no, not you. You pretend to care about him just enough to keep him trying, but really all you want is for him to keep cleaning up your messes while you impersonate a real Pennaeth. Probably still hoping Lilibet will one day lose all sense and stop noticing how her onetime sperm contributor can't seem to understand the word *no*, and on that glorious day she'll finally let you call the banns and the three of you can play happy families. Well." Milo shrugged. "At least until you gamble everything out from under them, I reckon. Anyway." He downed the rest of his wine. "All things considered, the fact you're a raging bigot and just a *really awful person* besides shouldn't be all that shocking."

Smiling, all teeth, Milo put his glass down with rather more force than he'd meant; the stem snapped with a small chime. He ignored it, dropped the rest of the glass to the table and tried to stand, but Folant's meaty hand closed on Milo's forearm, wrenched him back down. Milo's palm flattened on the broken glass but he ignored that, too.

"That arrogant tongue of yours is going to get your skinny arse flattened one day, you mark me on that. You need a bit of Rees in you before you can think to get away with talk like that in Wellech."

A slow smirk worked its way unbidden to Milo's face. "I've plenty of Rees in me any time I want it. Seems to me that's what this is really about, anyway."

Drunk and somewhat stupid or no, Folant couldn't miss that one.

"*What* did you just say to me?"

"I think you heard me. Or maybe you didn't. I reckon it *would* be difficult to hear with your head up your arse like that."

"You shifty little by-blow witch. You'd best watch that mouth of yours, my lad, else you might find it one tongue and a few teeth lighter."

Milo tried to heave his arm back, couldn't. "I am not *your* lad and I will thank you—"

"What in the *world*..." Ellis's voice and, with no small measure of ugly satisfaction, Milo watched Folant's eyes widen. "Milo, your hand!"

Milo dragged his glare away from Folant's hateful stare and looked down. It wasn't until Milo saw the small blossom of blood seeping into the white tablecloth that the pain flared through his palm and began to throb up his wrist.

"Oh. Well. That's... sort of pants." Milo shrugged out of Folant's by now looser grip and stood.

"Just got a little clumsy." Folant never took his eyes off Milo. "Priddys never could hold their liquor."

Maybe not. But at least they could hold onto their money And their pride.

Ellis snagged up Milo's bloody hand. "You've a shard or two stuck in there." There was tension beneath the smooth tone.

Milo shot a quick glance to Ellis's face.

Ellis wasn't looking at Milo; he was looking at Folant. His brow was drawn down, eyes narrowed down to chary little slits. Keeping his gaze on his tad, Ellis dug a handkerchief from his pocket and placed it gently over Milo's palm.

"Don't press it just yet." Quiet. Concerned. "We'll want to get the glass out first." Ellis finally turned his gaze to Milo's, his eyes instantly softer, though sharp and watchful. "You're pale. And your hands are shaking. What's going on?"

Folant's hostile gaze was burning holes into Milo's nape. Ellis's too-observant one was burning holes into Milo's conscience.

"Tch!" Folant was still lounging in his chair at the table, sneering now. "Careless and clumsy as he ever was. Useful as a fart in a jam jar, him."

Milo pulled at his hand. "Elly, it's fine, I'll just—"

"I know anyway." Ellis tightened his grip. "Just say it out loud and I'll fix it."

Fix it *how*? Ellis could kick Folant's arse from here to the nether and back, and Folant would *still* think Milo was scum for no other reason than he'd been born Dewin. There was no *fixing* that.

Milo tugged at his hand again. This time, Ellis let go.

"You can't fix everything, Elly." Milo couldn't quite meet Ellis's eyes. "Nor should you have to." He stepped back. "I'd better go and get this cleaned up." He kept his back to Folant as he angled out from between them and turned for the kegs.

He shouldn't have come. He hadn't even planned to; in fact, he should right now be in Whitpool, getting ready for the Reaping migration season since Ceri wasn't there, but.... Well. Ellis had been so *convincing*, damn it all, and it had been a whole month since they'd managed a visit to Brookings, and Milo had missed him and... and he was a bloody pushover, all right, *fine*, and when Ellis had asked Milo to come to Wellech for his birthday, Milo had *wanted* to say yes and... and so he had.

He hadn't even spared a thought to Folant. Which only proved that Milo was a gormless nit whose brain spent most of its time in his trousers.

At least the... whatever it was with Folant had sobered Milo up. All right, almost sobered him up, but he certainly wasn't as drunk as he'd been—only angry and stupid and a little bit in pain, and he really just shouldn't have come.

His hand rolled into a fist and he almost yelped out loud. He turned it down to a quiet hiss as he slipped into an empty space between the kegs and waved down one of the men tending the taps. He requested a dipper of water from the melted ice, but then thought better of it and changed the request to a pitcher. There was an empty table on the outskirts of the party; Milo took his pitcher to it, flumped into a chair, and trickled some water over his palm. It wasn't so bad; the cuts were rather deep but the shards were large and easy to see. Once he got them out, he could stop the bleeding with the handkerchief and the worst of it would be that he'd have to wear gloves next week out in the pastures. Maybe do without his violin for a bit. His shirt was ruined, though.

"That shirt is ruined."

Ellis set his broad hand to Milo's shoulder as he angled around the table. Diffident, he pulled up a chair and set it in front of Milo.

"Here, let me see."

Milo didn't look up. "I've got it."

There was a long sigh from Ellis. "Milo, just let me have a look, all right? I can see your eyes crossing, for pity's sake. You're only going to drive it in deeper and make it worse."

And why did that seem to Milo as though it had more than the one meaning? Cold anger washed through him, and it made no *sense,* damn it. He didn't know what he was angry about exactly, or at whom, but it filled his chest and thumped behind his eyes.

"I *said* I've *got* it," he grated, poked a little too vehemently, and bloody *damn* if he didn't sink the sliver deeper.

"Blight it *all*, Milo, stop being such a *bloody* stubborn child and give me that hand!" This time Ellis didn't wait for Milo to surrender his hand—he merely snatched it up, and yanked it closer to the pool of yellow light thrown by the lantern.

Milo tried to pull back but Ellis's grip was tight and insistent. "'M notta child." Sullen. Peevish. *Embarrassing.*

"Right, yes." Ellis squinted, carefully prodding at a chunk of glass. He paused at Milo's hiss and flinch but didn't let go. "Because the adult thing to do here is to stomp off and try to do this yourself with no help, even though you're so sauced you can't see straight."

It seemed sarcasm ran in the family.

"I am *not*—*Ow*, hoy!"

"Just sit still, I've almost got the one."

Milo slumped back, scowling at the top of Ellis's head. "I am not *sauced*. And I am not a child."

Nine save him, he was proper pathetic. And why was it suddenly almost impossible to shut his mouth?

"No, you're not." Ellis slipped the first splinter free and held it out on the tip of his finger for Milo to see. "But you're acting like one." He flicked the shard onto the bloodied handkerchief and went back to work. "Since when do you let what my tad says bother you?"

"I don't know what you mean." Milo's voice was all at once too quiet, tentative, and if his mouth was going to keep running without his permission, Milo would prefer that the things that came spewing from it didn't sound quite so feeble, thank you.

"Right." Ellis's tone was tight. "Because you always jam your hand into broken glass and don't even know it until it's called to your atten—will you *please* hold *still!*"

"Then don't dig in there like you're mining for treasure! That *hurts*!"

Ellis peered at Milo, jaw set hard. "Mam is over at the Bluebell tonight. Shall I go get her?"

He *would* go get his mam, wouldn't he? And *Milo* was the child.

Milo scowled. "Just go easy, all right?"

"I'm going as easy as I can." Ellis's fingers were once again working carefully, gently trying to pry the last splinter free. "But you've gone and sunk it deeper and it will take a moment." He took up the pitcher to rinse some of the welling blood away. "If you'd've let me see it when I—"

"All *right*, so I'm sauced and I'm a child and I'm clumsy and useless and I don't—*OW!* Blood and *rot*, Elly!"

That one really *hurt!* Milo tried again to drag his hand away but Ellis wasn't letting go.

"Sorry," Ellis said quietly.

He didn't look sorry at all. In fact, Milo was fairly certain Ellis had meant that last vicious jab.

"There. All done." Ellis held another shard out for Milo's inspection. "That's a big one. Must've been part of the stem." He dug into Milo's coat pocket, fished out his handkerchief, pressed it to Milo's palm and closed his fingers over it. "Hold that there until the bleeding stops. Press firm, now."

Milo huffed. "I *know*." It came out with a truculent bite again, and... bloody *damn*, what was *wrong* with him?

Ellis rolled his eyes. "Uh-huh."

Milo looked away, face hot, but he could feel Ellis's gray gaze running through him, digging deep beneath his skin, slipping through his ribs like a knife, seeking. Milo shifted, drew his hand away, and this time Ellis let him.

The silence stretched too long between them, the noise of the festivities a dull background hum. Ellis only kept staring, waiting, and for a moment, Milo wanted to clock him one for nothing more than making him feel so bloody exposed and naked beneath that stare. The almost pleasant haze of alcohol Milo had worked so hard to develop had dissipated; now he only felt tired, drained, and... and quite miserable, now that he thought about it.

"You should get back to...." Milo waved his uninjured hand about. "Your dance partners will be looking for you." He winced.

All right, he *was* a child. A twelve-year-old whingy little creadur, petulant and jealous and—

Damn it, they had a courtship contract with a conjugal rider, that was it, nothing exclusive, and for all Milo knew, it was all only a casual shag now and then when it was convenient for both of them. And he'd never even *asked*, had he, because... because it hadn't occurred to him that he should. And maybe he didn't really want to know because he didn't *want* more than that anyway—he *didn't!*—except apparently he *did*, and hadn't had a clue. Which still didn't mean Milo had any bloody right to expect that just because Ellis had invited him here it meant they were to be joined at the hip for the duration.

"And what is *that* supposed to mean?" Ellis wanted to know.

Humiliation made the heat in Milo's cheeks flare hotter. "Nothing. Stone me, Elly, I'm sorry." He shook his head in a vain attempt to make his brain start working again then he stood. Ellis only watched him, new anger sparking in his eyes. "I'm *sorry*. It isn't meant to mean anything. Only... you've duties, and guests to keep happy, and..." *And bosoms to dance with and skirts to lift* and Milo needed to escape, *now*, before he said something *really* bad and made more of a fool of himself than he already had. A lump was suddenly clogging his throat and he swallowed it down. "I... the privy and...." He turned and walked away.

All right, so he fled. But, just to spite Folant, he threw a magelight up as he headed... somewhere. Away.

The river was as good a place as any, he supposed. It was sort of in this direction, wasn't it? There was the road, and trees and things, and... yes, the river was that way. Maybe he'd just dive in and see what happened. At worst he'd drown, but at best he'd be washed somewhere downriver, and he wouldn't be *here* anymore.

He needed his violin. He needed to stop thinking.

And also, he needed to stop getting drunk in Wellech. There was clearly a developing pattern of it not ending well.

This had been *such* a bad idea. He had to have known, somewhere deep down, what it was he'd been pretending he didn't want. He had to have known, somewhere yet deeper, that he *did* want it, apparently very much, and wasn't likely to get it.

Because people didn't stay, nothing *ever* bloody *stayed*! Tads died before they even knew you existed, nains died just when you were beginning to understand how badly you needed them, mams went away because *everything I do is for you*, and lovers... well. Milo didn't really know—Ellis was the first real lover he'd ever had.

He was lonely, that was what it was. Celebrating Ellis's birthday reminded Milo that his own was coming up. There was no sign of his mam coming home. Howell and Glynn were about the place all the time, but it wasn't the same. Milo was... worried. He could admit that now, once the anger had curdled and dried up, still leaving him confused and somewhat empty but no longer tamping. He was worried. Not only because his mam had left, but because she'd left without telling him, without giving him the chance to... he had no idea, and now he had no way of knowing if he ever would, and it *burned*.

There was no possibility of going home and having his mam there to rant to. About Folant. About the growing hostility toward Dewin in general. About having his nose shoved in the fact that he'd been assuming things and perhaps had no right to. About how *angry* he was that his mam had left, and how it had apparently knocked Milo's balance out from under him, and he hadn't even known it until bloody *Folant* of all people had slung it in Milo's face and made him see it. And now he couldn't even seem to track the novel contours into which his own life had shifted.

That was what this was. Confusion and disquiet and resentment that had nothing to do with Ellis. Wanting the reassurance of something more, something solid, but not entirely sure he wanted anything *but* the reassurance of an offer he had no right to expect Ellis to make when Milo didn't have the stones to pony up and make it himself. And that wasn't fair. Milo had no business taking any of that out on anyone but himself. So it was probably best he just steer clear of anyone he might catch in the blast radius of the sudden and unfathomable smoldering angst he hadn't even known was burning in his gut somewhere and corroding his reason until Folant took a stick and poked at its coals.

Tomorrow Milo would sober up and realize that he liked his life, he loved spending the time he was given with Ellis, and Milo had no business getting himself into a twist over something so incredibly foolish. Probably after he got done throwing up.

Nine save him, he was a useless git, and why wouldn't the ground just open up and swallow him?

"Milo, wait!"

Milo didn't want to. Well, he did, but. No, he *really* did, or at least something in him did, because before he knew what he was doing, he'd swung around, distractedly pleased when he didn't stumble, and stalked up to Ellis, who was walking fast toward him but pulled up short when he saw Milo coming at him with his little magelight bobbing along behind him. Ellis looked wary, concerned, confused, and Milo couldn't blame him, since Milo's hands were suddenly clenched in the silk of Ellis's spendy waistcoat, and Milo's mouth was already running without thought to what came spewing out of it:

"I don't want you to sleep with Alys Hughes dy Evans."

Ellis's eyebrows shot up his forehead. "...All right?"

"I don't want you to sleep with anyone."

Now they came back down and twisted. "Can I sleep with you?"

Milo gave Ellis a bit of a shake. "This isn't *funny!*"

"It is a little." Ellis set his hands over Milo's. "What happened?"

It was so soft. So concerned. It screwed into Milo's chest, and made it *hurt*.

"I.... He...." Milo's eyes were burning, blurring, and damn it all, he *refused* to cry like an infant, except he thought maybe he already was. "Elly." Thick and choked. "*Elly*." She—" Milo broke off, chest tight, head pounding, so many things pushing at him he hadn't even known were there, and now they wouldn't let him breathe. "She left. Elly, she *left*. It's been months, and I don't even know where she is except from stories in the bloody *newspaper*, and I don't even know if those are true, or about her, or when she's coming back, or if she's even all right, because bloody *Alton* won't even let me into his office, and Kymbrygh's MP won't admit to even knowing she's gone, but after that woman in Brookings I've just been so... *so*... except I don't want to be the 'Dewin vermin' that comes between you and your tad, but he—"

"Did he actually *say* that?"

"—wants you to court *Alys*, or really anyone but me, and we never talked about the contract, we never said no one else ever, and I don't want to hold you back, but that's a lie because I really really do, and I'm sorry, I really am, but everything is... my whole bloody *life* just sort of went doolally, and I didn't even notice until your tad took it apart between shots of liquor like he was bloody dissecting my sad little corpse, and Elly... *Elly*. It—"

Hurt. It *hurt*.

"Shh, Milo." Ellis let go of Milo's hands and pulled him in tight against his chest. "It's all right."

"I'm sorry."

"Milo, it's all *right*."

"It's *not*. Nothing feels all right but *this* and *you*. And I'm really sorry. I don't mean to put so much on you. I don't mean to—"

"D'you think I'd rather be anywhere else but here with you?"

"No, because you're probably the best, most generous person I've ever met, and a gormless numpty besides, who'd rather be a rock for someone to dash themselves to pieces on instead of enjoying your own birthday party." Milo snuffled. "Also, I'm getting snot all over your waistcoat, and I'm pretty sure I'm bleeding on it too."

Ellis laughed, startled, but deep and real enough that it jostled Milo's head against Ellis's shoulder. He pushed Milo back, squinted into his eyes; whatever he saw must've been rather pathetic, because his whole face softened, and he set his broad hand to Milo's damp cheek.

"Is this you asking for a cariad contract?"

Milo opened his mouth. Closed it. Said, "Yes?" He shook his head. "Some day? Maybe? I don't know." Ellis frowned, cautious, and slid his hand away. Milo reached for it with the hand that wasn't a bloody mess and laced their fingers together. "The logistics would be a nightmare. You can't leave Wellech for more than a week or so. And I can't leave Whitpool."

"True." Ellis was still looking at Milo like he was trying to see into his skull. "Brookings is nice."

"But neither of us could live there."

"Right. Yes. We have responsibilities."

"People depend on us."

"And dragons."

"And dragons."

Ellis stared at Milo, thoughtful. "The Sisters would never approve a cariad contract unless one of us agreed to move."

"It can't be you."

"It can't be me. And they'll never let it be you, not unless you've got another dragonkin up your sleeve."

"I haven't."

"Then the Sisters—"

"The Sisters can go hang!"

Ellis smiled, muted and pained. "Except it's not that easy."

"I know. Don't you think I *know*?"

"Milo...." Ellis looked away. Hesitant. Uncomfortable.

"...Oh." Milo's stomach swooped. "Oh, blood and rot. You're trying to think of a way to say no without hurting my feelings, aren't you?"

"What?" Ellis blinked. "Where in the world—?"

"It's all right." Milo tried to pull his hand away... couldn't. "I'm so sorry. You were having fun, and I've gone and spoilt it all with all these—"

"No, that's not what—"

"—stupid *feelings*, though to be fair I wouldn't've even known they were there except your tad's a stonking great arse, and save me, Elly, you're so damned *lovely*, and you make me laugh, you make me feel *important*, and I didn't even know this was in me until—"

"For pity's sake, Milo, *belt up* already!" Ellis gave Milo a little shake, just enough to jostle his flapping mouth shut. "Whatever all that was," Ellis said slowly, "has nothing to do with what I was going to ask."

Milo tried to make his nod bracing and not as forlorn as he felt. "We can still be friends."

"For the love of—" Ellis rolled his eyes. "I really might have to murder you. With knives." Exasperated. "It has nothing.... Only." He sighed, teeth clenched, and peered up into the heavens as though looking for strength before he leveled Milo with an even stare. "Tell me all this isn't only because you're drunk and sad, and my tad—"

"No. Elly, *no*." Milo squeezed Ellis's hand. "But I can't pretend he didn't make me see some things I don't really want to see. Things are changing. Most of it not good. Folant isn't the only bigot in Kymbrygh, and associating yourself with Dewin right now probably isn't—"

"I don't actually want to know how you plan to finish that sentence." Ellis's jaw was set hard.

"You can't make it not true."

"I can make it less true. I *am* making it less true."

"Which is why you're needed in Wellech."

"Except I want the same things you want."

"You...." Milo got a little lightheaded. "You do?" He'd been sure five seconds ago that he'd ruined everything, and now—

"*Yes*, you bloody *idiot*. And apparently for longer than you have, but I'll take 'better late than never,' because you really are unfortunate in the head sometimes." Ellis huffed and ran a hand through his hair. "So now that that's settled, thank every goddess—what do we do?"

Milo looked away, trying to wrap his gooey thoughts around the abrupt shift in his brain and his stupid, *stupid* heart, while also trying to figure out what could come next.

Because, yes. What *did* they do?

"I guess...." Milo shut his eyes, leaned in, and set his head to Ellis's shoulder. "I don't know. I don't *know*. I don't know anything right now except I want you for mine, and I don't care how selfish it makes me."

"All right." Ellis wrapped his arms around Milo, squeezed good and tight. "Good." He pushed Milo back. "Then let's do this as properly as we can." His frown was musing as he jammed his hands into his pockets, searching, then a waggish grin bloomed when he came up with something small and shiny, glinting in the magelight as he held it out in his palm. "An exchange of tokens upon the signing of a cariad contract is the done thing, yeah?"

"But we're not signing—"

"Because we don't need a piece of paper to tell us how we're allowed to feel."

The sharp tone of it made Milo a bit wibbly. He tried not to look too besotted as he peered down into Ellis's hand. He blinked.

"It's a key."

"To my heart."

Milo gave him a flat look.

Ellis grinned. "Sorry, couldn't resist." He didn't look sorry at all. Because apparently the poetry of Ellis's soul was one half poignant, passionate sonnets and the other half was dirty pub song lyrics. He did soften the grin into something more sincere, though, when he took Milo's hand and dropped the key into it. "It's to the Croft. To my home. Because you're my home now. Wherever you are. For as long as you want to be."

All right, that... very nearly made Milo melt. He swallowed past the giant ball of emotion clogging his throat and dove into his own pockets, looking for something, anyth—Ah!

"Have you got one?" Milo had asked that long-ago day when Nain had told a wee Milo to *Look* at a dragon, and the dragon had *Seen* Milo in return and claimed him as kin.

"I had," Nain said. "I gave mine to Bamps." Soft. Melancholy.

Milo only knew he'd had a bamps once, back when he'd still been in Mam's belly, but Bamps had been in the ground by the time Milo was born. "Did he not give it back?"

Nain smiled, sad but fond, and tugged at the short bill of Milo's bobbled knit cap. "It's exactly where it belongs."

Milo didn't even know if he'd thought about it before, that Nain had buried her cariad with her dragonstone still in his pocket. Now that he did, now that he understood....

It would hurt to let it go. But he reckoned that was partly the point.

"It's a dragonstone." Milo dropped it into Ellis's outstretched hand, feeling his magic swell all around him—easy, safe, because that's how things were with Ellis—a soft reach first then a flare outward, winding right into Ellis's nimbus, and turning every mote of him a lovely warm gold. Milo made himself not stare. "I've had it since I was tiny."

"I remember." Ellis's voice was quiet, and his gaze was intent on the stone in his palm. He shifted, shoulders stretching loose, as though he could feel Milo's misbehaving magic curling around him like an overly enthusiastic coat. "You showed me when we were boys."

"Did I?"

"I can't believe you still have it."

"I've never parted with it. Not once." *So I hope you understand how much I mean this* went unsaid. "Nain said it was a way for the dragons to bind my heart to theirs, and...."

Milo hoped the rest of the sentiment was obvious, because he couldn't make himself finish it without blubbing again.

Apparently it was, because Ellis sucked in a soft breath and closed his fingers reverently over the stone. "It's warm."

"Always. And gets more so when a dragon is near."

"Yeah?" Ellis brought it closer for inspection, smiling and holding it like he'd never received anything finer. "It's perfect."

Milo tugged at his ill-mannered magic, made it behave, and didn't say *So are you* because it seemed he was always at risk of dying of twee these days.

But he hoped Ellis heard it anyway.

Chapter 9—Glissando
: *a rapid slide between two distant pitches*

Every moment is infinity turning
faster than the heart's hasty crawl

Milo had heard that once. Or read it, maybe. Song lyric? He couldn't remember. But he thought he might understand the poetic contradiction of it now.

Reaping migration kicked his arse. Besides the fact that it seemed every single dragon on the continent made at least a short stopover before moving on, a ridged snapper—*well* west of the path it should've been flying—got stranded with a torn wing in Goodcrest just north of Tirryderch. Part of the clan lingered with it, which made the locals jumpy. Everyone was fine with flyovers—enamored with them, really—but no one except those who lived on or near preserves were used to such a large wild animal stalking their borders. And because it was a snapper, and because it was a wounded snapper, it was an *unpleasant* large wild animal.

"She's *gorgeous*." Dilys had come up from Tirryderch to see. Bored, she said, having completed her Warden training in Wellech. Ellis had insisted she take a month before assuming her fellowship in the Tirryderch division, and it was chafing her something wicked. So much so she'd managed to talk Milo into taking her little half brothers camping a few weeks ago when Ellis had to cancel a meetup in Brookings. And though it hadn't been completely awful, a day and a half in Tirryderch's wilderness with two so-bright-they-bordered-on-obnoxious little creadurs, plus Dilys and her relentless wit, did manage to convince Milo he really had to stop being such a pushover.

"Can I?" Dilys gave Milo a pleading look. "Please, please, Milo, can I?"

Milo laughed, charmed, and got Dilys as close as the snapper would allow. Which turned out to be nearly eye-to-eye, but she didn't let Dilys touch. Dilys was a bit disappointed but not deterred.

"You can't keep a *dragon*, Dillie, you absolute minger."

"I don't want to *keep* her." Dilys rolled her eyes. "I'm only saying it would be fun to have one about Tirryderch." She waggled her eyebrows. "I've a proper *list* of knobs I could feed her."

The logistics of getting the dragon to Old Forge involved a lot of negotiation with the railroads, a lot of soothing of the locals, a lot of pacifying the dragon, and a cursed lot of time spent doing all of it. Thank every goddess that Glynn loved everything about being an apprentice and had turned out to be so competent.

"I can't believe we've got a *snapper!*" Glynn was nearly starry-eyed. "What's she doing this far west?"

"Loading me with more work I don't need," Milo retorted, though he frowned as he said it, wondering the same thing, because it hadn't only been the snapper, but part of her clan as well. One dragon wandering from its path was unusual enough, but the ten or so that had accompanied this one? Milo was already composing in his head the questions he was going to need to ask those dragonkin in Central Màstira who were still answering his letters. It seemed like every predictable thing about dragons was becoming less so by the day.

"She likes me." Glynn grinned at Milo from atop the stepladder as she examined the repairs she'd helped Milo do on the snapper's wing. She smoothed her hand down the wing humerus and snorted when the dragon gave a pleased little shiver. "I bet I could do this without you here, even."

Milo shrugged and handed her up a pot of salve. "Let's not find out just yet, yeah?"

"You're a proper killjoy, Milo."

"It'd be a doddle to magic you up a tail, Glynn."

By the time Highwinter rolled around, Milo was in serious need of a holiday. Ellis was charmingly accommodating, managing to arrange an entire week in Brookings where they attended so many festivals and fairs they were both probably a stone heavier when they parted at the train station.

"The almanac says this'll be a bad winter." Ellis adjusted Milo's scarf, gave it a little tug to pull him closer. "But let's try for two weeks?"

Milo's frozen nose defrosted just a touch when he leaned into Ellis for a proper kiss. "Yes. Let's."

It turned out to be four weeks, but it was four weeks of bonfires in the pastures, and persuading reluctant cattle into the feeding pens because the dragons could barely move in the cold let alone fly, and chipping ice off the outer fences so Milo could feel the wards properly. Someone was still now and then mucking with them, occasionally breaking through one in particular. The Whitpool Wardens had been no help at all in finding out who or how. There was at least one of them patrolling almost as often as Milo did these days, and yet no one had yet been caught or even seen.

Well. Cennydd had been nabbed nosing about the perimeter again, but this time Milo let the Wardens deal with him, because Milo simply didn't have the patience. And maybe the Wardens would do a better job of scaring Cennydd off for good this time.

When it came to actually solving the problem, though, Milo was no closer than he'd been when the whole thing started. No one in

Whitpool had the magic necessary to challenge those wards. No one Milo knew of, anyway. And the parish council agreed.

It was unnerving. And annoying. And *bloody* time-consuming.

Months of dragons and Wardens and apprentices and mad dashes to Brookings, and Milo barely managed the space to breathe between it all. So it was odd that the year slipped past him so fast his memory of it was an indistinct haze, and yet slurred with the speed of cold honey at the same time.

*Every moment is infinity turning
faster than the heart's hasty crawl*

Too bloody right. And Milo hadn't even realized it until he'd picked up the newspaper and registered the date. Which was absurd, since he'd had it marked in his diary for a month, ever since Ellis said he'd bought his ticket, determined to visit before Sowing migration was over, even if it meant he had to leave the overseeing of the tail end of Wellech's planting to someone else. And yet Milo hadn't made the connection until the date was coupled with headlines like **Queen Orders Blockade in Gulf of White Sands**, and **Refugees Bring Harrowing Tales of Tyranny and Oppression**.

Something is always brewing, Ceri had said. And she still hadn't come back.

It had been a year. A *year*.

She hadn't been in touch. At all. Alton wouldn't tell Milo where she was, how she was, when she might be coming home, or even admit he had anything to do with her being gone—he wouldn't even let Milo in the cursed door! The sly suggestions of the Black Dog Corps in the newspapers weren't nearly as reassuring as they probably should've been. It wasn't as though Ceri Priddy was the only mage who could conjure a beast out of smoke and magic, and the Black Dog Corps were legend—of *course* their tactics would be copied and used. So who really knew who if it was her out there? And the way she'd left, the way she and Milo had been when she'd left, ate at Milo.

So did his want for a cariad contract. His ache to have more of Ellis than a few days every month. His absolute helplessness when it came to figuring out a solution that could work without one of them having to give up everything. Not that they'd be allowed to. It would be no less impossible to find dragonkin to replace Milo than it would be to dig up a future Pennaeth to replace Ellis; even if the Sisters approved the contract, the local governments would contest it, and likely win. And unless the distance between Whitpool and Wellech somehow magically shrank....

Milo sighed dramatically and closed his fingers over the key in his pocket. He'd arrived at the station too early, overly excited—a bit jumpy, even—that Ellis's long-awaited visit to Whitpool was finally happening. He'd thought a cup of tea and the newspaper at the station's teashop might help pass the time and calm his nerves. The date, the headlines, the state of the world in general—it only ramped up Milo's anxiety and sent it sprawling through his stomach, his chest, every vein, every artery, until his tea felt like acid bubbling through every inch of him.

Save him, he was like those barky, jittery little terriers, so busy vibrating all over the place they didn't even notice they were pissing on everyone's shoes.

Milo huffed out his tension, shut his eyes, and took a long, deep breath. He was being irrational. What did he have to be nervous about? It was *Ellis*!

When he opened his eyes again, it was to the surprised face of Cennydd, staring at Milo from across the teashop as though Milo had just stolen his wallet. It only lasted for a second or two, the strange shocky anger morphing into a smile so pleasant Milo wondered if he'd been seeing things.

"*Haia*, Milo!" Cennydd grinned, and made his way over to Milo's table. "How've you been?"

"I'm well, Cennydd, thank you. And you?" Milo didn't see Cennydd much these days. As far as Milo knew, Cennydd had kept clear of the preserve since the Wardens had scared him off, and there hadn't been a peep from Glynn about trouble between them since that day at the forge. "School's going well?"

Glynn had another two years to go, so Cennydd must have at least one.

"Oh, you know." Cennydd waved his hand around, but didn't really answer the question. Instead, he tilted his head and asked, "So what brings you to the station today? Are you off somewhere again, or...? Oh!" Cennydd's eyes widened. "Is your mam coming home, then?"

Milo tamped down the jab of worry that spiked at the question, then sidestepped it. "I'm meeting my...." He hesitated, weirdly shy about saying it out loud. "My cariad is arriving on the afternoon train." He pulled out his watch. "I was a bit early." *A bit* was ridiculously optimistic. He still had a good wait. And that was if the train was running on time. "Oh, sorry." Milo stuffed the watch back in his pocket and moved the newspaper aside. "Would you like to join me?"

Cennydd's eyes had gone narrow. "You've signed a cariad contract?"

"Oh. Well, no. Not yet." Milo felt his cheeks go hot. All right, so *this* was apparently why he'd been shy about saying it out loud. "No paperwork or anything, only. Well, there are some things to figure out first. You know how it is." In point of fact, Cennydd probably didn't, seeing how he was still so young, but that didn't stop Milo's mouth. "Schedules"—(which were fairly insurmountable)—"and contract approvals"—(which they hadn't actually applied for yet, and likely wouldn't get, anyway)—"and plans to make, and things to think about, and... well, you know, things just sort of get in the way, and..." And they barely lived on the same island, the distance between them was so great.

For pity's sake, *what* were they *thinking*?

"Hmm." Cennydd was frowning, hazel eyes curiously sharp as he pulled out the chair across from Milo and sat down. He stared at Milo, opened his mouth several times to say something then apparently rethought it, until finally he looked down at the newspaper and... paused. Clearly thinking. Clearly assessing. "Milo." Cennydd's hand was warm and sweaty when he set it atop Milo's, astonishingly presumptuous for all it was gentle. "This... cariad." He said it with a pinch of lips, like a disapproving auntie. "Are they...? Can they...?"

Milo was abruptly incredibly uncomfortable, sitting here with Cennydd's hand over his as though... well, Milo didn't know, but he didn't like it. There wasn't much custom in the shop just now, but there was some, and this little display was right out in the open. It was mildly shocking and proper discomfiting, and it didn't help that Cennydd was acting exceptionally oddly, even for him. So oddly, in fact, that when Milo tried to pull his hand away, Cennydd's clamped down on it so firmly Milo thought he felt bones scrape together.

"Cennydd, I don't think this is the place—"

"You don't, Milo. Think, that is. That's what I've always liked about you. I mean, you're sharp as split shale when it comes to dragons or books or getting one over on the parish council, at least that's what my mam says."

Cennydd's mam had a seat on the parish council, and so should know very well that Milo absolutely did not "get anything over" on them. It was only that he had no issues with siccing Merfyn on them to fight tooth and nail for what the preserve needed. And what the preserve usually needed was for the parish council to get off its collective arses and approve the paperwork so it could move up the chain. And then *maybe*, when it had been so long Milo had almost forgot he'd made a request, someone in Llundaintref would finally approve it. Or refuse it. Which meant Milo would have to start the process all over again.

"Your mam should not be speaking about council business to—"

"Oh, let's not talk about my mam, yeah?" Cennydd grinned, but it was flat-eyed, a shark's smile, and far too mature a look for the boy he actually was. "My point is, Milo, you're impressively astute about everything except when it comes to what's good for you."

Milo again tried to pull his hand away without causing a scene. Cennydd's sweaty palm made the grip give a little but not enough.

"Cennydd, I need you to let go of—"

"This cariad of yours, for instance. Is it someone of good standing, at least? Someone who has useful connections?"

Ellis was probably of the best standing possible, and likely had more connections than even Cennydd's parents, though Milo refused to say so and be drawn into whatever this was. He had no intention of listing Ellis's assets as though Milo were anxious for the approval of bloody *Cennydd*, of all people.

"*Or*"—Cennydd was all smug confidence, puffed up and self-important like the *Somebody* he'd always wished he was—"is it merely someone who has nothing more to offer you than the love they profess to have for you?"

All right, *this*? Was getting utterly, breathtakingly bizarre.

"Cennydd, that's enough. You've no right to—"

"Because things are getting dangerous for people like you."

It shut Milo up, just like that.

Cennydd's gaze slid down to the newspaper with its blaring headlines of fear and unrest, and then—pointedly, Milo could *feel* it—up to Milo's earring. "And you're going to need someone looking out for you. Someone who *is* connected to the right people. Someone who has the means to keep you safe when things get.... Well. Shall we say... precarious." Cennydd squeezed Milo's hand. "I've always liked you. You've done me the odd good turn now and then. Let me do you this favor."

"That...."

Milo gritted his teeth and *yanked* his hand away. He paid no attention when his teacup went over and rattled against the saucer, sloshing tea across the doily and ruining the lace. He didn't even check to see if the shop's other patrons were paying any mind. There was an urgent need to wipe his hand off on his trousers, but Milo controlled it.

"If I didn't know better, Cennydd—and I had *better* know better—but if I didn't know better, I'd say that was either a very strange, very *premature* proposal, considering you're nowhere near of age for a contract, or... or it was some kind of threat. Though, if it was, I think you'd best just come out with it or leave right now."

"*Threat!*" Cennydd laughed, weirdly fond. "My dear Milo—"

My dear Milo. As though he were some middle-aged man of the world, and not the local butterfaced social outcast who wasn't even old enough to shave yet.

"—it's far from a threat. Honestly! And anyway, contracts can be got 'round, if you know the right people. Look at your mam." Cennydd held his hands up, harmless, when Milo shot him a sharp glare. "All right, all right, that was rude." With a blasé shrug, he set his elbows to the table and leaned in. "It's an offer of protection. Because bad times are coming, Milo, especially for someone like you, and you'll regret not having someone at your back who can keep you safe when it comes. I can do that for you."

There it was again. That same frisson Milo had felt on the bridge in Wellech, and then again at a festival in Brookings, and then again as he sat in the middle of a celebration and listened to Folant Rees tell him he wasn't good enough.

"Someone like me." Milo fisted his hands beneath the table. He flicked his glance to the newspaper. "You mean Dewin."

Cennydd sat back and lifted his eyebrows.

Milo tried to keep calm, cool his tone, but it was difficult. "That's half a continent away, Cennydd. Why in the world would I need 'protection' here in Kymbrygh?"

Cennydd grinned. "See, this is what I'm talking about. It's adorable."

Every goddess save him, Milo really was sitting in the Whitpool Railway Station's teashop, listening to a teenaged gobshite five years his junior call him *adorable*.

"The thing about Dewin is they stick together. And they own everything, including most of the powerful magic."

"That's absurd. The Natur Sect is known to be very nearly as powerful, and the Gwybodaeth Sect—"

"Yeah, sure, up in Harthoer, maybe, or down in Eskus, but here in Màstira? The continent is crawling with Dewin. They have all the magic, and all the money to go with it, and you know it. Everyone knows it. Dewin don't use magic—they *have* magic, they *are* magic. And they only breed within the sect so they can keep it all to themselves. How fair is that? They were protesting in the streets of Ostlich-Sztym, as though the world was being unfair to *them*, before Taraverde cracked down on them and put their—"

"You mean until Taraverde's 'Elite Constabulary' turned peaceful protests into full-out *riots*, Cennydd. They *killed* people, and Ostlich-Sztym let them—*their own people*. You can't honestly think—"

"Oh, please. They didn't let the few push the many around, which is as it *should* be." Cennydd waved it away, as though it was right, as though it was *nothing*, and tapped at the newspaper. "That's what all *this* is about. It's also where your problem lies, Milo. I mean, you're the only Dewin in Whitpool, yeah? Especially now with your Black Dog mam gone off only the goddesses know where. You've no friends except Glynn and her tad. I know, I notice, because I pay attention. You've not even joined the Home Guard. You've no one to… shall we say, have your back."

Only, don't show him your back.

Glynn's voice. Strangely resonant now.

Milo shook his head, a peculiar numbness seeping from gut to chest and out through his limbs. "Everything you just said is wrong. All of it. Dewin are under threat because for almost a decade their political clout has been the only thing between the dictator in Taraverde and his land-grab. He's made them a scapegoat with lies and hate-mongering."

"Then how d'you explain an entire country agreeing with him, and more falling into line with them every day?"

"Ignorant people are all too willing to hate someone for no reason, as long as the wrath isn't directed at them. You've no clue what the politics—"

"*I've* no clue! Stone the crows, that's rich from you. *You* don't *pay attention*, Milo. Not to the right things. And you really should. I know how you love those dragons. What would happen to them if—" Cennydd cut it off, though it was too clear what he'd been getting at. His grin had compressed into something sour and unpleasant, just like that, jaw set and eyes flat. "It started with Taraverde, yes. But then it moved on to Ostlich-Sztym. And now the Dewin are being chased out of Colorat too. If they're lucky. Błodwyl's next, you watch and see if I'm wrong. Their homes taken. Their businesses signed over to whomever the government chooses. They're fleeing like rats, Milo, and d'you know where they're fleeing to?"

He paused, eyebrows raised, but when Milo said nothing, Cennydd puffed a short laugh and shook his head with a *What am I going to do with you, you naïve simpleton?* It was all Milo could do to sit there and not knock Cennydd's apparently oversized head from off his scrawny shoulders.

"They're coming here, Milo. Not only to Kymbrygh, but to Preidyn and Werrdig too. Some have managed to sneak their way across the borders of Nasbrun or Proyya, but most of them are coming *here* because our Queen bloody *invited* them. And I'll tell you a secret." Cennydd dipped in close and lowered his voice. "There are quite a lot who don't like it. She's Offeiriad. She should *know* better. And some people...." He sat back, took a glance around, then smirked. "Well. Not everyone is content to allow it."

Something in Milo went utterly still, utterly cold.

A train whistled in the distance. Ellis's train. Had to be. Early when the trains were never early, but Ellis was nearly here.

Milo should be settling his bill, collecting himself, getting ready to meet Ellis on the platform. Joyful and eager.

He sat right where he was. Staring at Cennydd. Unable to move.

Cennydd was a bloody *teenager*. This was all Purity Party rot and nonsense he'd picked up from people older than he was, deliberately politically skewed, intent on othering anyone who didn't look and think and speak and worship exactly like they did. And the crude bit about "only breeding among their own" was just flat untrue, the rest twisted out of the clear shapes of reality and distorted into something sinister and depraved.

And for *what?*

Milo was the only Dewin Cennydd even knew, so what could Dewin in general have ever done to dredge this kind of hatred from a mere boy? There was no reason for it that Milo could see. None. Cennydd was a *child*. He couldn't possibly understand where most of the ignorance he was spewing even came from.

Except.

Cennydd's mam sat on Whitpool's council. His tad came from probably the wealthiest family besides Dilys's in the whole of Kymbrygh. If this was what Cynnedd had been hearing at home....

And here he was, offering Milo "protection" against... what, exactly?

"What...?" Milo cleared his throat, setting his teacup back to rights in its saucer to buy himself a moment. "What does that mean, Cynnedd?" He peered evenly at Cynnedd, and hoped for once he was managing to keep what was roiling inside him off his face. "How might someone go about stopping this... well, the way you're talking about it, it sounds like an infestation."

Cennydd's smile was so condescending it made Milo's teeth hurt. "Oh, Milo." He shook his head with a chuckling sigh. "You just don't *pay attention*." He stood, still smiling, and set his hand to Milo's shoulder. "I won't be old enough for a contract for a few years. But that doesn't mean I can't do things for those I care about in the meantime. And I've always loved the dragons." He gave Milo's shoulder a pat. "Think about it."

⁂

Milo did think about it. When he made it to the platform just before Ellis disembarked. When he clung to Ellis like he'd never let go. When he watched Cynnedd greet a stranger with a handshake and escort him to a waiting car, all the while eyeing Ellis with a narrow, contemplative scowl. When he told Ellis, "Let's go home," and pulled him down the station's steps.

He thought about it, couldn't *stop* thinking about it.

He was *paying attention.*

⁂

"And this is what you do all day?" Ellis was grinning, delighted, as the razorback calf snuffled at him and let him set his hand to the small, still-soft scales just below the nub of what would eventually grow into a horn behind the brow ridge. "Play with baby dragons?"

The calf's mam was watching carefully, wary but not hostile. Which rather made Milo's head explode a bit.

"I can't believe she's letting you near him."

Milo didn't think it was merely because he was here and watching. Nothing about this mam and her calf fit into what Milo knew was normal dragon behavior. Strangely docile and permissive, the cow, allowing Glynn right up close to her calf when Milo had never known a dragon to let anyone but dragonkin that near their young. But Glynn wasn't just anyone. The dragons saw her every day, knew her, and even if they didn't trust her like they trusted Milo, they at least knew she was no threat and never so much as growled at her, as far as Milo knew.

This cow, though?

Milo had told Ellis not to expect much. That he was a stranger, and the cow probably wouldn't allow Ellis much closer to her calf than twenty paces, if he was lucky.

And then she'd only stood there and watched when the calf trotted up to Ellis and butted him in the chest. Milo had nearly had a heart attack; he'd been watching the calf's colors carefully, and the cow's even more so, but there'd been no jags of anger or protectiveness roiling a warning. It happened so fast Milo hadn't even had time to whip the shield he had ready at his fingertips between the calf and Ellis. All Milo really saw was Ellis go flying back on his arse and the calf staring down at him like it couldn't understand why the puny new plaything was so easy to knock down. But the colors were all so *happy*, so *calm*, and Ellis was *laughing*, and then the calf was *nuzzling*, and the cow was just *watching*, and it was all so bizarre that Milo wondered if Ellis was somehow dragonkin and no one had noticed because he wasn't ever around dragons.

It would figure, actually. Lleu had been all over Ellis at first meeting like Ellis had bacon in his pockets, and Ansel hadn't even tried to go after Ellis's shins, not once.

It wasn't fair.

"And no, I do *not* 'play' with baby dragons all day." Milo huffed, trying to shake out the tension that had ramped all through him only a second ago. "We hardly ever even have a calf about the place. Not unless a cow breeds out of season, which this one did, and had the bad grace to brood here in the middle of Reaping migration." He jerked his chin at the cow, still only standing there and watching Ellis paw at her calf. "He's the one who hatched last winter. I know I told you, because I couldn't make it to Brookings for over a month."

"I remember."

"He's doing... all right, I suppose. It's only...."

Milo hesitated, frowning, because the brooding had gone fine, the hatching perfect, but the calf, though healthy as any other hatchling Milo had encountered when it kicked away the last of its shell, didn't seem to be quite thriving the way Milo expected. The way even the spitter had done, once Nain had found her. But this one wasn't growing, was sometimes moody and aggressive for no reason then playful and buoyant—like now—and seemed to have occasional stomach issues Milo couldn't explain. It walked funny sometimes, like its joints ached, but there was nothing wrong with its bones. And though the cow seemed to share the same troubles sometimes, it wasn't often, and none of the other dragons showed symptoms, so whatever it might be, it apparently wasn't contagious.

Maybe the cow had got into something before she'd arrived last year, and it had seeped through her egg's shell before it hardened prebrood. Milo didn't know. There was nothing in his books, Rhywun Collins was no help, and none of the other dragonkin were having issues, at least those who answered his letters. And though both cow and calf occasionally flared odd moody colors for no reason, the tempers came and they went, a weird overhang of soup-green and gray now and then that Milo didn't know how to interpret. All it told him was there was something wrong one minute and not the next, and he couldn't get a handle on it.

Milo pushed a sigh through his teeth. "It's only, they grow so fast in the first couple of years—he should be twice his size already. He should be strong enough to make the flight up north before the end of this season when the rest of the clan goes, but the way he's going I don't think he'll be... ehm...."

The calf used the claw on his wing thumb to tap curiously at Ellis's broad-brimmed hat, all gentle care, but playful still. The colors wafting off him were all warm pastels. Affectionate. It made Milo blink.

"That.... That's not...." He shook his head. "Sorry, only this is very strange. They normally don't do this. And you aren't *that* charming, so I can't figure—"

"Oi, I'm charming as a basket of kittens with bows on!" Indignant. "And you know you love me, so no surprise they do." *Arrogant.* "But I think it's more they sense the dragonstone." Ellis grinned over at Milo, one hand exploring the knots that would grow into horny plates down the calf's back, and the other patting at the breast pocket of his day coat. The calf tilted his head and snorted out a thick puff of smoke from his nostrils. "It's been warmer than usual since I got here"—Ellis coughed and waved the smoke out of his face—"but now it's only this side of hot. And he keeps sniffing at it."

"Oh, for—" Of course. *Of course.* "You're clan!" Milo's smile was probably a bit daft and dazed, but he couldn't help it. "They know you're mine. Ha! According to them, I *own* you!"

He laughed when Ellis lifted his eyebrows and flashed him a look that said *Oh really?* Because yes. *Really.*

Dragons were clan animals. They'd made Milo part of their clan when Nain's old "friend" had created a dragonstone for him. And Milo had, apparently, pulled Ellis into the clan when he'd offered the stone as a cariad gift.

He couldn't say he'd meant to, really. He hadn't even thought about it at the time. The stone was important to him, and it had been just as important to give Ellis something of himself, to seal what wasn't really a contract, not legally, but... was there such a thing as a contract of the heart? Said out loud, it would make Milo cringe with twee, but in his head, it seemed entirely fitting.

And he *still* couldn't stop *smiling*.

"No getting out of it now," he told Ellis, smug. "The dragons say you're mine. And who wants to argue with dragons?"

"Not I." Ellis slid his hand over the calf's nose and stepped back. He looked down at his boots, smile small and easy, then peered up at Milo, gray eyes bright. "Who needs the Sisters to approve a contract when you've got dragons?"

Milo very nearly did a pirouette in the mud, he was so giddy.

Because who indeed?

⁂

Glynn and Ellis got on perhaps a bit *too* well.

"Oh, he did *not!*" Glynn's jaw was hanging, her wide-open grin crinkling her eyes into crescent moons. "*Milo?* I don't believe it. You made that up."

"Why would I?" Ellis's smile was evil as he waggled his eyebrows at Milo across the table. He stabbed up a bit of popty. "I see he's got all of Whitpool swottled with his 'upstanding young squire' game, but Wellech knows better. It took the locals years to stop hiding their cabbages when they knew Milo was visiting." He jammed the potato in his mouth, still managing to grin smugly around it.

"Not *all* of Whitpool is fooled," Howell put in mildly with a sidelong glance at Milo and a quirk at the corner of his mouth. When Milo shot him a betrayed look, Howell merely sipped at his beer and put all his attention on his braised lamb.

Glynn, however, was not to be deterred. "What?" She leaned in toward her tad, clearly tickled and far too eager. "Tad, *what?*"

Milo had felt a bit awkward about playing host to Ellis by himself. So he'd thought it might be nice to invite Howell and Glynn to have supper with them.

Every goddess in the pantheon, had he been wrong.

Howell shrugged, apparently fascinated by the way his knife parted the lamb on his plate. "It's only that I'm not surprised he pulled the same stunt in Wellech." He took a bite, chewed thoughtfully. "Though it seems p'raps that was mere practice, because he managed to pull it off here."

"*No!*" Glynn sat back, gleeful. "Who?"

"Ta, Howell," Milo muttered, gulping more beer than was probably wise, but he figured he deserved it. He sighed at Glynn. "I was practicing my aim at the time." He shrugged at Ellis. "Remember the onions?"

"Oh, my heart." Glynn was practically vibrating out of her chair. "*What about the onions?*"

Milo ignored her, and said to Ellis, "It was like that, only I'd just learned how to catch something without actually exploding it."

"*Exploding!*" Now Glynn was bouncing.

Milo rolled his eyes. "It was Nain's fault. She made me come to the markets with her. And she knew I *hate* figs."

"Who hates *figs?*" Ellis actually seemed offended as he looked around the table. "I ask you!"

"*I* hate figs. And Nain knew it. And still, she made a point of loading up her basket with a bloody armload of them, *smirking* at me. And then she said I had to carry it because it was too heavy, laden down with *figs* as it was, and wasn't I always saying I was a big strong boy?" Milo huffed. "I was trying to grab at it with my magic. Nain had been all but drilling me on it, after all. But I couldn't stop thinking about all the otherwise perfectly edible dishes she was going to put the awful things in, and I... might've got a little... angry about it." He shrugged, cheeks warm. "I didn't actually *mean* to send the basket pitching across the market." He couldn't help the tiny smile that was ticcing at his lip. "And I *certainly* didn't mean to smash the figs into pulp and then blow them up so they smeared all over Rhywun Catrin's storefront. It just... happened."

It had been satisfying and hilarious for about five minutes. Until Nain decided that scraping and washing the storefront—"*Without* using magic, Milo, is that understood?"—would teach Milo a lesson while at least partially appeasing Rhywun Catrin.

It hadn't, really. Milo *still* got chary looks from her whenever he ventured past her shop.

Glynn was nearly breathless, face almost in her dinner as she laughed and laughed.

Ellis looked almost proud. "I admit, that does rather put the Cabbage Incident to shame."

"The cabbages were your mam's fault and you know it!" Milo pointed accusingly at Ellis. "She *said* to use them as targets!"

It only got worse from there. Or better. Milo reckoned it depended on one's perspective. He had to admit everyone seemed thoroughly entertained, even if the entertainment consisted mainly of exaggerated retellings of embarrassing incidents from Milo's own life. But it did put paid to Milo's anxiety over immersing someone like Ellis in the mundanity that was Milo's bucolic life. That and Ellis's clear fascination with the dragons. Milo always forgot they were rather exotic to those who didn't have to shovel their shite once a week.

Milo sat back, enjoying the homey atmosphere, laughing and eating and giving as good as he got when he could, and looking ahead to when Glynn and Howell would retire to their little cottage but having no desire to rush it. He'd have Ellis all to himself later. Right now, this kitchen hadn't heard so much cheer and familial laughter for more than a year, and Milo intended to savor it.

Chapter 10—Variation

: the compositional process of changing an aspect of a musical work while retaining others

He couldn't sleep. That was the only reason it happened the way it did. Simple coincidence; random serendipity. He couldn't sleep, so he carefully extracted himself from Ellis's squiddy limbs and went downstairs to make himself a cup of tea.

Lleu couldn't be bothered to follow, tucked up against the backs of Ellis's knees and peering at Milo as though to chide him for disturbing the night's peace and comfort. With Ceri gone, Lleu had taken to sleeping in Milo's room, in Milo's bed, and not only would he not be displaced by an added body, he had his ways of making it clear he was not pleased with the need for substitution in the first place. Namely by chewing the corners of the sheets and cushion slips, something he hadn't done since he was a puppy. And though he never actually chewed through them and ruined them completely, there was still nothing like the experience of turning over in one's sleep and coming into sudden unexpected contact with a cold, slobber-sodden lump of linen.

At least he hadn't regressed to pissing everywhere. Milo thanked the goddesses for small favors.

He didn't bother with lights. Another tick in the Random Chance column. Old Forge was too far out from the village proper to justify having electricity run, and erecting the poles and stringing the necessary cables along a property where dragons wandered was only asking for trouble. Milo was tired, he *wanted* to sleep, so he reckoned it was better to keep his eyes adjusted to the dark. He only lit a tiny magelight by which to see as he found the tea he wanted, filled the infuser, moved the kettle from the warmer to the cooker, and then propped himself against the kitchen window to wait. And because he hadn't bothered with lights, he could see it clearly when the mist rose.

Not uncommon, of course. Fog was as ordinary on the northern coast as sand. And there was always at least a light mist hovering over the thermal spring. This one, though... this one was....

Milo blinked, clearly seeing things, then squinted, because no, he didn't think he was. A murk really had just bloomed out of nowhere.

Ty Dreigiau sat atop the highest point of Kymbrygh's northmost cliffs like a battered old jewel in a cragged and pebbled crown. And though one couldn't see every detail of the preserve from the tower house's vantage, it did claim an overview of the constant downward slope of the expansive estate, pastures and pens and fences and forge. The high, sheer drops of the cliffs down to rock and sea were enough of a deterrent on the west and north, but the horseshoe thicket—ash and silver birch and evergreen—formed a natural barrier between the inner and outer fences on the eastern and southern perimeters. And all of it could be easily viewed from Ty Dreigiau's kitchen window. On a clear day, Milo could see all the way down to Whitpool. On a clear night, he could just make out the lights all the way to Maura.

So he marked it when the fog rolled up not from the ocean, or even the pools and streams that hugged Whitpool like a mam's sturdy arms as they burbled north and west and out to sea. This haze sprang up all at once from inside the preserve, moving not *from* the thermal spring, but *toward* it.

It made no sense.

The thing was, that spot, that origin point from where the mist was rolling... he knew that spot. And not only because he knew every inch of the preserve and could tell you which dragon liked to sun on which particular rock, or which ones had been fighting and clawed up which patch that needed a fill before the ground turned hard and frosted. He knew *that spot*, because he'd had to fix and reinforce the wards too many times over the past two years. He knew *that spot* because someone had broken the wards, several times, and no one had been able to figure out who or how or why.

And now there was this queer fog springing up from *that spot*, reaching distinctly north and a touch east, and blossoming out toward....

"The thermal spring."

Something in Milo's gut dropped, and he didn't quite know why.

The kettle jostled on the hob, just waking to a simmer. Milo jolted at the sound, huffed annoyance at himself, and pushed open the window. Stuck his head out and listened.

The silence was... complete. Unnatural. As though he'd gone deaf in the space between the kitchen and the window's sash. No muffled dragon calls. No night sounds. No soft coos or clucks from the chicken coop across the yard. No constant crash of waves. It was as if the entirety of the world outside the kitchen had abruptly misplaced the very idea of sound.

Milo pulled back, the ordinary hum of a lived-in house colliding with his eardrums all at once like a whip cracking in his skull. The tinny hollow wheeze of the heating kettle was a warning bell pealing behind his eyes. Ellis turning over in his sleep two floors up was the startling din of a rockslide.

"Magic."

Elfennol magic, at that.

He didn't even think about it—Milo opened himself and Looked. Saw the tendrils of it right away. Foreign and off. Milo could See it now, how the magic sought out the vibrations in the air, reached out with shards of violet and pierced them, silenced them. It stretched in a band that had to be deliberate, because it didn't cover the whole of the preserve—the entire eastern side of Old Forge was fine. Unaffected.

Not so to the west, though. A wide ribbon of nebulous amber swept from the southwest corner of the preserve, up and up, and stopped just short of the house itself. Generations of wards and protections laid over ancient stone repelled it in a strangely beautiful clash against a barrier of indigo.

But it was what was underneath that odd insentient conflict that made Milo suck in a breath and take a step back. Slam the window shut.

Murky grays with silver shoots winding out and out; fuzzy jades coiling into muddy corals, and fizzing into a broad swath of friendly saffron belied by the hostile garnet creeping beneath it. Except it wasn't all magic. There was... something else there with it, mixing with it. Gaseous, invisible to the corporeal eye yet thick as smoke to Milo's. Merged with the magic, it rolled into something else, something more, something patient and frighteningly resilient.

Sleep, the fog said. *Hush*.

And whatever the vapor it was fused to was, the magic that carried it pulled and pushed. Insistent. Seeking. Never letting up.

He was already throwing open the door to the mudroom, shoving his bare feet into muddy boots, pulling a shield around him against the alien magic, and snapping up the rifle on his way out the door before he'd decided to even move. Lleu's soft warning *whuff* from upstairs was cut to silence as Milo crossed the mudroom's threshold and took off across the yard.

The preserve was big, widespread, and pocked with dips and ruts and hillocks made by massive claws or whipping tails or enormous feet smacking down in hard landings. Any number of things lurked to catch at one's ankles or knees and break a bone or worse. Luckily it was also all downhill. Luckily Milo could spread his magic ahead of him, around him, See it all, and let the downward momentum pull him along as he crashed through pastures and copses, leapt gulleys and furrows, trying to ignore the strain of his lungs and the hard jolts up through muscle and bone.

He was winded, side cramping and legs going to rubber, when he approached the thermal spring, slowing before he reached the nearest cave mouth in case the silence wasn't affecting the dragons. It was possible. Magic was chancy with dragons—one never knew what charm might work on which dragon, and even that wasn't consistent. And it wouldn't do to startle a sleeping dragon in its nest.

Caves spring-carved from ancient limestone. Warrens and pockets and crags that dropped abruptly into nowhere. Warmth for creatures that weren't quite coldblooded, but close enough. Trust for creatures that chose dragonkin based on things even dragonkin didn't understand. Safety for creatures that placed themselves in the care of a preserve and depended on their dragonkin to stand the watch.

They were sleeping. All of them. Milo shouted, just to check, and though he could hear himself clearly inside his shield, the thick haze outside it caught the sound, snapped it up, and slashed the vibrations to shards until they scattered into nothing at all. There wasn't even an echo against the cave walls. Not one dragon stirred, curled in their piles. Not one so much as twitched in its sleep.

He was going about this all wrong. He could See the magic, and yes, it was powerful. But so was he. And maybe he hadn't even really known this kind of magic existed, that anything could do what it was doing, but Seeing it, being able to pick it up from its endpoint and trace it backwards, decipher its weave, was how he'd managed to excel at school. *Cheating*, his mam would call it if she knew, if she even suspected. And then she'd have some choice words and ready lectures, worried eyes and angry glares, until he promised he'd never do it again. But was utilizing a natural talent "cheating" any more than a person using superior strength in a physical contest?

Milo had never believed so. And he was bloody good at it.

He sucked in a calming breath, waited until his heart stopped hammering in his ears. Reached out and... touched. Found the prickly jags at the tips of the charm—no, not charm—the tips of the *hex* that overlaid the physical fog. Plucked at them. Prodded at them. And when he found the strand that led back to the foundation of the hex's weave, he twisted it, ever so gently, until he got a good grip and—

The careful tug wrenched immediately into a forceful yank, so quickly Milo had to pull back a bit to avoid getting snapped with the recoil. Like coaxing glittering fragments from a filament inside an electric light, the initial draw was the hardest part. And once Milo had hold of the end of it, everything started to unravel. It was like combing lambswool—forcing his own magic through the foreign power sealing hex to haze, and raking it through the tangles, separating one from another. And once he had the two in his own hands, he sent them spiraling, unwinding, whirling up and away skyward.

The fog began to lift. Magic and material both wafted into a slow-rolling vortex, and though it wasn't moving as quickly as Milo would like, it was probably just as well. He didn't know if the sorcerer on the other end of this magic could feel it unwinding from this distance, but if they could, Milo had just lost any surprise advantage he might have had.

He backed away, determined now, and pushed his magic ahead of him as he took off down the slope, rifle still clutched in hand—not that it would do him any good if he managed to find who or what was causing this. This magic was powerful, demanding acknowledgment, and worse, obedience, nudging constantly at his hasty shield as he plowed through the mist his own magic hadn't unraveled yet. He was moving faster than his own charms—it would be smarter to move with the haze, or just behind it. But whatever this was clearly had no good intent, and he couldn't take the time.

The goats were all down when Milo flew through the south pasture, tearing headlong past the pen and leaping the inner fence where Cennydd had been caught trespassing only a few years ago, and Milo had thought treating him like a person would help somehow. Now Cennydd's voice wavered in Milo's head—*You don't pay attention, Milo*—and Milo....

Milo'd had no idea how portentous that would prove to be. Until he skidded to a halt at the very edge of the trees that turned to bracken then scrub as the land rolled out and down to the cliffside of Old Forge's western boundary. Until he spotted the shapes of two men in that same spot where the wards had been impossible to keep intact for two years, and now Milo thought he knew why.

Because there was Cennydd, crouching against the inside—*inside*—border fence. The razorback cow was down, apparently deeply asleep, as her calf accepted... something from Cennydd. A hunk of meat, maybe, something the calf happily lipped from Cennydd's hand like Poppy accepting a carrot. Whatever it was, whatever Cennydd was feeding that calf, it had the same strange muddy-green and gray colors wafting from it that sometimes clung to the calf and its mam in shapes Milo had never been able to decipher. And the little razorback was accepting it like a treat. Happy. Content. Serene as old friends.

...*Old friends.*

The wards on the fences closest to the caves, warped and picked at for years, right where the fences ended and the cliffs began. Cennydd caught trespassing, and all Milo's suspicions dismissed because it was Cennydd, and Cennydd was only an awkward little gobshite who had no magic. And then a razorback cow brooded on the preserve, a new calf hatched, and the picking turned to actual breaks.

A man stood behind Cennydd, watching, wary. Powerful Elfennol magic all but poured out of him, fueling a protective bubble around himself and Cennydd and the calf. *Here* was the source of the gas-and-magic miasma that had settled over the preserve in a soupy haze and pressed at Milo's shield like a sentient being demanding entrance. Milo had seen that man before. Cennydd had picked him up from the train station right after he'd got done telling Milo he wasn't safe.

There was a winch. The shape of it in the dark was distinctive. Assembled, ready, and sitting just at the lip where scrub gave way to cliff-drop. Strength charms were crawling all over it; Milo could See the sharp reds spiking through the structure. Because no wagon or lorry or even tractor could have made it through the rough landscape of this part of the preserve, and the winch was clearly meant to lift something heavy.

Milo would bet there was a harness or a sling, just the right size for a young undersized razorback, at the end of the winch's ropes. And a small pontoon boat waiting on the rocky beach beneath the cliffs.

The fog was unrolling farther up the slope, Milo could See it lifting a furlong or three up. The man didn't seem to have felt it yet, but it would only be another minute or two before Milo's charms rammed against the source of the hex and alerted him. Milo kept his shield up, set the rifle's butt to his shoulder, sighted down, and waited.

It took longer than Milo thought it would. The sorcerer wasn't paying attention, keeping a close eye on Cennydd instead. Cennydd cooed at the little razorback, grinning as the dragon stumbled sideways then sat with a thump and a querulous little grunt. It listed, sick or sleepy Milo couldn't tell, but the greens and grays were winding through the dragon now, so Milo suspected it was a bit of both.

"There you go, little chap," Cennydd singsonged, for all the world like a tad soothing a child to sleep. "That's the way."

It was Cennydd's hand on the little dragon's snout that somehow woke Milo's rage and flared it hot up his backbone. That familiarity, that soft manipulative tone, that pleased look on Cennydd's face: satisfaction with a job nearly done.

And the job's intent was plain now. Somehow Cennydd had managed to get past the wards. Somehow he'd got close enough to at least this young dragon and its mam that they'd allowed him to approach and had even taken food from his hand. Milo didn't know how—neither Cennydd nor his accomplice were dragonkin, Milo would bet his life on it—but Cennydd had nonetheless clearly insinuated himself into the graces of these two razorbacks. And the winch and the attempt to make sure the whole of Old Forge slept through this little mission told Milo why.

No wonder these two dragons had been so complacent with Ellis, dragonstone or no, clan or no. Cennydd had doubtless been training the calf to this since it hatched.

Milo's teeth set tight. His hands on the rifle tensed.

He Saw it when his magic collided right up close with the sorcerer's. The sorcerer clearly felt it—he jerked back with a frown. Unable to See at least, Milo could tell, because the man shut his eyes, groping for the shapes of his magic, and flinched back when he touched Milo's instead.

"Hold right there, both of you," Milo growled, magic flaring at his back, spiking up and out in warning as Cennydd spun in his crouch and the man whipped a thorny little hex at Milo. It whapped Milo's shield with a flutter of sparks but flattened against it and fizzed into nothing. Milo barely felt it.

A test. A cautious prod more than an attack. The hex reeked of Elfennol magic, thick with fire and crazyjane whorls of barbs and glinting arcs.

Milo sent a magelight high above him, pulsing in steady flashes to hopefully attract the attention of... someone. The Warden assigned to keep an eye on the preserve, maybe, but if this sorcerer had managed to put dragons to sleep....

"Ah, Milo." Cennydd stood slowly, that smarmy smile slicking his mouth, and his hands out to his sides. He took a step toward Milo. "I see you've—"

"Stop, Cennydd. Not another step." Milo adjusted the rifle at his shoulder. "I've heard getting shot in the kneecap really hurts. I don't have to kill you to stop you. But I will if you make me."

Milo had no idea if that was true.

Cennydd seemed to think he did—he laughed. Took another step. "Oh, come on, Milo. *You*? You couldn't kill a fly, let alone—"

"Yeah? For the dragons?" Milo let it curl through his teeth. "I'm dragonkin, Cennydd. You know how much I love them. I feed things bigger and smarter than you to them every day." He pulled the hammer back with a deliberate *click*. "You really want to try me?"

"No, no, you're right." Cennydd was still smiling, trying for charm, or... something, but not getting even close. "How about another trade, yeah? For old times' sake."

"A *trade*." Milo snorted, derisive. "Like the one where you trespass on a protected preserve and I don't let a dragon eat you for it? Which, I must say, I'm rather regretting just now."

"Well, I was thinking more like you walk away, and my friend and I will let you. But I'm sure we can—"

It was distraction. Milo only realized it when the hex punched the wards of his shield with a force that was no small testing jab this time—it *stabbed*, hitting with a sharp impact that sent pain into

Milo's thigh, right where the hex hit the shield and tried to burrow its way in. Milo stumbled at the hot throbbing sting of it, maybe cried out a bit. But he kept his head and shot a return volley full of his own tiny hexes that covered the sorcerer's shield and bonded to its construction, gnawing in and working at the foundations of the wards, not even bothering to try to pull the threads apart, but ripping through them with sharp little teeth.

Distraction again. Cennydd had moved in right up close, only paces away from Milo now, and still edging in.

Milo bared his teeth and jerked the rifle. "*Stop!*"

Cennydd finally did. Still too close. Within arm's reach now. The pulse of the magelight made the set of his face something feral and ugly.

But Milo could handle this. He could keep them both at bay for quite a while, he decided. Unless Cennydd forced Milo to shoot—and Milo would, at least to wound, and maybe that would actually be better, take one of them out of play. Milo would decide that when he was forced to, but he could hold against the sorcerer for a long time before he was forced to rethink an open stand.

He was using a lot of magic—still unwinding the last of the hex that guided the fog, maintaining the wards of his shield, holding the flashing magelight, working at the sorcerer's shield to at least pull the dragons from behind it—but Milo *had* a lot of magic. And though his didn't come from the infinite elements around him, something he could instantly replenish by robbing power from elsewhere, it was still a considerable well. He had a while before he started to flag.

The haze had lifted completely now, the last of its clinging tendrils wisping up and away, the gas it cleaved to dissipating high above in the constant sea winds. So there was one thing down.

"Whatever this is about, Cennydd, it's done." Milo set his stance, legs apart and gun snug to his shoulder. "Back off. Now."

"Or... what?" Cennydd slid his gaze to the sorcerer, jerked his chin, then took a step to the side. "You don't seem to understand, Milo. You're not in charge here." It was a snarl.

"I'm dragonkin on a sovereign preserve. What are you, Cennydd?"

A roar rumbled from up the slope—blurred with sluggish confusion, but anger shot through the deep-throated call that followed. Milo had never heard this particular call before, but the feel of it, the colors that seeped into the still-swirling airstream, were clear.

Danger. Warning.

The cow beside the fence stirred.

The sorcerer took a step back, gaze flitting everywhere while trying to keep one eye on Milo. He'd noticed.

Cennydd hadn't. "What am I? What am *I*?" Outraged. "What are *you*, Milo? Besides a Dewin by-blow who lives off *my* taxes and thinks he has the right to—"

"For pity's sake, Cennydd, you're *seventeen*! You've never worked a day or paid taxes in your bloody life!"

"—dictate everything about the national bloody symbol of *my* country, taking—"

"It's my country just as much as—"

"—over things you've no business touching, let alone—"

A fountain of raw power hit Milo square in the chest. His shield kept it from doing physical damage but it certainly didn't feel that way. The impact rocked him so hard he almost toppled backward. It knocked the breath from him, nearly made him drop his shield altogether. He did drop the hex working against the sorcerer's shield. The magelight plummeted several lengths before Milo caught it, shoved it back up, and tried to redirect a stream of power at his failing hex. Cennydd moved in, and though Milo's wards prevented Cennydd from actually grabbing the gun, it dinged Milo's concentration badly enough that Cennydd's quick shove at the shield was enough to make Milo stumble.

The cow lifted her head. The calf shook his, as though trying to clear it.

Two dragons roared up the hill this time. Three.

And somewhere, not too far, Lleu barked.

Milo wished he could stop time. Freeze everything in place only for a moment so he could regain his bearings. Everything was happening too fast. And then nothing at all made sense as Cennydd's nimbus flared, carmine to russet shadowed with black as dark as well water, then surged out in spiny trails that all but screamed hatred and fury and ill intent. Milo was still trying to process it, get his mind to accept what he was Seeing, when Cennydd—*Cennydd*—pulled a thread of power from the ground between his feet, curled it into the shapes of a hex Milo'd never seen before, and hurled it at Milo.

Hot and bloodshot, with hobnail edges tipped in pitch. Malicious. *Deadly*. And from far too close.

Natur magic. Cennydd was a witch. *Cennydd*.

It hit Milo's shield dead-center. Seeking out and chewing at the spaces in his protection charms. *Hurting* as it tore and shredded, and changed direction every time Milo adjusted to counterattack.

"You—"

Milo couldn't finish the accusation—*You've been hiding this all this time*—because the sorcerer took the opportunity to intensify his own attack. The ground beneath Milo shook, shuddered, rising up just as Milo took panicked steps back, and gouging a strip that could've buried him. *Would* have. Because these two weren't only throwing painful hexes and deflecting wards at Milo—they were striking with lethal intent.

Assaulted on two fronts, magic flying everywhere. Milo tried frantically to tighten his shield against the shards of the hex patiently tunneling through it, shaped his magic into dual blunt-force barbs and slung it outward. It smacked Cennydd down to the ground, and forced the sorcerer back right up against the fence. Milo *shoved*, pinning them both where they were, and gritting his teeth against the sweat dripping down to sting and blur his eyes as they fought him.

He was fading. Tiring. Hurting enough to start losing his focus.

Cennydd shouted—"Let me up, you've no right!"—but the sorcerer had gone still, his eyes on the razorback cow that was on her feet now, swaying only paces away from him and clearly moving herself between him and her calf.

The cow growled. Fire lit in her belly.

Milo should be hoping the sorcerer's shield would hold against a potent blast of concentrated flame, but right now he was sort of hoping the opposite. He could use a hand here.

As though he'd called it, the sound of hoofbeats echoed down the hill, with throaty yips from Lleu, and a rough shout, a simple but deep and commanding "Hey! *Hey!*" that could only be—

Milo whipped around.

Fearsome in the uneven pulse of the magelight, bareback astride Poppy at full gallop, bent low over her neck, teeth bared, hands tangled in her mane, and hair whipping out behind him like a Wild Man from legend.

Ellis.

Relief teased at Milo for only a second before dread took over. These two were deadly dangerous, not aiming to merely wound or incapacitate Milo but to actually kill him. And Ellis had no magic. Milo had the gun. *Had* the gun. He had no idea where it was now and no recollection of having dropped it. Didn't matter. Ellis was heading for the heart of this fray with nothing but his forceful will and good intentions.

And the dragons were waking up. Confused and angry dragons were *waking up*. A dragonstone wasn't going to protect against that.

Milo couldn't allow it—absolutely *could not* allow Ellis to barrel into this with no protection. And yet Milo was already stretching things far too thinly. His magic was split in four different directions, and the constant barrage at his shield was scattering his concentration.

He could scarcely protect himself. There was no way he could protect them both.

It wasn't even really a choice.

Milo rammed out a burst of power, enough to finally kill the malicious little hexes gnawing his shield, then disentangled it from around himself and bunged it at Ellis. More power, pouring into the shield as it found and gathered at Ellis, and once it was secure, Milo allowed himself to breathe again. It turned to a wheezing laugh when the shapes of a howler and a blackhorn came swooping down the slope, low enough that their powerful wingbeats blasted dirt and grass across the ground and whipped it all into gritty dervishes. Fire glowed in their bellies, piping up their throats, silhouettes nearly flanking Ellis like outriders as he just kept on coming.

It was beautiful. The stuff of paintings and fireside tales. The laugh burbled out of Milo, rose a giddy octave or two, then turned to a scream when pain like a burning brand sizzled between his shoulder blades and sent him to his knees.

Everything just sort of… blurred.

Cennydd sneered—"It's what you get"—as he sent another jab of power through the hex, spotty face pale as dough but pulled into satisfied shapes when Milo's shirt started to smoke at the edges of the magic. The spiky pain trebled.

Milo couldn't hold back a shriek that turned to a breathless grunt as he doubled over.

Ellis shouted, "*Milo!*" and leapt from Poppy's back.

The blackhorn roared overhead.

The sorcerer said, "Bloody damn, kid," in a thick Verdish accent and backed away as Cennydd shouted, "I had to, he made me, you saw it!"

The hex burrowed through skin, muscle, burning, clawing, eating its way toward Milo's spine. *Agony.*

Milo tried to scream again but he had no wind.

The cow stretched her neck over the fence, opened her mouth. Milo had only enough time to register the petrol and sulfur smell, the fuel dripping over her teeth like drool, before a jet of fire shot from her throat and strafed the ground between her calf and everyone else.

Ellis ran *through* it, right toward Milo. Milo gritted his teeth, trying to keep the shield tight and strong as Ellis charged toward him.

Cennydd shrieked, crouched behind his shield for one second, two, before he turned and legged it into the trees.

The blackhorn circled 'round and followed.

The sorcerer was already gone. Somewhere.

Thank every goddess, because Milo couldn't hold the shield around Ellis anymore. The pain wasn't letting him concentrate. It wasn't even letting him move.

The blackhorn disappeared over the treetops then bellowed, presumably at Cennydd, because Cennydd's magic dissipated all at once and took the violent, spiteful hex with it. And while it stopped trying to chew its way through Milo, the pain went nowhere. It kept ripping through him like he was being flayed, like he was on fire, and maybe he was.

Screeching, the howler made a quick descent then lofted into a dive at the razorback, talons reaching out and grazing scales, and then again, until the razorback stopped spewing fire and lowered her head. Growling. Feral gaze flicking everywhere. One wing extended to cover the calf, who was only sitting there, blinking.

There was a high shout from up the hill. Glynn. Running toward them, three more dragons winging behind and past her to skim by overhead.

A swath of fire, high and hot, was eating the ground. Not at the tree-brake yet, but it would only be a few minutes.

"Milo!" Ellis skidded to his knees at Milo's side, patting at the smoldering hole in Milo's shirt. "Oh no." Patting more gently when Milo yelped and seized at the pressure. "Bloody—don't move. All right? Milo! Just stay still, don't move, I'll—"

"Can... hardly... *breathe*"—barely a whistle, forced from between teeth clenched tight—"let alone... *ah*... move."

Milo shut his eyes, reached out with his magic, put everything he had into dousing the fire, because Old Forge was too far out for the fire brigade to do much good. And anyway, the dragons were riled—it wouldn't be safe. It wasn't safe now.

Ellis was still grizzling at Milo—"D'you hear me? *Answer* me!"— but Milo couldn't listen, couldn't understand, couldn't do anything but try to hang on to his mind through the staggering pain, and... *there*.

Found the shapes of the fire. Twisted them. Changed them. Obliterated them.

It was all Milo had. Everything that was left. He tried to hear Ellis's voice telling him he was all right, everything would be all right, but the pain flared out, expanded, mutated into a leviathan that snagged him in jagged claws and dragged him down.

It was almost a relief to let it.

Chapter 11—Development

: *the central dramatic section of a sonata form that moves harmonically through many keys*

He was out for three days. Or so he'd been told.

He woke to Lilibet, leaning over him with her cool greens and serene blues, pushing healing charms into him with tender touches and calming whispers.

Whitpool had no hospital but for the surgery on the Home Guard's base, so Ellis had hunted down Rhywun Collins in the middle of the night to come sedate Milo and keep him that way until a proper Natur witch could be found. The damage was magical and so must the healing be. But there was no one in Whitpool who had the magic necessary—*Cennydd*, Milo thought groggily, *Cennydd's had it all along*—and instead of wasting time trying to track down someone else, Ellis had intended to send word to Lilibet the moment the telegraph office opened in the morning. He instead received an odd look from the man at the counter and a message just finished transcription: *Arriving a.m. train.*

"Of course you are," Ellis had muttered, thrown some money at the man anyway, and gone to the railway station.

"Because, unlike me," Ellis told Milo, "Mam has *useful* Dreams."

It was quick after that. The pain was still there but not nearly as mind-bending, and the bleariness came and went but was manageable. There would be scars, but, "Every hero needs a scar or two," Ellis said, smirk trying for cocky but too tender and worried to get there.

Milo didn't feel heroic. He felt... odd. Removed. Hurting but calm. Glad beyond sense no one else had been hurt and the dragons were all safe, though thoroughly nettled and restlessly taking it out on each other.

Lleu's barking had woken Ellis, he'd said. That, and the kettle screaming on the cooker. And then he'd seen Milo's light, and just....

Every goddess save him—what if Milo hadn't thrown the shield at him? What if one of the dragons, drugged and angry and frightened, had gone after him? What if—?

What if?

Lilibet let Milo up two days later. Partly because Glynn had sworn to not allow him to resume any of his duties yet, and Howell had backed her up with a stern glare and a somber "We have you, son." But mostly because Dilys showed up, a one-person army of cheer and sarcastic humor, and commandeered the subdued mood like a diminutive, domineering general.

"How are all you people getting in and out of the preserve?" Milo wondered.

They were in the upstairs parlor with its shabby couches and sea-facing windows, open now to catch the fresh breeze and "Put a bit of color in your cheeks" according to Lilibet. "You are not to move," she'd told Milo, "until you've finished a pork pie and drunk two cups of tea." She'd deposited Milo on the fat armchair Lleu agreed to give up in return for making a bed of Milo's feet, then demurred the impromptu tea party to "you young folk" and retired to Ceri's study.

"Oh, well, ehm." Weirdly sheepish, Ellis dipped into his waistcoat pocket and pulled out the dragonstone. He held it up with a shrug.

Milo's gut curled. "Oh, *Elly*. You can't... that's not enough protection for—"

"We're being very careful," Ellis cut in, tucking the stone away again with a glare at Dilys's muttered "Like a bloody anxious auntie," but for the most part he ignored her, and told Milo, "I bought a car to keep at the forge, and we—"

"You... bought a car."

"Well, you don't have one."

"You *bought* a car. To keep at the forge." Milo shook his head. "Elly, you can't just—"

"Except for the part where I can. And the part where I did." Smug. "And anyway, I bought it for Howell, so you have no say." Ellis shrugged with a waggish grin. "I need some more moles made for subsoiling, and all the blacksmiths worth anything in Wellech are full-up with backorders, what with Her Majesty's agro-boffins cracking the whip. Howell agreed to knock some together for me and ship them on, and I suggested I pay for it with a car."

Milo frowned. He was pretty sure they were called *agriculture executives*, and not *agro-boffins*, but—"What the deuce is a mole for subsoiling?"

"Oh, it's this iron... thing. Shaped like a bullet. About yea big." Ellis spread his hands shoulder-width apart. "You drag it under the soil to create drainage in heavy lands where there's clay layered—"

"Elly, it would take several *thousand* 'iron things' to equal the cost of a car!"

"There are brackets, too." Ellis caught Milo's incredulous look and rolled his eyes. "So he'll owe me a few. And I need them."

"Where's he supposed to get the iron? I thought there was a shortage."

Ellis shrugged. "I have a great deal to do with running Wellech. Wellech has mines."

Save them all, he had an answer for bloody *everything*. Which might not be so annoying if they weren't all so inarguably and damnably reasonable.

"It's not like a car will go to waste," Glynn put in with a halfway moony glance at Ellis that just wasn't fair. "He's got the money, and now Tad's got a car. Play your cards right and maybe we'll get a decent tractor next to drag that winch Cennydd left behind up to—"

"*Glynn.*" Milo rubbed at his brow. "We can't just accept—"

"Family can. Family does." Dilys wagged a finger at Milo. "Now hush or I'll buy Glynn the bloody tractor just to watch you squirm."

Ellis tried, Milo could tell Ellis *tried* really hard to stifle the snort, but it came out anyway. He coughed to cover it, and went on, "It wasn't a whim. We couldn't go traipsing up and down the road with no escort, not with the dragons only just settling down, and yes, I'm well aware the stone isn't a substitute for dragonkin. So we improvised, since—"

"*You* improvised," Milo muttered, strangely embarrassed but grateful too. And maybe he was embarrassed because he was grateful. He couldn't tell.

"Yes, all right, fine—*I* improvised, since buying the car will end up costing me less than keeping a hire car handy, and something was necessary. It's safer for us to come and go in a covered vehicle, you know it is. Plus, try getting a driver to come stay at a dragon preserve to be at our beck and call. For pity's sake, even the people who've lived here all their lives don't come near the fences unless they have to." Ellis paused, scowling, perhaps reminded, as Milo was, that Cennydd had lived here all his life too, and look how that had worked out. "Anyway." Ellis shook it away. "I'm the official escort until you're… ehm." He waved at Milo's general state of bedclothes and blankets and endless cups of Lilibet's healing tea. "Mam didn't want to mess with the wards so we've been using the forge's access road. Though she did what she could with the ones that were broken."

"I laid some of my own over what Lilibet did." Dilys shrugged and propped her socked feet on the tea table. "It should hold until you're up and about." She sat back and dug her shoulders into the cushions of the settee across from Milo, nudging Glynn with an impish smirk. "Though this one was just as much a Nervous Nellie as Ellis while I did it."

Glynn nudged right back. "It's barely two furlongs from the springs, and I'm not dragonkin. If one of the dragons had—"

"If one of the dragons had wandered down to see what we were up to, I would've dazzled them with my native charm, no doubt."

"No doubt." Glynn rolled her eyes with a good-natured snort. "Give them a laugh and a grin while they snaffle you down, why don't you. They'll have fond memories when they burp you back up."

"You're one to talk. Give your tad a heart attack, you will." Dilys turned to Milo, wide-eyed. "You'd think that little razorback would've been put off people altogether, but *no*, not when it comes to this one." She hooked a thumb at Glynn. "Followed her around the pasture like a lost duckling until his mam came and shuffled him off. *That* one's got more sense than a fencepost, at least after what almost happened, but the calf—"

"I just don't *understand* it!" Milo's outburst may have been a bit too strident, because it shut Dilys up. *Nothing* shut Dilys up. Milo shook his head, at a complete loss. "It's possible to endear oneself to any sort of wild animal when it's a baby, I suppose, imprinting and all that. But the mam? It doesn't make sense. And Cennydd, a witch all this time. I mean, I can understand hiding it. People do it all the time."

To avoid the draft in Ceri's generation. For a lack of trust in cases like Dilys's mam who didn't so much hide the talents of the people of Tirryderch, but merely refused to accept any higher authority when it came to what was good for them. And considering what Milo had been hiding all his life, none of it was that unfathomable.

"But trying to *steal* a dragon?" Milo threw his hands out. "*Why*? It isn't as though Cennydd could keep it for a pet. What had he planned to *do* with it? And who was that sorcerer? And that gas—what even *was* that? And how did they manage to weave the magic into it like that? And what was he *feeding* them?"

He slumped back, a bit winded, and peered at the other three in turn, blinking back at him with varying expressions, but mostly just as confused as Milo was.

...Except for Ellis.

"Young Princes, they call themselves." Ellis's tone was rife with derision and ire. "They're an offshoot of the Purity Party, because of course they are. That boy, that *Cennydd*"—he spat it—"was recruited several years back because his mam is a known Purity sympathizer, and because Cennydd apparently never shut his gob about how you let him in to see the dragons." Ellis ran a hand through his hair, clearly annoyed. "His mam won't admit she knew he has magic, but I'm hearing that his tad—"

"His mam." Milo frowned. "Why are they questioning his...? Where is Cennydd?"

"Personally, I'm still hoping the blackhorn carried him off somewhere to eat him in private." Glynn wasn't kidding—her glower was dark and fierce. She shot it up at Milo. "Don't show him your back—didn't I say that, Milo? *Didn't I?*"

Milo stared. "I didn't think—"

"Yes you did. You *thought* you could fix everything by being the good person you are. You *thought* he was only a decent boy who needed the occasional kind word, and there's everything sorted. You *thought* he couldn't possibly be capable of what he tried to do because you know *you* couldn't, and you can't understand that everyone's *not like you*, Milo! People have black in their hearts sometimes, they just do, and if you haven't learned that yet, you'd best get used to having holes blasted in your back, because—because you—"

It cut off with a near-sob.

Milo only kept staring. Apologies were necessary somehow, Milo knew they were, but he wasn't quite sure for what, and even if he knew, he was too thrown to try.

"All right, there, pet." Dilys set a firm hand to Glynn's knee. Squeezed. "My, my, *that's* a right fiery bit of temper. I take it back—if a dragon ever tried getting shirty with me, I'd want you there to scold it into submission."

It made Glynn laugh, a watery burst that was still part blub, but the smile was real. "I'm sorry." She shook her head. "Milo, I'm *sorry*. It's only—"

"He knows, *cyw*." Dilys lifted her eyebrow at Milo. "And he knows you're only saying what we're all thinking anyway."

Milo hadn't, actually. He kept that to himself, because he didn't know what else to do. Luckily, no one seemed to be expecting anything of him just yet.

"No one knows where Cennydd is," Ellis said after a moment. "*Or* the other man, *or* whoever was waiting down on the beach for them. The Wardens here took Cennydd's mam and tad into custody, but the Colonel-in-Chief of the Home Guard apparently stepped in with some convenient orders from Llundaintref, so he's got them now."

"Alton?" Milo narrowed his eyes. "What's the Home Guard got to do with it?"

Alton is Colonel-in-Chief of the Home Guard, not some secret spy organization.

Ceri's voice, derisive, but.

But.

It had been Alton who'd come to see Ceri that day—the day Milo was in retrospect *certain* she'd decided to leave. It was Alton who'd asked about dragons disappearing. And it was Alton who was so determined not to let Milo ask him about Ceri that his lieutenant wouldn't even let Milo past the Home Guard's outer office.

"He wouldn't say." And Ellis was deuced annoyed he couldn't find out, Milo could tell by the way his jaw clamped tight and his eyes flashed. "But I had a chat with your First Warden. You know her?"

"Yeah. Eira. She's a friend of Mam's. She's been trying to help figure out who'd been at the wards."

"She said, yeah. She also said one of the Wardens had caught Cennydd out there once. But everyone knew he didn't have—"

"Everyone knew Cennydd didn't have magic, so it *clearly* couldn't have been him." Milo had been such a blind idiot. Maybe that was what he was supposed to be apologizing for. He hadn't been *paying attention*. He clenched his hands into fists. "*Damn* it!"

"And when she mentioned it to you, you told her—"

"*Yes*, bloody—" Milo couldn't help the growl. "I told her he just did that sometimes. That they should put a scare into him and leave it. *Yes*, Glynn, I *know*, like a calf, unfortunate in the head—I get it, all right?"

Glynn put up her hands, all innocence. "I wasn't going to say anything."

"You don't know *how* to not say anything."

"Hey, just because you're—"

"*Anyway*." Ellis gave Glynn a quelling roll of his eyes and turned back to Milo. "Eira tells me she's heard some things. Nothing official, only rumor and scuttlebutt, but word is a man who's dragonkin came through the immigration office in Llundaintref. A refugee from Colorat with stories about preserves taken over, dragonkin brought down from Taraverde, and dragons gone missing."

Dilys sat forward. "How does a *dragon* go 'missing'?"

"And why didn't she tell *me* this?" Milo wanted to know.

"Because she didn't know until the other night happened and word started to leak back from Llundaintref." Ellis shrugged. "She says she doesn't know if it's connected, and Llundaintref's not saying. But how could they *not* be? And that's not the only reason, and not even the interesting bit."

Dilys huffed. "Blood and rot, there's *more*?"

"Always is." Ellis put out a hand. "The other reason is because she's been told not to say anything to anyone. Something called the National Secrets Act, if you can believe it. They made her sign a contract and everything. But the most interesting bit is that she got that order—"

"Alton." Milo's teeth clenched. "She got the order from Colonel-in-Chief Alton."

Because everything, *everything* kept coming back to Alton.

◉

Poison, it turned out. That was the report from Eira, or at least as much of it as Llundaintref would allow her to tell Milo. Hunks of meat laced with lead, coated with Natur magic, to make the dragons more biddable. And Cennydd had been feeding it to those two dragons right under Milo's nose. For *months*.

Milo had raged when he'd read it. Exhausted himself. Accepted what comfort Ellis could give, but it hadn't helped any more than the cup of tea going cold by Milo's elbow now.

Tea helped *everything*.

"He'll stay as long as you want him to."

Lilibet's tone was kind, her fingertips gentle as she traced the edges of the burn on Milo's back. He hadn't seen it yet, not up to the contortions he'd need to do to stretch his neck in front of a mirror. And anyway, he didn't actually care. The pain receded every day. By next week, Milo figured he'd be able to resume his duties around the preserve, though perhaps go a bit more lightly than usual. Maybe even pull out his violin without gritting his teeth through a sonata or two.

"He'll stay until you convince him to go."

It hadn't really sunk in the first time she'd said it. This time, it pricked at Milo, made him frown.

"Are you saying I should? Make him go, I mean?"

Lilibet hummed, finished applying the salve, and stepped back with a soft pat to Milo's shoulder. "I'm saying he won't leave until you tell him to. Because that's what Ellis does. He stays where he's needed."

"And he's needed in Wellech. More than...."

More than I need him.

Milo didn't know if that was true. He could get along without Ellis if he had to. But he wasn't about to even try to deny that having Ellis here—right beside Milo, in his house, in his bed—was a balm more important to him right now than salves and teas and blankets and bandages put together. And wasn't that good enough as far as "need" went?

Lilibet shrugged and headed to the basin to rinse her hands. "Needs are so personal, randomly skewed by fact and emotion and any number of things, and therefore impossible to quantify one against another."

"But you think—"

"What I think doesn't matter."

"Except clearly you think it does." Milo pulled his shirt on, feeling abruptly vulnerable in his own kitchen, like a dragon without scales.

Ellis and Dilys had gone to the forge with Howell to watch him dole out the rations. Glynn was taking advantage of the dragons being elsewhere to unload some fresh hay for nests outside the thermal spring. They were alone, Milo—exhausted and sore and a little bit fuzzy—left to Lilibet's tender mercy. At the moment, she didn't seem to be in the mood to spare him much.

"Do you...." He set his teeth. "Do you not approve?"

Lilibet's eyes shot wide. "Of you and Ellis?" She huffed a high little laugh. "*Fy ngwas i*, that is absolutely the wrong question. You've loved each other since you were boys; now you love each other differently, and clearly very deeply. Enough," she said with a sly glance, "to try to skirt the Sisters' consent and redefine a contract." She ignored Milo's sputter, opened a hand. "So why in the world would you *care* who might approve and who mightn't?"

She raised her eyebrows, expectant, and her gaze was, it seemed, deliberately calm and warm. And that bloody *smirk*. Ellis took mostly after his tad in looks—same build, same straight nose and strong jaw—but he'd definitely got his coloring and that damnable smirk from Lilibet.

"I'm... not entirely sure I do." Milo looked away. "Folant doesn't. Approve, I mean."

"Well, Folant wouldn't."

They left it just lying there, the *thud* in any conversation in which the subject of Folant arose.

When the silence grew cloying, Milo said, "Then I don't understand."

Lilibet dried her hands slowly, seemingly taking far too much care, before she sighed and set down the cloth. "You do. Only, you don't want to. You Priddys are practically made of duty." It was bitter. "It only depends on what particular strain of it has infected you." She gave Milo a small, cheerless smile. "You're very much like your mam in that way, Milo."

Again, Milo looked away. His throat was tight. "Do you know...?" *Where she is? Why she left? Have you Dreamt of her?*
...Is she still alive?

Lilibet came to sit in the chair across from him. "I promised her, years ago, not too long before you were born, that I would never Dream of her. For her. Never again. And never once for you."

That made Milo look up. "Why?"

"Because she asked it of me."

Milo put aside the fact that Lilibet would apparently refuse to Dream for Milo if he asked it—and he might've done, if he'd thought of it before now. But even if he had, Lilibet wouldn't, and all for the sake of Ceri, even though it wasn't Ceri's right. It was annoying, but right now not the point.

"No, I mean, why would anyone ask that at all? If I had a way of making sure the people I love stayed safe and happy, I'd use it."

"Would you, though?" Lilibet tilted her head. "Dreams are not life. And life has a way of changing things from one Dream to the next. Every choice you make has infinite alternate choices unraveling from them like skeins of thread. Multiply that by every person around you and all their choices. That's a lot of thread you can get tangled in by simply trying to touch one strand enough to set it wobbling.

"If you spent all your time trying to shift life to one side to align with a Dream, you'd one day find yourself merely pretending at the motions of life, fitting them into the shapes the Dream gave you, rather than living it. And if you tried to shift the other way, against a Dream, who's to say that the moves you make aren't precisely what would lead to what you were trying to undo?"

"But you did Dream for her. You said *never again*."

"I did. Long ago. When we were girls and thought it fun and daring. And then when she was off to war, and I couldn't help wanting to know if I'd ever see her again." This time Lilibet's smile was warm and fond. "Imagine my surprise when I Dreamed of you."

"…Oh." Milo blinked. "And what did—?"

"Ah-ah." Lilibet wagged her finger, chiding. "Did we not just decide these sorts of questions are not entirely healthy?" She rolled her eyes at Milo's displeased huff, then seemed to take pity. "Nothing more than that you would exist when she did finally come home." She sighed. "And that she would need…." There was a clear struggle for a moment, between what Lilibet apparently wanted to say and what she thought she could or should, before she settled on, "That she would need." She tapped at Milo's nose. "And we already know that needs are *personal*."

Milo pinched his lips tight to prevent a curse from sliding through them. It was a variation on the same old nonanswer he'd been getting from his mam all his life. Which was why he refused to feel guilty when he asked,

"Did you ever Dream of my tad?"

"No." Too quick. Lilibet seemed to know it, because she shook her head and said, "She was already mourning him when I Dreamed. I only ever saw that she'd loved him."

"She won't ever tell me anything about him. But I've always wondered if… I mean, I had the impression…" Milo clenched his jaw, annoyed with himself. "What I mean to say is, I'm pretty sure he was the enemy. And I can't help thinking… Well, she's a spy after all, and… I mean. Did she…?"

Milo had never allowed the question to the surface. Had pretended it would never even occur to him to wonder. But that was back when he'd still been telling himself the Black Dog was a myth that would be somewhat terrifying, though also rather brilliant, if true but clearly couldn't be. Because people didn't go off to war and strike terror into the hearts of enemies, and then come home to be mams who nagged their sons to collect the eggs in the morning and to stop pinching Glynn, even if she was an annoying little creadur sometimes.

Except now Milo was pretty sure people did, or at least Ceri had. And with what his mam had said, way back on that train ride from Wellech—*someone who in another life you could've loved, get them to trust you while you're looking for the right place to slide the blade in*—well. With something like that still bumbling about in Milo's head at odd moments, he couldn't make himself not wonder.

"Would it change anything if she had?" Lilibet's voice was soft, curiosity rather than judgement.

Milo had thought about this too. "I don't... think so."

It was war. People had to do awful things in war. And spies had to do things Milo couldn't really imagine. If Milo accepted that Ceri had been a spy—was a spy—then he had to accept that she'd done things that would likely curl his stomach. But it didn't make her not his mam. It didn't make her not the woman who'd loved him and taught him and watched him with cautious pride as he grew.

Lilibet studied him for a moment, dark eyes narrowed, thoughtful, before she sat back with a shrug. "No. I don't know what might've happened if she'd been put to it. I only know he was killed before she had to make the choice. And that she mourned him after."

Milo looked down at his clenched hands atop the table, a bit relieved, but other than that, unsure what to feel.

They were quiet again, Lilibet scrutinizing Milo, and Milo unwilling to say or do anything to provoke what she so clearly meant to say. Because she'd waited for this, for everyone else to be scattered about the place, for Milo to be alone and tired and vulnerable. To make sure she got honest answers, maybe. Or merely to ensure he was past the point where he could just get up and walk away before she'd got what she wanted out of whatever this was.

Maybe Lilibet got tired of waiting. "You understand that war is coming." So bald. And yet so tender.

"You don't need Dreams to know that."

"No," Lilibet said softly. "Maybe we only need to know ourselves. And each other." She paused, perhaps waiting for Milo to look her in the eye, but he didn't. "I know you, Milo. I don't have to Dream of you to know what you've been debating in the back of your mind, while pretending even to yourself you're doing no such thing. Because I know your mam, and I know what she'd do. What she *did* do. And you're far more like her than you sometimes like to think. Duty, you know." She tapped at the table until Milo finally looked up and met her gaze. "Which is why I'm telling you—he'll go where he believes he's most needed, and there he'll stay." She paused, one eyebrow raised and mouth turned down in an unhappy frown. "Or follow." She looked away, looked down. "Right now I reckon your need and Wellech's are about even. But Wellech when Preidyn's at war?"

It clicked, then, what she meant. Why she'd said it.

Because Ellis would enlist. He would. There was no question of an eventual draft when it came to Ellis, because he'd already be gone.

"You still Dream for Elly. Or of him, at least." Milo's voice was hoarse. He swallowed the burn working at the bottom of his throat. "You knew what happened the other night long before anyone could've told you."

She didn't deny it. She didn't flinch.

She knew. She'd Dreamed. And so, here she was, doing exactly what she'd just got done cautioning against—tweaking at a strand, setting it awobble.

Milo clenched his fists tighter. "And what if I've a duty to him, then?"

"Oh, *anwylyd*. Of course you do." She looked sad. Full of compassion, but determined too. "Only it's not the sort either of you would choose, is it?"

Save him, Milo couldn't even look at her.

It was odd that, even after what happened with Cennydd, *this* was what decided him.

Or maybe crystallized what something inside him had already been resolved to do when Cennydd sat in front of him and told Milo things were getting dangerous for people like him.

Made of duty. Infected by it. And, well. Maybe so.

"You've Dreamed it all through. All the ways it could go." Milo had to clear his throat. "And he needs to stay in Wellech."

"Yes." Not even a second's hesitation, but an underpinning of urgency that rattled like a warning. "Wellech has to need him to."

Wellech already did. But, it seemed, not enough just yet to convincingly outweigh the needs of Preidyn when the declarations started rolling. Or the needs of Milo when Ellis found out what Milo was only just now realizing he intended to do.

It was a lot to expect, a lot to ask, for Milo to even know how to set a finger on one side of an imagined scale, to know on which side to place it, how much pressure to apply. It was a betrayal of sorts to merely consider it, manipulation at best, and shocking hubris to imagine he even had the right.

The funny thing was, he already knew how to tip this particular scale where it needed to go. It... didn't make it any less awful.

Milo nodded, slow and heavy, and looked away. "I need time."

Lilibet set her hand atop Milo's, her grip strong, almost safe. "You have some. Not enough."

"Yeah, well." Milo tried to swallow the thousand emotions tangled in his throat like snarled skeins of thread. Couldn't. "It'll have to do."

Ellis was the last to leave, and yes, Lilibet had been right—Milo had to argue him into it. Even though it had been over a week since Lilibet had left, and four days since Dilys had. Ellis had been in Whitpool for over a fortnight now, when usually he was lucky if Wellech could spare him four or five days.

"Elly, I'm *fine*. I promise."

Ellis had already handed his bag over to a porter. He had his ticket fisted in his hand, as though he was contemplating just throwing it to the floor of the platform and stomping it. In fact, he probably was.

"Are you *sure*, though? I can stay for another—"

"You can't. You know you can't. You should've been back last week."

"Maybe. Yes. But damn it, I'm *bloody* tired of everyone else getting to decide when and how much I get to see you." Ellis took hold of Milo's shoulders, careful not to squeeze or jostle, because even though Milo really was fine, mostly healed, the odd movement still set him to hissing when he was surprised into it. Ellis leaned in until his brow was set to Milo's. "You've been *hurt*, Milo. You were *attacked*. If you need me to—"

"I know, Elly." Milo set his hands to Ellis's lapels and a kiss to his cheek. "I know. And thank you. But I'm all right. I promise."

The fug of coalsmoke and engine grease was nearly overwhelming. Milo pushed his face into Ellis's shoulder, breathed in the scent of him, because Ellis always smelled like summer. Sandalwood in his hair, and cedar on his coat, and a touch of freesia at collar and cuffs. Good sweat and expensive soap and always, *always* the faintest trace of river silt.

Milo never wanted to let go.

But he made himself pull back. Made himself smile. Made himself lift his chin.

"You'll be able to make it to Tirryderch next month? You're sure?"

The Coven would be meeting there. And Milo had some things he needed to say to them. It was a long trip for Ellis, and Milo hadn't liked asking it of him. But he'd had to. *Had* to.

"Yeah." Ellis nodded, firm. "Or I can just come back in a fortnight, if that would be—"

"Elly!" Milo grinned, a real grin, because Ellis could pull them out of him without even trying. Without even knowing from how deep he was pulling. "Tirryderch. Next month. Dillie's already offered—"

"Pardon me, syr." The same porter who'd taken Ellis's bag was now trying very hard not to notice the rather public clinch. "We're boarding now."

"Right." Ellis pulled back. "Right. Yes. I'm coming." But he was still looking at Milo like he was only waiting for a sign that he should stay.

Milo wanted to give it to him. He was careful not to. "Next month." One more kiss. One more hug.

"All right. Next month." Ellis sighed, but he let go, backed up slowly, still watching, then turned and followed the porter.

Milo waited to wave him off, keeping his smile as Ellis lifted a hand on the other side of the window. Milo didn't move until the caboose rattled past him, and the smoke got too think, and there was nothing left to see but empty tracks.

He made his way to the car—Howell's car now, with Howell waiting behind the wheel, indulgent smile on his face and a chipper "Home, then?" when Milo climbed in.

"Not... yet," Milo said, unable to meet Howell's eyes.

He gnawed his lip, guilty, and thought of how Howell and Glynn had finished up the Sowing migration when Milo was next to useless, and did it without a qualm, without a second of resentment, because Milo was family and they loved him.

He thought of Dilys, who'd come running all the way from Tirryderch, because Milo'd been hurt and needed her sarcasm and refusal to accept he wouldn't be all right.

He thought of Ellis, and how he wouldn't leave unless Milo made him, how he'd follow if Milo didn't stop him, because love was not to be defined by clauses and riders on paper but was a contract of the heart, and Ellis's was the biggest and most generous there was.

He thought of the dragons, how they trustingly slurped from troughs offered by their kin, and how someone had found a way to twist that trust into something not only sick and despicable, but quite possibly world-changing if it couldn't be stopped.

He didn't think of Lilibet, drawing Milo a map of emotion to show him how not to drag her son to a place he didn't deserve to be. How he was needed right where he was, and Ellis always stayed where he was needed.

He didn't think of Ceri, out there somewhere and still trying to protect a young man who hadn't been her little boy for a very long time, but would still nevertheless always be.

"Will you drive me to the Home Guard's office, please?" Milo pulled in a slow breath for courage before he looked Howell in the eye. "I need to see Colonel-in-Chief Alton."

BOOK TWO: ACCELERANDO

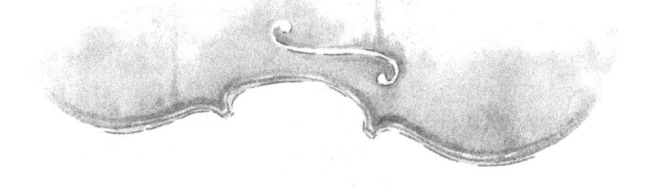

Chapter 12—Countermelody

: a secondary melodic idea that accompanies and opposes a main thematic idea

The thing about Tirryderch that always got to Ellis was the landscape. Rolling greens and lush grassy hills that tumbled out and up into mountains that cycled from peacock to verdigris to deepest carmine, depending on the weather or the angle or the set of the sun. Not tall enough to be snow-capped except in the deeps of winter, but grand and sprawling all the same. It was gorgeous.

He'd been here a handful of times, most of them when he was a boy, back when long trips were more exciting adventure than inconvenient necessity. Though, he reckoned as the train rumbled through the last pass and toward Tirryderch proper, he'd likely make it a point to visit more if the railroad had a more direct route from Wellech. As it was, Wellech up to the Kymbrygh Central Station then back down to Tirryderch took nearly an entire day and evening. (Because the Kymbrygh Central Station wasn't *central* at all. If it was, it would be in Wellech, but that was a sticky argument Wellech was never going to win with Kymbrygh's MP.) As a result, it was well into dusk when Dilys picked Ellis up from the Tirryderch Station.

"I thought Milo might be with you."

"Well, *haia* to you too." Dilys grinned, waving away Ellis's apology as she snagged his small valise and left the larger bag for him. "He's holed up with Tad and Steffan over some…" Dilys paused with a twinkle, leading Ellis from the platform and down to a waiting car. "Actually, I don't think I'm meant to tell you. I think it's meant as a surprise." She tossed the valise in the boot, waited for Ellis to load his other bag in, then jerked her chin as she slammed it shut. "Get in, then."

"Wait." Ellis paused with his hand on the door, a sinking feeling burbling in his gut. "I see no driver."

There was that grin again, rather pleased this time and full of wicked promise. Dilys put her arms out, caroled "Ta-da!" and hopped into the driver's seat.

"Oh," said Ellis slowly. "Well. Crap."

"Damn it, Dillie, cars have headlamps for a reason!"

"Yeah, for great wibbly boys who have no sense of adventure. It's not even dark!"

"Not— Are you—? The bloody stars are out!"

"Oh, *fine*, you massive whinger."

"What are you—? Watch where you're going!"

"D'you want the lamps on or d'you want me to watch where I'm going?"

"*Both!*"

Ellis took it back—the landscape was not gorgeous. The landscape was full of twisty roads and blind curves, and he'd be happy if he never had to see it again. Or Dilys.

His hands were still gripping the dashboard, fingers cramped into claws, when Milo opened Ellis's door and stooped down to give him a welcoming smile and a pair of raised eyebrows.

"*Haia*, Elly."

Rugged was the first thing Ellis thought. Milo was the kind of person who looked too young and too fair for even peach fuzz but could actually grow a beard by just thinking really hard about it. Still, this was more than the four-days scruff Ellis was used to. Full and thick though neatly trimmed, black beard on pale cheeks capped by dark blue eyes sparking open welcome. More sinew-strapped bone than bulk and brawn, but the lean structure of Milo was put together like a fine, elegant house built on a scaffolding of solid steel. No hat over black hair gone long and just gathering a slight curl at the ends, but the durable walking trousers and the shabby but still somehow natty tweed coat and the casually open shirt collar...

Ellis opened his mouth. Closed it. Swallowed. "*Haia*, Milo."

"Are you, ehm...?" Milo was smirking. Because he was a terrible person. "Are you getting out?"

"Soon as I can trust my knees."

Dilys dipped down next to Milo with a contemplative look. "Is that green, d'you think?"

"Nah." Milo shook his head. "He's too lush for plain old green. More like viridian."

"That's not a color. You made that up."

"Didn't. It's still green but richer and with a tinge of blue. Deeper. More striking."

Terrible. Person.

"You're only saying that because you're a sop and too twee for words." Dilys looked back at Ellis, eyes narrowed, then tipped a sharp nod. "Green."

Ellis unclamped his hand from the dash and latched it over Dilys's face instead. He gave her a shove back.

"*You* are a vile minger who shouldn't be allowed behind the wheel of a car, and I hate you."

Dilys stumbled back, laughing. "That's what Milo said!" she crowed, then popped the boot and skipped up the steps to Ty Mynydd with a bounce to her step that was just flat insulting.

Ellis glowered over at Milo, who was peering back at him with a glint Ellis really didn't want to melt at seeing, but it couldn't be helped. This Milo was a far cry from the one Ellis had left at the Whitpool station a month ago, still tired and shaky and far too pale then, and looking as though his world had been yanked from under him.

Then again, it rather had been.

It was dark, but the lamps on the drive and front step were lit, so Ellis had no problem seeing that Milo's color was better. And the way he was still leaning down, relaxed and cheerful, told Ellis the sting and stiffness must be gone as well.

"*Haia*," Milo said. Soft. Happy.

"*Haia*," Ellis said back, smiling because he couldn't help it, then finally hefted himself from the car.

He hadn't been kidding—his knees really were a bit unreliable. And Dilys really was evil and shouldn't be allowed to drive.

Milo waited for Ellis to straighten with a huff, before—smile crimping, eyes gone urgent—he moved in close and wrapped his arms around Ellis's neck. Tight. Pressed together as though Milo were trying to fuse them into one person. Full of some fraught emotion Ellis could sense but didn't entirely understand.

"I'm here," Ellis said, gripping Milo back, and stuck his face into Milo's shoulder, home again, no matter where he was. "Missed you." Hushed and heartfelt, and said into Milo's neck.

"Yeah. Me too."

It lasted until Ellis heard Ty Mynydd's front door swing open again, and one of the valets politely clearing his throat as he descended the steps. Milo pulled back, hands to Ellis's arms, and gave him a bright-eyed grin as the valet took Ellis's bags from the car and stood to wait.

"They gave you a room next to your mam's." Milo jerked his head at the valet. "I was hoping you wouldn't need it."

Lilibet had left Wellech last week to arrive a few days before the Coven. Ellis couldn't help wondering if Dilys had driven Lilibet from the train station too, and if she had, if the experience had been as nerve-shattering as it had for Ellis.

Ellis made a show of thinking about Milo's unspoken but quite obvious question, then shrugged. "Can't think why I would."

Milo grinned and shut the car's door. He tugged at Ellis's arm. "C'mon, they held supper for you."

⚬

The pile that was Ty Mynydd couldn't be easily classified. There was an ancient longhouse underneath there somewhere, but each generation of Mosses had added to it according to their own tastes with no thought toward keeping one style harmonized with another. Thus, from the outside, it was as though a child had stomped through a pile of building blocks, albeit very expensive and well-made ones. On the inside, though, it was like walking through history in stasis.

The wing that belonged to Nia and Terrwyn and Steffan was expansive yet somehow cozy, predictably more modern than the rest but still warm and homely. Room upon room, each a lesson in taste and comfort. Bare-beamed ceilings lofted high over polished oak floors that lay beneath thick woven rugs in rich reds and deepest blues. Overstuffed couches and plump chairs sat in clusters around hearths, all of it accented with gleaming cherrywood tables and bookshelves overflowing with carefully chosen titles.

Supper had been simple by Dilys's request and to Ellis's delight. Rarebit made with a savory mix of sharp and mild cheeses, and a cawl so full of beef and lamb chunks and more vegetables than Ellis knew existed there was hardly room for the broth. Good, dark Tirryderch apple ale set it all alight on his tongue, and finally relaxed him enough he could unclench, unwind. And possibly ward off the headache that had started building on the train and Dilys hadn't helped even a little bit.

All of it eased Ellis into a wonderful warmth, and he was sort of sad to see it end when Steffan sent the boys off for baths. It seemed to be the signal for everyone to adjourn. Ellis barely remembered leaving the table, since he was now in the process of becoming one with the couch, oozing into the cushions, and merely watching the conversation around him rather than participating. Or really even paying attention.

"It's not about *politics*, Mam." Dilys sighed, retorting to something Nia had been saying about... Ellis had lost track again. The last time he'd been listening the conversation had been veering into... hm. Schools, maybe?

"Everything is about politics," Terrwyn put in, diffident. "Our existence is political." He gestured between himself and Steffan and Nia, then smirked with a jerk of his chin at Dilys. "So's yours and your brothers'."

And, well, that was true. Tirryderch had gone a bit insane, back when Nia (its Pennaeth for only less than a year at that point) and Steffan had pulled Terrwyn (too young to have won a seat on the parish council, but nonetheless won it he had) into their arrangement, skipped a courtship contract altogether and gone right for cariad. And then it rather exploded when Nia took advantage of ancient and very ambiguous bylaws in Tirryderch's charter to change the Pennaeth position from an inherited post to an elected one, co-equal with Tirryderch's council. Traditionally more of a support system for the Pennaeth than an independent body, the council stepped right up to its new remit, and was now more loyal to their Pennaeth than they'd been before.

The Sisters only just barely endorsed the cariad contract, but that was nothing new. Allowing the union of the magic-rich Rydderch bloodline with the Moss wealth and political stature, alongside the prestige of the Hill ancestry Steffan brought to the mix, was just asking to one day be deposed. Or, in Nia's case, ignored. But as long as no one publicly or actively opposed the Sisters, they were content to pretend it was all their own strategy and let things lie.

Ellis would admit it gave him ideas his tad would never approve of, but Ellis could likely take the Wellech position of Pennaeth from Folant any time he chose. He just hadn't chosen to yet. But if he did, and if Milo—

No. Milo couldn't. Probably wouldn't. The dragons meant too much to him, and anyway, it wasn't as though Kymbrygh was enjoying a surplus of dragonkin.

It still stung, though, made Ellis by turns angry and impatient and sad and frustrated. He wasn't used to feeling at a loss when there was a problem to be solved. It wasn't right and it wasn't fair, and the dragonstone in his pocket was lovely but not *enough*. He calmed himself by setting his hand over Milo's on the couch cushion beside him. Milo didn't turn to him, unusually quiet but paying very close attention to the conversation, looking sad one second and tamping the next. But he spread his fingers until Ellis threaded his own between them, and curled them tight.

They'd retired to Nia's... well, Ellis wanted to call it a study because of the giant walnut desk in front of the windows, but it was more of a parlor with its four couches and enormous cabinet dedicated solely to an overly generous variety of potables. Ellis was sticking with the apple ale they'd had at supper. Milo'd had a glass of single malt in his hand for over an hour now, but Ellis had yet to see him take a drink from it.

"Well, everyone has to do their duty as they see it, don't they?"

The question from Dilys didn't seem terribly shocking or

provocative, but it still, for whatever reason, made Milo stiffen beside Ellis. A quick flick of Milo's gaze toward Lilibet then away had Ellis frowning, bemused, and paying attention again.

"You can't fault anyone who wants to serve their country," Dilys went on. "Watching out for Tirryderch's magical folk doesn't mean you can dictate whether or not they enlist."

"The council doesn't *dictate*, for pity's sake." Terrwyn rolled his eyes. "We merely discourage our citizens—*all* our citizens—from signing any contract before they're made aware of all possible repercussions. That's not dictating—it's being responsible, and caring about those who've elected us to look after their interests."

"And yet most of the ones who've come to you with a request to endorse their contract application walk away with a much dimmer view of Her Majesty's Royal Forces. And we barely have enough in the Home Guard to justify a Tirryderch division." Dilys lifted her eyebrows, practically daring Terrwyn to deny it; when he didn't, Dilys put out a hand. "You don't want your people in danger. All right. It's a mark of your kind heart and your care for Tirryderch. But you've also a duty to Kymbrygh in general, and a time is coming when—"

"Could it not be said," Nia cut in, "that by doing our duty—how we see it—to our magical folk, we are, in turn, doing our duty to Kymbrygh?" She shrugged. "Tirryderch is more or less the granary for the Preidynīg Isles. We need our Natur witches to monitor the crops for blight or infestation, our Elfennol sorcerers to find water in times of drought, our Dewin mages for power and protection, and just generally adding skill where necessary. Who would it serve if all those folk went off to war and our crops failed? Tirryderch could no longer provide grain to the rest of Preidyn. We couldn't provide the excess we trade with the rest of the world, and therefore put taxes in the Queen's coffers so she can pay for a war we have no say in waging."

"And were the council and our Pennaeth to assist such an exodus," Steffan put in, "if Tirryderch were to encourage its magical folk to heed the Queen's call to enlist, Tirryderch would then lose its ability to lend more practical support. We couldn't feed ourselves, let alone provide for the troops we send to war the goddesses know where."

"That's not... ehm." Ellis tried not wince, since everyone was looking at him now; it was somewhat difficult, because he hadn't really meant to speak up in the first place. He cleared his throat. "Only, you're talking as though you couldn't get along without magical folk, and Wellech—regardless of how misguided and dogmatic its Pennaeth's policies—has rather proven that untrue."

Terrwyn set a skeptical gaze on Ellis, complete with raised eyebrows. So did Milo.

Steffan was clearly trying not to snort. "Has it, though?"

"Well, I mean." Ellis sat forward. "I'm not actually defending my tad, because there really isn't a good defense, and I've no interest in trying to find one." He shot a look at Lilibet, who was smirking at him from her chair by the fireplace. Ellis gave her a glare back. "And I'm not denying that Wellech could be doing much better for itself if its policies on magic weren't so strict. Believe me, that's a fight I'm still in up to my neck, and one I intend to win." He couldn't help the glance sideways at Milo, but Milo was frowning down into his drink. "I'm only saying that Wellech does manage to feed itself without magic as an integral part of its production, and I imagine Tirryderch could do too, should it ever have a need."

"Wellech manages to feed *itself*," Terrwyn put in. "And yes, I've no doubt Tirryderch could do, as you say. Though that's a question we won't need answered for quite some time, thanks in no small part to the influx of magical folk from Wellech over the past two decades." He waited, daring Ellis to disagree, but when Ellis didn't, Terrwyn went on, "Nia's point is that the extraordinary volume of our output is dependent on magic, and Preidyn is dependent on that output. Steffan's point is that Preidyn is, therefore, dependent on our magical folk right where they are, and isn't it thus *our duty* to do what we can to keep them here?"

"But you're arguing a *fallacy*, Tad." Dilys had the exasperated attitude of one who'd had this discussion before. Many times. "You say that as though Tirryderch has no need of defense for itself and no obligation to contribute to Preidyn's should the call get more strident. I'm not saying any of you are wrong in protecting the citizenry—I'm saying you're only protecting us from our own government without conceding that a threat to Preidyn is a threat to Tirryderch, and you're hugging the very edge of the law by doing it. If this enlistment drive turns into a draft, you'll be breaking it."

"Unjust laws need breaking, or at least a good solid challenge. Especially ones that put undue and unfair onus on magical folk to die in wars we didn't want started in the first place. How many died in the last one? It'll take generations to replace the witches and sorcerers Tirryderch alone lost, and our mages have always been too thin on the ground." Terrwyn skimmed a quick look at Milo, as though expecting him to start doing his part to replenish Kymbrygh's stock of mages right this minute. "What good will it do our magical folk to defend a country that doesn't seem to care if we go extinct in the doing?"

"Well, it'll keep you out of prison for a start!" Dilys snapped, angry, before she pulled in a calming breath and sat back with a huff. She scrubbed at her face, shoulders slumping. "I just don't want to see the three of you end up arrested. It'd make those Gray

Party knobs too smug to bear, and then I'd have to punch them all in the face and get *myself* arrested, and where would it end?"

It burst the bubble of tension that had been building, gave everyone a good chuckle and reset the temperature to something less smothering.

Until Milo asked, quiet, "So you don't agree that sometimes one's duty ought to go beyond one's own dooryard?"

He wasn't looking at anyone, still staring down into his untouched drink, apart somehow, even with his hand still in Ellis's, and reserved like Ellis had never seen him. Waiting for an answer.

"Oh, save me," Dilys said, grin tweaking at the corners of her mouth, but eyes wide and uncertain. "You're not thinking of *enlisting*, are you?"

It seemed to startle Milo. He jerked his head up, shot a surprised frown at Dilys, and stammered out a "Wh... what?" before he huffed and finally took a drink from his glass—all of it in one go. He coughed, the burn of the whisky clearly more than he'd been expecting, so when it became evident he couldn't answer, Ellis did it for him.

"He couldn't even if he wanted to." Ellis freed up his hand and absently patted Milo's back. When Milo made a grab for Ellis's ale, Ellis handed it over and said, "Her Majesty is rather stingy with her dragonkin." He couldn't help how his lip curled a little as he said it, thinking of a cariad contract application still sitting unfinished somewhere on his desk back in Wellech; he tried to cover it with a shrug. "The Home Guard slapped him with an exemption before he'd even got through the application process, so I doubt the Royal Services would do different."

"All the better." Nia took Milo's empty glass and got up to refill it. "And it's his good luck he didn't inherit *everything* from our poor Ceri."

"*Nia!*"

It was the first word Lilibet had spoken since they'd sat down, her voice so loud and so sharp, it startled everyone. Nia nearly dropped the whisky decanter. Lilibet merely sent her a glare then a significant look at Milo, done coughing now, but bent over his knees and breathing deeply. He didn't look up.

Lilibet raised her eyebrows. "I'm sure Milo would appreciate it if you didn't speak of his mam as though—"

"I'm speaking of *my friend* as though her *duty* is well past done." Nia brought Milo's drink to him, gave him a sympathetic smile when he took it, and ran her fingers briskly through his hair before she sat down, aiming a level look at Lilibet. "Ceri answered her country's call. More than once. She did her *duty* as she saw it. And where is she now? We're all supposed to pretend we don't know she's been pulled back in, that we're not worrying about her every day, as though we're dense or just don't care. It's *rot!*" Her green eyes flashed with anger. "So you'll forgive me if I refuse to pretend I'm not pleased we won't have to one day do the same for Milo." Her shoulders sagged, and she sent Milo a soft look. "I'm sorry if I've upset you, pet."

"Ta, Nia." A murmur, once again into the whisky glass. Ellis could actually see Milo setting his teeth and making the decision to don a brave smile. "She'll be fine. She always is." He took a drink—a sip this time, though it looked to Ellis as though Milo would really like to toss this one back too.

Abruptly melancholic on Milo's behalf, Ellis slid his arm around Milo's shoulders and pulled him as close as propriety allowed. "She will be, you know." Quiet, and only for Milo. Milo's smile when he gave Ellis a glance was still a bit forlorn but grateful too.

"Preidyn cultivates her magical folk," Steffan said, husky and with a contemplative look into the fire. He shook his head, lips pursed. "She smiles when she births them, raises them up and gives them good schools to teach them, good laws to protect them. She gives them everything they need to meet their promise. To be the very best they can be." He pulled his gaze from the fire, somber, sent it to everyone in the room, one by one, before settling it on Milo. "And then, when she needs them to die for her, they do it willingly. Because she's made them believe she's a loving mother, grief-stricken but still in need of their willing sacrifice, when really she's merely a butcher, eyeing her shepherds' flocks for the—"

"Bloody—*Steffan!*" Dilys. Shocked. And livid. Apparently on Milo's behalf if the look of furious apology she was shooting him was any clue. She glared at Steffan. "Why would you even *say* something like—?"

"Because it's true, *cyw*." Nia's tone was firm. "Putting flowers on a cairn doesn't make it less a cairn."

"Could we," Milo said slowly, tone harsher than Ellis had ever heard it, "possibly *not* discuss my mam in terms of butchers and cairns?" He shot a hard look all around, set his glass down. "You have your views on duty. I understand. I don't even disagree. But I won't have you judging my mam's views of it simply because—"

Terrwyn harrumphed. "We're not judging *any*—"

"—*simply because*," Milo said, louder, "she chooses to do her duty as she believes necessary." His chin was quivering. "They're killing people like me. Like her. A ferry ride away from Preidyn, they're *killing* people."

"*Milo.*" Nia shook her head, mouth turned down in a disbelieving scowl. "You can't know what—"

"Except I *do* know. I *know*. And, apparently, at least a few of my neighbors, people I've known all my life, think it's all perfectly—"

He choked, gave his head a violent shake, then gritted his teeth. "You don't know—you don't know *why* she—" He shrugged Ellis's hand off his shoulder and stood. "You don't *know*. Maybe she thinks whatever needs doing is bigger than just her. Maybe she knows things you don't, things that convinced her she had no choice. Maybe she believes she's the only one who can do whatever it is she left to do. *You don't know*, and I'd appreciate it very sincerely if you wouldn't decide that 'our poor Ceri' is wasting her life on something *you* apparently think isn't worth it, when to her, it's clearly worth *everything!*"

He was breathing too heavily into the hush that descended on the room with a reverberating *thud*. Shaking a bit too. Clearly at a loss as to what to do now that he'd said his piece and stunned everyone around him into the breathtakingly uncomfortable silence. That was it, it seemed, all Milo had, and now...?

Ellis felt like a side character in a school play, filling up a space but ultimately useless. He didn't know what to do, when Milo plainly needed someone to do *something*.

Terrwyn was looking at the fire again, jaw set, clearly still convinced he had the right of it, but unwilling to continue pushing his point. Nia looked thoughtful, eyes on Milo, concerned though not dissuaded. Lilibet just sipped her wine, cool and unmoved and no help at all, while Steffan merely sat beside Nia, shaking his head as though disappointed in everyone. Dilys was the only one halfway useful, boring holes into Ellis's forehead and widening her eyes with a purposeful tilt of her head at Milo.

Do something.

So Ellis... did. He stood, set a hand to the small of Milo's back, and gave him a nudge. Said, "Well, then. Ta for supper. Could've done without the entertainment, though," and shot the room a grin that was nothing but bared teeth.

Lilibet rolled her eyes, mouth flat, chiding—Ellis could almost hear the exasperated *Manners, boy!* but ignored her. Kept nudging until Milo finally moved, nearly stumbling as Ellis led him from the room and pushed him up the hall. And up another hall. And... down another, and...

Ellis should say something. Offer some kind of comfort. He knew how badly Milo had been taking Ceri's absence, and Terrwyn and Nia and Steffan had done nothing just now but make it worse. And all right, Ellis could see their point—Ceri was a lifelong friend to them, they were clearly worried about her, and no one could deny she'd done more than her share. Whatever the circumstances behind her leaving, it truly wasn't fair.

He'd never say it out loud to Milo, but Ellis was just as happy that the Queen *was* stingy with her dragonkin. And, though he knew very well how hiding his Sight had always chafed at Milo, Ellis was grateful beyond sense that no one but a trusted few knew about it. It would be a difficult choice for the Queen's Council, he reckoned, deciding if it was more important to keep a rarity that was dragonkin tending to dragons, or to send another even rarer rarity that was a Dewin Seer into whatever hole Ceri had disappeared into. Except Ellis was pretty sure he knew on which side that debate would land. And he couldn't help the relief at knowing it wouldn't happen.

Selfish, yes, no question. Because he couldn't imagine the absolute agony of being the one left behind. Not if the one leaving him was Milo.

"Ehm." Milo slowed, squinting around as though he'd just woken up. He frowned. "Where are we going?"

Ellis stopped, turned to Milo, and shook his head. "I've no idea. I don't even know whose wing we're in." He looked behind them, then ahead. "I've been lost for at least six hallways now. What kind of house even *is* this? Is there no end to the thing?"

Milo stared. Blinked. "You..." He stared some more, then... snorted. Blinked again. Surprised. Seemingly at himself. The corners of his mouth were twitching. "We're... lost."

Ellis looked around again, just to be sure. He nodded. "Seems like it."

"You got us lost."

"I mean, you'd think there'd be one of those maps on at least one of the walls, yeah? Like at a railway station. With a helpful arrow and all. *You Are Here.*"

"Lost. In Ty Mynydd."

"And me with no breadcrumbs."

Milo laughed, one of those bright bursts that turned his eyes into crescent moons. It was an unexpected surge of sunlight on an overcast day, and just as quickly gone. Milo looked away. Pained.

"I'm sorry for..." He lofted a directionless wave. "I've gone and made everything awkward now, and you've only just got here."

"Pfft." Ellis snagged up Milo's hand. "Life lesson, boyo: it's only awkward if one acknowledges awkwardness. If one, however, chooses to bully one's way through it with oblivious smiles and crass commentary, it turns into entertainment." He waggled his eyebrows.

"Ah, I see." Milo's mouth turned up and his gaze went sly. "I begin to understand Wellech's obsession with its favored son."

"I should hope so." Ellis squeezed Milo's hand, pulled him closer. "Otherwise, there's more than two years' concerted effort to sway you to my charms gone wasted."

Milo's smile now was soft, though his eyes had turned... sad, maybe, and his voice was thready when he said, "Never that," and set a light kiss to Ellis's mouth.

There was something there, something just beneath Milo's surface that Ellis couldn't quite get hold of. As though the mess with that Cennydd git had punched a hole in Milo's spirit rather than his back, and the physical healing hadn't taken hold on the emotional end. And Milo was trying so hard to patch it every five seconds Ellis didn't have the heart to call him on it.

He'd wait. He'd give Milo the space he needed, and wait. It would come, eventually, like it had at Ellis's birthday party. Because Milo was absolute crap at understanding his own depths, and even more crap at hiding them once he found them. But he was very good at turning to Ellis when the smolder turned to a blaze, so Ellis would just make sure to be there when whatever this was finally dawned on Milo and burst from him like dragonfire.

Milo pulled back and set his hand to Ellis's sternum. "You understand. About duty. You understand." His eyes were so solemn, misted and overbright, tiny chips of green and hazel fracturing through the blue like metal in water.

Ellis frowned, not quite following the turn, but said, "Of course," because duty, at least, he knew. "I bloody live it, Milo. You never have to explain something like that to me."

Milo smiled, small and pressed-lipped, but it was a smile. "You're too good to me."

"I really am."

It made Milo grin, startled. "So I can rely on you to be thoroughly though hilariously offensive for me the next time I enter a room and everyone stops talking to stare uncomfortably into their cups?"

"It's like you've never met me."

Ellis grinned when Milo laughed out loud. It was real, too—open and surprised, and it made Ellis wrap his arm around Milo's neck and drag him in.

"There'll be apologies all 'round at breakfast tomorrow, and then everyone will pretend nothing happened." He set a kiss to Milo's forehead. "Stop worrying."

"Oh, no." Milo's eyebrows went up, and his smile took on a crafty glint. "I've plans for you for breakfast."

Ellis's brain immediately took a trip south. "*That's* what I like to hear."

"Not that sort of plans." Milo shook his head and pulled away, not even a little bit apologetic. "Though it does still require you to be up early."

"If it's not in the fun way, I don't see—"

"You will."

Ellis narrowed his eyes. "Is this the surprise Dilys was talking about?"

Milo huffed, exasperated. "I swear that girl could only keep a secret if she were dead. And even then she'd find a way to snitch." Milo took Ellis's hand and turned them both around to start back down the hallway. "I'm not telling." He gave Ellis a sideways glance that was nothing but suggestive challenge. "Though that doesn't mean you can't use those charms you're so smug about to try to pry it out of me."

"Great goddesses." Ellis grinned and started walking faster until he was the one tugging Milo. "Figure out where we are quick, or I'm going to just pick a room, and we'll end up shocking one of Dilys's multitude of cousins."

Milo laughed, squeezed Ellis's hand, and lengthened his stride. "Follow me."

"Anywhere," Ellis said, and let Milo lead him.

Chapter 13—Motive

: *a small musical fragment used to build a larger musical idea*

Ellis eyed the ladder with a grim frown, peered up farther and glared at the loft beyond. Rain pounded against the roof, almost drowning out the occasional protest of a sleepy cow. A flash of lightning temporarily illuminated the whole of the loft, bales and pitchforks and hay hooks all strobing stark blue-white against the mounds of hay strewn over the length of it. Thunder clapped, loud and violent, making him wince then roll his eyes.

He sighed. "This is *your* fault," he said over his shoulder as he took the first ascending step to what was to be, regrettably, his bed for the evening.

"I know," was all Milo said.

"That woman—what was her name?"

"Rhywun Catrin."

"Rhywun Catrin was all ready to let us stay the night in her parlor." Ellis tossed his pack up into the hay then swung into the loft, careful not to stand straight and whack his head on the low slant of the roof or the even lower slant of the rafters. He squinted past the shadows cast by Milo's magelight. Another clap of thunder pounded so close Ellis could almost feel it echo in his chest. "A little less awkward hemming—"

"I was *not* being awkward!"

"—and we could be sleeping somewhere dry—"

"This *is* dry."

"—*and* might have even managed a hot supper."

Milo's pack came bouncing up into the hay, just before his dark head crested the top of the ladder. "I *told* you, I brought supper."

Ellis peered pointedly around the loft, trying very hard not to snort, and lifted an eyebrow as another great roar of thunder blatted above their heads. "Are you going to cook it?"

No answer but a roll of the eyes from Milo as he slid that *stupid* gigantic bloody hamper he'd been toting the whole way—*and* had kept closed and latched, and wouldn't let Ellis get a look into—to the floor of the loft and hoisted himself up fully after it.

"A little bit of charm, that's all I'm saying." Ellis plopped down into the hay, flipped his pack over and began unlacing his bedroll from its ties. "You can do it, I know you can, I've seen you. You've charmed me right out of my—"

"Gah, Elly, not now." Milo ran a hand through his damp hair, clearly frustrated. Strangely angry.

Still behaving oddly and pretending he wasn't, and Ellis was still waiting semipatiently to find out why. And trying, in the meantime, to at least jolly him out of it.

Ellis waggled his eyebrows. "A bit of a smile here, a quick touch to the arm there, an unspoken promise I'd have no choice but to prevent you from keeping, and we'd be inside that *warm* kitchen, probably even now scoffing stew or whatever that heavenly smell was coming from Rhywun Catrin's stove."

Milo sighed. "You're right. I'm sorry."

...So, that wasn't really what Ellis had been going for. The mood had been coming and going with no pattern Ellis could find, and he was no longer sure it stemmed from what happened in Whitpool last month. Something at the coven last week, maybe? That disconcerting discussion in Nia's study last night?

Whatever it was, it was clearly weighing on Milo at odd moments, and Milo wasn't talking. Yet.

Ellis had thought maybe that was the point of this walking-trip-turned-comic-tragedy. Except Milo didn't seem to think any of it the least bit funny.

Face closed, head down, Milo shook out his bedroll with a firm *snap* then spread it out over the space between them. "Anyway, Rhywun Catrin happens to be Rosa Evans dy Critchett's mam, in case the name didn't dawn on you. If I'd tried this charm you seem to think I possess, and it by some stretch of the imagination actually worked, the contract offers would never stop."

"Stone me, *that's* who that is?" Ellis laughed out loud. "I take it back. No charm. Ever."

Rosa Evans dy Critchett had been sending conjugal contract offers to Old Forge since Lilibet's party two years back. The arrival of a new one every six months like clockwork made Milo squirm so badly he'd asked his solicitor to not even notify him anymore, just politely refuse them.

"We've never even *met!*" Milo'd told Ellis, mystified, the second time it happened. "For all she knows I'm hunch-backed and full of the pox!"

Ellis had laughed and laughed and laughed.

"Rosa Evans dy Critchett." Ellis shook his head, unable to hide a chuckle. "Only you, Milo. Of all the places in all of Kymbrygh, and you end up in the one—"

"What was I supposed to do, build a house?"

"Nooo," Ellis replied, teasing, "because that would be absurd, while stopping here has to be the most inspired—"

"Well, *someone* had a massive huff when I suggested we might find a bit of shelter in the lee of the cliffs farther uphill. And this is the last farmstead I know of until we get to... where we're going."

Ellis ignored that last bit—he'd tried everything he could think of all day long, but Milo refused to tell him exactly where they were heading, only insisted that Ellis would be rewarded for his patience when they got there. Ellis couldn't remember ever having been rewarded for patience—mostly because he possessed very little of it—but hadn't had much of a choice: when he wanted to be, Milo was as enigmatic as Ellis was impatient.

"I did *not* have a *huff*," Ellis protested. "I only said that if there was standing water on the floors of those cliffs, I was going to throw you off them."

"You're right." Milo dug into the hamper and emerged with a bottle of wine. "Murderous intent is much more respectable than a huff. I stand corrected." He gave Ellis a grin that was... off, too distracted around the eyes, then flumped to his bedroll, propped his back against the rough wood of one of the rafters, and set about working at the cork.

Ellis frowned.

There was an ease between them, always had been. It had perhaps been on holiday during the years they'd been apart, but had slotted right back into place as they lay on the rug in Ellis's rooms and watched a sea made of fire roll across the hearth. It was... maybe not entirely missing now, but strained, as though Milo had to try too hard to catch it.

Something at the coven, Ellis decided, or what happened at Old Forge. One or the other, had to be. Ellis was going to lay his money on the attack. And if he happened to win that bet, no blame to Milo. The incident with Cennydd had been shocking and awful, and no doubt shook Milo at a fundamental level.

Ellis *knew* he shouldn't have left Whitpool so soon.

The label on the wine bottle, when he caught sight of it, immediately distracted him.

"You brought La Belle Blanc? On a walking trip?"

A rather expensive import for enjoying in someone's barn.

Milo grimaced as he twisted at the cork. "It was to be a... Well, I thought... I was *trying* to..." He paused as the cork slipped free then he shrugged, muttered something that sounded like "special" then took a long swig from the bottle.

"Special?" Ellis grinned, anticipatory.

All right, Ellis's birthday was months away yet, and Milo's was after that, so Ellis hadn't missed one of those. Highwinter was ages away, and there were no gift-giving occasions Ellis could think of between. And they'd never really celebrated their sort-of-contract, considering its official unofficialness. With the secrecy, that ridiculous hamper, the wine, Milo's very clear displeasure that none of this was going how he planned...

"Special how?"

Milo ignored the question, only handed the bottle over to Ellis, said, "I forgot cups," then leaned back and glared at the low-slung ceiling.

It rather thumped Ellis's anticipation. And his mood in general.

He peered over at Milo, still staring at the rough slope of the ceiling, his profile carved in blue from the magelight and illuminated occasionally when periodic flickers of lightning burst across the sky. Ellis took another swig from the bottle, leaned across and tapped at Milo's elbow with the mouth of it; Milo took it without looking, necked it and drank more deeply than Ellis knew was his wont. Milo usually made it a point to savor good wine.

Confused, getting a bit broody himself, Ellis stuffed his pack and his bedroll up against the nearest bale, slumped down and closed his eyes. If nothing else, the sound of the storm would lull him to sleep, and if it passed the way Ellis suspected it was going to, they could get the bloody blazes out of here before anyone came in to start milking in the morning.

"Are you hungry?" Milo asked, quiet.

"Mm," was all Ellis replied.

Maybe it was bit too terse, a bit too hostile, because everything went silent. For quite a while. Until:

"Elly?"

Milo's low voice was accompanied by the nudge of his foot into Ellis's shin. Ellis dragged his leg away.

"No."

"But—"

"*No.*" Ellis drew his knees up, well away from any further advances, just in case Milo didn't get the point.

"But you *always* want... you know."

Ellis opened his eyes, rolled them. "It's called sex, Milo. You *are* allowed to say it out loud in front of cows, you know, I doubt you'll shock them."

"Fine. You always want *sex*, so what—"

"I do *not* always want sex!"

A pause—Ellis could almost hear Milo's eyes crossing. "All right, perhaps you don't want sex right after you've *had* sex, but otherwise—"

"I'm *tired*. I've been up since before dawn, and I'm—"

"And whose fault is that?"

"It comes from decades of living on a farm. We don't all get to sleep 'til midday if we want."

"*Who* sleeps 'til midday? An hour or two after sunrise is *not* midday."

"Well, you've been dragging me halfway across Tirryderch since even before lunch—"

"Godwick Vale! Not even a day's march!"

"—in a bloody *gale*—"

"A *thunderstorm*, for pity's sake!"

"—and I said, I *said* it was going to rain, I *told* you—"

"Six *thousand* times."

"—and now I'm *tired* and not at all in the mood to go rolling about in all this bleeding, scratchy *hay*, when all I can smell is cow and dung!"

"You live on a *farm*, for pity's sake!"

"Right." Ellis sat up to give Milo a flat look. "And I always make it a *point* to sleep with the cows. You know—except for the bit where I don't." He snagged the bottle, took a long, slow gulp before shoving it back into Milo's hands. Then he turned, punched at his pack a couple of times and flopped his head to it. "And it's more than just a *farm*."

"*You* said farm."

Ellis thought back... All right, so he had. But still. "Well, it's more."

"I know."

"The Croft, you know."

"Yes, I've heard of the place."

Ellis sat up again, scowled at Milo. "Lots of people depend on me, you know, it's not just a *farm*. Acres and acres, as well as the whole of Wellech, *and* the Wardens, and I—"

"You work very hard, yes, I know."

Ellis narrowed his eyes. "Helping or hurting, Milo?"

"I was *agreeing* with—" Milo scrubbed at his face, blew out a long breath. "Right." He peered about himself with a dubious slant of his gaze. "I'm sorry. I really am. This hasn't turned out at all like what I'd thought."

Well, Ellis would have to be a complete dolt not to know that. He deflated.

This wasn't them. They didn't do this sort of sniping and bickering. And Ellis still didn't understand it. Any of it. Milo had *planned*... well, something, anyway, and even if it still irked Ellis a little that Milo wouldn't tell him what the plan had been, the fact that he *had* planned something was really quite touching. Despite the disconcerting feeling that Milo had thrown some kind of barrier up between them that Ellis couldn't puzzle out, the realization of that fact alone served to soften Ellis's mood considerably.

"I know, Milo. It's not... Well, I don't *know*, but, Milo." He huffed.

"I wish you'd just tell me. Whatever this is, whatever's had you all arse-about-face, you *can* just say it. You know that, right?"

Milo looked away. "I'm bodging this so badly." Quiet. Defeated.

"Bodging *what*, though?" Ellis scrubbed at his face. "No, never mind, keep your secret. But whatever's bothering you, Milo, whatever's got you all…" Ellis flailed a wave at Milo's current lack of Miloness. "Whatever's got you not yourself, just *say* it, yeah? It'll be like popping a blister."

It made Milo's mouth quirk. "That's… kind of disgusting."

"Though helpful."

"Is it?" Milo looked away for a moment, contemplative, before he straightened his spine, and gave Ellis a smile that was almost right. "Hopefully it will all come clear in the morning. *Without* the pus." He peered again at the ceiling. "If this lets up, anyway." He took another drink of wine then held the bottle out to Ellis. "Hold this. I imagine you must be starving."

Considering the fact that Milo had almost literally shoved him out of Ty Mynydd this morning with a couple of pasties in hand for breakfast, and hadn't thought to pack more than a few apples, some leftover rolls and a sack of walnuts for lunch, yes, Ellis *was* starving.

"I don't suppose it makes sense to save this until we get there." Milo unlatched the lid of the enormous hamper (*stupid*, enormous hamper, Ellis's petulant side insisted) and set about digging supper from it. In light of what began steadily emerging from it, Ellis didn't pursue the subject of where "there" was this time, only took a nip from the bottle and watched.

A plate of cold beef, perfectly pink in the center, appeared from within several layers of cheesecloth, along with a large loaf of crusty brown bread. Sliced ham came next, followed by baby asparagus, freshness confirmed when Milo jammed a stalk in his mouth and crunched it down as he continued to pull what Ellis had to admit appeared to be a rather significant supper from the hamper that was looking less and less stupid as each dish emerged. Just-off-the-vine snap-peas joined the asparagus, along with three early cucumbers. A great slab of lemon cake had survived with minimal squashing; Milo set it down next to a few apple squares Ellis remembered from supper last night.

"I appear to have forgot silver, as well," Milo said, head nearly submerged in the depths of the hamper as he hunted about for something to use as utensils. In the end, he only shrugged, dug out his pocketknife, and began slicing up the bread. "No plates, no cups, no silver. I reckon it wouldn't've been entirely perfect after all." The knife was too small—he was smooshing more than cutting. Milo growled, tossed the knife down next to the plate of beef and simply tore the loaf in half. He thrust a hunk at Ellis.

Ellis took it, gulping more wine before handing the bottle back to Milo.

"Keep it." Milo dipped back into the basket and came up with another. "If I get you drunk enough, maybe you'll forget where you are and who's responsible for dragging you there."

Ellis almost said, *I doubt it*, but... well, Milo was... Ellis sighed. Milo was Milo and almost impossible to stay annoyed with. Ellis only took another swig from the bottle, slapped a slab of beef and one of ham on top of the hunk of bread and took a bite. He leaned back, stretched his legs out and snugged his shoulders more firmly into pack, blanket, and hay. He reckoned it wasn't *that* uncomfortable.

Anyway, it was first-rate wine.

⁕

Good food, both bottles of wine, and some excellent distraction later, "See?" Milo mumbled into Ellis's ear. "You *do* always want sex."

If Ellis could have moved, he would have thumped him.

⁕

"Well." Milo shrugged, eyeing Ellis with a weirdly timid set to his gaze. He swept his arm out in front of him with a small smile. "This is it."

Ellis stepped up beside Milo onto the rocky outcrop, and directed his gaze below. And made a concerted effort not to frown. *This is what?* was on the tip of his tongue, but he held it back.

Milo had woken with a headache—no real surprise, because wine—full of apologies for the day before, but grinning wide any time the night before came up. Ellis's propensity for waking before dawn worked in their favor this time, as they were able to get their gear together and be gone from the barn before anyone came to tend the cows.

Still, even with their good luck, the clear skies this morning, and the memory of last night, Milo was even more pensive today. If Ellis didn't know better, he'd think Milo was silently panicking. Having second thoughts about having planned... whatever it was, maybe, nervous about how Ellis would react when he finally found out what it was; Ellis didn't know, but he'd resolved that, whatever it turned out to be, he was going to react with smiles and enthusiasm.

Except, now that they were here and he was actually being presented with whatever it was, he *still* had no idea what it was. Now *Ellis* was starting to panic a little. He peered about, looking for some kind of sign that would tell him exactly what he was supposed to be seeing.

They were just outside of Godwick Vale. Once they'd left the barn and got back on the road, Ellis found himself assessing the lay of the land out of habit and had grown more dubious despite himself, because there was nothing out here. The current view didn't disabuse him of that notion.

It was nice enough, rolling green and rocky hillside almost as far as the eye could see, a great swath of tall grass. Wildflowers dotted the landscape, spring blossoms still laden with the morning dew, swaying indolent and ponderous in the soft, warm breeze. The sky was gorgeous this morning, indigo-amethyst shot through with traces of crimson, and still heavy, like it was dipping down to touch the skin of the world.

Ellis's smile was sincere when he turned it on Milo. He breathed in deeply, thankful there wasn't a cow to be found amidst the clean scent of morning.

"Very pretty."

Milo peered at him sideways, a rueful smirk curling up one corner of his mouth beneath his beard. "It's mine."

Ellis blinked. "Yours."

"I've been wanting it for some time now, but Steffan, with Terrwyn's rather reluctant backing, only just yesterday agreed to sell it to me."

Ellis looked again, his frown deepening. "But..." He shook his head, bit his lip. He really didn't want to ruin whatever this was for Milo—investment, maybe?—but, "Milo, there's nothing *here*." He turned around, eyeing the landscape in every direction. "There's no water inlet, and with all this rock, I don't think you'd be able to get a well dug. The only thing you *might* use it for is grazing for livestock, but it's too far away from any farmsteads to lease it out for that. This is the middle of nowhere!"

"You sound just like Steffan." Milo's smirk turned to something softer, lighter. "And Nia, actually, when Steffan told her what I was haranguing him about."

"Well, I should hope so!" Ellis was edging near outrage. "What were they *thinking* selling this to you? You can't *do* anything with it, and you'll never be able to sell it again. What did you pay for this?"

"Far less than what it's worth to me." Milo leaned in, smiling, and planted a firm kiss to Ellis's mouth.

All right, now Ellis was *really* confused. "Milo—"

"I paid exactly 2p for the land because they wouldn't take anything more. They finally agreed to sell it to me because Steffan's too soft for his own good, and at least Terrwyn grew weary of telling me how worthless it is. I was, apparently, quite annoying." Milo grinned, waggish and proud. "He finally ended up bunging a berry tart at me at breakfast the other day and told Steffan I was old enough to choose how I threw away my own money." He shrugged, still smiling but more thoughtful now as he looked out over the land. "I don't care about water rights or wells or leasing or livestock, because I don't intend to *do* anything with it, and I don't intend to sell it, either. This wasn't an investment. I just... I wanted it. And once I had it, I wanted you to see it."

Ellis couldn't help it this time. "*Why?*"

Milo ducked his head, a light flush creeping up his high-boned cheeks. "Because when I saw this place, it was at sunset. It's much prettier at sunset, you understand. I'd meant for us to arrive just before, but you know—the rain." He sighed. "Anyway, Dillie brought me out here last autumn. That camping trip for the boys—you got held up in Wellech sorting that boat full of refugees and couldn't make it, remember?" When Ellis nodded, still frowning, Milo grinned. "Noisy little creadurs, those two, bloody *endless* questions and just *not listening* about running ahead or shoving each other off boulders, and I just needed a moment, you know?"

"So I climbed up to this very spot, right here on this bit of a cliff, and looked out over it and... well, the first thing I thought of was how"—Milo's voice dipped down low, and his cheeks brightened—"how I wished you were here with me." A deep, long breath, like he was looking for courage; Milo looked Ellis in the eye. "At that moment, I wanted nothing more than to kiss you, right here on this spot." His gaze slipped down to his feet and he shoved his hands into his pockets. "And once I had the land, I wanted... well, I wanted to..." Milo rocked on his heels, kicked a small stone and sent it clacking down over the cliff. "Anyway, things didn't really go to plan, did they?"

Ellis's jaw had come unhinged about three halting sentences back. The trip and the hamper and the wine and the odd secretive mood. The truth of what Milo was saying without saying it burst in Ellis's head like a firecracker.

Milo must have misinterpreted Ellis's no doubt gobsmacked expression, because he rolled his eyes and chuffed a growling sigh. "I know, all right? I'm sorry, it was... I mean, I didn't—"

"*No.*" Ellis took a small step closer. "Don't... don't take it back."

"I'm not. I couldn't if I wanted to. Elly. *Bloody*—" Milo stepped in so fast it startled Ellis, though there was no time to react before Milo's arms were strapped around Ellis's ribs, and Milo's face was tucked into Ellis's neck, and Milo's breath was bleeding warm down Ellis's collar as he said, "Elly. *Elly.* I've so much I need to tell you, and I'm just... I'm not brave enough. I can't stand the thought of you not knowing, of you not understanding why I... and yet I can't just *say*—" He squeezed tighter. "I *miss* you. You know that, right? Every second we're not together, I *miss* you, and I'll never stop, not ever. Duty or no, you have to know that. Never doubt it, no matter what."

"What—?" Ellis held Milo tight. "I do. Of course I—"

"You have to *know* it, Elly. Always. All right?" Urgent. Quavering.

"Yeah." Ellis squeezed harder. "Yeah, Milo. Me too. Always."

And it was odd, and it was strangely dramatic, out here on this peaceful spot of worthless land that had just been made priceless, but it was also… all right. The blister had well and truly burst, and Ellis didn't need to understand everything that poured out of it. Everything was going to be all right.

The gesture itself was profoundly touching, but the relief at being the subject of it, at Milo's clear sincerity in offering it, was beyond precious.

Ellis had learned a lot of things about Milo over the years—some things more slowly than others—but one of the more recent things he'd understood was that, of all the many things of which Milo was capable and at which he was skilled, romance was not one of them. Not in the sentimental, heart-on-the-sleeve sense of the word, at any rate. He wasn't opposed to the idea of it, but had never seemed terribly interested in mastering the practice. Milo couldn't say the sorts of things people said to each other in penny romances; his tongue would tangle and his cheeks would flame. Milo thought it made him a coward, not brave. Ellis thought otherwise.

Because Milo *did* say those things, only not in words. He said them by dragging a gigantic hamper halfway across Tirryderch. By buying a useless parcel of land because he thought it looked beautiful at sunset. By letting Ellis get annoyed with him, complain all the way here, because Milo had once thought it would be nice to kiss him here.

Ellis's eyes were stinging and his chest was hurting from lack of air. "I may have, ehm…" He pulled back, had to blink several times, then swallow until his throat didn't feel so tight. "I think I've come over a bit sentimental." He gripped Milo's arms. There were so many things he could say, so many things he *wanted* to say, but only one seemed like it fit: "D'you want to wait 'til sunset? Because I'm not sure I can go the whole day without kissing you until I make you understand how breathtaking you are."

Milo's eyes were overbright, gaze churning with emotion, searching. Whatever he was looking for, he must have found it, because he gave Ellis a wobbly smile, small and poignant.

He leaned in, scrutinized Ellis like he could see right through to his soul, then… well, pretty much snogged the life out of him.

Chapter 14—Modulation

: *the process of changing from one musical key to another*

"Petra." Ellis frowned down at the map spread across two hay bales in the main barn he used as a field office on the western edge of the Croft's boundary. Fingertip planted to the basin where the Afon Wisgi fed into the Aled, he slanted a narrow look up at Petra, took in her resigned expression, and knew the answer before he asked, "Why are the Ffrwythlon fields still marked for drainage?"

Petra pursed her lips. "Because they need draining?" Clearly noting Ellis's glare, she held up her hands. "Look, you can't keep Folant's boyos on as managers and expect them to listen to me over him. They won't—"

"I *expect* my second to speak for me while I'm not here to do it. If you can't manage a couple of obstinate—"

"I can manage *them* just fine. What I *can't* manage is *your tad* sliding in behind me and changing orders on *your* supposed say-so."

Petra's round face had gone the color of new brick and her voice had risen with each syllable. Tall and dark and broad as an oak, silt-brown hair wild as a crown of leaves, she was whip-smart and sweet-natured unless you got her riled, and then she turned mean. Which was why Ellis had hired her three years ago as farm manager for the Croft, and why he'd since made her his second in Pennaeth matters when he wasn't around. But if she couldn't be counted on to help Ellis keep Folant in line...

Ellis clenched his jaw, took in a long, deep breath. "So what you're telling me is the Ffrwythlon fields still need draining because the mole subsoiling never got done."

"Because Folant—"

"*Yes*, Petra, because we've established countless times already that Folant thinks he can ignore orders from the bloody Queen herself, let alone you and me, which is why it's our job to make sure he doesn't!" Furious, Ellis swept the map off the bales, though it wasn't terribly satisfying—no startling crash, nothing broken. "We can't—"

"No, *you* can't. *Your* job." Petra wasn't shouting anymore, but her tone was just as effective. She shook her head, stern though not entirely unkind. "I ken the pressure you're under, Ellis. I ken how hard it is to do what you do to keep Wellech running—sometimes doing it three or four times because your tad's gone and undone it as soon as you walked away." She sighed, weary. "But I'm not you. I'm not Pennaeth in all but name. He is. He's *Pennaeth*, Ellis. And when your Pennaeth tells you to just ignore what 'my upstart know-it-all sprog' told you to do, you do it." She waved out the barn door. "Or at least they do. And when Folant's 'upstart-know-it-all sprog' is off again on one of his trips…"

She let it hang there, not *quite* condemning because Petra never balked at taking over when Ellis wasn't in Wellech or out on patrol with the Wardens. But she *did* balk at being held accountable for limitations that weren't her own.

Ellis set his teeth and looked away. She wasn't wrong. Which really didn't help.

"Have they finished planting, at least?"

Petra crossed her thick arms over her chest. "The fields have been leased to Baughan from the weir side."

Baughan raised sheep. A lot of sheep.

Ellis shut his eyes. His fists clenched. So did his jaw.

Nia hadn't been wrong when she'd pointed out that Tirryderch was the granary for the Preidynīg Isles. The problem was, over the past fifteen years or so, that had come to include Wellech as well. Once equally productive, a good chunk of Wellech's yield followed its magical folk to less oppressive parishes, and now Wellech received most of their grains from Tirryderch like the rest of the country. One of the few smart things Folant had done in the past two decades—or ever, as far as Ellis knew—was to change gears and focus on mining and, more importantly, raising livestock instead. It kept Wellech prosperous and competitive. It also limited the available growing spaces for food crops, since mine works and livestock were taking up a great deal of the useable fields.

Which wouldn't be a problem, had the order not come down from Parliament's Agricultural Executive Committee that Wellech, among other parishes across the Isles, was to increase its yield of barley, wheat, and three kinds of beans by nearly sixty percent by Reaping, and it was under no circumstances to decrease its ore output. The boffins on the Committee, of course, had lots of advice on how to accomplish all that, but none of it based on applied experience or even reality. Ostensibly, the increased yield was meant as benevolent relief for those countries in Central Màstira under siege, and others accepting refugees; practically, it was all but confirmation that war was inevitable. Because Preidyn would need to feed its troops somehow, and one couldn't ship livestock to a battlefield.

All of which meant Wellech needed to convert grazing fields to growing fields. They also needed better drainage systems to deep-cultivate the heavy lands where water sat atop a layer of clay beneath the wild grasses. The subsoiling for those particular fields had been started when Ellis left for Whitpool at the end of Sowing—it should have been well underway while he'd been busy praying Milo didn't die, and completed when Howell shipped the moles and brackets two weeks ago. The plowing and planting were to have been done right after. And now there were apparently flocks of sheep grazing the acres and acres where barley should already be growing.

"Well, there's lovely, yeah?" Ellis sucked in a calming breath. "Right, then." He straightened and turned to Petra. "I want the sheep moved across the river to Corstir."

"But..." Petra frowned. "The Corstir fields are more bog than not."

"Then Baughan will just have to make sure his herders are worth their contracts, won't he?" Ellis cut off Petra's inevitable protests. "Lambing's done, and there's plenty of grazing, as long as someone's watching and pulling the odd laggard out of the mud now and then. We'll reduce the terms by ten percent for the trouble, but I didn't sign that lease, which makes it not worth the paper it was forged on, and Baughan bloody well knew it. If he doesn't fancy getting spanked in front of the council, he'll move his bloody flocks, keep his lip pinned, and never cross me again.

"Now." Ellis bent and retrieved the map, spreading it back over the bales. "Draining now will cost us enough time we'll never get a second harvest out of Ffrwythlon. But if we plant beans instead of barley..." He trailed off, tracing the available spaces on the map and collating the information with the land characteristics in his head. He tapped at the southern end of Wellech. "I wanted to rest the Hollywell fields until next Sowing, but I've little choice now if we're going to make the quota. Get them planting barley in those fields, and we'll use the Ffrwythlon space for beans—they'll do well enough in the clay soil, and the tile drainage system that's already there will keep everything just dry enough."

Petra tilted her head, eyebrows raised. "Unless we get a wet season."

"In which case, I've got two Dewin mages from the last batch of refugees who said they're willing if I need them. I've already been holding Nia off about scooping them up for Tirryderch, and they've family here in Wellech—they're looking for a reason to stay."

"Folant's not going to like that." Petra didn't look like she disapproved, though—she looked like she was hoping it became necessary. And that she had a good view of the inevitable clash when it did.

"Folant," said Ellis, rolling up the map and trying to keep his jaw from tightening again, "is not going to like a lot of things that are coming his way. And sooner than he'd like."

Petra's eyebrows shot up. "Are you—?"

"It's come to the point, finally, yeah?"

"And not through anyone's doing but his own."

Ellis had to admit it at once warmed him and broke his heart a little. It wasn't as though what he intended to do was something he actually wanted. He'd never wanted it. Except he'd somehow always known it was unavoidable.

He should talk to all the farm managers. The union heads. The growers and the miners and the tenants and the crofters and the inspectors and the livestock handlers.

He should talk to his mam.

...To Folant.

He wasn't going to.

He huffed a heavy breath. "The council has their regular a week from tomorrow. I'll file the request to add me to their agenda." When Petra didn't object, didn't lose her small smile, Ellis merely pursed his mouth and tapped the map against his palm. "It's gone beyond a nuisance and slid right into a serious problem. If you hadn't shown me this when you did, it would've been too late. I can't have the whole of Wellech paying for the spanners he keeps throwing into the works, and if we don't make these new quotas, the agro-boffins will tax us to death." Ellis wanted to look away, but he kept his gaze even and his chin up. "I've been left little choice, yeah?"

Not necessarily asking for reassurance, but... yes, wanting it anyway.

Petra kindly obliged.

※

His tad found him, unfortunately alone, at the back of the Grange's common room two days later. Bumble and Bella—Lilibet's herding dogs, who truthfully were more Ellis's tagalongs and only deigned to occasionally check in on Lilibet's goats—stood to happy attention when they spied Folant. Bullish as ever, he swaggered through the sparse crowd, most of whom were preoccupied with sampling the elderflower ale brewed for the upcoming Dydd Duwies festival. There were plenty, though, who paused to greet and glad-hand as Folant made his way by.

It was easy to mark the exact moment Ellis was spotted—Folant's eyes went narrow, and his politician's smile turned to a sour grimace. Ellis merely tipped his jar in sardonic salute, sighed out a resigned "Here we go" under his breath, and told the dogs to sit and stay while he subtly adjusted his sprawl from "relaxed" to "bored with a touch of arrogance." It never paid to give Folant an insecurity to snag hold of.

Bumble and Bella sat waiting at the entrance to the snug, chests out, tails lazily sweeping the floor behind them while they watched Folant fill a jar from the keg and saunter his way over. He didn't look at Ellis, instead greeting the dogs and giving each a friendly scritch to the ears before he joggled the chair across from Ellis; Ellis slowly removed his feet from the chair, sent the dogs a hissed *chh-chh*, and kept his eyes on Folant as Bumble and Bella settled once again by Ellis's side.

Folant didn't even take a sip from his jar before he leaned his elbows on the table and got right to it: "Baughan came to see me."

Ellis snorted. "I'm sure he did."

"So did Taffy."

It didn't surprise Ellis, but it did make him have to concentrate so he didn't clench his jaw. Taffy Leyshon served on the council. Ellis was pretty sure she was also a member of the Purity Party.

"And what did Taffy want your help with?" Ellis lifted his jar. "Some immigrants need threatening? A contract needs forging?" He took a slow sip.

Folant rolled his eyes. "For pity's sake, boy, I thought we were putting all this bad blood behind us. 'Sort our relationship,' you said."

"We were. Or I was, at least." Ellis shrugged. "Turns out, though, that if we did put bad blood behind us, we'd have nothing to base a relationship on at all." He leaned in, mirroring Folant's pose, elbows on the table and drink between his hands. "You don't want sorting. You want me blind and docile while you keep chasing a battle my mam refused to fight years ago. You want—"

"Your mam used me for—"

"Of *course* she bloody did! That's what conjugal contracts are *for*!" Ellis sat back and threw out his hands, so bloody *tired* of having this same conversation and never getting a different result. "And because she didn't fall in love with you *or* your cock, you've been obsessed with trying to punish her ever since. Except you're *not*. Nothing you've tried has worked—*none* of it. Her school still stands, her students are still exempt from your crap regulations, and she still. Doesn't. *Want you!*"

He'd got louder. By the time he was done, he was shouting, and it was plain everyone in the place had heard at least some of it. Most merely raised their eyebrows and attended their drinks; some stared until Ellis shot his glance their way, and then they pretended they hadn't been caught gaping; one man, a stranger, met Ellis's gaze with a blatantly interested one of his own. Ellis knew just about everyone in Wellech, but not this man. Average looks, average build, clothes not expensive but not cheap. Unremarkable but for the thick white scar down one cheek.

One of the newest refugees, maybe, in which case, it was a little embarrassing to have him hearing something like this, but... probably for the best, in the end.

Ellis dismissed him. He had enough to deal with.

Folant didn't even bother to turn when everything went quieter. He peered at Ellis with his usual bravado curling his lip, but there was something else there, too, something Ellis didn't quite ken. Disappointment, maybe, but Ellis was used to that from his tad. Something that looked like melancholy, but Ellis had never seen anything like that on Folant before, so he wasn't sure he was reading it right.

With a soft, grim chuckle, Folant looked down into his ale, swirled it against the sides of the jar, before he set it carefully down and folded his hands. "I can't believe you've made it all these years, in a place where everyone knows everyone else's business, and you still don't know what your mam really did. What it means."

It was all Ellis could do to just sit there and not flip the table like an irate drunk. "Tad..." Ellis sighed, already exhausted. "Bloody—" He set his jaw. "You've no idea how very much I *do not* want to have this conversation with you again. She offered you a contract. You signed it. You have no right—"

"She never wanted a cariad." Folant jabbed a finger at the table with every syllable, apparently determined to dig up the bones of this long-dead corpse and reanimate it once again. "It was her right, I've never argued otherwise."

Ellis willfully swallowed the disbelieving snort, but he couldn't just let that one pass by unchallenged. "Everything you've done since I was old enough to wonder why you two hate each other says otherwise."

"Oh, I don't think she hates me." Folant huffed a dry laugh. "I don't think I've ever warranted anything better than indifference as far as she's concerned."

That was... probably true, actually. "Fine, so you hate her. Can we move on now?"

"I thought I could've loved her, once." Folant peered at Ellis, calculating. "And then I found out what she'd done. Why she offered that contract."

It was that calculation that made Ellis hesitate. Because he was pretty sure that, whatever Folant said next, it wasn't going to be a half truth to gain Ellis's sympathy, or a flat lie to try to turn him against his mam. Ellis'd had plenty of experience with both, and he knew what they looked like. This was different. This was Folant offering a truth, or at least truth as he saw it. Those were sometimes harder to hear. The venom that habitually came out of Folant's mouth was one thing, but to be forced to admit he actually *believed* the vitriol...

Ellis took a drink from his jar. "All right, then." He sat back, giving Bella room to lay her head on his lap. He obligingly stroked her ears, and tipped his head at Folant. "She offered a contract because she wanted a child without a cariad to go with it. Why is that a bad thing?"

"Oh, no." Folant shook his head, one corner of his mouth turning up. He looked like a spider that had just had its web jostled by something big and juicy. "She didn't want a child, boyo. She wanted *you*."

"...All right?" Ellis blinked. "Last I checked, I *am*, indeed, her child, so if that's—"

"She *Dreamed*." Folant said it with a weird vehemence. "She holed herself up in that great pile of hers with a list of men who could give her what she wanted, and Dreamed for *weeks*. Watched children she'd never birth grow up, live their lives, and die, one after another. Watched herself raising them, caring for them, loving them, then woke and started it all again. Like they were nothing. Moving on to another contract, another Dream, as though each time she moved on she wasn't killing some child who'd never even have a chance to be conceived."

"That's..." Ellis shook his head. "Stone me, Tad, that's... *really* not how it works."

"It's what happened."

"It isn't, because it's bloody impossible. That's not how Dreaming even *works*!"

"It's what *happened*!"

"For the love of—" Ellis wasn't sure if he was amused or horrified. He was definitely scunnered. "Even if it did work that way—which it *doesn't*—what of it? You might as well say every woman who doesn't conceive every time she's ripe is killing a child that'll never be. That's not how any of it works. You can't just—"

"She watched babes born, she watched them grow, she watched them die, until she Dreamed you. *You*, Ellis. She Dreamed you and said, 'Yes, that one,' then binned all the rest like they didn't matter. That's not love, that's not a mam, and *no one* should have that kind of power."

And there it was.

"Ahhh, now it comes to it." Ellis huffed a snort, not entirely surprised, but all at once glad Folant's "grand revelation" was really just the usual bitter refusal to accept rejection in a slightly different wrapper. "It's always going to come down to the magic, isn't it?" Ellis shook his head. "And somehow I think that if she'd accepted your cariad offer, you'd be all right with it after all. Because it's not that you don't like that anyone has that kind of power—you just don't like it that *you* don't. Not only that you don't have it, but that the woman who does wanted nothing from you but the son she'd

Dreamed, and never had any intention of sharing that power with you. Bloody *damn*."

He shooed Bella away and scrubbed at his face, halfway between laughing and snarling. "Every goddess in the pantheon, you actually thought telling me that would make me sympathize with your Purity Party blather, didn't you? You thought telling me it wasn't about being spurned as a lover but being denied power was going to, what?—get me on your side? Make me agree that those with magic are less than people and deserve your scorn like you're someone special?" He threw his hands out. "No wonder the Dewin make you insane. You just can't—"

"The Dewin don't *have* magic—they *are* magic. D'you know what would happen to a witch or a sorcerer if you stuck them in a cell away from anything they could pull power from? Nothing. They'd sit there and rot. Dewin could just wait until your back was turned, open the door and stroll out."

It was both hilarious and terrifying.

Hilarious because it was so completely wrong and pathetically uninformed. A Natur witch could pull energy from anything living, right down to a rodent in the walls; an Elfennol sorcerer borrowed from the elements, and unless there was no air in these hypothetical cells, finding a source to draw from wouldn't be an issue.

Terrifying because the way Folant said it was so sure, so specific. Which meant he'd thought about it. About putting people with magic in cells.

"Unless, of course," Folant went on, callously oblivious, "you kept them in pain, but we wouldn't want to be *cruel* about—"

"You... Sweet Duwies, save me." Ellis had started snorting—half sincerely and half in horror—by the end of Folant's tirade, but that last dried up any humor and turned it to shock. "You tried to rearrange an entire parish to hate magic as much as you do, and for years I just didn't understand it. And then I thought I did, and I actually felt sorry for you, just a little, because loving someone who won't love you back must be dreadful and near to tragic, and maybe a man can be forgiven, *maybe*, for letting it obsess and ruin him. Except then—*then*!" Ellis threw both arms out wide, nearly smacking Bumble in the side of the head. "It turns out it's all because you want magic and can't have it. Bloody *damn*, I admit I didn't see that one coming." He propped an elbow to the table, dropped his head into his hands and rubbed at his temples, shoulders shaking, laughing again, semihysterical now and well aware of it, but for pity's sake! "I can't believe you've nearly run your ancestral land into the ground because other people have something you don't, and you can't stand it."

"I want nothing from any of them." It came out from between

Folant's clenched teeth, a barefaced snarl, which only made Ellis laugh harder, until Folant said, "And I won't have them here—d'you understand me, boyo?"

That finally killed the laugh, and made Ellis sit up straight, eyes narrowed, fists balled tight.

"You'd best think," Folant went on. "And you'd best do a thorough job of it. Because that Dewin of yours? You make him cariad, you'll be wanting to get used to dragon shite, because you won't be bringing him to Wellech and letting him call it home. The rest of the world can do what they like with all the witches and sorcerers and mages, but I won't have them here, and you won't—"

"I think you'll find I'll do what I like. Because the only one who doesn't seem to understand how badly you're hurting Wellech is you."

"I'm making Wellech better! I'm clearing out the—"

"You're chasing off valuable resources! One of which, though I know you'd prefer to forget it, is *me*. Because I Dream, Tad. Not well enough to be one of those good-for-nothing witches you want run out of Wellech, but if I could, you're bloody right I'd do it, and what's more—*I* wouldn't give someone like the you the power of knowing what might be coming either."

It wasn't new information. It was just something they never spoke of. And Ellis had allowed it, had participated in the denial, had allowed Folant to pretend, because some tiny part of Ellis had never stopped hoping for some kind of reconciliation he knew now was impossible. He'd just killed it himself. He was going to kill it even deader before the week was out.

It didn't matter. It wasn't the point.

Folant went still, disbelieving at first, and then... revolted. Only for a moment, and then it cleared the way for his fallback smirk. "Well, then. Seems spending all that time with Dew—"

"Don't you bloody say it. I hear 'Dewin scum' out of your mouth one more time, I swear I'll punch it so hard you'll be shitting teeth for a month. And I'm beyond done, *finished*, with how much you *care*, how much you *do* for Wellech. Forging contracts, queering crop rotations, delaying planting"—Ellis pounded his fist to the table—"and that's only today! All you're doing is dragging us into your clumsy, vengeful snake pit with you, and I'm *done*, Tad. D'you understand? I'm not having it anymore. We've got bigger problems now than your pride—Wellech, Preidyn, the bloody *world*.

"A ferry from Llundaintref with a cracked paddlewheel stranded for hours half a furlong from our shore because Wellech's bloody *Pennaeth* heard there were two immigrants on it and tried to have the fishing boats confined to moor and the captains detained so they couldn't go help—did you think I wouldn't hear about that? I hear bloody *everything*, Tad, every malicious word, every moment of pettiness, and the time for all your spite and duff is *over*!"

"Is it, then?" Folant shook his head, narrow-eyed and still smirking, completely unruffled. "Ah, boyo, you've so much to learn yet. You think because I handed over First Warden without a fight, I'll just—?"

"You handed over nothing. I *earned* First Warden, and then I took it, despite every single obstruction you tried to throw in my way. You can try to salve your ego with a different story, but that's how it was, and everyone knows it."

"And you think taking Pennaeth will be as easy?" Ellis's clear but as yet unspoken threat had left Folant remarkably unperturbed. His gaze was shrewd, amused, and it didn't look like mere bluff and bluster. It looked like confidence. Folant sat back in his chair, drained his jar, and set it with a smack to the table. "You need two-thirds of the council. You probably think you have it."

He stood. With a smug grin and a condescending pat to Ellis's cheek, Folant gave the dogs a last scrub between the ears before strolling, unhurried, from the table and then the Grange.

It took a while for Ellis to stop rubbing at his temples and gritting his teeth, but when he did, when he risked a look up and outward to see who was still paying a bit too much attention, he found only the stranger with the scar willing to meet his eye. Ellis merely stared back, not in the mood, until the man twitched his lip into an apparent attempt at something friendly, raised his jar, then finally stood.

Coming over to introduce himself, likely, and Ellis should care, should make the time, should offer a welcome. He didn't. He shoved out of his chair, chirped a sharp whistle to the dogs to follow, and left.

✦

He'd been home from Tirryderch for just shy of a fortnight when news arrived that the Duchess of Newbrookshire, ambassador to Błodwyl and first cousin to Preidyn's Prince Consort, had been assassinated. Gunned down, along with her son, in a tearoom in Venetia by a man with ties to the Young Princes and, more damning, Taraverde's Premier.

It was personal. It was meant to be. Preidyn had led the way in resisting the advances of the Central Confederation, had formed what was now being called the Western Unified Alliance along with several other countries, and though those other countries had yet to enter the fray, the Central Confederation was making sure Her Royal Majesty knew it was not pleased.

Two days later, while the continent was still reeling and only just drawing new and deadlier sabers to rattle, a Verdish biplane dropped, literally, out of the sky, smoking and sputtering and shearing low over a Preidynīg cruiser patrolling the Blackson off the southern coast of Ynys Dawel—one of Kymbrygh's minor islands only a half-day's ferry ride southeast of Tirryderch. It struck the water just off the cruiser's bow, harmless to all but its pilot, but the audacity of its presence so close to Preidynīg shores struck a grating chord across the country. It shuddered especially through Kymbrygh.

"It's a dragon flight path," Petra said, thick slice of bread in her hand while she pored over the newspaper and ignored the rest of the breakfast the Bluebell's holder had delivered moments ago. Petra shook her head, waved the bread around like she'd forgot she was holding it. "What was a plane even doing there? And how'd it get all the way from Taraverde with no one seeing it?" She frowned up at Ellis. "Surely *one* of the ships in the blockades would've done."

In the far corner, a group had clustered around the radio for the local news; voices rose, each offering strident suggestions as to how to get it to stop squawking out ear-piercing whines and deliver sounds understandable to more than the local dogs. Ellis had no idea why they thought it might work today when it hadn't for as long as he'd been patronizing the inn. The reception in this part of Wellech was utter shite.

"Unless it didn't come from Taraverde." Ellis had read the paper over tea before he'd left the Croft this morning, so he'd had time to ruminate.

"Of course it came from Taraverde." Petra rattled the paper. "It says right here the plane was—"

"I know what it says." Ellis twirled a greasy sausage on the end of his fork. "Frankly, it's what it doesn't say that worries me." When Petra merely gave him an impatient glare, Ellis shrugged and leaned over the table. He lowered his voice. "It wasn't only a plane—it was a biplane. One of those two-seaters that have no range to speak of because they can't carry the weight of two people plus the petrol necessary to get them anywhere far."

Petra gave him a squinty little frown, skeptical. "How would you know?"

"That's the funny thing. I wouldn't normally. Except Milo was telling me about strange things going on with dragons on the central migration paths—the ones over Colorat and Ostlich-Sztym—and how there'd been an incident a couple years ago with a collision between a small plane and a dragon. One dead pilot, one crashed plane, and one annoyed dragon, is what Milo told me. But it made him start paying attention to the sorts of planes that were being built, where they were being tested, and the like. Were they minding the flight paths, were they putting dragons in danger, were dragonkin going to have to start protesting to their respective governments—that sort of thing. And I remember him getting *blindingly tamping* when he learned the planes in question barely had enough range to cover a trip from Preidyn to Werrdig."

"It's what the bloody *ferries* are for!" Milo had raged, pale face gone red and dark, and blue eyes blazing. "They're putting dragons in danger for *nothing*! Save a bit of time getting from one place to another, sure, but for what? Take a train! Take a bloody *airship* if you're that impatient! What could be that bloody important they'd risk crippling or even killing a dragon for it? They can't fit more than two people in the biplanes, and those don't even have the range the smaller ones do!"

And then he'd found out Preidyn was building and testing her own planes—"What d'you want to bet me that's where all the ores are going? No bloody wonder Howell's gnashing his teeth over the rations!"—though they had the sense to do it on Werrdig's west coast, well out of any flight paths. Milo had only been slightly mollified.

Ellis couldn't help the fond smile, remembering, and then the slight frown when he realized it had been a bit too long since he'd heard from Milo. Ellis had wired last week about a date for their next trip to Brookings, and so far, nothing.

"So you're saying it couldn't have come from Taraverde." Petra's brow drew down, bemused. "Except it was Verdish. The wreckage—"

"It could've come from Taraverde. It did come from Taraverde. Originally." Ellis shot his glance around the inn, checking for eavesdroppers, but everyone but for those arguing with the radio was doing the same thing he and Petra were—debating over the newspaper and looking worried.

...Except.

There was that man again, the one with the scar, a mug of what was likely tea on the table in front of him, newspaper ignored by his elbow. Watching Ellis again, and not even trying to look like he wasn't. Ellis had been seeing him around for the past week. Turning up at the mercantile when Ellis went to pick up a pair of boots he'd ordered over the winter. The teashop when Ellis dropped by to check if they'd managed to procure any of the Eretian blend they hadn't been able to get since the blockades went into effect, but it never hurt to ask. It was strange, though, enough for Ellis to notice, because he'd never seen the man before last week, and now he seemed to be everywhere.

One of Folant's gofers, maybe? Trying to figure out if Ellis had the backing from the council he was hoping for when he sued them for Pennaeth in only a few days? Not if the man was a refugee, though maybe Ellis had been wrong about that. It still didn't explain where the man had come from or why Ellis couldn't seem to stop not-really-running-into him.

Ellis scowled, annoyed, and turned back to Petra. "The waters around all the Preidynīg Isles are bloody lousy with the Royal Navy. You're right, that plane couldn't possibly have flown over any of the blockades without being spotted."

"And it couldn't have gone 'round over Desgaul. They cut ties with Taraverde before we did. They wouldn't have stood for it."

"Yeah, but *when* did they cut ties? And what did they allow before they did?"

Petra huffed and rolled her eyes. "For pity's sake, Ellis, just say it, would you? It's too early in the morning for guessing and political intrigue, especially when my brain is otherwise occupied with how I'm meant to get to Wastings Brook and back with the seed you want before dark if this conversation gets any longer."

"You get the seed by making Cai do his job and make the trip for you. But fine." Ellis quit playing with his breakfast and bit the sausage in half. "I'm only saying—a Verdish plane showed up where it didn't have the range to be. Desgaul hadn't closed their trade or their borders to Taraverde until last year, and Vistosa right after, well after the plane-versus-dragon business Milo was telling me about. So who knows when that plane made the trip that brought it so close to Preidyn's waters? It could've been ages ago." He paused to gulp some tea. "And if it was, if that plane—and who knows how many others—slid down and over the continent without Preidyn noticing, but couldn't just sit and wait somewhere in Vistosa for the opportunity to try it on with our navy, where, in all the Blackson between Vistosa and Kymbrygh, could it have taken off from?"

Petra narrowed her eyes. "The only thing there is the Surgebreaks." A small island chain south of Preidyn's outer isles, largely unclaimed but ostensibly controlled by Vistosa because they were an ally. Preidyn never saw the point in fighting over a scattering of rocks in the ocean that couldn't even support a vegetable patch. Petra shook her head. "Except there's nothing there. It's all rocks and cliffs."

"Yeah." Ellis nodded and chomped a bite of bread. "So nobody pays it much mind." He lifted his eyebrows. "I wonder when's the last time Vistosa even remembered it was there. And I wonder if the big island is perhaps long and flat enough to serve as, maybe, a runway."

A chuckle came from a few tables over, loud enough it made Ellis look—that man again. Not looking at Ellis this time, but quietly snorting down at his newspaper, shaking his head, as though he'd read something amusing.

It annoyed Ellis all over again. There was nothing in the paper today that was the least bit funny. He was going to have to make a point of introducing himself sometime soon, figure out who the man was and why he kept popping up when Ellis wasn't looking.

Not today. There was too much to get done before Ellis met with Ioan over in Gwynedd to try to get him to break with Folant.

Ellis stacked his tomatoes on top of what was left of his bread, shoved it all in his mouth, and washed it down with the last of his tea. He stood.

"You ready?"

Petra glared up at Ellis then down at the cockles she'd barely had a chance to touch. She sighed the sigh of the tragically long-suffering and dropped her fork to her plate.

"I hate you."

Ellis merely grinned, obnoxious, and with a full mouth. "You love me. Everyone does."

"Everyone also loves kelp cakes and blood sausage." Petra took her time making a messy pocket with her bread and dumping her cockles in to take with her. She lifted an eyebrow at Ellis. "Doesn't stop me chundering just looking at them."

"Petra!" Ellis set a hand over his breastbone and took a staggering step back. "My poor heart."

"Fie." Petra brushed past Ellis and made for the door. "That's been living in Whitpool for years. Along with... other things." She smirked as she opened the door and waved Ellis through. "Well done, you, keeping the brain, though."

"Yeah, well." Ellis waved a farewell to the room in general, spared one last bemused glance for the stranger, and quit the inn. He huffed at Petra as she followed. "I've still got Ioan tonight. I'll be needing it."

✺

Ellis didn't get a chance to try to twist Ioan's arm. He barely had a chance to buy him a drink. Ioan hadn't even sat down and taken his first sip when a young boy, white-faced and panting, burst through the doors of the shabby pub that was Ioan's local.

"Her Majesty..." The boy gulped a breath and waved a telegram. "It's war."

Chapter 15—Inversion

: a variation technique in which the intervals of a melody are turned upside down

They'd invaded Błodwyl. It wasn't a surprise. Błodwyl had been screaming for support from the World Court for close to a year now, insisting it was inevitable, and they couldn't be expected to hold the line against both Taraverde and Ostlich-Sztym by themselves, did no one understand what was happening here?

Everyone did, everyone knew, everyone watched. Some, mostly Preidyn, tried every measure short of war to halt it. Still the onslaught came, and the brutality described in the initial reports was staggering. And the descriptions of the horrifying deaths from magically enhanced gas attacks were sick-making.

Ellis was rereading an article he'd skimmed earlier, looking for mention of the 153rd Kymbrygh, his cousin Matty's unit that had shipped out last autumn. They'd been headed for the continent, though Matty hadn't been able to say precisely where. Peacekeeping, he'd said. "Likely only getting to know the locals, eating their food, and keeping an eye on some border somewhere. I'm not worried." Matty'd shrugged, the shoulders of his dress uniform stiff and straight. "Them Verds'd have to be blind dafties to actually attack when the Royal Forces are on the job."

Ellis had agreed. Everyone he knew had agreed.

Except "them Verds" *had* attacked. And the fighting, from what Ellis was hearing and reading, was vicious and horrifying.

"Well, if they do," Ellis had told Matty, "expect me within the week."

And he'd meant it. He'd done well in his schooling, and more, he was a Warden. If he did go into the Royal Services, he'd go in as an officer.

The call for enlistment had already grown into a full-out campaign by the time Matty had shipped out, and Ellis had no doubt it was going to turn into a draft any second now. He wasn't so sure about joining anymore, he realized as he keyed open the backdoor to the Croft and shuffled into the kitchen, still reading. He had to squint through the early evening dusk to make out the words on the broadsheet he'd folded and unfolded countless times through the day, so often the already flimsy paper was beginning to give at the creases.

It was darker in the house, the setting sun on the wrong side. He groped out for the knob on the wall to turn on the light, grateful all over again he'd had electricity installed when he'd taken over the ancient farmhouse that had been his nain's. Entrusted not to Folant, her son, when she died, but to Lilibet until Ellis was old enough to claim it, and the valuable farm on which it hunkered. Nain had never had any illusions about who and what her son had become, and she'd been determined that her grandson would have at least this much of his inheritance, if not the chunks of it Folant had already squandered or gambled away by then. If the law had allowed it, she'd've willed Ellis the title of Pennaeth too.

Which was the crux of Ellis's current indecision. How, after all, could he enlist like he wanted to, like he should, and leave Wellech in hands that became less capable by the day? As it was, the cleanup Ellis found himself needing to do every time he got back from a trip to see Milo sometimes took longer than the trip itself. That wasn't even counting the time away on patrols with the Wardens. And it was getting worse.

It took a moment for the light to warm up, the hum low and strangely pleasant just before it bloomed across the kitchen, and lit—

Ellis jerked back, only managing not to actually loose a startled squawk because his throat was abruptly too tight to get a noise through it.

The man—the stranger with the scar—was sitting at Ellis's kitchen table, calmly staring at Ellis and waiting for him to gather the wits to move, to ask, "Who—?" Nope, too high-pitched and squeaky. Ellis jerked his chin and demanded, "What in the name of every goddess d'you think you're doing?"

All at once he found himself annoyed that, for the first time since he'd been back in Wellech, Bumble and Bella hadn't followed him home. Not that they'd do much besides stamp muddy paws on the stranger's clothes and beg for pets, but they could sometimes at least *look* like they could possibly be moved to consider violence.

"Please pardon the intrusion, Rhywun Ellis. But you're a difficult man to get alone. I wouldn't normally be so… rude." The man shrugged, unperturbed. "But in light of last night's declaration, things have become rather more urgent, and I've no more time to spend waiting for the entirety of Wellech to leave you be for five minutes." He shook his head, wondering. "How d'you stand it, anyway? *I* get more time to myself."

Temper flared hot behind Ellis's eyes, and he bristled. "Who in the world are you, and how did you get in my house?"

The door had been locked. In a parish where no one had to worry about leaving their doors open, the First Warden of Wellech locked his—and his desk, and his filing drawers, and anything he deemed valuable or sensitive—because the former First Warden couldn't be trusted not to waltz in and help himself to whatever he pleased. Ellis knew this because he'd had to buy back the bespoke saddle and monogrammed billfold—presents from Bamps once upon a time—after Folant lost them in a game of dice. The door had been locked. Ellis had heard the tumblers roll and give as he'd unlocked it.

The man waved a hand, negligent. "You'll find I have many talents." His tone was level, and his mouth was quirked—nothing quite so disrespectful as a smirk, but halfway amused nonetheless. He nodded to the chair across the table. "Sit down."

Something prideful and insulted joined the temper. "Sorry, did you just invite me to sit down at my own kitchen table?"

The man sighed. "This would go a lot easier and more pleasantly if you did."

"Easier." Ellis surreptitiously closed his fingers into a fist and let the shafts of the keys poke through the gaps by his knuckles. He adjusted his stance, ready for a rush if it became necessary, abruptly and for the first time ever regretting that his rifle was locked in the shed with all his other hunting gear. Didn't matter. The man seemed built well enough, but Ellis was pretty sure he could take him if it came to it. "I'm not certain I've any interest in making whatever you're here for easier. In fact, I may just dedicate myself to making the next few minutes extremely difficult for you."

"I wish you wouldn't." The man turned his hands palm out. "I'm not here for ill, Rhywun Ellis. Though ill has come." He lifted his eyebrows, hazel eyes intent. "We're all going to need to do our parts now. A mutual friend in Whitpool told me you'd be the best choice and, more importantly, willing. What I've seen and heard the past week has persuaded me to the same opinion."

Ellis narrowed his eyes. "Friend."

Milo was the first to come to mind, but... with the way this man had clearly broken into Ellis's house then proceeded to be vaguely threatening and threateningly vague at the same time, this was quickly seeming a bit cloak-and-dagger. And that suggested Ceri more than Milo. Possibly Eira, Whitpool's First Warden, but information traveled fast between the Wardens, no matter who was in which parish; if Eira had sent this man, Ellis would've heard about it days before the man even showed up in Wellech.

Slowly, the man lifted a hand, open and harmless, then tugged out the lapel of his coat. He waited for Ellis to note the white of an envelope sticking out of the inside pocket before he pulled it out and offered it to Ellis.

Frowning, Ellis took it. "This is Milo's handwriting." He narrowed his eyes. "It's unsealed." Which meant anyone could've stuck anything in there and claimed it was from Milo. Paranoid, perhaps, but Ellis had been dealing with Folant for more than two decades.

"Open it, please."

Ellis did, still frowning, to find another envelope, this one sealed, along with a slip of folded paper.

"Open the other after I've gone," the man said. "Only the note for now, if you would."

It was short, though Milo's natural warmth was somehow all over it.

> *Elly—*
> *I know this is odd. I also know there's no one else who can do what you're about to be asked to do. You're the best person I know. There's no one I trust more.*
> *Listen to him.*
> *Yours,*
> *Milo*

Ellis shook his head, read it again, then peered at the man, bewildered. "Who *are* you?"

He was as normal-looking as the other times Ellis had seen him—plain heavy jumper, trousers well made but not too spendy, hair neither short nor long but neat and respectably trimmed. Unremarkable. Ellis wondered now if the effect was *purposefully* unremarkable.

The man all but confirmed it when he said, "My callsign is Mastermind."

Ellis stared. "...Seriously?"

The corner of the man's mouth turned up, sardonic. "I wouldn't judge, if I were you. Yours is Prince."

"Mine." Ellis blinked. "*Mine?*" He skimmed his gaze around the kitchen, as though someone—likely Petra, because she was a smartarse cow—might jump out and yell "Gotcha!" When no one did, Ellis threw his hands out. "What are you even *talking* about?"

"You're in a unique position, Rhywun Ellis." The man sat back in his chair. "As First Warden you know Wellech's every weakness or potential weakness. Moreover, you're in regular contact with the Wardens of the other parishes, and I'm betting you know those weaknesses as well. On top of that, you're doing the job of Pennaeth, which in your case means you not only know everyone, but their politics, their weaknesses, their motivations."

"You seem to be rather fixated on weaknesses."

"In my line of work, I've little choice."

"And what is your line of work?" Though Ellis was beginning to think he knew.

The man tipped his head, as though conceding a point, though he didn't answer the question. "It's worse than you think." He paused, waiting for a reaction; when Ellis didn't give him one, the man quirked an eyebrow as if to say *All right, we'll do it your way.* "This isn't the first time people have turned on their own. It's not even the worst. Not yet, at any rate." His mouth crimped, a flash of anger so quickly smoothed back into the detachment that had been so persuasive just a second ago, Ellis marked the slip he wasn't entirely sure *was* a slip. "It's easy to scare folk," the man went on. "All you have to do is give them a bogey. It doesn't even really need to be credible—they'll take care of convincing themselves, once you start blaming all their ills on it. Start it out small, whispers and rumors and not-quite-accusations. Add in resentment they didn't know they felt, and sprinkle in a good dose of fear. It doesn't have to be reasonable fear. That's the beauty of it, really—you never have to prove any of it, you only have to keep repeating it. Once it takes hold, all you need do is sit back and wait for people to start turning this bogey you've built into something not quite a person. It's very quick after that. Neighbors turning on neighbors, children on parents, cariad on cariad."

"That's..." Ellis shook his head. "Listen, I'm not sure what kind of game you're trying to get me to play here, *Mastermind*. But if you're confessing to being some evil villain right out of a penny dreadful, you'll have to give me a moment to dig up something to restrain you with because I'd have to arrest you, and I don't know where I left my—"

"*I'm* the vil—?" The man huffed a curse, appearing truly offended, then truly annoyed. "Boy, open your eyes. I've been watching you—I know you're smarter than that. You know what this is."

Ellis thought he did. He stared at the man, narrow-eyed, and gnawed the inside of his cheek.

"All right." He glanced down at the note still in his hand—*Listen to him*—and all at once wondered what Milo had to do with all this, and why Ellis hadn't heard from him in too long. He held up the note. "Why did Milo give you this? Why didn't he just tell me about"—he waved the note around—"whatever this is supposed to be?"

The man seemed to chew that over for a moment or two, then didn't answer it.

"You were right about the planes." He lifted his eyebrows when Ellis frowned. "There's a base in the Surgebreaks. The broad strokes of it will be in all the papers in two or three days, but I'll tell you this much now for free." He tapped a thick finger on the table. "Two months ago, in secret and directly contrary to World Court convention, Vistosa signed a treaty with Taraverde granting them unencumbered use of the islands. In exchange, Taraverde will leave Vistosa out of all aggression, and acknowledge and respect Vistosa's neutral status."

"That's hardly *neutral!*" Ellis's spine had snapped rigid. "Those islands are nearly right on top of—"

"Yes. I'm aware. And I'd very much like to tell you more about it and what it has to do with why I'm here." The man reached into his coat pocket again, and drew out... a contract. "But I'll need you to sign this first."

"Oh, yeah, of course." Ellis snorted, finally set his keys down on the bench, and reached for the contract. "I'll just have my solicitor go over it and get back to you soonish, yeah? Thanks for stopping by, I hope you won't mind finding your own way—"

"Ah-ah." The man pulled the contract back. His brow was furrowed but his mouth was tugged up at one corner. "I'm not sure I like your tone."

"I'm not sure I like you in my kitchen."

"Fair." The man waved the contract. "This is something called the National Secrets Act. You're familiar with it."

It wasn't a question, and yes, Ellis was familiar with it, because Eira in Whitpool had told him she'd had to sign one shortly after the mess with Cennydd. Except how would this man know that?

It rather confirmed the *spy! spy! spy!* flashing in bright, furlong-high letters behind Ellis's eyes. And ramped up the *what does this have to do with Milo?* that hadn't stopped pattering at him since he'd seen the handwriting. Ellis clutched the still unopened envelope tighter in his abruptly clammy hand. Jaw set, he tore at a corner—

"You open that now, I leave."

It shouldn't have been a threat. And yet it stopped Ellis before he'd got the envelope open.

Which seemed to please the man, because he relaxed back into his seat again, and held the contract out, tilting his expression into something halfway conciliatory when Ellis glared.

"Not a demand on my part," the man said. "A condition on his." He waved the contract. "Please."

Ellis stared at the neatly folded papers in the man's hand, then down at the crumpled, torn envelope in his. Foreboding welled, heavy and thick, and he wasn't sure which otherwise innocuous-looking bit of paper it was focused on.

Angry now, impatient, and swamped by intrigue and dread both, Ellis snatched the contract out of the man's hand and held back a curse.

"Let me find a pen."

The plane had been reconnaissance, though there was no way to tell exactly what it had been sent to scout. Gaps in the coastal patrols, most likely. The point was, it hadn't meant to be seen, likely blown off course by a sudden sea squall, and hadn't had enough fuel to get back. It was pure luck it went down where it did and with a Royal Navy cruiser as witness.

Preidyn's main island was just across the gulf from Taraverde. Ellis had assumed it an obvious target, but—

"The Isles are too scattered," the man said, patient.

Mastermind, Ellis reminded himself, but he couldn't even think it without wanting to snort.

"And too independent, for the most part," the man went on. "They don't want Llundaintref because it's strategic—they want it because that's where Her Royal Majesty is. They don't want to take it, they want to raze it. Even if they did take Preidyn's government seat, all the other islands would likely just nod along with whatever the invaders say, and then do as they please anyway just to be difficult, because we do love our Queen and we don't like it when anyone crosses her. No." He shook his head with a sour curl of his lip. "The smartest way to take all of the Preidynīg Isles at once is to take—"

"Tirryderch," Ellis said, a bit breathless and a bit sick. "You take Tirryderch, you take Kymbrygh. Because if you control the food, you control the people."

The man tilted his head with a lift of eyebrows, approving.

It didn't settle the rush of acid sloshing in Ellis's gut. "Then, with what Vistosa just pulled, why aren't you there telling all this to Tirryderch's Pennaeth?"

"What Tirryderch knows or doesn't is not what we're here to discuss."

Ellis gritted his teeth. "Then would you mind getting to what we *are* here to discuss? Because I still have no idea what any of this has to do with me. Or Milo, for that matter."

That wasn't entirely true. He had a suspicion. The Wardens were meant for keeping local and regional law and order, but everyone knew they were also meant to become another arm of the Home Guard, should there be a real threat to Preidyn's borders. It was only that, as far as Ellis knew. A *just in case* backup. Because nothing like it had happened since the wild days of raids and pirates, before all the clans scattered across the various islands became the United Preidynīg Isles. And that had been centuries ago.

The man folded his hands atop the table and leaned in. "We're here to discuss Wellech, Rhywun Ellis. We're here to discuss the information leaking out of it. Important information."

"Leaking." Ellis sat bolt-upright. "What kind of information? And to whom?"

"Its mining output, for a start. Its crop yields. Its defenses." The man lifted a hand when Ellis frowned. "As well as the names and whereabouts of just about every citizen of Kymbrygh who's got even minor magical abilities." It wasn't until the man paused, sympathetic, and said, "Including those who've recently immigrated," that Ellis knew.

Knew.

Still, he breathed "*No.*" Painfully small, embarrassingly shaky, because it was... it was too much. Too horrible.

"Wellech has not been helpful or useful in structuring a home defense for quite some time now." The man pursed his mouth, the scar puckering with the narrowing of his eyes. "Council reports that go into the Pennaeth's office and never come back out—never make it to Kymbrygh's parliament, let alone Llundaintref—and instead show up in the hands of people who don't have Preidyn's best interests at heart. Ore production, harvest productivity, river traff—"

"I fill out those reports myself!"

"Yes. I know. I've checked. But who's meant to sign them and send them on?" When Ellis merely stared, *knowing* but unwilling to actually *believe*, the man sighed. "I don't know what the goal is, if that means anything. It could be as simple as bigotry, or just plain incompetence. Sometimes it is, and in this case there's certainly evidence of both. And I haven't yet had proof enough to warrant an arrest. Which, I feel compelled to point out, could well lead to summary execution without the nicety of a trial. But if—"

"*Execution?*" Ellis reared back. "This isn't bloody Tarav—"

"We have cause to believe sensitive information is being sold or given to a hostile entity, which could end in injury to our citizens, our government, our nation, and our Queen. That's treason, Rhywun Ellis."

The word—*treason*—hit with a sharp thump to Ellis's solar plexus. He could hardly breathe. And he didn't know if it was the shock of hearing it, or the absolute *certainty* that his own tad was the one guilty of it.

The man gentled his voice. "We need Kymbrygh united. We need a network of people we can trust that stretches from Wellech to Tirryderch to Whitpool, and every minor parish, village, and hamlet between. We need everyone watching our shores and each other's backs." He lifted his eyebrows. "We need a Pennaeth in Wellech who isn't working against us, for whatever reason."

Ellis shut his eyes, trying to calm the rabbiting of his heart, slow his breathing. The thought of what Folant was doing—*had been* doing... it had been bad enough when Ellis thought it was merely arrogance and bitterness and misguided blame. It had made him angry at his tad, *furious*, and even made him feel a little sorry for someone who'd based his prejudices, his *life*, on things so shockingly wrong yet so thoroughly embedded there was no talking him out of them.

But *this*.

Even if there were some way of understanding it, there was no excusing it. Whether Folant knew what he was doing, what he was endangering, or not, there was no coming back from this.

Ellis hadn't had much hope of having a tad for most of his life; he'd never fooled himself that owning Folant as his sire would be anything but a series of compromises and overlooking things unpardonable from anyone else. Last year, last week, right up until that discussion at the Grange, he'd been willing to try, to keep trying, because Ellis rarely gave up on something he wanted, and he nearly always got what he was after in the end.

There was no looking away from this. There was no compromise possible. Not for Ellis.

He sucked in a long, deep breath, let his hands curl into fists, and opened his eyes.

"I don't have the votes to take Pennaeth."

The man smirked. "You do now."

Ellis didn't want to know how, but he was willing to accept the truth of it. He nodded.

"What d'you need from me?"

What "Mastermind" apparently needed was for Ellis to abandon any idea he might have had of enlisting. For him to present his case for Pennaeth to the council, and not even hint at a foregone conclusion.

There would be clandestine meetings and secret codes and covert communications, everything anyone who'd read even a single spy novel would expect. But there would also be things Ellis never would've guessed.

"You want to leave Folant just running about, doing as he pleases? You *just said*—"

"Everything he's done or said for the past year has been predicted, monitored, and carefully controlled. Every boyo he's spoken with, every rumor he's bred, every letter he's sent, we know about it. There's a value to knowing what information is making it into whose hands. There's even more value in deciding exactly what information will get through, and what the source thinks they know."

Ellis stared, rather stuck on the middle bit. "You've been monitoring the post? What, like opening personal letters and things?" He thought of the letters Milo sometimes sent and scowled, the thought of anyone besides Ellis himself reading them extraordinarily offensive.

The man squinted. "What exactly d'you think spies do?"

And that was... fair. Ellis supposed. No less intrusive, but fair. Ish.

"Yes, all right, but I'm still not clear on what you're asking for here. You want me to read Folant's letters? Eavesdrop on his card games?" Ellis shook his head. "Once I petition the council, and if I get the votes like you say I will, he's not going to let me anywhere near him."

In fact, it was likely he'd file his own petition to disinherit Ellis and remove "dy Rees" from his name. Not that Ellis didn't intend to do that last bit himself, but he hadn't even yet got used to the idea of the complete break that was in his near future, and this man wanted him to... what? Try to somehow get closer?

Impossible.

The man was peering at Ellis keenly, as though he could tell what Ellis was thinking. Though, Ellis supposed, the man was a spy. Maybe he could.

"The problem," the man said, slow and thoughtful, "is that your views are too well known. You've been trying to out-shout your tad with them for too long for anyone to believe you might've changed your mind. And mark me, if the worst happens, it's going to make you a target."

"The worst." Ellis narrowed his eyes. "Are you seriously expecting an invasion?"

"First lesson." The man held up his finger. "Always expect everything, and try to plan accordingly." He lowered his hand and knocked his knuckles against the table. "Right now I need you for contacts, for information, for opening Wellech to the system already in place through the rest of Kymbrygh. All you have to do is give me the information. Because if the worst does happen, it'll be best if you don't know what I do with it."

Ellis blinked. "So you're saying if we get invaded and I get arrested, at least you'll have what you need."

"Listen, son." The man leaned in, expression grave, tone even. "You are just now on the edge of coming to understand that a quarter of the people you've known all your life would like to see another quarter gone or dead, and yet another quarter would be so paralyzed or apathetic they'd do nothing but watch. That leaves only a last quarter to do something about it." He sat back, eyebrows raised. "It's time to choose a place to stand and decide which quarter you belong to."

It was too close to what Milo had said back in Nia's study, his whole body vibrating with it, and his eyes already seeing things that would hopefully never come to pass. And yet Milo hadn't seemed to have much hope at all, too sure there wasn't any, because he'd seen at least the stirrings of it up close—in a hostile woman in Brookings; a bitter boy in Whitpool; neighbors who'd casually and genteelly excluded him as though he were a leper but a nice one, so they didn't quite have it in them to be cruel about it. And those were only the ones Ellis knew about. Who knew what Milo had seen and just never talked about?

Ellis sat back. "Milo sent you to me." The man didn't answer, but Ellis didn't need him to. He tapped the unopened envelope against the table. "You know what this says. You read it."

"The condition was I wouldn't be in the room when you opened it."

Because Milo would've thought of Ellis wanting privacy, but he wouldn't have thought of anyone having the audacity to read something he'd specified was private. Milo was not his mam, he wasn't a natural dissembler, so the betrayal of discretion wouldn't have even occurred to him.

Which really made Ellis worry about what this man—this *Mastermind*, save them all—had dragged Milo into, when everything Milo thought or felt was always telegraphed all over his face. Milo was no spy.

But whatever it was Milo had agreed to, he'd wanted Ellis with him, which had rather decided Ellis before the man had even started his pitch. Because Milo thought it was worthy, was willing to risk himself for it, and he believed in Ellis enough to send this man to him.

And that... well.

It was one of the reasons why having Milo in his life was imperative for Ellis. Even back when they were boys, Milo had always seen the very best in Ellis, had believed everything good about him, had believed in *him*. It made Ellis want to be the person Milo saw when he looked at him. It always had.

Ellis huffed and tapped the envelope on the table again, impatient this time.

"All right. You have your source." He lifted an eyebrow. "But 'Prince' is out of the question."

It wasn't. Out of the question, that was. Ellis was stuck with it whether he liked it or not.

He really, really didn't.

Dearest Elly—

Please don't be angry with me. I don't think I could bear it. I won't blame you if you are, of course—how could I?—but...

This is so much more difficult than I thought it would be. I tried so very hard to tell you in Tirryderch, but I'm afraid I've turned out to be more of a coward than I thought I was. Which is going to make doing what I have to do very difficult indeed. But I came to realize I couldn't tell you without explaining why, because you deserve that, you deserve so much more. You would've wanted answers, and I couldn't give them to you. But I think I would've, had I taken the chance. I think I could endure tortures and torments and cruelties, but I could never endure hurting you without at the very least telling you why.

Since you're reading this, I reckon you know now.

By now you've had a discussion that was likely as unpleasant as it was necessary. I won't apologize for orchestrating it, because I meant what I said—you're the best man I know, and the situation couldn't be in better hands. I will apologize, though, for what it means for us, and how I've gone about it.

Your mam told me not too long ago that I'm more like Ceri than I think I am. I'm beginning to understand what she meant by that. It's not an entirely happy revelation, but quite possibly a useful one.

We're each in unique positions. Please just remember that. There are things you can do that no one else can, just as there are things I can do—hope I can do—that no one else can. I need you to keep that, to hold to it, when you grasp what I must say next.

I'm keeping the key. Do you understand? I'm keeping the key, because you will never not be my home. But I've filed for a dissolution to our contract. It's done. You'll receive the paperwork from Merfyn by month's end.

Please, Elly, please think about it all with your head and not your heart, and I know you'll come to understand why. Maybe not now, today, but you're cleverer than most, and I know it won't be long before you see the sense.

We can't know how any of this will end, we can't know what will happen, and I won't leave you wondering and waiting. I know too well what that's like. I won't do it. We each have our duties that are bigger than those we have to each other, but I won't balk from this one duty I have to you—I won't have you waiting. I won't.

I love you, Elly. I don't know if I'll ever see you again, but if I don't, I hope you'll make that your memory of me. I'll always be the man who didn't deserve you but loved you 'til the end.

Yours always,
Milo

Chapter 16—Improvisation

: *"on-the-spot" creation of music (while it is being performed)*

The first thing Ellis thought after reading the letter was *No. Absolutely not.*

The second thing he thought was rather incoherent, with a lot of furious swearing and threats aimed at the devious bloody gob of grem who called himself *Mastermind*, of all things, and skulked out of Ellis's kitchen—out of Wellech altogether, for all Ellis knew—before Ellis opened the letter and understood bloody *Mastermind* was in serious need of a good throttling.

The third thing Ellis thought was, again *No*, and then *No*, and then *I'll kill him.*

And that was how Ellis found himself on the overnight train out of Wellech and on his way to Whitpool, jaw set so hard his teeth hurt and his head was pounding. He slept, fitful and badly, right there in his uncomfortable seat in the main car, and Dreamed, though it was odd and gauzy and made him wonder if his mam had missed something in her instruction of Ellis's meager talent. All broken and bizarre, it didn't seem like a Dream at all—Milo was playing the violin, of all things, and quite well. Milo didn't play. Ellis would know.

He woke with a headache, sore neck, and the dragonstone all but burning a hole in his pocket. He distracted himself by peering at all angles out the train window, trying to spot the dragon that must be flying close, but couldn't find it.

The afternoon sun was bright and the sky, for once, nearly cloudless when Ellis stepped onto the platform in Whitpool and barreled out toward the waiting rank of hire cars, that same expression of *Ugh, do I have to?* on the driver's face when Ellis gave the preserve as his destination. Ellis had found it rather funny when he'd been here last, and then frustrating enough that reasoning his way into buying Howell a car had seemed worth the wrath from Milo. But the people of Whitpool were funny ones, with a core of those who'd lived here all their lives and viewed the dragons as just another part of the scenery, albeit a part needing practical caution, and another entirely different assemblage that—

"Oh, for pity's *sake*." Ellis nearly slapped his forehead.

Maybe it was that he'd had his eyes opened last night to something he hadn't known to look for. Maybe it was the ostensibly insignificant fact that Whitpool seemed to attract more transplants from the rest of Preidyn than any of the other Kymbrygh parishes. Maybe it was the simple existence of Ceri and the knowledge of who and what she was—and why hadn't Ellis ever wondered about her presence here and the more or less open knowledge of it? Did spies retire? Really? Could they?

And if not, how would that work?

Whitpool's Home Guard was the command post for the divisions of all the other parishes. Whitpool's Home Guard was the specialized training ground for those who'd done their obligatory stints in the ranks of whatever parish and were meant to move on to the Royal Forces. Whitpool's Home Guard had stepped into a matter for the Wardens when Cennydd had tried his audacious abduction, had shut it all up with contracts and secrets and disappearing parents—disappearing *Cennydd*, for all anyone knew. Whitpool's Home Guard apparently had more power than the Royal Forces when it came to orders direct from Parliament and information that couldn't have come from anywhere else before it was cut off. Whitpool's Home Guard had a relationship personal enough with Ceri Priddy that they refused her son admission by her request.

Milo was of age. Refusing his application was borderline illegal. Ceri's word should've meant nothing. And no one was rejected from the Home Guard, not if they were fit for service. Everyone did their stretch, everyone but the Wardens, and even they were subject to Home Guard rule in times of...

"Ohhh," Ellis breathed, "well, what d'you know," not entirely surprised he'd never noticed, never even thought about it. Why would he? Why would anyone, unless they were one of the many citizens of Whitpool who were not from Whitpool?

He eyed the car's driver and wondered. Hair trimmed short and neat, shoulders back, spine straight, even in the car's plush driver's seat. And, just like almost every other driver Ellis had hired to take him to the preserve had done, eyeing the sky every five seconds like he was afraid a dragon might swoop down on the car once they turned on to the access road to the forge.

Military or former military. Clearly.

Not from Whitpool. Clearly.

Because, honestly—who would purposely move to a place crawling with dragons, a place with one of the few *dragon preserves*, if one was afraid of dragons?

It was a good way to keep an eye on things, Ellis reckoned, an entire network of people who could keep track of who was coming and going merely by waiting for someone to hire them and tell them. What other jobs could a person do that would provide information no one would even realize was being noticed? Someone in the telegraph office, maybe? Post office? Servers in the tearooms and pubs and inns?

Were these people training to become spies, or were they actively spying? And what would they be spying *on*? Whitpool wasn't exactly a hub of intrigue and political interest. It didn't even have a port!

Then again, Ellis supposed, what better place to plunk a secret web of spies or potential-spies-in-training than somewhere no one would think to look? Ellis certainly hadn't. He didn't think Milo had, and Milo lived here.

Ellis was looking now, though, watching the driver through the rearview. Thinking back to Eira telling him everything he wanted to know, First Warden to First Warden, until the Colonel-in-chief of the Home Guard told her not to. Remembering last night in his kitchen and a stranger with delusions of "mastermind" grandeur telling him they needed a united Kymbrygh, *from Wellech to Tirryderch to Whitpool*, and now Ellis wondered if the placement of Whitpool in that arrangement of seemingly careful words had been incidental or indicative.

And also—*Mastermind.*

For pity's sake, the man had done everything but semaphore and interpretive dance!

Ellis didn't try to be clever with the driver or sneak in a few leading questions. Firstly, he wasn't even sure he'd know how. Secondly, everything that had just barged through his head was important and a bit terrifying, but not why he was here. He merely sat quietly until the car chugged its wobbly way up the bumpy, pitted access road that in truth was little better than a deer path, and pulled into the forge's yard.

"Shall I wait?" It was dubious and reluctant, said with an eye out the windscreen and pointed at the sky, tracking a dark shape coasting slow and lazy over the ancient but still stately jut of Ty Dreigiau.

Every child in Preidyn, and especially Kymbrygh, was schooled on dragon breeds and dragon habits and dragon dangers, though Ellis couldn't tell one from another in the sky the way Milo could. He'd got to know the shape and build of a razorback fairly well, since he'd had such up close and personal acquaintance the last time. And the spitters were easy to spot just by the frill. He wasn't sure what this one was. Spear-shaped and slick, it moved like a snake with wings, curling into updrafts and widening into thermals with all the grace of a silk banner in a warm breeze.

For a moment, Ellis considered demanding that yes, the driver should wait, just so he could point and laugh when he finally cornered Milo and told him exactly how numb-brained he was being. Then again, Ellis didn't suppose there would be much laughing, and he could see Howell's car poking its shiny grill from one of the outbuildings by the barn. Ellis didn't suppose Howell would begrudge him a ride back to the train station, should he need one.

"No. Thank you." Ellis heaved himself out of the car, and swung the door shut. "I'll figure it out from here."

Except he couldn't.

"Wait, explain it to me again. More slowly, please."

Glynn heaved a breath that was more like a growl. "This isn't an explanation, because I don't have one! I'm only telling you what happened!" Clearly frustrated; angry tears were misting her eyes.

"All right. Yes. I'm sorry." Ellis tried to make his tone soothing. "Start from when you noticed something was off with him."

He skirted a glance at the strange man standing in Milo's dooryard, hovering behind Glynn and looking concerned and anxious while occasionally muttering heavily accented Preidish. His syntax was formal, borderline archaic, and broken by a language with a cadence blurred at the edges, swaying on the vowels and smudging the gutturals. Ellis wasn't any more alarmed than he'd been since Mastermind showed up in his kitchen—too young, too skittish, this man hardly seemed a threat, and if Ellis had understood Glynn correctly, he was dragonkin fled from Colorat. Ellis just didn't understand why the man, barely more than a boy, was *here* and Milo wasn't.

"Something's always been *off* with Milo," Glynn groused, that same familial annoyance-affection Ellis had seen between her and Milo when Ellis had been here at Sowing. "And I thought that after... well, after Cennydd"—her mouth crimped tight—"it wasn't all that surprising, yeah? Of course he'd be... different." She wrung her hands, dirt in the creases from whatever she'd been doing before Ellis showed up. "But it was... I mean, he got... *calm.*" She frowned, shook her head. "That sounds daft, but he got calm. And sad. And he kept *sighing.* Like a character in a tragedy." Her hands were pulling at the hem of her shirt now. "I thought about writing you, actually. I thought maybe something... that you two maybe..." She huffed. "But then he went off to Tirryderch, just like he planned, and he came back like he was supposed to, but then he just... left. All he took was his violin, and I—"

"Wait, his what?"

"—don't know where. I don't know *why.*" She stopped there, clearly trying to keep her tears at bay.

"You said—" Ellis had to pause to swallow down the clump of disquiet gathering in his throat. "You said he took his violin." He leaned in. "He plays?"

"Well." Glynn looked taken off guard. "Yes?" She waved out toward the preserve. "Mostly to the dragons, but sometimes..." She trailed off, frowning. "You didn't know?"

Ellis didn't answer. Couldn't.

It wasn't only the Dream that came flaring back to life, Milo in some dim-lit tavern, turbid with smoke, one musician among four playing something quick and lively. It was the hollow realization that no, Ellis hadn't known. Because Milo hadn't told him.

Such a small thing, some new facet Ellis would've been pleased to learn any other time, would've been fascinated by and insisted Milo play something for him, just for him, right now. Hearing it like this, like a secret betrayed, when there were apparently so many of them Ellis hadn't even guessed were there...

He tried to stay calm. It was unclear if the roiling in his chest was worry or wrath. Wrathful worry, probably.

Howell hadn't been in the forge, though the fires had been burning when Ellis wandered through, and the runner had been in place in preparation for rations later. Ellis had been just as glad he wouldn't have to explain his unexpected appearance and small-talk his way through the forge before making his way to the house.

Except, when he'd climbed the porch steps and pounded on the door, righteous and livid and organizing everything he'd decided he wanted to say, it hadn't been Milo who answered the door. Aleks, the man was called, young and swart and disturbingly fit, and blinking at Ellis from the other side of the door like he was the one who belonged there.

So many things had gone through Ellis's mind—*No, Milo wouldn't*, and *Would he?* and *How could he?* and *No, he wouldn't*—and none of them came out his mouth, seeing as how it'd been busy flapping like lackluster bunting in the warm sea wind. But then there had been Glynn, tearing in from the pastures, breathless and flushed but looking strangely relieved at seeing Ellis, and maybe a bit guilty, explaining that this was Aleks, dragonkin from Colorat, helping to look after the place while Milo was gone.

Ellis was still trying to wrap his head around that "gone" bit when Glynn started bossing him into the house. He couldn't help frowning at Aleks, moving much more agreeably than Ellis, as Glynn bullied them through Ty Dreigiau's backdoor.

"Here," said Glynn, pulling composure around her as she shut the mudroom door and waved Ellis into the kitchen. She set her shoulders, blinking away her obvious disquiet, determined, and nudged at Ellis until he moved from in front of the stove. "Sit down, I'll make tea." She set the kettle on the cooker and pulled out the tea tin.

Aleks, looking thankful to have something that would remove him from beneath Ellis's probably somewhat hostile scrutiny, pushed out a string of babble and took the teapot from Glynn's hand. He smiled, polite and gentle as he said... whatever it was he was saying, but Ellis definitely heard "tea" in there somewhere, and he was pretty sure there was "let me" in amongst the muddy glottals and slippery diphthongs.

Glynn seemed to understand it well enough, clearly pleased and maybe even charmed. Smiling, she allowed Aleks to take the makings from her hands and shoo her to the table across from Ellis. When she sat, her smile slid down into something troubled.

"He started teaching me to run things." She shrugged when Ellis frowned at her. Like it was habit, she slicked a glance toward Aleks as he clinked and measured and absently hummed something low and offkey, before she looked back at Ellis. "Balancing the books. Reports to the council. Requisitions and applications. That sort of thing. Told me someone else should know how to do it." She smiled, wistful. "I was really happy. I was a *real apprentice*, you know? And he thought I was smart enough, and good enough, and that I *could* learn to..." Her eyes teared up again, and she blinked. "When Aleks came, I just thought Milo was being generous."

Aleks's humming quietened at the sound of his name, and he stilled, as though worried about what was being said. He looked over his shoulder, searching out Glynn, and when she peered back with a reassuring smile, his shoulders relaxed, and he went back to the tea.

It had almost been fearful, the look on Aleks's face, wary and alert, like it had been when he'd reluctantly opened the door to Ellis's pounding. Ellis reminded himself this man—this *boy*—had managed to escape a warzone where his neighbors had literally tried to kill him. And one look from Glynn had coaxed the guarded apprehension away as quickly as it had been triggered.

Ellis started to wonder if Howell had witnessed any of this, and if he had, why he thought leaving these two alone in the same room was a smart idea.

Glynn shook her head, fond, as she turned back to Ellis. "He told me and Tad to keep it quiet. Milo, I mean. Told us Aleks wouldn't want the notice, and maybe not everyone in Whitpool would be happy to have a foreign Dewin up here with the dragons. But Milo said it was the kind thing, the right thing. And I thought he was thinking about how he would feel if he got chased from his own home and the dragons he loves so much. Dragonkin with no dragons—how sad is that? But really, he was only—" Her hands balled into fists on the tablecloth, and she leaned in and lowered her voice. "He planned this. He brought in a *replacement*. Trained me as one, and didn't even *tell* me." Her bottom lip wobbled, and the tears sprang to her eyes again. "It's like Rhywun Ceri all over again, and I was going to write you, Ellis, I was, but I didn't know what to say. I mean, what was I supposed to—?"

"You weren't supposed to do anything, Glynn." Ellis reached out, intending to take up Glynn's hand, comforting. "It wasn't—"

Aleks was there instead, setting the steaming teapot in the middle of the table and laying his hand to Glynn's shoulder with soft, shuddering words, stresses in all the wrong places but nonetheless discernable as a question. He gave Ellis a narrow-eyed look.

Ellis pulled his hand back, eyebrows high as Glynn patted at Aleks and gave him a smile. Aleks shot one more glance at Ellis—warning, if Ellis wasn't very much mistaken—and went back for the cream and sugar.

Ellis leaned in. "D'you speak Coloran?"

A true grin bloomed on Glynn's face, bold and unabashed. "Nope."

"And he doesn't speak Preidish."

"Nope. Well, some."

Ellis merely leaned back when Aleks brought over the cups and saucers. Three of them Ellis noted, and he thought there might've been some kind of warning in that too, a subtle "I'm joining you because I belong here" that Ellis had no intention of arguing with. He did smirk a little, though, and try very hard not to snort.

"He's learning, though." Glynn said it with a flick of her glance toward Aleks. From under her lashes. And with a bit of color high on her cheeks.

And every goddess save him, Ellis was going to choke on all the sweetness and twee. He sighed, thoroughly entertained but also still thoroughly swottled and angry and sixteen different kinds of worried.

That was when Howell came in, windswept and cranky and peering between Glynn and Aleks in a way that let Ellis know in no uncertain terms Howell hadn't missed a thing when it came to this too-obvious prelude to a courting contract.

How old was Glynn, anyway? How old was Aleks? Were they even old enough for contracts? And how did contracts work in Colorat? Did they even have them?

When Howell's gaze landed on Ellis, there was no surprise there—more like expectation realized as he nodded, pursed his lips, and waved down toward the village.

"You'll be wanting Colonel-in-chief Alton."

◉

Alton was, of course—*of course*—Mastermind.

Now that Ellis was here, slouching in the chair across from Alton's desk, he realized he really should've thought of that. He *at least* should've clued in that something was coming when Howell had sighed at him and told him he was surprised—Ellis heard "disappointed"—that Ellis hadn't shown up sooner. "Like mother, like son," Howell said, morose, while he navigated the car he so clearly loved, probably wanting to smack some intelligence into his passenger but refraining because his passenger was the one who'd bought him the car.

Sometimes being wealthy and generous came in handy.

"Where have you sent Milo?" Ellis allowed the sharpness, the indignation, the sheer bloody *anger* to bleed through every syllable.

Alton, stone-faced as he'd been last night, merely lifted an eyebrow. He didn't answer. Made it clear he wasn't going to.

He looked different in his Home Guard uniform, all buttoned down and polished, with medals stretched across the lapels that spoke of a very long career, and a scar and demeanor that spoke of a violent one. Strangely, the uniform didn't add gravitas or credibility to the remarkably unremarkable man who'd shown up in Ellis's kitchen last night—Alton already had that, effortless and natural, whatever he decided to dress it up in.

The narrow-faced lieutenant almost hadn't let Ellis in. Ellis'd had to pull the "I'm First Warden of Wellech, and I Have Important Business" tone. Even that hadn't been working entirely until Alton had called from the other side of the door to let Ellis pass before he shouted the place down. As soon as Ellis heard the voice, he'd known.

"I know it was you." Ellis tried to keep his hands from fisting, gripping his hat between them to remind him it was expensive and he'd be displeased with himself if he ruined it. "If I find out you've sent him after Ceri, I'll—"

"You'll what?" Alton folded his hands atop his desk and leaned over them. His expression was flat, but his gaze was sharp. "No, please, I'd like you to go on. I'm very interested to know exactly how much power you think you have here." He waited, watching Ellis closely, and when Ellis had no answer—because he had *no* power, none, and he knew it—Alton sucked a tooth and sat back. He tipped his head. "I'm surprised it took you so long, actually. I'd been expecting you all morning, and then most of the afternoon."

Ellis barely held in a growl. "How'd you get here so fast, anyway? You weren't on the train." Ellis may have been bleary-eyed and laughably distracted, but he would've noticed *that*.

"Really?" Alton's eyebrows went up. "That's what you want to ask me?"

"It's one of the few questions I think you might answer."

"And yet." Alton smirked in the face of Ellis's glare, but he did eventually let it drop and turned more serious. "I didn't pull him in.

He came to me. Other than that, there is nothing I can tell you besides he's doing his duty to his country, and asked that I find a way for you to do the same."

"Just like his mam tried to do for him?"

"Contrary to what you and your nearest and dearest seem to think, I am not here to arrange a war around the shifting whims of mams and cariads." Alton shrugged. "You happen to fit a space I need filled. You'd be more valuable to Preidyn in Wellech, at least for now. If you choose to enlist instead, I won't stop you. I'll forget everything you agreed to last night, and we'll pretend we never met. Either way, you won't be sent after Milo. That's not how this works. But if enlisting is what you want..." He waved a hand, negligent, before he paused with a hard look. "Although I'll remind you that you'd be leaving Wellech to its Pennaeth, with no one between him and whatever havoc he might choose to wreak without you there to stop it or fix it. Kymbrygh needs Wellech. Preidyn needs Kymbrygh. Preidyn's allies need Preidyn." He put out his hands. "How we each fit into the duty we choose is up to what we have to offer. And how willing we are to offer it."

Ellis let that stew for a moment, teeth set hard and head once again pounding, before he said, "So you're not even going to tell me if you've turned him into a spy like his mam."

"No."

"Or where you've sent him."

"No."

"Or tell me I'm right when I say I know he's gone off to Central Màstira."

Because that was where dragons had gone missing, and Milo loved his dragons. That was where a coven had gone dark, and Milo had been outraged and terrified on behalf of every member of it. That was where they were killing Dewin, and the memory of Milo's insistent words about duty and *say you understand* had been a stubbornly dismissed subvocal hum at the bottom of Ellis's brain since he'd read that letter. Now they flared and blared and clamored 'til his ears were nearly ringing with it.

"No," said Alton, calm and even.

Ellis had known it was coming. It still *hurt*, like skin rubbed raw.

"Then can you *at least* tell me," Ellis ground out, *this close* to seething now, "how you expect a man who can't even lie properly to infiltrate a country where they're *killing* people like him?"

Alton stared, for quite a long time, evaluating, calculating, before he finally looked to the ceiling, muttered, "Give me strength," and then something about amateurs before he looked back at Ellis. "I will tell you only that you'd do well not to underestimate what a person can do when given the proper tools, the proper training, and

"No, that's not—*no*." Ellis shook his head, trying to clear it, but all it did was make the pounding worse. "The dragons. Old Forge." When Alton only continued to glower at him, Ellis set his teeth and made himself speak calmly and clearly. "They've been stealing dragons. And now they're attacking Kymbrygh."

And the only ones there to defend the preserve were a young girl, an old man, and a refugee dragonkin who didn't even speak the language.

It was the closest Ellis had seen Alton come to an actual, genuine smile. He thumped Ellis on the shoulder, said, "And if they try it on at Old Forge, they'll meet two of my better assets," and shoved Ellis out the door. "Tell Brimstone and Jackrabbit hello for me." There was a definite grin when he slammed the door in Ellis's face.

Ellis barely noticed.

Because Brimstone. Jackrabbit.

Codenames.

And.

Well.

All right, then. There it was. Apparently everyone Ellis knew was a spy.

He couldn't help himself when he got outside and saw Howell waiting for him, leaning against the car's front fender and polishing away a speck on the paint with the cuff of his sleeve. Ellis merely walked toward the car, and stopped in front of it. He waited for Howell to look up, and when he did, Ellis bunged his ruined hat at him.

"So. Are you Brimstone or Jackrabbit?"

Chapter 17—Prelude

: a free-form introductory movement to a fugue or other more complex composition

Howell, it turned out, was neither Brimstone nor Jackrabbit. It was only that Alton was an arse.

Of course, Ellis only realized all this after having thoroughly insulted Howell by more or less calling him a liar when he denied being a spy, and then thoroughly infuriating him by implying Glynn was.

(In Ellis's defense, he could totally see Glynn as a Jackrabbit. And now that Howell was basically breathing fire at him, Ellis could see Brimstone too. That was apparently neither here nor there, now that Ellis understood Alton had merely been winding him up.)

Howell grizzled all the way to the telegraph office. He grizzled some more while he waited for Ellis to send his messages—one to Petra with instructions to assist the mining camps in doubling security on Ellis's authority; one to Tomos, one of the senior Wardens, to step up patrols with special attention on the railroad tracks and beaches. And Howell flat outdid himself grizzling when Ellis insisted on buying him an early supper at one of Whitpool's better inns to make up for the imposition Ellis had made of himself.

All of which made Howell's offer to drive Ellis to Wellech in the morning less appealing than it might otherwise have been. Anyway, it couldn't wait for morning, and it was getting late already. Alton said Ellis was needed in Wellech *now*, and Ellis figured Alton would know. And, frankly, it wasn't as though Ellis fancied the idea of staying in Milo's house, likely Milo's bed, when Milo—

Damn. Ellis had to swallow it down and shunt it aside or he'd end up blubbing all over Howell's leather seats.

And anyway, Ellis wasn't up to being in the company of anyone who might expect him to hold up one end of a conversation for a drive that was at least eight hours if the roads were in good repair, but probably more like ten, since it usually took well into summer to repair all the damage from spring wash-outs. His head was still spinning, and aching, and he hadn't yet even managed to accept the fact that Milo was gone—*gone*. Ellis had spent last night and this morning not getting his head around spies and Pennaeth and war, but preparing himself for a honking great row in Ty Dreigiau's dooryard that would likely alarm Milo's precious bloody dragons and result in Ellis getting exactly what he wanted.

None of it had gone the way Ellis thought it would, none of it, and he didn't know which bitter bone to clamp his jaw around and chew first.

"If you can get me to Hendrop before dark, that will do," he told Howell.

There was a brewery there that made nightly lorry runs to a string of inns and pubs and taverns from Hendrop to Corstir, always finishing in Corstir just before midday. Ellis knew this because Jac—the holder of the Stone and Sickle, last stop on the run—had celebrated the approval of his cariad contract with Alun, the lorry driver, by closing the pub and disappearing for a week. Which wouldn't have been a problem, probably, had he #1—told anyone, and #2—found his way out of bed to answer his door before Ellis and two other Wardens had shown up to look into why a well-liked pub holder had gone abruptly missing.

It could've been painfully embarrassing. It was actually disproportionately hilarious. Mostly because Jac had finally come to the door in nothing but a sheet to find three Wardens, his mam and brother, and about a dozen loyal and very worried Stone and Sickle patrons standing in his yard, staring then applauding when Jac somehow tripped himself out of the sheet and onto the porch. The ensuing blushing and stammering ended with an impromptu party in the pub's main room—drinks on the house—as well as great memories and several new friends for Ellis.

"Or," Ellis amended, conscious of the imposition on Howell, but unable to come up with a better alternative, "help me find someone who can get me to Hendrop. I know you've got to get back to the forge." Rations came right at dusk, and there was prep time to consider as well

It was too long of a drive for a hire car. And with what Ellis suspected about the drivers, well. Even if Alton already knew where Ellis was going anyway, and why, Ellis didn't want to give him the satisfaction. Petulant, yes, all right, but Ellis figured he had the right.

Howell grunted, still clearly annoyed but also clearly unwilling to be an ungracious host. "Aleks and Glynn can sort the rations. They'll know not to wait."

Ellis lifted his eyebrows. "Glynn can handle rations by herself?"

"Well, yes, but Aleks has been doing it since he was wee, apparently, so they'll likely do it together." Howell noted Ellis's bemusement. He shrugged and turned onto the high street. "Colorat wasn't a wealthy country before all the trouble, and once it started..." His mouth crimped. "From what I can gather from Aleks, it was only him and his tad on the preserve, and his tad was crippled up and dying of the waste. Aleks ran everything, including the forge, until they were both arrested." He stopped, ruminating with a bewildered frown. After a moment, he went on, "They brought in dragonkin from Taraverde, Aleks said. *Dragonkin. Willing*, or at least he thought so. Took over the preserve, and started feeding them what that nesh minger *Cennydd*—" It was bitten off through clenched teeth, like every other time that name came up. Howell shook his head, lips pressed tight and eyes on the road. "Dragonkin hurting dragons. Never thought I'd see such a thing."

"There are a lot of things I never thought I'd see." Ellis was still trying to figure out which one to allow space in his head. War, and enemy planes off the coast of Tirryderch, and now bombs *in* Tirryderch.

Alton had been right—they were going after the part of Preidyn that would cripple the rest. And with Tirryderch reluctant to risk its magical folk...

Ellis shifted uncomfortably in his seat and decided the first thing he needed to do when he got back to Wellech was to establish a safe way to communicate with Dilys. *She* certainly wouldn't be dithering over whether to allow volunteers to risk themselves. Ellis had already got a few reports from Tirryderch's First Warden with barely disguised whinging in the margins about his newest novice Warden, and *She says she knows you—can't you tell her I don't need her help running things?* Ellis had no doubt Dilys would only laugh at him if he tried, and anyway, she probably *could* run things, and quite well. In fact, with what had happened in Tirryderch only an hour or so ago, Ellis had no doubt Dilys was right in the thick of it, containing the fallout and hunting down whoever was responsible.

"His tad didn't last a month."

Howell's low tone jolted Ellis out of his musing. He glanced over to see Howell's knuckles were white on the steering wheel.

"He's younger than Milo," Howell went on. "Aleks, I mean. He's only a boy, still." His lips were pursed and his brow was furrowed. "He doesn't say, but I'm thinking there were a lot of things he had to do to get out of there that no boy should even have to think about."

Ellis looked down into his lap then out the window. "War doesn't care."

"It doesn't." Howell was quiet as he took the turn onto Queensway Road, but it was an uncomfortable quiet. So Ellis wasn't surprised when Howell cleared his throat and said, "I don't like that he went. Milo, I mean. I don't like that he went and I don't like how he did it. But I respect his reasons, and I respect him for living his convictions."

Ellis kept staring out the window. "I can do all that and still be angry with him."

"You can."

"And worried."

"Of course."

"And bloody *terrified* that he's going to—"

"*Fy machgen i*," Howell cut in, the endearment gentle, and unexpected enough to stop Ellis before he got going, "listen to an old man who knows, who's lived it from both sides—worry and fear will get you nothing but a dizzy head and a sore heart. And when it comes to Priddys, it always ends up wasted effort anyway." His expression turned soft. "If you'd ever seen my Ceri in action, you'd never doubt it."

"You... wait." Ellis blinked over at him, thoroughly diverted. "Did you... did you serve with her?"

He hadn't actually known Howell had served at all.

"And you *have* seen Milo in action," Howell continued, ignoring the question entirely. He was smiling now, for all the world a proud tad bigging up his son. "How many mages, d'you think, could hold off a witch, a sorcerer, and a raging dragon, all at once, and live to tell it?"

"He almost *didn't* live. That's the bloody *point*."

"Except it's *not*." Howell shook his head, smoothly rounding a curve in the road then wincing when a tire hit a rut. "The point is that a young man, untried and not expecting trouble, was taken off his guard and attacked out of the blue, in the middle of the night, by what should have been overpowering force—what *would've* been overpowering force for anyone else—and still managed to save his dragons while protecting his cariad and his home and my daughter.

"The *point*, boyo, is that there was no way in any nether all of that wasn't going to get out, one way or another, and once it did, that exemption Ceri arranged wasn't going to hold. Milo's time as a civilian was up the second he found Cennydd with that calf, and the cleverest thing he could've done was exactly what he did—going to Alton instead of waiting for the Royal Services recruiter to come get him. Because you don't want to know what Ceri saw in the Green Coast War before she fell beneath Alton's eye, what they expect of their magical folk on the frontlines, and that's the way it was all heading for Milo until the moment he asked me to drive him to the Home Guard's offices."

Ellis narrowed his eyes. "*You* drove him." There was betrayal in his tone, he knew there was, but he couldn't help it. Even if he knew Howell was right, that it all made sense, he still couldn't help it.

Howell sighed. "Ellis. Lad." He scrubbed at his short brown hair. "Say what you want about Ceri Priddy, think what you want, but you can't say she doesn't love her son fiercely. Which is why you can't pretend not to see that she's spent her life since he was born making him ready for exactly what he's just stepped into."

"That's..." Ellis stared, confounded, because what? *What?* "Actually, that's the biggest load of shite I think I've ever heard. From what Milo tells me, and from the little I've seen myself, Ceri did everything short of building barricades to make sure Milo never saw the other side of Old Forge's fences."

"Right. Of course." Howell smirked. *Smirked.* "Which is why she had her mam teach him control and your mam teach him magic. Which is why she sent him to the best, most prestigious and well-known school for Dewin outside Eretia. Which is why she made a proud announcement for his rites and threw him a very public party."

Ellis couldn't say *Which is why she pounded it into him since he was wee that he had to hide the Seeing* because he couldn't tell if Howell knew about it, and it wasn't...

Actually, it was a moot point now. The entire reason for keeping it a secret had already happened, and by Milo's own hand.

"She terrified him into hiding a part of himself so he wouldn't—"

"She tried to protect her son. It's what mams do."

"She conspired with Alton to—"

"*She tried to protect her son!*" Howell's hands were clenched on the steering wheel again. "D'you think for a second someone like Ceri Priddy—*the Black Dog*—didn't know how this was eventually going to go? D'you think she hasn't been watching this war coming, for bloody *years*, and trying everything she could to keep her son from it? Who *wouldn't* do that, if they could? What mam or tad wouldn't hide their sprog in a bleeding *root cellar* for the length of a war if they thought it could save them?"

Ellis thought of Nia and her mangling of laws to keep her citizens safe. He thought of Lilibet and how she'd got teary and shouty when Matty enlisted.

"She did everything she could," Howell said, quieter. "Even went back in when they tried to use Milo against her, though I think she might've done that anyway." He paused with a scowl before he shook it off. "But she always knew it was out of her control. She always knew that if war came, Milo would either find a way to go or be dragged. And so she made sure he was the very best at what he did. Made sure he'd be valuable to someone like Alton, because the life of a spy might be damnably dangerous, but the life of an infantry mage is several thousand times more so."

"Valuable." Ellis couldn't help the skepticism. "Valuable how?"

Howell lifted an eyebrow. "The boy speaks how many languages?" He snorted, didn't wait for Ellis to answer. "How many people d'you know your age who know as much about politics as

Milo does? About history, regional cultures, continental sects? How many mages d'you think there are who could've done what he did that night of the attack?" He paused, as though considering, then went on, "How many can Look without everyone around them knowing what they're up to?"

Well. That answered that question.

"You knew."

"I know a lot of things. Like, for instance, it never mattered if Alton found out about the Seeing, because he always knew. It's only that he and Ceri both pretended he didn't. And likely would've kept on pretending, had Taraverde not got too big for its tyrannical britches. What mattered was that *Llundaintref* didn't know. And now that Alton has snapped Milo up, the fight was over before Her Majesty's Royal Services even knew there was one. Because even the HMRS don't mess with the RIC."

RIC. Royal Intelligence Corps.

And here Ellis had thought himself so clever for making all those little connections between Whitpool and the Home Guard and spies and conspiracies. When really, it seemed Whitpool was no less than a key hub of Preidyn's entire intelligence network.

Whitpool, for pity's sake!

Ellis watched the road for a while, trying to settle it all in his head, but it was no good. *He planned this. He brought in a* replacement. *Trained me as one, and didn't even* tell *me*, Glynn had nearly wept at him, and yet—

"I'm not sure I can believe Ceri trained Milo up to be a spy without him knowing it."

Howell huffed, plainly frustrated. "She didn't train him to be a *spy*, for pity's sake. She merely developed his talents and facilitated an education that, should the worst happen—and it has—would destine him for something other than cannon fodder." He shot a knowing look at Ellis. "If you enlisted today, with your education and your time in the Wardens, would you go in as a lowly grunt sent right to the frontlines?"

Ellis looked back out the window. Because, all right, point taken.

"I'm only saying, boyo." Howell clapped Ellis on the shoulder before reaching to switch on the headlamps, squinting a little as light splashed out in front of them. "Never underestimate a Priddy. And never count them out." His mouth lifted in a half smile, fond and proud. "Don't imagine you know everything about Milo, what he can do, what he's capable of. And never doubt there's so much more you *don't* know."

Ellis thought about sorrowful letters and secret plans and, every goddess save him, bloody wretched violins. And decided he had no choice but to concede the point.

Like mother, like son, Howell had said.

Milo hadn't seen it, or at least Ellis didn't think so. Ellis certainly hadn't seen it, this apparent similarity that made Milo leaving something sad and worrying but not at all surprising to anyone but Ellis.

Now Ellis had to decide if he was relieved or even more pissed off.

Slumping, he blew out a long, weary breath. "Do you...?" He pursed his lips, shook his head, almost embarrassed to ask the question, but not enough to outweigh the need to know. "Do you ever stop being angry at her?"

Because Ceri had left Howell just as surely as Milo had left Ellis. And maybe she hadn't done it with a letter that purposely arrived much too late to do anything about it—Ellis had no idea and no intention of asking—but she'd still *left*.

"Never." Not bitter or caustic, and there was no hesitation or doubt in Howell's tone.

Well. That was... something. Comfort, in a way, though small—tiny really, miniscule, but *something*.

"You know a lot more about all this than I think you're supposed to, Howell." Ellis lifted an eyebrow. "You *sure* you're not Brimstone?"

Howell merely shot him a glare and grumbled under his breath.

Ellis smirked and rested his head against the window. He let himself doze to the sway of the car and the hum of tires on the road.

⊙

The thing about Dreams was that they weren't anything like people who didn't have them thought they were. They weren't anything like what Ellis had thought they were before he'd finally explained one to Lilibet in terms other than "nightmare" or "weird dream" and she recognized them for what they were. Even so, Ellis didn't Dream like other people who had the talent—he couldn't Dream about something on purpose; he couldn't determine where a subject of a Dream was, or when the circumstances he saw might occur, or if they already had; he couldn't always hear what people said.

He Dreamed faces and expressions, mostly; determined moods by the quality of light through which he saw. Stark and monochrome if someone was angry; soft-focus and amber-lit if they were melancholy; reds out of nowhere, possibility coloring in the gray spaces of something he should be paying attention to; golds flickering at the edges of laughter or love or just plain goodwill. It was like being in a picture show, only there was no music, and no one could see him. He was an observer, watching the ghost-trails of others step off in a hundred different directions as they mulled alternatives, and then solidify again when they chose one. And if he was attentive, if he cared about what he was watching, he could mark details, analyze them, remember them.

Milo was having supper in some place badly lit, terribly crowded—and loud, Ellis decided, because Milo kept leaning across the table, tilting his head as though he was having trouble hearing the person speaking. A violin case sat propped on the chair next to him. He was smiling, laughing, but... it wasn't right. Tension sat high on his shoulders. His smile was that polite one that looked bright and beaming if you didn't know him but alert and guarded if you did. His hand was tight around the knife that, by the state of his plate, looked as though he'd yet to use it to cut his meat. There was something else off about him, something...

The earring. There was no earring in Milo's ear, and from what Ellis could see, no hole as evidence there ever had been.

Milo's gaze slid somewhere over Ellis's shoulder then back again, carefully casual, unconcerned. Ellis turned to look, saw a roomful of featureless faces, everything misted and colorless but for two—a man and a woman—outlined in the red of possibility so vague and blurred Ellis almost didn't catch it. Unremarkably dressed, a bit shabby, even, plain and ordinary, but not quite pulling it off. They both had the stiff postures Ellis had only earlier recognized as someone normally in uniform suddenly out of it.

Something burned against Ellis's chest, a hot knob searing at his ribs, like someone had dropped a smoldering coal down his shirt. He patted at it. Set his hand over it. Reached into his waistcoat pocket, and pulled out the dragonstone. It glowed. Bright and hot enough to sting his eyes, his hand, except it didn't.

Milo sat up straight, head turning one way then the other, eyes narrowed. Frowning. Wary. Confused.

The person across from Milo—a man, Ellis could see now, dark-haired and swart like Aleks but more widely built—said something. Milo shook his head, smiled, that careful one again, and said something back as the Dream began to break apart, fog bursting through Ellis's vision and cracking it like glass.

He woke, surprised and disoriented, to Howell shaking his shoulder and telling him, "This looks like something you'd best handle."

The dragonstone was in Ellis's hand. It was hot. Reflex by now, he blinked out around him, looking for the dragon that must surely be near, but...

"This," Ellis said slowly, squinting past the overbright beams of mining torches and harvesting lamps aimed into the car, "is not Hendrop."

It was, in fact, Newridge, well east of Hendrop and more than halfway to Wellech. The car was stopped at the intersection where the road met the tracks of the Central line.

"What...?" Ellis sat up straight and jammed the dragonstone, cooling now but still warm, back into his waistcoat pocket. He turned to Howell.

"Ah," said Howell. He shrugged. "So."

He'd decided to just keep going and take Ellis all the way to Wellech, he explained. And had further decided that Ellis didn't need to know about this decision, that he'd let Ellis sleep, until they got there.

Which might've been fine, had it not resulted in a severe cramp in Ellis's neck that ran all the way down his spine and into his hip, extreme gritty-eyed confusion at being the apparent focal point of a lot of suspicious gazes in the dark, and also a healthy dose of guilt for the inconvenience he was, albeit unwittingly and unwillingly, causing Howell.

That wasn't even counting the Dream he was going to have to pick apart and examine for every remembered detail later.

"What is this?" Ellis finally managed to ask, waving out the windscreen at the... it looked like ten or so people out there, glaring lights all 'round, and if Ellis wasn't very much mistaken, there were a few guns pointed at the car too.

"Some kind of checkpoint," Howell ventured. "Though I can't say it looks official."

It wasn't. Couldn't be.

Frowning, Ellis got out of the car. Half the lights stayed on Howell; the other half moved with Ellis. It wasn't much better, but some of the glare dissipated, and now Ellis could make out a small flatbed lorry parked on the other side of the tracks. There were people seated in the bed, more lights and guns trained on them.

"What is this?" Ellis asked again, putting authority in his tone this time, and censure, because none of it looked right or innocent. "Who are you people, and what d'you think you're doing out here?"

One of them stepped forward, an older man, thick-boned and redheaded, pale skin lighting up near white in the dazzle of the lamps. He had a rifle too, a fat snubbed shotgun that hung in his grip like a truncheon.

Ellis wasn't armed, he reminded himself. He wasn't in Wellech where all the Wardens and pretty much everyone else knew him. He tugged the brim of his crumpled hat down to shield his eyes as he pulled himself straight, feet apart, and tried to watch everything at once.

"Who're *you*?" the man wanted to know, bold and arrogant as he stepped up right in front of Ellis, thin lips pressed flat and eyes narrowed. "What's your business in Newridge?"

"We've no business in Newridge, hence why we were attempting to drive through it. Not that my business, or lack thereof, is any of yours."

Ellis peered around again, the shapes of it all coming into clearer focus now that he was getting used to the light. It was a motley little crowd—men and women, all armed, whether with some kind of firearm or merely a good solid staff, even down to what looked like a long, curved hunting knife in a teenaged boy's hand.

It had every appearance of a nascent mob.

He looked again at the lorry, at the people hunched in the bed of it, at the people apparently keeping them there. His chest got tight, and his heart knocked a quick staccato against his sternum.

"Who are those people?" Ellis asked slowly, though he was fairly certain he knew.

"Tirryderch was bombed today, or hadn't you heard?" This from a woman with a wicked little pickaxe propped against her shoulder. She looked remarkably young and rather delicate, like she should be in a well-appointed parlor somewhere waiting for someone to bring her tea.

"I heard." Ellis jerked his chin at the people apparently being... well, there was no point in trying to dress it up—being held prisoner. "Are you telling me what looks to me like two old men and three children no older than twelve did it?" He lifted his eyebrows all 'round, though he still couldn't see some of the people lurking behind the rest of them, nor could he tell how many were surrounding the lorry and what kind of weapons they held. "Capture a dangerous ring of saboteurs, did you?"

"Word's come down it were a couple'a Dewin Verds." The man puffed out his chest. "So we're collectin' 'em fer when a Warden comes through."

"Collecting them." Ellis's hands fisted and he had to deliberately keep his jaw from clenching. "I see." He put on a smile, nothing but teeth. "Tell me..." He raised his eyebrows, all cool command and expectation.

The man shifted uncomfortably, but offered, "Kane."

"Kane." Ellis nodded. "Tell me, Kane—those bombs went off this afternoon. One all the way down in Littlederch, and the other not far from Tirryderch Station, which, granted, is a little closer, but not by much. And since the trains weren't running, I'd say a car or lorry might get those responsible somewhere around Newridge by now." Ellis paused, and made a show of peering around with a frown. "So where's the car these people were driving?"

Kane set his teeth and lifted his chin. He didn't answer.

"Oh." Ellis tilted his head. "I... see." He put out a hand. "Well, a fast horse, maybe, but you're still talking another few hours. And walking would take..." He blinked inquiringly at Kane. "How long d'you think it would take someone to get from Littlederch to here riding shank's mare, Kane?"

Again, Kane didn't answer. He looked away this time.

"I'd say it'd take someone at least until sunrise. No, actually, make that early afternoon." Ellis looked around again. The guns had lowered but not enough. There was confusion, maybe, on the various faces, but not shame. "That's if they walked steadily at a good clip and didn't stop to eat or sleep. So here's what I think happened." Ellis let his gaze shift slowly, meeting every eye that would look back at him. "I think you heard about the bombings and decided someone needed to pay. And since everyone seems to think that somehow the Dewin in Colorat and Taraverde getting killed by their governments for being Dewin, *somehow* that makes the Dewin Preidyn's enemy. So you took it upon yourselves to drag five people from their homes because, you know, maybe they're Dewin. I mean, you don't know they are, but you think maybe. But that's good enough for you, because what they *definitely* are is immigrants." He stopped, flashed the same toothy smile. "Aren't they?"

He didn't even pretend to wait for an answer this time, because he already knew it and he no longer cared. "Hoy, over there!" Everyone was already looking at Ellis, but right now he only cared about those in the lorry. "Any of you Verdish spies? Saboteurs, maybe?"

The three children—two girls and a boy, now that Ellis could make them out, all of them younger than he'd first thought—only stared at him, clearly terrified and confused. One of the men, though, glared, snarled, "*No*," through his teeth then spat to the side. "I've lived here all my life, Nerys Bennett, and you bloody well know it!"

The woman with the pickaxe set her chin and looked out into the darkness. Which probably made her Nerys.

"Your *cariad* hasn't!" she snapped back, derisive, like the word tasted bad, but she still wouldn't look at the man. "And those creadurs can barely even speak the language, only that Verdish chatter!"

"He's my *cousin*! And they speak *Coloran*, because they're from bleeding *Colorat*!"

Right. The picture was becoming clearer with every word. The other man and the children were relatively new immigrants, and these people likely didn't appreciate them "mixing" with one of their own. So they'd watched as they'd taken in all the Purity Party venom, and they'd built a bogey, just as Alton said they would, and when the opportunity to do something about it arose...

"All right." Ellis clapped his hands, once, then walked deliberately through the gauntlet of farmers and miners with weapons toward the lorry until he was close enough to lay a hand on it. "Here's what's going to happen. This is mine now." He patted at the back fender then turned with his hand out. "Who has the keys?"

Silence.

Then: "Who d'you think you—?"

"Ellis Morgan, First Warden of Wellech, pleasure to meet—well, actually, not so much a pleasure, if I'm honest. I don't generally like it when people kidnap and threaten their neighbors. Sort of reminds me of what Taraverde likes to call their 'Elite Constabularies' but most people of good conscience just think of as monsters and murderers."

The word—*murderers*—out in the open and satisfyingly loud like that, did the trick. Mouths fell open, heads turned, eyebrows went up. All as if to say *How dare you!* and *I would never!* even though every one of them were clearly capable of at least considering it. It was only that it hadn't had a chance to progress that far yet.

What might've happened if one of those men had tried to run? What would have happened if one of them had fought back? The gratifyingly mouthy one, the one from here in Newridge, might've got away with a beating, but the other one? And even if none of these people had the heart yet to hurt a child, they plainly had no trouble with scaring the life out of these three. If the mob had grown big enough that those making it up felt almost anonymous, if this situation had gone on much longer...

Ellis didn't want to think about what might've happened. Mostly because he was afraid he knew.

"But anyway," he went on, still holding his hand out, "you said you were 'collecting' your neighbors for a Warden. And, what luck, now you have one. So what we're going to do is this: we're going to put these people in that car"—he pointed over toward Howell, still watching everything through the windscreen—"and my friend over there is going to take them away. In the meanwhile, I'm going to start thinking about what I'm going to say in my telegram to Eira." He paused, smiled. "She's the First Warden of Whitpool, in case you didn't know, which makes her *your* First Warden. A good friend of mine. I'm sure she'll be... interested in what you've all been up to tonight."

"So..." This, tentative, from a boy leaning against the lorry's driver-side door. Young, probably a local peer of the children he was meant to be guarding, and armed with a rifle almost as tall as he was, though it rested upright and harmless against his shoulder. He shifted uncomfortably beneath Ellis's questioning gaze. "Why d'you want the keys to the lorry?"

Which meant he had them.

Ellis took a step toward him, and set his mien firm—not menacing, exactly, but he was more than done with these people, and flat tamping that someone in this crowd thought it a grand idea to involve a boy who wasn't even old enough to shave yet, give him a gun, and tell him to use it against someone they told him he should hate. Ellis held out his hand again, crooked his fingers.

"Because I don't like the use it's been put to. Because I can. And because I still need to get home." He turned on the crowd again, and raised his voice. "So I can make sure the people of Wellech haven't already descended into craven brutes like the people of Whitpool, specifically the people of Newridge, have apparently done." He shook his head, and allowed his disgust to show clearly. "Bloody damn, war's not even two days in yet, and look what you've already become. P'raps you'd do better to take all this zeal for guns and violence to the recruiting offices. Oh, but then there's a chance you might come up against someone who's not a child, who's armed, and capable of *shooting back*." He said the last through his teeth, then spun on the boy again, hand out. "Give. It. Here."

The boy swallowed, shot a quick uncertain look behind Ellis, presumably to his mam or tad, and frowned. He hesitated; Ellis didn't look back to see what kind of silent communication was going on around him, only kept staring the boy down, waiting. The boy's facial expressions went from mulish to indecisive to angry and back to uncertain again. But he fished in his coat pocket and came up with the key.

"You're not a Whitpool Warden, though," he said as he handed it over. "Are you allowed to steal a lorry when you're not in Wellech?"

Ellis snatched the key out of the boy's hand. "Report me." He peered up at the people in the lorry's bed. "Let's go."

When they only stared at him, Ellis jerked his head with a look that said *Hurry up!* and reached up for one of the little girls. He didn't pause when one of the men cried out in those same rolling gutturals Ellis had heard from Aleks, but he did try to look compassionate and unmonsterlike as he carried the girl toward Howell's car. He watched over his shoulder as the two men gathered up the other children and climbed warily down from the flatbed, eyeing everyone around them. Hesitant. Watchful. Scared.

Ellis kept a careful eye on everything. Waiting for the now silent crowd to object. For the mouthy man to say something at exactly the wrong time. For a bloody *mole* or owl or something equally ludicrous to stumble out into the center of it all and startle these people out of their confused paralysis before Ellis could get everyone into Howell's car and away.

Right now the only things holding them back were the new, as yet unanalyzed knowledge of who Ellis was, and the bravado he was spewing all over the place like a tom spraying his territory. He needed to move very fast before it occurred to anyone else besides that boy that yes, Ellis *was* out of his jurisdiction, and yes, the First Warden of Wellech *did* intend to actually steal the lorry.

"Get them out of here," he said through the open door as men and children piled in around Howell. "Don't back up and turn around—just circle 'round the yard, then drive like a hole to the nether is opening up behind you. I don't think any of them will follow you, but don't take the chance."

Howell pressed his lips into a stubborn line. "Not until you've got that lorry started."

It took two seconds for Ellis to decide it would be a waste of time to argue. He nodded, said, "I don't think they should go home yet. Take them to Eira. And..." He lifted his head to scan the crowd again—some skulking off, but most still watching—then dipped back down and lowered his voice. "No one knows about Aleks?"

"Milo was afraid..." Howell didn't finish, only gestured out the windscreen.

Ellis knew exactly what Milo had been afraid of. Now Ellis realized it was far more insidious than Folant's boyos in Wellech and an unreasonably bitter little woman in Brooking.

We need Kymbrygh united, Alton had said, as though it was just that easy. Ellis was a little embarrassed that, until now, he hadn't understood exactly how difficult it could be.

"Right. Well. Good. Keep it that way." Ellis tapped a restless drumbeat on the car's roof as he thought about Aleks in Milo's kitchen, looking wary and afraid, but still *opening the door* to someone he didn't know. "And tell him to stay out of sight. He shouldn't answer the door for anyone but you, Glynn, and possibly me, unless there are others you know you can trust with his life."

Howell nodded, waited for Ellis to walk calmly across to the lorry and get in. Waited some more until Ellis keyed the ignition. Ellis watched through the rearview as the lights of Howell's car circled 'round and headed west while Ellis navigated the lorry slowly onto the road east.

He didn't stop clamping his jaw and watching his back until he took the sliproad toward Bamwell and crossed into Wellech. He breathed in deep, convinced he could smell the river in the chill, misty air, and made himself unclench.

Thought about Alton and his assertions that all cruelty and brutality needed was a bogey on which to focus fear, upon which to build power. About Milo telling him that frightened people were a bigger threat than whatever it was they were frightened of. About Folant building an entire worldview on something as small in scope and petty in nature as personal rejection.

And concluded that Wellech needed a lot of work before it could become what Alton—and Kymbrygh, and Preidyn—apparently needed it to be. Deciding how he was going to start made Ellis feel marginally less helpless and outraged.

His head still wouldn't stop pounding, though.

※

It was a hot spring, though Ellis couldn't feel the heat and humidity against his skin the way Milo clearly could. The steam was thick, though, curling Milo's hair at the ends, sticking it to his forehead. A magelight drifted above and before him, slicking shadow to cave walls damp and rough.

And empty.

It took a bit for the import of that to hit Ellis.

Straw old and mildewed wilted in nooks that once must have been nests. An egg the size of a small boulder lay abandoned, cracked but not broken, and half buried beneath hills of old hay and clover gone brown and brittle.

Milo knelt, eyes overbright, and laid his hands to the shell. Stared down at it. *Looked*, perhaps, but Ellis couldn't tell, not like this. Whatever Milo felt, whatever he Saw, it made his jaw set tight and his fists clench as he pulled away.

There wasn't time for more than that. There was no sound in this Dream either—it happened that way sometimes, one sense gone and another hyperactive—but Milo jumped and whipped around to narrow his eyes at the darkness behind him. With one last angry look at the dead dragon egg, he snuffed the magelight, and...

Well, Ellis didn't know. Everything went dark, and the Dream broke, giving Ellis just enough information to increase his already constant worry, and the frustration that he couldn't do a blessed thing about any of it.

The headache was still there when he woke.

"And how would you even know what your Pennaeth has and has not been doing?" Folant's sneer was full of contempt.

A bigger bogey. And here it was.

Ellis stood back, straightened his spine, and allowed one corner of his mouth to turn up. "Indeed," he said, hushed and grim. "How would I know?" He cut his glance away from Folant and toward the councilmembers. "Certainly not because our Pennaeth has been keeping your First Warden apprised. It's really a good thing for all of us that I don't rely on our Pennaeth for anything more than a nice pint down the pub now and then and perhaps a spot of cards or dicing when his pockets get light." He shrugged. "Despite the lack of proper forthcoming, I'm well aware of what's out there, what might be coming, and what needs to be done about it. I'm also well aware of why our Pennaeth has done nothing to protect us from the worst, should it happen."

Folant narrowed his eyes, not even a little bit shaken by the implication, but angry now. "So well informed about 'reasons' that don't actually exist."

"Oh, they do. And I am." Ellis held Folant's gaze. "And, I'm afraid, I don't think Wellech would take kindly to merely rolling over and welcoming their new foreign overlords." Several soft mutters went up from around the table. Ellis only kept watching Folant. "Good thing I've planned ahead, yeah?"

"You might," Folant said, soft and dangerous, "want to plan for your defense when I bring a charge for false accusations."

Ellis tilted his head. "I might do. If I wasn't quite confident I could prove it."

Folant stared for a moment, fury blazing behind his eyes, before he jerked his chin, dismissed Ellis altogether with a finality Ellis knew was going to stick. Forget Folant's anger at what he'd see as another betrayal, that Ellis was trying to take Pennaeth, just as he'd taken First Warden. This, what Ellis had just done, the open accusation of treason he'd just thrown like a gauntlet, might as well have been an axe severing every last tie between them but for the genetic one neither of them could do a thing about.

"I've my own plans." Folant sat back. "If you had your way, *dyn bach*"—Ellis made himself not bristle at the derisive slant to that; *little man*, indeed!—"Wellech would be overrun from the inside, all those rats deserting their sinking—"

"That analogy might hold more water," Ellis cut in, "if those rats, as you call them, were actually deserting and not being run out. *Which*," he said louder when Folant opened his mouth, "is beside the point."

It wasn't, not really, but Ellis couldn't let this get sidetracked into a debate about prejudice and its justifications. Because Ellis knew these people, and he knew whatever Alton had threatened wasn't going to get through some of their biases. Not unless Ellis gave them something bigger to worry about.

"The point right now is that Wellech's Pennaeth has left us defenseless in the face of a very real and very dangerous threat. And if any of you think for one second that any invasion that might be coming *wouldn't* include magical strikes—against which, we've *also* been left nearly defenseless—then Wellech will deserve what might be coming to her.

"I'll be kind, for now, and assume it's mere incompetence that's left us open to what an enemy might try to bring down on us. But kindness only works while a Pennaeth serves as nothing more than a figurehead like Whitpool's—someone to cut ribbons and smile at school children." He paused and swept the council with another hard look. "When *our* Pennaeth has not only refused to do his duty by the people he's meant to protect but has actively worked against his country, I *will not* choose kindness, and I will not stand by and watch it done. You have a decision to make here, one that's likely to be one of the most important ones you'll ever make, and it *will* affect each and every one of us here and everyone we love."

He'd allowed himself to become angry. To all but shout toward the end there. Because he couldn't help seeing Milo's face every time he thought of those "rats" Folant wouldn't shut up about.

Sighing, Ellis slowly took his seat, and shrugged as nonchalantly as he could manage. "You don't decide when enemy ships show up in our harbors, and you don't decide based on who's bought you the most cups of cider over the years. You do it now, and you do it based on who can actually lead when a leader is needed. *A fo ben, bid bont.* Who d'you trust to build that bridge, then?"

He left it there, making it clear he was done, and waited for someone to call a vote. It only took a few minutes of uncomfortable silence and meaningful looks skidding back and forth across the table before Watcyn knocked his gnarled knuckles against it and motioned that the vote be secret this time, rather than the usual voice vote. No one objected as Cled scrounged up enough slips of paper and pieces of graphite or charcoal to go around.

Folant was smirking, overly confident, because he still had his boyos around him, he still had no reason to worry he didn't have the votes he thought he did. He didn't even bother to look around the table at the councilmembers as they bent their necks and marked their slips. He wasn't insightful by nature, he didn't pay attention, so he hadn't seen the shock of understanding on several of their faces as Ellis had leveled his accusations. The anger on several others when Folant hadn't bothered to deny them. Or even the betrayal on at least one of the men who'd likely never have dreamed of voting against Folant Rees until a man who called himself Mastermind had paid him a visit.

Ellis could've told Alton he hadn't really needed to threaten anyone. Rah-rahing along to hateful rhetoric that fed one's bigotry was one thing—understanding that the person feeding it to you was also willing to feed you to it was entirely another. Folant had given them their bogey, but Ellis had just delivered a bigger one in Folant himself. And Folant clearly didn't know it.

Folant said nothing while the votes were collected and counted, still assured, still self-righteous and smug. Until the tally was announced. *Then* Folant had a lot to say.

Ellis merely sat back, silent, and let it all wash over him. Folant's rage, Folant's betrayal, Folant's rude slings and vicious barbs at the councilmembers who were "supposed to have my back!" He didn't say a word about Ellis. He didn't even look at him. It was as though Folant had wiped his son entirely from his world. Except for one moment amidst the raving when he shook off the hands of the two trying to lead him out and turned on Ellis. Folant's fists slammed the table, and he leaned over them, right in Ellis's face.

"You bring that Dewin scum that's twisted your head around here and I'll kill him."

Ellis ignored the gasps from the others at the blatant, public threat, and looked steadily back at Folant. "Your friends already tried. With *magic*, you bloody hypocrite. Didn't work. But try it again, and I'll make sure I'm the one to arrest you. That's *if* you don't give me a reason before that."

It was the lack of surprise on Folant's face. The narrowing down of wrath to cold calculation.

Ellis hadn't been sure before. Alton hadn't implied Folant had been involved in what happened at Old Forge. But once Ellis's eyes had been opened to just how far Folant would go to get something he wanted—or be rid of something he didn't—the immoral deviousness he'd employ when thwarted, all while convinced he was perfectly righteous and justified, it only made sense.

Horrible, awful sense.

There were the congratulations still to get through once Folant was escorted out of the council offices. There was the swearing-in as Ellis set his hand over his heart and promised to guide and protect Wellech as its Pennaeth or die trying. There were the invitations to the Grange to celebrate, the toasts to raise his cup to, the smiles to return.

And all Ellis could think about through all of it was that he missed Milo with an ache so deep and painful he wasn't sure he was going to be able to keep breathing through it.

"How d'you manage a clever codename like Wildfire, and I get a crap one?"

"Maybe 'cause I *am* clever, and you're... well, we'll leave that one unsaid, shall we?" Dilys's voice was distant and tinny, but the grin behind it was clear even through the static.

Ellis rolled his eyes at the box of plugs and switches and dials he only still barely knew how to work. The book of instructions that was delivered with the equipment was thorough, but it wasn't as though Ellis had the time to study it like he needed to.

He adjusted the headset that never failed to pinch at his ears and leave them red, sometimes even bruised if he left them on for too long. "Tell me how things are there."

Ynys Dawel was still occasionally suffering assaults coming from the Surgebreaks, but according to what intelligence came through—along the ad hoc but still growing underground network across Kymbrygh—the Royal Navy had already decimated most of the planes stationed there. What they missed, the Tirryderch magic folk sent to defend the island took care of. Between the wards and the focused battlemagic and the sheer numbers of those wielding it, nothing had broken through to Tirryderch like the attacks clearly intended.

There was a pause before Dilys's voice came back, more subdued. "Let's say that many here have come to the realization that it was perhaps a good thing in the end that citizens of one place became citizens of another."

Ellis almost laughed, but it wasn't really funny. Who knew Folant more or less running nearly anyone with magic out of Wellech for over a decade would one day be a blessing? For Tirryderch, at least.

He didn't say it was starting look like it might come bite them all on their collective arses before too long. Dilys would know that. Anyway, it wasn't something one should say on uncoded chatter over open radio waves. They were speaking in Kymrae, erring on caution's side, but Folant had taught Ellis the very hard lesson that one couldn't necessarily count on one's own countrymen to keep the good of the country in mind.

"El—*Prince*." Dilys had lowered her voice, her tone holding none of the good-natured mockery that had been there when she'd greeted him with *Prince? Really?* through open laughter. "Every parish needs its citizens right now. So how are things *there*?"

Ellis paused, going over the numbers in his head. Again. He didn't have enough actual witches and sorcerers, and only two mages who'd been refugees from Ostlich-Sztym in early spring whom Ellis had managed to talk into staying put. If Ellis could get Lilibet to work with all of them, along with those who had magic but not enough of it to qualify for a coven, Wellech might be all right. Maybe.

"We'll be fine," Ellis managed, and tried really hard to believe it.

They exchanged what information it was safe to exchange. The first reports of dragon attacks were coming in from Nasbrun, seemingly orchestrated by dragonkin who, yes, really were commanding dragons in a way no one had suspected was possible. Verdish warships had broken through the blockade in the Gulf of White Sands and made a play for the southeastern shore of Preidyn; the Royal Navy had taken heavy losses but hadn't given an inch of ground, and the Royal Forces had deployed its infant Air Brigade from Werrdig for the first time to back them up. Other Western Unified countries were finally entering the various theaters. Desgaul and Eretia had at long last ratified their own war declarations against Taraverde and placed whole divisions under the Western Unified banner, *finally* deploying naval support to Preidyn and ground troops to Błodwyl and Esplad to try to staunch the flow across the continent. When word spread that Taraverde was using dragons as weapons, even Macran had made it official, wary of Taraverde marching down through Proyya once it was through with Nasbrun, and arriving at Macran's borders.

The only relatively good news coming out of the continent lately was an unconfirmed report of some kind of attack on a garrison in Colorat, a lot of explosions, and a small clutch of sickly dragons flying off while the whole place burned. Ellis had Dreamed very little, had seen no reports from Alton or anyone else that even mentioned it, but he *knew* it was Milo. Somehow.

"The entire continent will be at war by the end of the summer," Ellis said, morose and missing Milo and rethinking yet again whether staying here to look after Wellech "just in case" had been the right choice.

Dilys was quiet for a while, long enough Ellis started to wonder if she'd gone out of range, before she said, "Listen, I need to tell you something."

Ellis waited, but when she didn't go on, he frowned. "So tell me, then."

It took another moment, somehow tense over blank staticky airwaves, but finally Dilys said, "I can't *tell* you what I don't really know is true. Right? But." Static. Silence. Then, "We found a stray hawkweed. It was really hard digging it up, and it got mangled a bit. So we couldn't really tell for sure. Anyway, it turned out to be poisonous."

Ellis narrowed his eyes at the radio's control panel. Nonsense. All of it. But this was Dilys, and Dilys, for all her wry wisecracking ways, didn't babble nonsense for no reason. And certainly not here, now, like this.

So. Coded. Somehow.

Hawkweed wasn't poisonous. It also didn't grow in Tirryderch. It didn't grow anywhere in Kymbrygh except in Wellech, in the crags of the cliffs along the River Chwaer. Which was why the autumn riverboat race through Silver Run Valley was called the Hawkweed Sprint by the locals.

There'd been scuttlebutt a couple days ago that three Tirryderch Wardens had raided what should have been an abandoned fishing camp on the southern coast. It turned out to be occupied by a group everyone suspected were the ones who'd bombed the mining camp and railroad tracks only weeks ago, hunkered down and waiting for their Verdish comrades to break through the navy and Ynys Dawel to storm Tirryderch.

Hard digging it up. The suspected spies had been questioned.

Mangled. Bloody damn, had they been tortured?

Poisonous. Well. That was fairly clear.

It didn't surprise Ellis that Dilys had been one of the Wardens who'd captured the spies, if indeed that's what they turned out to be. It didn't surprise him that if something happened in Tirryderch, Dilys would be in the thick of it.

It also didn't surprise him that she'd bend the rules to warn him that something might be coming Wellech's way.

"Glad you caught it before it could hurt anyone." Ellis took his finger off the *transmit* toggle to clear his throat, then pressed it again. "That stuff will give a person nightmares."

Ellis hoped the *I'll get Lilibet on it* in that bit came through.

"*Yes.*" The grin was back in Dilys's voice. "Yes. That's it."

It had.

Ellis grinned too, a bit winded without having even moved, until Dilys said, "Prince," sober now, and soft, in a way that made Ellis sit up straight and brace himself. "It was..." Static again, the hesitation longer this time, before Dilys finally continued, "It was the thief who tried to steal your cariad's treasure."

There was no need to pause and try to parse it.

Cennydd.

Caught. Finally. But only after he'd crossed the line completely into murderous sedition.

Ellis just stared at the radio for a moment, breathless, before he managed, "And will he be trying to steal again?"

"No." Harsh. Clipped. "Never again."

Dead, then. Tortured to an end just as horrible and painful as what he'd tried to do to Milo, maybe, or a summary execution because *That's treason, Rhywun Ellis.*

Again, Ellis only sat there, staring at dials and wires, unable to decide how to feel about any of it. Except for the chunk of knotted grief behind his breastbone that Dilys had been a part of it.

"I'm sorry," was all he could think of.

He was unsure if Dilys's terse "I'm not" was the whole truth. He let it go. Because, really—what could he do?

"I've got to go," Dilys said, her tone once again cheerful enough if you didn't know her.

Ellis hesitated, deciding he owed her at least this, but unsure how to word it. Eventually he just said, "Blight it," and toggled to transmit again. "Listen, he was all right last time I saw him."

Dead air for a long moment, a staticky whine as Dilys likely toggled on then off again, before she answered, "Yeah, last time I saw him too. What does that have to do with how he might be now?" Gloomy. Tired. And a bit annoyed.

Again, Ellis had to think of how to say it, and settled for, "A person can dream, yeah?"

Not just Milo having supper with strangers this time, or Milo playing the violin Ellis hadn't known he could play. No, this last Dream had been soundless, as they sometimes were, and fuzzed out in places that probably mattered. But Ellis had seen clearly when Milo had set his hand to a chain as thick as a giant's thighbone, shoved a pulse of power through it. And though Ellis saw very little of anything else, the broken chain and the dragon leaping into the sky, Milo grinning as he watched, had been sharp and well-defined.

He's freeing dragons, he wanted to tell Dilys. *He's doing the one thing I think he would've left me for, the one thing he'd willingly die to accomplish.*

He couldn't say any of it. Not over the radio.

Dilys was silent for quite a while this time before she ventured, "We're going to have a very long talk next time I see you."

Ellis shut his eyes, smile soft and wide. "Wildfire..." He paused, shook his head, and kept his eyes shut tight because the knot in his throat was making them burn. "I honestly can't wait."

✺

"Ah." Lilibet stopped pushing the bath chair up the walk, looked Ellis up and down from over the top of her tad's head, then wrinkled her nose in disapproval. "That's not the tie I saw you wearing."

Ellis barely kept himself from adjusting his tie, though he did manage to withhold his growl as he signaled for Bella and Bumble to calm the deuce down and *sit*.

"Mam, if you don't stop doing that, I'm going to forbid you from Dreaming for me. Ever."

Not an idle threat. He'd nearly demanded it when he'd shown up at Rhediad Afon after he got back from Whitpool, and she'd taken one look at him and said, "Ah. So that's today, then." And he'd known—seen it all over her—that she'd Dreamed what Milo was going to do. It hadn't occurred to Ellis, though, not until she volunteered the information—guilty, maybe, but still unapologetic—that it had been her who'd told Milo that if he went, he needed to make sure Ellis stayed. Ellis had only just started speaking to her again a few days ago when he'd decided how he wanted to go about fixing Wellech, and that only because she was part of the plan.

Bamps smiled up at Ellis from his bath chair. "*Fy machgen!*" He held out his arms.

Ellis returned the endearment with one of his own—"*Haia, hen ddwylo*"—and bent to give his bamps a kiss on his wrinkled cheek and a quick embrace. *Quick* because Ellis was nudged out of the way by Bella a second later, paws gentle on Bamps's lap. "It's good to see you out," Ellis said as he straightened.

He was thinner than the last time he'd been out of his rooms, but Bamps remembered who Ellis was this time, so that was an improvement.

"It's good to *be* out on a fine day like this." Bamps stroked Bella's silky head and gestured at Bumble, parked against Ellis's leg. "That one was stuck to me like a burr until ten seconds ago."

"Well, he's always been a been of a barmcake." Ellis scratched Bumble's ears. "Will you stay up for tea? I've some business that needs doing, but after, I can come up to your rooms."

Bamps hooked a thumb at Lilibet over his shoulder. "The General says it's the solarium for me."

Lilibet rolled her eyes but she was smiling. "The General is a title I'm thinking is about to be handed down." She shot her glance behind Ellis, eyebrow lifting. "And there are your troops."

Ellis looked toward the ornate little gate that separated Rhediad Afon's private grounds from the formal gardens that flanked the main road to the Reescartref Bridge. Petra was letting herself through, speaking low and serious to Andras, who was anxiously twisting his hat in his hands as she stopped him and waited for a signal from Ellis to approach.

"Are you sure about that one?" Lilibet was eyeing Andras openly, making him squirm.

Ellis didn't chide her. "Not entirely, considering the last time I spoke to him for more than giving him orders now and then was a few years ago when I gave him a formal reprimand."

Both Andras and Bethan—not only for accosting Milo the way they'd done, but for potentially embarrassing Wellech. If Milo had followed through on his threat to make a report to Kymbrygh's MP, which by rights he probably should have done, it would've been a bloody circus. But Ellis had been watching both Bethan and Andras closely since then, and if he could make Andras into someone useful to what Ellis wanted to happen next...

He looked at his mam. "If I can convince someone like him to take up my cause, I've a chance with the rest of them. We need everyone."

Lilibet merely gave Ellis a fond look and started pushing Bamps's chair toward the house again. "I'll tell Grwn to set up the private dining room for lunch for six, shall I?"

Because Dyfan from the miners' union and Wynny from the farmsteaders should be arriving any moment now, and Ellis had forgot to mention them when he'd told Lilibet of his plan.

Ellis rolled his eyes. "We both know you already have done."

Bamps twisted in his chair to smirk at Ellis over his shoulder. "If I had a copper for every time I've said as much to her over the years..." He turned back around, cackling.

Ellis watched them, smiling, until they rounded the curve toward the service door. He turned back toward Petra and Andras, and gestured them over.

"Come inside. We'll have some sherry while we wait for the others."

◉

Ellis had chosen to have this meeting here at Rhediad Afon partially because Lilibet was part of his plan and it was just easier to come to her. But mostly because he'd never hired household staff for the Croft, and he couldn't be bothered with organizing an impressive lunch. The staff at Rhediad Afon was little changed from even before Ellis had come along, and they ran the place with both love and military precision. Lilibet often accused Ellis of visiting as often as he did because of Martyn's skill in the kitchens. She wasn't entirely wrong.

The cawl was enough to stop Andras gawping and start him using his mouth for more savory purposes. The leek and bacon tart sent Wynny into paroxysms of ecstatic delight. Dyfan, always reserved and generally cynical by nature, knew exactly what Ellis was up to but still quietly allowed that the sewin and steamed samphire with watercress sauce was better than his nain's. Petra merely inhaled everything in front of her while cutting amused glances at Ellis.

The red ale and scrumpy served alongside the courses probably wasn't hurting. The cream liqueur served after would hopefully do the rest of the job of loosening postures and reserves and, more importantly, tongues.

Lilibet, because Ellis was her son and she loved him, had helped to put everyone at ease and keep the small talk going while Ellis went over in his head what he wanted to accomplish with all this. So when Grwn emerged from the dining room's service door with the honey cakes and tea, Lilibet waited for everyone to be served and for Grwn to make his way back out before she sat back and gave the gathering one of her most brilliant, charming smiles.

"It's so good of you all to make the time to join us. We know you've all got important matters to attend, and not enough daylight to attend them." She tipped no more than a dewdrop of milk into her tea and stirred with a delicate *tink tink tink* of silver on porcelain. "But we know that all of you, especially, would understand the even more urgent matters your new Pennaeth has brought you here to discuss."

> Feed them—check
> Charm them to within an inch of their lives—check
> Acknowledge their importance—check
> Point out your own—check
> Imply they're already informed enough to know why they're here—check
> Suggest you need help they're uniquely qualified to give—check

It was all Ellis could do not to grin at his mam. Instead he sat back, stuck the tip of his spoon in the cream atop his honey cake, and proceeded to dig a small channel. Thought about Alton and his bogeys. About how alarmingly effortless it had been to make one out of Folant.

About Milo saying fear was easier to catch than pox. How he'd left his life, his dragons, Ellis, to walk into things at which Ellis was only getting worrisome glimpses because it was what was *right* and *necessary*. How he'd understood Ellis down to bone and left behind just enough of a map to show him where he could go, where he *should* go, stopping short of making all but one of Ellis's choices for him.

How Ellis *missed* him with a soul-deep ache that didn't get easier as time went on. In fact it got worse every time he caught a hazy glance of things he was pretty sure he wasn't meant to be seeing.

It solidified things, though. Ellis didn't use his Dreams the way Lilibet did. He couldn't. It wasn't the same for him. But he could learn from the lessons of them. Take vague, ephemeral ideas and outline them in the reds of Dreams that meant *this is important.* Shut his eyes, watch the possible steps a person could take, follow each trail, then decide which was the one that might be most useful.

He'd thought very carefully about what each person here had to offer. What their connections were and how influential they might be when it came to it. What might be eked out of them if given the proper motivation. How all of them together might cultivate the nascent little seeds Ellis had been carefully sowing since even how his nain said Milo's heart was inside it, and bound to the dragons'. But Ellis had looked it up since then, pored through the little information he could find on it.

Clan, of course, but he'd known that already. *Protection* too, but only minimal, and that was implied in *clan* anyway.

He was grateful for it in an entirely new way, though, when he found himself standing on the edge of a ridge just south of Caeryngryf, looking down into a meadow where what he was pretty sure was a massive horned redcrest crouched, watching him back.

"And you..." Ellis gave himself a moment to swallow his surprise and clear his throat. "You say it's been here since...?"

"Three days ago," Olwyn said. Her weathered face was barely visible beneath the brim of her wide floppy hat, but since she was pale as milk and bald as an egg, Ellis figured it was for the best. The summer had turned out to be one of the more intense Kymbrygh had seen, and autumn wasn't offering much relief so far; today it seemed the sun was actually trying to blind them first then roast them. "Ate up nine of my flock and at least three of Arawn's, but he hasn't managed to get a proper count yet."

The sheep had since wisely fled the scene, and from what Olwyn had told Ellis, Arawn was still out trying to catch them all. Or what was left of them.

It was luck Ellis even happened to be in the area. He'd had reports from some of the Wardens that folk were gathering on the bluffs overlooking Caeryngryf. Setting out camp chairs and picnic rugs and settling in with their field glasses to watch the Verdish ships try to take on the Preidynīg Navy's blockade several leagues off the coast. Ellis had been moved to break it up and warn the looky-loos off. Those battles were getting closer and closer, after all, more worrying, and one stray shot...

"Why hasn't the dragon followed the flock, I wonder?" Ellis shook his head. There was nothing here for it to eat now, after all. "And what's it doing here in the first place?"

Wellech got the very occasional flyover, certainly, with Caeryngryf getting the greater part of the few, it being the largest port town. Sat on the northeast tip of Kymbrygh, a sort of corridor on the very edge of the western migration path, it had good whaling in the warmer months if a dragon was so inclined. So spotting one in the sky or skimming the sea now and then wasn't unprecedented. But Ellis had never heard of a dragon actually landing anywhere east of Whitpool. Dragons knew very well where their safe havens were, and Wellech had never been one of them. And redcrests—if that was what this one was; he'd have to look it up later—redcrests weren't supposed to be in these parts at all. They flew the central migration paths, and as far as Ellis knew, didn't venture this far west of the continent. Ever.

"That's what *I* want t' know." Olwyn squinted up at Ellis. "Think yer cariad'd fancy a trip out?" She waved down to the meadow and the bulk of the wary dragon hunkered among the ragwort and thistle. "Don't know how we're t' shoo it, else. It won't move."

Ellis ignored the pang at "yer cariad" and focused on the amusing mental picture of Olwyn trying to "shoo" a dragon. And she *would* do. Might have done already, though the fact she was standing here probably said otherwise. Dragons were unpredictable at best; it was unwise to approach one in any circumstance, and this one looked... angry.

...No.

"Sick," Ellis muttered. "It's... I think it's sick."

There was a bare patch where scales should be riding the shoulder of its right foreleg, and another that circled its neck. A wide swath of what looked like moss clung to the spiky ridges on its knotty spine and all the way down its tail. Its massive wings looked intact but they were splayed out and drooping around its body like mastless sails instead of tucked tight to its back. As though they'd simply collapsed and the dragon didn't have the strength to collect them. Its sides were heaving, as if breathing was a chore. Most telling of all, the dragon was just *sitting* there, watching them—cagey, of course, and clearly ready to defend if it had to, but dragons tended to retreat in the face of anyone but dragonkin. They were skivers, rather than provokers. Like prizefighters walking away from a scuffle because they knew they had nothing to prove and could hurt someone if they participated.

"D'you smell anything?" Ellis asked Olwyn.

Olwyn frowned, pursed her lips, wrinkled her nose. She inhaled, long and deep, then scowled up at Ellis.

"Flowers. Sheep dip. Dirt. Grass."

"Not petrol." Ellis nodded, concerned now.

Even this far away, his nose should've been twitching with the sharp scent of dragon. This one clearly hadn't had its fire fed in a while. And it was sick.

Lead had been the verdict after the ruckus at Old Forge. Cennydd had been lacing legs of lamb with massive doses of lead coated with magic, and feeding it to the mam dragon first, ingratiating himself, before she let him feed it to her calf.

"*Poison*," Milo had spat, clutching the report from Eira in a fisted hand. "He'd been *poisoning* dragons. And for *months*."

Stomach pain. Confusion. Difficulty concentrating.

"Chaotic mood shifts," Milo had growled. "It apparently sometimes makes the one who's been poisoned quite mad and violent. It also sometimes makes them more *biddable*." He'd thrown the report at the desk, and when it didn't result in a satisfying crash, he'd swept the books and inkpot after it, not even pausing when the movement apparently pulled at his wound and made him grimace. "It's a gamble, Eira says, but Llundaintref told her it's possible to spell the metal with a bit of Natur magic so it feeds off the energy of the dragon itself."

Ellis had frowned, confused. "But I thought magic didn't really work on dragons."

"It doesn't. Mostly. But these spells work on the metal, so it rather evens the odds."

Cennydd had been working with the Purity Party. The sorcerer with him, according to Milo, had a foreign accent. Dragons were disappearing in Central Màstira. Horned redcrests flew the migration path that took them right over it.

They were clan animals, dragons. And an animal that sickened could lose the sharper edges of its instincts. Could lose its clan. Could lose its way home.

"Right." Ellis shoved out a breath and set a hand to Olwyn's shoulder. "Come with me. I've suddenly got a lot of work that needs doing, and I don't trust you not to get yourself eaten."

Olwyn huffed but allowed Ellis to steer her away and back down the ridge. "Will ye send fer yer dragonkin, then?"

If only I could, Ellis thought, but merely patted at Olwyn's back and kept walking.

Chapter 19—Polyphony

: music with two or more sounds happening simultaneously

The good thing about not having the time to so much as think was not having the time to so much as *think*. And while there was a lot to think *about*—like Wellech and Milo and Dreams and war and Wellech and *Milo*—there were only so many things upon which Ellis could have an impact.

This, he decided as he peered up at the banner, was one of those things.

Wellech Unedig, Kymbrygh Unedig, Preidyn Unedig
United Wellech, United Kymbrygh, United Preidyn

It wasn't terribly original as slogans went. Most countries dragged into the troubles of the world had adopted some variation on the theme. But it was simple, it was succinct, it placed Wellech as the keystone to success, and most importantly, it was in the native Kymrae.

"*Mae cenedl heb ei llais yn genedl heb ei henaid,*" Wynny had pointed out when they'd discussed it all months ago in Lilibet's dining room, an adage so old it was said to have emerged, already woven into the soil, as the isle of Kymbrygh rose from the ocean. *A nation without its voice is a nation without its soul.* And considering that every child in Kymbrygh learned Kymrae before they learned Preidish, or at least alongside it, using the language in what Ellis had worked his arse off to make Wellech's new motto seemed to bolster the sentiment behind it.

"Here, you look like you could do with one." Tomos, a toddler clinging to his shin and an infant in a sling across his chest, nudged at Ellis's elbow with a jar of what looked like some of that fizzy lemon stuff Ellis hadn't had a moment to try yet. "'S like champagne for tweenies."

Ellis frowned as he took the jar. "Where are their mams today?" He waved at the children, the elder of them now trying to climb Tomos's leg with one hand and making grabby gestures for Tomos's drink with his other.

"Oh, they're about. Cristyn is helping her mam and brother get the boat ready for the second race, and Lynnie's off to find this one"—he lifted the toddler, laughing now, by the seat of his trousers—"something he'll eat without grizzling." He raised the boy up until he could grin and rub noses with him. "I'm convinced no such thing exists." The little boy was screaming laughter now, high-pitched and thoroughly entertained with his little feet off the ground and his bum in the air.

Ellis grinned and took a sip of the lemon fizz.

Tomos had wanted to be a tad but had no interest in being a cariad. Considering there was a plentiful pool of women who felt the same, he'd had no problem arranging conjugal contracts and negotiating shared parental responsibilities. It so happened, though, that Tomos was one of the most pleasant, lovely people Ellis knew, and he'd chosen conjugal partners who seemed equally so. Thus, it wasn't often one saw Tomos and his creadurs out without said creadurs' mams.

Folant could've taken a lesson, Ellis mused, though he kept that to himself. Obviously. There were very few cautionary tales about carefully selecting one's contract partner as effective as the one of Lilibet Morgan and Folant Rees.

Thin-lipped, Ellis shook it off and raised the jar for another sip—the stuff was quite good—but paused when he caught sight of Andras and Zophia on the edge of the crowd. Clearly arguing. Clearly anxious. Clearly relieved when they spotted Ellis and started pushing their way toward him.

Ellis narrowed his eyes, pushed the jar back at a barely paying attention Tomos, and said, "You might want to go find Lynnie. Now. Quick."

Because Zophia's expression of urgent dread might as well have been a flashing bright sign that said *Trouble Brewing*.

Ellis didn't wait for an answer, only started weaving his way through the knot of people waiting on the banks of the Chwaer for the boats to line up for the coracle class race, the first of the day. And maybe it was stupid of Ellis to be reacting the way he was, on instant alert and *knowing* something was in the process of going wrong. Lilibet had Dreamed as he'd asked, had done it three times to be sure, and had come up with nothing that would justify Ellis cancelling the Hawkweed Sprint altogether—the whole damned Riverfest, to be honest—as he'd toyed with doing.

But his covert "put propaganda to good use" campaign had been going so well, better than he expected. A change was rolling over Wellech, propped up no doubt by the clear threat from outside, but also by the subtle push from the inside. Wynny had family in Tirryderch and had become an enthusiastic source of news about how its magical citizens were keeping the wolves from Tirryderch's, and thus Kymbrygh's, doors. Dyfan was using the quotas and the abolition of Folant's policies to deploy what magical talent he had in his ranks, thereby improving Wellech's mining output while also making the mines safer.

Changes that once would have gathered angry protest before, likely out of nothing more than habit fueled by ignorance. With Ellis's constant beating of his *The Enemy is Coming!* drums, there'd been nary a lifted eyebrow.

Wellech, for now at least, no longer seemed to think in terms of "magical citizens -vs- good citizens" and instead had begun to rally as a whole against anyone who wasn't them.

Which was why, Ellis decided, it was throwing him to see Andras and Zophia so clearly at odds. Andras was probably Ellis's greatest success thus far. A boy who'd grown to manhood in Folant's Wellech and—by virtue of being not only drawn into the new Pennaeth's "inner circle" but also being assigned the responsibility of mentoring a refugee Dewin and making her a reliable Warden—was now ardently embracing Ellis's.

"Rhywun Ellis!"

Andras was pushing through a clump of tweens who seemed to have acquired jugs of something Ellis suspected they were too young to be drinking. At the sounding of Ellis's name, they all looked up, confirmed it absolutely was their Pennaeth and First Warden carving a path in their direction, and promptly scattered.

It gave Andras and Zophia a clear lane, at least, and they pulled up in front of Ellis, both of them wide-eyed and breathless.

"Syr!" Andras gulped a breath. It gave Zophia time to jabber something in Ostlich, which was a bit inconvenient since Ellis had only had a year of Verdish in school and though the languages were similar, they weren't similar enough. To Ellis's surprise, Andras seemed to understand her because he snapped, "I *know*, Zoph, just belt up for *moment*, would you!" He shook his head, and told Ellis, "She forgets her Preidish when she gets excited."

Ellis gave Zophia a level look. "I expect my Wardens to keep their heads, regardless of circumstance, and I expect clear communication. Is that understood?"

The tone of it straightened Zophia's spine. She nodded, said, "Yes, syr, sorry, syr," in heavily accented Preidish, but it was calmer than thirty seconds ago. She was tall and pale and thin with a shock of black hair and vivid blue eyes that made it necessary for Ellis to deliberately keep thoughts of Milo from blooming. That became a bit easier when Zophia went on, "We have patrol the estuary, yes?" Broken and thickly inflected, but Ellis understood it this time, so he nodded. Zophia twitched her chin toward Andras. "There was man. He wear Warden coat. Badge. But he's not watch people, yes? He's watch water."

Ellis frowned. "I'm not sure I understand what you're saying."

"Not *people*. *Water*. You say watch *people*, yes? Watch for trouble." Her Preidish was breaking in places. "But he's watch water. So I watch him. And I see." She pulled up her sleeve and turned up her wrist. "*Saw*. I *saw*." She set her teeth, getting agitated again, and apparently frustrated that she had yet to make her point understood.

"There's a particular sort of mark," Andras put in, broad hand subtly set to Zophia's shoulder. "She's seen it. A tattoo that some of the Elite Constabularies wear."

Something in Ellis's chest went into freefall as Zophia nodded, emphatic and relieved, and pointed at her wrist. "Is here."

Ellis had never seen one but he knew of their existence. From what he'd read, Western Unified troops were using the marks as a way to identify captured enemy soldiers. It had only made the news services because those enemy soldiers were apparently cutting them from their skin when capture was imminent, and the idea of it was so sick-making reporters couldn't seem to stop mentioning it.

"That…" Ellis lost what wind he still had in his lungs. Lieutenant Colonel Crilly, Wellech's Home Guard commander, had assured Ellis that the vague threat Dilys and her compatriots had managed to extract from the captured spies had been baseless. That it had been merely a last-ditch effort to confuse. Lilibet had seen nothing in her Dreams. Ellis had tripled the patrols for the whole of the festival, and quadrupled them for today's races. Every Warden in the northeast quadrant of Wellech was watching *everything*. "What did we miss?"

Zophia either didn't understand the question or ignored it. "I saw." She kept pointing, blue eyes intent on Ellis, *willing* him to understand. "Not same—not *the* same. But close. And I feel—*felt* magic."

"All right." Ellis was already walking, compelling both Andras and Zophia to walk with him. "So you think someone from Taraverde's Elite Constabulary, someone with magic, is at the estuary watching for something in the water. Wait." He stopped short and took hold of Zophia's sleeve. "Water. You said he was watching the *water*. D'you mean the river?"

His heart sank when Zophia shook her head. "The sea."

Shite.

"Our frigates are still patrolling just past the buoys." Andras apparently knew exactly what Ellis was thinking. "I *saw* them this morning."

And yet it seemed that not only was someone waiting for something to get past them, but that someone had already managed it himself.

"C'mon, move." Urgency clipped Ellis's tone sharp as he tugged Zophia into a fast walk. Andras hurried to follow.

Cursing under his breath, Ellis steered them back the way he'd come, peering ahead and spotting Tomos looking back at him. Tomos must've twigged that something was up, because his children were nowhere to be seen, and his badge was now in plain sight on his waistcoat.

"And did you report all this to Tilli?" Ellis jerked his chin at Tomos in a curt *follow me.*

"*Fin,*" Zophia said, "I mean *no,*" followed by a string of rough, jagged chatter that Ellis recognized as Ostlich but was streaming by like a whirlwind jig, and the only word he understood of it was Tilli's name.

Andras rolled his eyes at Zophia and shook his head at Ellis. "She couldn't find Tilli, so she came to me. I was trying to tell her she shouldn't have left her post"—he shot a glare at Zophia; Zophia merely glared back—"but by the time I got the whole story out of her, we'd spotted you."

Well, that explained the arguing earlier.

"Right, then." Ellis stopped walking and waved Tomos in closer. "Go find Wylt and see if he can raise Tilli on the wireless. I want everyone looking for a man with—" He paused and turned to Zophia.

"Brown hair." It was prompt, and clear this time. She waved at Ellis. "Color like Syr. Warden coat and badge. Tall as..." She peered between Ellis, Andras, and Tomos before she said, "Taller than me, shorter than Tomos." Since Tomos was the shortest of the three men present, it surprisingly served to narrow it down fairly well. "Wide, though." Zophia put her hands out to each side of Andras's shoulders. "Bigger."

Grand. So they were looking for someone who sounded like he could probably be a prizefighter.

Ellis turned back to Tomos. "Relay all that to Tilli. I want every Warden up that way looking for this man. After that, I want whatever troops the Home Guard has in the area at the estuary and reconnoitering with Tilli if they haven't already been keeping in touch."

Which they better have been, but Crilly was a friend of Folant's and seemed to have issues with sharing authority with Folant's son. And Ellis was getting *bloody* tired of having to placate someone who was supposed to be on his own side into cooperating when an order came from anyone other than Alton. Ellis was going to have to talk to Alton about that, and soon.

"Also, I need someone to get hold of one of those frigates and tell them what we know. Don't wait for Lieutenant Colonel Jackass to do it, we haven't the time for his bosh. But do make sure it's someone who knows how to call the alert without anyone else who might be listening figuring out we're on to them."

Because whatever was going on here, it was looking to be something big. And Ellis would be damned if a single Wellech citizen came to harm on his watch.

They couldn't raise Tilli. Which became even more worrisome when Ellis understood that the man Zophia had spotted had Tilli's rifle strapped to his back. That came out in the stilted conversation that ensued as Ellis urged Calannog faster, *faster, damn you*, and Andras and Zophia tried to keep up on their own colder-bred horses.

He'd ordered a delay of the races before they'd started their mad dash to the estuary. And just in time, too—the emcee had been calling for the pistol to start the coracles on their way when Ellis had accosted him.

Maybe it was the delay that served as some sort of signal. Maybe it was the abrupt rise in chatter on the radio waves. Maybe it was that more than the one man Zophia had spotted had managed to infiltrate Wellech, and the First Warden suddenly taking off in the direction of the estuary told them they'd been found out.

Whatever it was, it did the job—Ellis was just barely within sight of the estuary, rounding the curve of the meander that would be the final leg of the Sprint, when the clamor went up.

Once the River Chwaer narrowed back down from the oxbow and wove its way through the interlocking spurs, it was all cliffs from there until it reached the Chwaer Bach Estuary and flowed out to sea. The rockface was steep and sheer, for the most part, but this channel had been river-carved in stages, leaving the cut bank side terraced in places in a sizeable step formation. It afforded room for a crowd to muster on the wide rocky treads for a good, if slightly precarious, overhead view of the boats that sped their hopeful way past.

It was why more spectators gathered here than at the estuary itself where the finish line was. The concave shape of the cut bank made the steps into an overhang from which one could see everything on the river below.

The hordes that had amassed here, waiting to spot the first coracle as it sprinted downriver, were screaming, and not in the way they should be doing. A swell of anxious shouts, amplified by the curved wall of toothed rock, rolled up and out just as Calannog skidded to a halt and Ellis jumped from his back. Heart a hard knot in his throat, Ellis pushed through the mash of confused people on the bank, telling them, "Back up! Out of the way!" until he could peer down on the panicked spectators who were all at once turning and trying to climb the steps and each other. Screams whelped out as a shout of "*Bomb!*" echoed up from somewhere. And then everyone started pushing.

Not thirty seconds later they were bottlenecked. The only way up to the bank from the steps was a natural channel in the rock, a long gentle slope that at its narrowest point was wide enough for two or three on a good day. Now, with the press from behind, five or six were trying to squeeze through at a time, and almost no one was getting past.

Ellis started yelling—"Stop! *Be still!*"—before they all shoved each other off the edges. It was a long drop to the water from up here.

He swooped down to snag up a child someone was holding above their head before they dropped her. There wasn't even a moment to make sure she was on her feet as he roughly put her down behind him before more were being held out toward him. Others began to claw their way up the too-steep rock.

Two more Wardens came barreling in from downriver, thank every goddess, their horses' hoofbeats loud on the cliff top's sedgy path. Ellis called out, "Marston! Willa! Get over here and help!" but he hadn't really needed to—Andras, along with some of the would-be spectators, was already heaving people up, and Marston and Willa immediately dismounted and dropped to their knees at the edge to start pulling.

It wasn't helping with the panic—it seemed to be making it worse. "Stop!" Ellis shouted again, and again every one of them ignored him. Probably didn't even hear him, too busy screaming and belling at each other and jockeying for space on rock steps that had looked a lot wider and safer only a moment ago. Ellis pushed his way to where bodies were clogging up the way out, and just started tugging. "*Stop!*" It was sharp, angry, almost despairing, because they weren't *listening*, they were making it all so much worse, and—

And then Zophia was taking hold of him, *yanking*, until she pulled him away with such shocking force he almost went over on his arse. She snapped, "Hurry, it's there," then shot away and up the edge of the cut bank at a run. Ellis didn't know what "it" was, but someone had shouted "Bomb!" before, so he went.

Zophia was fast, but Ellis's legs were longer. Good thing, too, because he caught her up as she pelted toward the cliff edge, hands out to either side and ahead of her, face screwed into a look of fierce concentration. Ellis had to grab at the back of her coat to keep her from running right off the cliff. She didn't seem to notice. She leaned over the edge, shouting something in guttural Ostlich that sounded furious and vicious as she windmilled her arms as though winding up for a bloody good throw then sliced her hand through the air.

Ellis hadn't even seen who she was yelling at until a man went flying backward at the base of the cliff where the bitten-apple contour of it sprawled back outward. The man landed just at the edge of the water in a wrecked-looking heap and went still.

"Knew I feel magic," Zophia muttered as she twisted her brow and frowned harder. "Fuse. Is burning."

Which meant it was too late. Ellis could smell the faintest whiff of charcoal rising from just beneath the lowest step of the cut bank. Whatever had been triggered, it involved black powder. And it was abruptly clear what the goal was here.

The point bar on the other side—the safer side—had been closed off. Signs told of dangerous erosion of the slip-off slope, Ellis could see the bold block letters from here. Thing was, the signs hadn't been there this morning when he'd ridden Calannog the length of the River Chwaer. And if there had been an erosion problem, he would've heard about it. Whoever that man was down there, he'd wanted everyone on this side of the river.

A sharp breath huffed out through Ellis's abruptly clogged throat. "It's going to blow up the steps." And all the people who were on them. Those who didn't get hit in the initial blast would die in the resulting rockslide or fall straight down the too-long drop to the water.

"*Fin*," growled Zophia, and shut her eyes, vibrating beneath Ellis's grip still fastened to her coat as she fisted her hands out in front of her. Opened them. Closed them. Turned them up toward her and pulled them in.

Gasps and new shouts went up from everyone who'd been scrambling below them as, in clumps of five and ten, they were lifted into the air and wafted up and over the top of the cliff. Ellis could do nothing but hold on to Zophia and watch as people were lofted right above his head, flailing and frightened, and dumped roughly down in the grass behind him.

Andras was helping people to their feet now, and directing them away, trying to instill calm, but almost none of them were having it. Panic made them irrational, and shock was probably not far behind. Willa dug a whistle out of her pocket, though, and once she started blowing it, sharp and shrill, everyone started moving in the direction she and Andras were waving them.

"Faster!" Ellis shouted to them. "We don't know what's down there!"

Zophia was still concentrating, ignoring Ellis and trying to shrug him off as he started tugging her back and away from the edge of the cliff before the bomb Ellis was now dead-sure was down there somewhere went off.

"Damn it, Zophia," Ellis snapped just as faint little *fwumps* sounded from beneath them, right under where the curve of the rockface cut off the line of sight. A small scree of pebbles plinked and plunked its way down as Zophia huffed a sharp "*Ha!*" and vibrated harder. Ellis stopped trying to pull her away and stared instead. Because those were...

"Bloody... *damn.*"

He had to choke back a faint, crazed little chuckle as small bundles of dynamite, blasting caps inserted snug and still fizzling, came loose from where they'd evidently been inserted into the crags of the rockface. Somehow. Magically? Maybe. There was no way anyone would've had the time to drill the holes necessary for the six—seven—*ten*, bloody *damn*, the bombs just kept coming, and counting them was making Ellis's gut hollow out. One by one the deadly packages drifted out from under the steps then sailed up into the sky like clay pigeons launched for skeet.

Up. *Away.* Out over the river and high above it.

The explosions were much grander than skeet, though—loud, frightening, and much too close but just far enough away.

The screaming ramped up again. People who'd been slowly letting the Wardens herd them out of danger all at once started running. Some took the time first to gather up family members; a few others were more interested in gawking, clearly awed, as Zophia continued to pluck out the trussed bombs and send them to explode just far enough up and out they would do no harm except to the ears of anyone close enough.

And there were a bloody *lot* of them. Enough that they would've taken out the entire cliff face, likely. It seemed like endless hours before the barrage finally stopped and there was nothing left but small clouds of smoke and ash catching the breeze to glide docilely downriver.

Zophia was still standing there—eyes closed tight, hands out, fists clenched—well after the last one had gone off. Ellis's ears were ringing; his heart hadn't yet seen fit to descend from his throat. He wanted nothing more at the moment than to park his arse on the grass and put his head between his knees. Maybe cry a little. Just a very little.

Except Zophia still wouldn't let him pull her back and away from the edge. Still didn't seem to know that she'd got them all, had saved everyone, had even caught the villain. She wouldn't move, wouldn't *be* moved.

Until Andras sidled up alongside her, peered down the cliffs, lifted an eyebrow, and said, "Well, being the hero's nice for you, Zoph, but you're still not getting out of calisthenics in the morning."

Ellis felt the shift in her, the abrupt swing from muscle strained tight and tense to a rude desertion of adrenaline and the rubbery infirmity it left behind. She laughed—just a quick, bright burst of it—then fell back into Ellis and passed out.

He'd been halfway expecting it, so Ellis was steady as he caught her and laid her on the grass. "Don't worry," he said before Andras could work himself up. "I've seen this before." And under similar circumstances, though with Milo there'd also been a life-threatening magical wound to add to the fun. "It's mostly exhaustion. She used a lot of magic but she'll be fine."

Shaking a little with spent nerves, Ellis peered around, spotted Willa, and jerked his chin. "Get someone to find a wagon or something." And then to Marston, "Ride ahead to Rhediad Afon and tell my mam to expect a guest."

Andras straightened. "Syr, I thought I'd—"

"No." Ellis shook his head and ignored the crestfallen look Andras gave him as Marston hefted Zophia up and took her away. "You did well, Andras." Ellis stood to set his hand firmly to Andras's shoulder. "*Very* well. But we're not near done yet."

⁂

Paddleboats. Bloody *paddleboats*, for the love of every goddess.

The man who'd planted the bombs, whoever he was and however he'd got into Wellech, had indeed been expecting company—twelve people in three paddleboats had been caught trying to slip past the coastal patrols in the dead of night three days ago. There'd been a series of attacks planned. Railways, of course. Any roads and bridges they came across on their way down to Tirryderch, because that was what these people really wanted. But the worst of it would have been the planned bombing of the Millway Dam, which would have flooded a great deal of the Hollow Valley. Ellis didn't even want to guess at how many might've died in the resulting surge and flood.

And because the lieutenant colonel who commanded the Home Guard's Wellech division was an arse who liked Folant better than he liked Ellis, no one reported any of it to the First Warden. And because no one had reported any of it to the First Warden, his people had been unprepared.

"Tilli was beaten nearly into a bloody *coma*, Crilly! D'you not get what you've done here?"

"You keep telling me your Wardens don't fall under my purview, and I'm not—"

"Not under your purview does *not* mean you can withhold information that almost gets one of *my Wardens* killed!" Ellis could barely breathe, he was that tamping. "That's not even *counting* how many might've died today if one of *my Wardens* hadn't spotted what *you* missed!"

"Ah, yes, your... *Warden*." The curl to Crilly's lip told Ellis he was probably going to have to clamp down tight on his temper for the next thing that came from Crilly's mouth. "Zophia Weber, I'm told. Dewin from Taraverde."

"Ostlich-Sztym. Not that it should bloody *matter*."

"That part, no."

Which meant the part that did matter, at least to Crilly, was that Zophia was Dewin.

Crilly eyed Ellis, challenging, one corner of his mouth turned up. "Are you quite sure she's not—?"

"I think," Ellis cut in, soft and very, very calm, "you'd best not finish that sentence."

Ellis found himself with his fists pressed to the edge of Crilly's oak desk, looming, though he hadn't done it consciously. Crilly was trying to look unaffected, but he'd shifted back in his chair, gaze sharp on Ellis's hands.

Once Ellis pulled away, Crilly seemed to bolster himself to say, "Every angle should be explored, Rhywun Ellis, and I assure—"

"I'll take Rhywun Morgan, thanks."

Petty, perhaps, but they weren't friends, and Ellis merited the respect, even if Crilly saw him as nothing more than Folant's wayward brat who needed a lesson. Today was no bloody *lesson*.

"Of course." Crilly actually smiled. "Please expect one of my inspectors to call on you in the next day or so, *Rhywun Morgan*. And on your... Warden." He made himself busy with shuffling papers around and not looking at Ellis. "As I said—every angle should be explored. We're at war, after all."

"Yeah. We are." Ellis nodded, watching carefully. "So why don't you tell me how the search for the other three spies is going?"

Crilly blinked. Frowned.

"Three boats captured," Ellis said softly. "Four in each." He paused, tilted his head. "So where are the three our bomber was with?"

He watched Crilly's face go blank. And he wasn't sure if it was because Crilly sincerely hadn't thought of it, which was bad, or was dismayed that Ellis had, which was much, much worse.

"Tell you what." Ellis opened Crilly's office door. "You send your inspectors to investigate me. I'll send mine to investigate... well. Every angle, I reckon."

He left it there, smiled with all his teeth, and quit the room.

Four days later, two frigates patrolling the small upper islands off Preidyn's eastern coast were bombed in a massive air attack that finally broke through Her Majesty's Navy's lines. This was not an expeditionary force. This was not a stray plane accidentally caught outside its supposed airspace. This was numerous battle squadrons with air power no one had until now suspected. They came in coordinated waves, and were led—shockingly, though it shouldn't have been by then, probably—by two colossal, seemingly feral bellwing cows. *Seemingly* feral because, though they were vicious and crazed as any animal gone rabid, those who saw them up close—the ones who survived, at least—testified that the dragons wore collars, of all things. And seemed to be taking direction from a cruiser that sat behind the battle lines and never engaged.

By the time Preidyn's own fledgling Air Brigade arrived from their base in Werrdig, the islands were devastated. The pictures in the paper of the destruction were hellish and shocking. The loss of life hadn't yet been calculated. Ellis had heard more than once that the Central Confederation's attempts against Preidyn were less strategy and more the Verdish Premier's personal antipathy for Queen Rhiannon. This attack convinced him.

Preidyn won the battle in the end. The flotilla of Royal Navy patrol ships already cruising the Goshor converged with the destroyers that sped in to join the fight. The planes from Werrdig sported not only bombing capacity but gun turrets with crack gunners Taraverde's planes just didn't have. All of it meant more of the Confederation's forces—planes and ships both—ended up at the bottom of the ocean than did Preidyn's.

The silence in the crowded pubs said it was a hollow victory. The laments sung in the common rooms said it was a costlier one than most had imagined. They had, until now, only read about Western Unified victories in other parts of the world through newspaper reports, or heard them described each week's end through the Queen's calm, plummy tones on the radio. The realities of the damage done even in victory had just been made acutely clear, and the collective pain of it was stunning.

It brought the war *home* like even the attacks in Tirryderch hadn't done, like the attempt at the Riverfest only days ago hadn't managed.

Ellis lost another five Wardens to enlistment. He was sure he was about to lose more, and it hit him unexpectedly hard because, though everyone had known conscription was coming, having it enacted into immediate effect was sobering. And Ellis knew, with a guilt and weird longing he didn't quite understand, he wouldn't be getting one of those letters with the sharp coat of arms of Her Majesty's Royal Forces on the envelope.

After a week of frantic preparation, covert reports to Alton, and an argument with Lilibet over whether she should take Bamps to Whitpool where it was relatively safer—which did not go as Ellis had hoped—Ellis camped out alone in a field in the Hollow Valley. The redcrest had somehow managed to make its way southwest from Caeryngryf to skulk the floodplains outside Millway. When there'd been evidence it had tried to squeeze its way through the too-small-for-it entrance to the Red Whisky Mines, Ellis guessed what it must be after. He arranged with Dyfan to have a ton of coal dumped by the banks of the Aled where the dragon seemed to be slurping up enough fish that Ellis was expecting complaints from the fishing villages downriver any day now.

It was hunting for itself, so that was good, even if "hunting" meant it was merely dipping its snout in the water and waiting for it to fill up with fish. And it was clearly looking for the minerals it needed, though coal wasn't going to be enough.

Can send instructions to smelter for fire. Best I can do, had been Howell's answer to Ellis's probably somewhat tangled and definitely fretful telegram when the dragon had shown up in Olwyn's pastures. *No kin before Reaping end.*

And. Well.

There'd been no way to arrange things with the closest forge because the dragon wouldn't stay in one place. And it wasn't as though Ellis could tell it to "Go wait over by the forge at Red Whisky" and have it understand that if it did so, he'd see its fires relit. So he merely kept an eye on its movements, and spent time around it when it let him. Aleks was arriving on the morning train, intending to try leading the dragon back to Whitpool using the lorry Ellis had appropriated. Which, Ellis supposed, was good, since Eira had been sending cables complaining "The longer you keep that rattletrap, the worse my paperwork." Ellis would've thought getting rid of two nuisances at once would be a relief. No more harassment from Eira, and no more dragon to worry about. Instead, he was just glad the dragon had stayed where he could find it before what would be a very strange goodbye tomorrow.

"This is it, I'm afraid," Ellis told the dragon. She—because Ellis had looked up the markings—she was peering over from the levee across the channel where Ellis had set up camp. Just sitting there. Watching. She didn't look wary, though. And Ellis *had* brought half a side of beef and lit the coal for her. "Just you and me. For now, anyway. Your kin will be coming to look after you until..."

Until Milo comes home, he didn't say, because it was stupid and probably had more to do with the now half-empty flask of single malt in his hand than reality. Even if—*when* Milo did come home... well, the dragon would likely be dead by then. She was still dropping scales. Though she'd emerged from her attempt to camouflage herself behind the too-thin tree cover so she could scoff the smoldering coal pile as soon as Ellis set it burning and moved back, there was no resulting glow to her belly. She smelled of rotten ash and mildew rather than petrol.

Then again, maybe Aleks could work miracles as well as Milo could. The little razorback and its mam had recovered. Or at least they were recovering. Glynn said Aleks expected they might even join the clan at Reaping migration. If the same thing that had happened to those dragons had happened to this one, only worse, so much worse—

"Maybe there's hope for you," Ellis said softly.

Then again, those razorbacks were safe on a preserve right from the beginning, being cared for by dragonkin who loved them simply because they were dragons, being fed good rations and fat cows and goats before retiring to their secure, sturdy hot springs caves. This one had been sick and mostly fending for herself for... well, who knew how long? Who even knew if she *could* be saved?

"Bloody—" Ellis scrubbed at the stubble on his cheeks and chin. "I'm sorry."

He wasn't sure for what. For not knowing what to do to help the poor beast. For not being dragonkin. For not understanding what *his* dragonkin was up to until it was well past too late.

Again, the dragon merely watched him, blinking slowly, her posture relaxed in the lush grass of the levee, lying with her back legs tucked beneath her and her chin on her forepaws like a cat on a hearth. Her tail swished slow and lazy through the grass, her wings splayed out to her sides. The dragonstone was a comfortable, familiar burn in Ellis's pocket, and when he took it out to curl it into his palm, he could swear the dragon shivered and melted a little more into the grass.

Ellis tipped a sympathetic smile, said, "Well, at least you don't seem to be in pain," and when she merely closed her eyes, tail swooshing to an eventual sluggish halt, Ellis drifted off to sleep wondering if it meant something that a dragon would trust him enough to sleep so close to him.

He dreamed of Milo, but he'd hoped he would. He wanted comfort. He wanted to feel close. Connected.

He didn't get any of it.

It was dark wherever Milo was, and fogged over so thick Ellis thought maybe Milo had done it. Ellis couldn't get a clear idea of where Milo was, but it was somewhere with a river or at least a wide stream, because Ellis could hear the water flowing. Could see Milo's boots sinking into ankle-deep mud as he ran. Toward? Away? Ellis couldn't tell.

And then he could, because Milo broke through the wall of fog and into—

"Oh, Milo, no." It made no sound, but that didn't stop Ellis from saying it again, "No!" and then shouting it, "Milo, *no!*"

Even if Milo could hear him, Ellis suspected he wouldn't have listened. Because *this*...

It was nothing like caves or hot springs or anything that resembled a preserve. This was like stables, or... no, a kennel. A strange open-air kennel that was clearly less about caring for the occupants than it was about controlling them.

Nine dragons sat nearly shoulder-to-shoulder, no room to spread massive wings or even turn around in place. Not that they could anyway—collars circled each neck, chains running from one to the next with links as thick as tree trunks. Because there was probably nothing one could stake a dragon to strong enough to keep it down. Except, apparently, other dragons.

One of them looked dead, its lax body forced upright by proximity but its long neck twisted sideways on the ground in front of it, head skewed to one side, and milky eyes open. Two looked like they were on their way to the same fate, scales even now dropping from blotchy bared patches all over their bodies, and necks practically naked where thick iron collars rubbed away armor and scraped the hide beneath raw and bloody.

All of them looked angry. All of them were snarling, eyes wild and half-mad. All of them had clearly had their fires fed, glowing trails piping up their throats. And all of them were now entirely focused on Milo.

Ellis might've shouted some more. He couldn't tell. Not with the chaos that rose up and swatted the scene with confusion and madness and violence that didn't show Ellis trails of red possibilities and steps not taken. Because this was Milo, and it could only go one way. And damn him if Ellis didn't recognize the determined set of that jaw, even beneath the beard he'd likely never get used to.

Teeth set, Milo ran in, throwing up a shield but not stopping, *not stopping*, when three blasts of fire hit him at once. He just kept going, yelling something Ellis didn't hear, one arm up over his head as though to hold the shield, and one hand reaching for the chain closest to him. He laid hold of it, gritted his teeth, snarled, and the chain broke in three places and slithered groundward.

Milo yelled something—"Back off, the lot of you!" it sounded like—but the claws and fire and teeth still came at him when he darted for another chain. "Damn it, I'm kin, you *will* listen!" except they didn't.

They were going for each other now, as well as Milo, great jaws clamping onto whatever was closest, claws extended and swiping. Cries went up alongside screeches high and loud enough to burst eardrums. Milo's shield held when two dragons snapped for him at once, but Ellis could see how Milo staggered backward with the force of the blows. It still didn't stop him—he dove into the midst of angry dragons again, reaching for another clump of chain, expression turned once more wrathful and resolute as he broke the chain then went for another.

Light flooded the... field, Ellis could see now it was a field. Out in the open with nothing around it but the stream Ellis had heard before chaos ensued, and what he recognized as a forge.

...And possibly a military fort. An old castle being used as one, anyway.

And didn't that just figure?

"Damn you, Milo!"

Ellis had never felt so helpless in his life.

The fog had scattered once Milo had stopped paying attention to it. The lines of sight would be clear now. Ellis had never heard machinegun fire before, but when he saw the bright sporadic flashes in the distance, he thought that was probably what he was hearing now. Shouts rose in what he recognized as Verdish beneath the warbly wail of an ear-splitting siren.

Fortunately for Milo, the dragons seemed more pissed off at the gunfire than they'd been at him. They turned toward where the shots were coming from and snarled, venom dripping from bared teeth, heads jutted forward and wings pulled back, clear attack stances, and... that was all. They stood there—glaring, yes, ready, yes, but still waiting.

It wasn't clear for what until a small ball of light wafted from above where the flashes of gunfire were strobing the dark. Not small and a friendly blue like a magelight; silver-white and sharp, crackling like a firework, and sailing out of the dark ahead of the nimbus it dragged behind it in a fizzy tail. Every dragon's eye watched it come, still waiting, until it smacked into Milo's shield without a sound, and then kept pushing in.

Milo looked at the little ball. Looked at the dragons, their eyes on him now, mouths opening, fire pulsing up their throats, flames igniting the dribbling venom and lighting small fires around their feet. Looked back at the ball.

Jaw set, Milo dropped his shield, snatched the ball, and lobbed it back to where it came from.

The dragons didn't wait this time. They watched the ball land just in front of the soldiers still shooting, then splash out and stick to every one of them like hoarfrost on glass. The soldiers started yelling, backing away, but the dragons seemed as though they'd been anticipating exactly this—they dropped their jaws with roars that were abounding rage made sound, and razed the ground in great gusts of flame like blazing rivers bursting from half a dozen dams.

Milo took immediate advantage—he put his head down and concentrated on working methodically through the chains.

The castle... fort... whatever it was, it was now on fire, already an inferno beneath the dragons' concerted, very clearly *furious* onslaught. Everything was going up, even the wet grass trampled into mud by multiple sets of huge clawed feet. When the brilliance leveled off, lumps of what Ellis suspected had been people thirty seconds ago lay burning in the mud. Some of them were still moving, though slow and tortured, so Ellis stopped looking.

Milo ignored it all, ignored everything, dodged talons and tails and fire and bullets and teeth until he'd broken every chain, set every dragon free.

It took a moment in the chaos for them to realize they'd been set loose, apparently for them to even notice Milo was yelling "Go! *Go!*" at them. It took another for them to stop breathing fire or fighting with each other long enough to try their wings and take off. Dragon-song spiked the air above the violent skirmish, incongruously smooth and lyrical as dragons took to the sky, wings for a moment blotting out the bright lights flooding away the dark and making a clearer target of the man who'd freed them.

Until he turned toward it, waved both arms in a quick, disdainful sort of gesture, and every light flared overbright, sputtered, then went out in brilliant fountains of yellow-white sparks.

Ellis couldn't see what happened next. The flash of exploding lights was too bright. He only saw vague silhouettes against the shifting framework of rising flames. One of them running, gun in hand, raised, getting closer; one of them—*Milo*—not turning in time. Ellis saw the flash from the gun's muzzle before he heard the *crack* of the shot. Saw Milo jerk forward and to the side, hand flailing up to grip at his shoulder, before he heard the cry and pained grunt. Saw Milo complete the staggering spin, arm whipping out as though for balance, but it wasn't—the figure with the gun went swirling back as though caught in a dervish, brutal and powerful, each limb thrashing out in its own helpless spiraling wrench.

It was a woman, Ellis could see when she landed with a violent, sickening twist, arms and legs splayed or wrung in unlikely contortions, head turned the wrong way, neck screwed nearly all the way 'round, eyes open and staring up into a sky dark and heaving with the beats of dragons' wings.

Milo's stare looked no less lifeless, fixated on what he'd just done, disbelief and incomprehension coiling into something numb with horror.

His magic, Ellis thought, frantic. Pain made using magic impossible for some, extremely difficult for others, sucking up energy and crowding out concentration. Ellis didn't know how getting shot might compare to magic eating a hole into one's back. He did know, though, that Milo was going to find out any second.

If only he would bloody *move*!

Gunfire was still rat-a-tatting from the other side of the conflagration, shouts were still sounding, and the enemy was trying to flank Milo now, getting closer, because Ellis could hear their footsteps squelching through the mud. And Milo was just *standing* there, staring at the twisted body on the ground, breathing too fast, still clutching at his shoulder.

Ellis couldn't tell what finally brought Milo out of it. It certainly couldn't have been his own shout of "Move! Milo, *go*!" but something in the chaos got through the too-clear shock.

Milo turned around and ran, hand red and glistening with blood from where he'd been gripping his shoulder, head tilted back and mouth open as fog started pluming from it like breath. Thicker. Heavier. It rose from Milo's mouth as he ran, then curled down over his shoulder like water, dripping to the ground, rising, spreading. A moment, mere seconds, and it nearly blanked out sight altogether into nothing more than gauzy midnight-gray bloodshot by fire in lurid waves.

Well, that answered the *Is he in too much pain to use his magic?* question, at least.

And then, like but unlike the stories Ellis had grown up with and only half-believed, the dark shape of a massive beast with glowing red eyes emerged from the mist, bellowing and snarling as it wrought itself from shadow, and glided beside Milo on wings that hadn't even taken shape yet. It paced him, thick muscle made of fog and magic flexing and pulling beneath its smoky black scales, wings making themselves seemingly out of the night itself, widening, expanding, until Milo flung his arm toward the formless dark haze behind him and shouted, "*Go!*" The dragon curled upward, circling over Milo as it grew and grew and grew, gained substance, plucked sooty detail from vapor, then *boomed* out a roar that could shatter eardrums. As though pleased by Milo's command, the dragon spun, wide jaws made of smoke opening, dripping with mist like venom, and winged off toward Milo's pursuers.

The dragons—the real ones—were still singing as they glided away into the night sky, calls soft with distance now, and weirdly sweet, considering. A direct paradox to the sounds of a great savage dragon made of magic and the shouts of those who watched it come for them out of the dark as Milo ran for his life.

So it was *exactly* the wrong time for Ellis to wake to the redcrest crooning out a similar song, crouching not a person's length away from him, and with its nose stretched out toward Ellis's hand, still gripped around the dragonstone. But that was what happened anyway.

Chapter 20—Transition

: a bridge section between two musical ideas

Crilly had been gone within two weeks after Riverfest. Ellis didn't know if he'd been dismissed, arrested, or merely disappeared into whatever hole Alton favored, and he didn't care. The new commander of the Wellech Home Guard was Colonel Saoirse Walsh, transferred in from a Werrdig post, and Ellis liked her the second she asked him, "What are we doing about the missing three?" Perhaps a bit less so a second later when she told him her callsign was "Hammer," then called him "Prince" and didn't bother to hide her smirk. Still, it made the covert parts of what he'd been doing much easier.

He put Petra on coordinating with Walsh on the parish management portions of the missing spy problem, Tomos on the parts that intersected with the Wardens. For the first time Ellis was confident in leaving at least that crisis to people he knew would solve it.

And they did. Mostly. Within a week, two of the missing saboteurs were caught trying to steal explosives from the Mali Bracer mine up by Caeryngryf. Still with their eye on the Millway Dam, no doubt, though Walsh's people hadn't yet got anything of value from questioning them. And absolutely nothing on the one both Ellis and Walsh were sure was still out there, though there'd been no way to confirm it. Still, the presence of the two indicated the likelihood of the third, so they kept looking.

Unfortunately, they'd been looking for months now. If there was a spy somewhere in Wellech, they were holed up in a place no one knew to look.

"It's getting..." Dilys didn't finish, static taking up the space where words should have been, but Ellis knew what she didn't say anyway.

Winter had set in hard, as though making up for the unusually hot summer and mild autumn. It worked in Preidyn's favor, though—the Blackson turned vicious in the cold months, and the islanders who lived in the middle of it were of tough stock by necessity. Coastal waters took on lethal edges, and the tides came and went as though they had a personal grudge against the shores.

The attempts on Ynys Dawel and Tirryderch were thus rendered ineffectual and sporadic, but they hadn't stopped. The air raids on Preidyn, though, had broken through too often now for any citizen of the Preidynīg Isles to keep believing comprehensive invasion and annexation hadn't been Taraverde's goal all along. Though the dragon attacks had stopped, since dragons could barely move from their caves in the winter let alone fly forced sorties, aerial bombings were still devastating coastal villages and ports. A small force had temporarily taken Greater Brisland, a minor island off Preidyn's eastern shore. It was the first truly strategic loss Preidyn had taken, and though the island was won back within days, the shockwave was still rippling through the other islands.

All of it was compounded when Western Unified lost control of the Gulf of White Sands, though the battles still raged over it. Desgaul had wasted no time once they entered the war; they took the burden of holding the Lauxauhn Strait, and freed up the Preidynīg Navy's Southern Fleet to move north and west to fill in gaps around the rest of the islands, and renew the fight in the gulf. With Eretia now all-in and focusing their naval forces on the Eretian Gulf and the Goshor Sea, and sending more troops to Błodwyl than there were Błodwyl citizens, Taraverde had been forced to draw back. Eretia was now a liberator, the heroes of Błodwyl, and the people of Błodwyl responded by surging the ranks of their armed forces, every new enlistee startlingly bloodthirsty and now bent on vengeance as well as justice.

The letters had started to arrive, just after Highwinter. Innocuous-looking envelopes with the Official Royal Seal carried by stoic young officers to family members who hadn't known until the letter's arrival that they were surviving family members. Seven Wellech families had received them so far, offering condolences to loved ones of men and women Ellis had known, played with as a child, run with as an adolescent, worked with and drunk with as a young man. Three of them had been Wardens from Ellis's own ranks.

Bad, Dilys didn't have to say. It was getting very, very bad.

"I know," Ellis said into the radio. He took his finger off the transmit toggle, shut his eyes tight and clenched his jaw, before he had hold of himself enough to ask, "How are you, though?"

Dilys laughed, a sharp humorless bark of it that sounded like the edge of a sob. "How d'you think?"

Less than a month later, as Wellech was deep in the throes of the worst of winter, a break came in the form of Folant, of all people. And if randoms didn't stop showing up at Ellis's kitchen table uninvited, he was going to find someone to set some damned wards, see if he didn't.

"What are you doing here?" Ellis was too tired for this, too busy for it, not even a little bit in the mood. Teeth set, he shut the door that had bloody well been *locked* when he'd left this morning, and threw his coat at a peg. "And how d'you keep getting in? In case it's escaped you, you're not—"

"I know where the spy is."

It stopped Ellis. Made him blink. "You... Sorry, what?"

"The one you've been looking for since Riverfest. I know where she is."

Ellis narrowed his eyes, more suspicious than hopeful, because life with Folant had taught him to be. But Folant wasn't looking smug and up to his thick eyebrows with hubris. He only looked tired.

"She." Ellis leaned back against the bench, arms crossed over his chest. "Go on."

Folant looked away, gaze roving unseeing all around the kitchen before settling on his own wide hands, loosely fisted on the table. Uncomfortable. Even fearful, maybe, but Ellis wasn't sure he'd ever seen Folant afraid of anything, even when he should've been. It threw Ellis, because this was not the man who'd snarled animosity and anger and ill grace as he'd ceded the position of Pennaeth.

"First," Folant said, eyes still on his hands, "I need to know who I'm talking to." He looked up, clear-eyed and expressionless. "Am I speaking to Wellech's First Warden? Her Pennaeth? Or my son?"

Ellis's eyebrows shot up. He bit back several retorts—*You disowned your son*, and *What does it matter when you don't respect any of them?*—and merely said, "Let's go with Ellis Morgan for now." He shrugged, deliberately indifferent. "I reckon the need for any of the others will depend on what you've got to say."

Folant nodded, as though he hadn't expected anything else, and blew out a slow breath. "I never intended—"

"I don't care."

"It *matters*. None of this—"

"I. Don't. *Care*." It took all Ellis had not to shove it out between his teeth. "And the less you tell me about any motives you may or may not have had for things you may or may not have done, the less chance there is that your First Warden will have to step in." Folant's mouth clamped tight, anger this time, and Ellis didn't care about that either. "Say what you came to say, and be done with it, or get out."

"You're that tamping with me that you'd see me leave without giving you information you clearly—"

"D'you think I haven't already guessed just from you showing up?" Ellis huffed a disbelieving laugh. "You were *selling information* to whoever happened to be on the other end of your coded messages. You're a bloody enemy contact. Of *course* any spy caught out in Wellech would eventually contact you. D'you think we haven't been watching?"

Ellis's efforts to unite Wellech under one banner had been working slowly but surely, but the hunt for the Riverfest saboteurs had done the rest of the job. And the continued search for the one who'd got away had entrenched it down deep. Everyone had been keeping their eyes open, everyone had been checking on their neighbors. Walsh had helped to throw a virtual net over the ports and waterways and rail stations. Even keepers of the smallest shops and grange halls had been on the lookout for unfamiliar faces.

The problem was that Wellech had a lot of wilderness. If someone knew how to live off the land, they could last years and never be found. But with the extraordinarily harsh winter digging in deep, Ellis had been hoping the spy would poke their head out for supplies, even for a moment, if they planned to try to ride out the rest of the cold weather in the wilds. And he'd known too well who they'd have no choice but to go to.

Folant looked away, fists clenched tight now, jaw set firm. "I'm not." He swallowed so hard Ellis heard the *click* of it from across the kitchen. "An enemy contact. I'm *not*."

"You were. And willing. You *sought* it. You bloody **volunteered**."

"Only because the damned—"

"*I don't care!*" It rang through the house, slammed a silence into the walls that echoed high and tinny in Ellis's ears. When Ellis could speak again without snarling, he said, "There are conversations I will never have with you again, Folant. That's one of them."

Folant flinched, whether at the "Folant" rather than "Tad," or the finality of the tone, Ellis didn't know. It didn't matter. None of this was what mattered.

"Now." Ellis kept his arms folded over his chest, kept his slouch against the bench relaxed. "You've got a location. Tell me."

Hollywell wasn't a surprise. There was almost a direct line through the Torcalon Wood from the Chwaer Bach down to Surrey-witch Sound, roads and villages easily avoided if one had a mind to do it. A minor port town, too far south to be of use to the mines or to those on their way to Llundaintref. It was quiet compared to the near "big city" feel of Caeryngryf, and like most of Wellech, everyone not only knew everyone else, but their business as well.

Ellis met up with the Home Guard contingent Walsh had assigned to Hollywell, agreed on a strategy with the lieutenant in charge, and pulled Zophia front and center.

"Anything?"

People with magical abilities of all sorts had been emerging from the woodwork over the past few months, most of them agreeing to allow Lilibet to teach them how to use the gifts they'd neglected or suppressed in a Wellech that didn't appreciate them. Ellis was perishing to get as many as would agree into his ranks, but they all still had a way to go before they'd be as useful as they could be.

Zophia, in contrast, had gone to a good school in Ostlich-Sztym—not quite as prestigious as the one Milo had attended in Llundaintref, but respected on the continent—and Ellis had come to depend on her when a situation called for magic or magical expertise.

She was staring at her knees now, crouched beside Ellis in the snow, concentrating, bobbing her head in a slow nod. "Wards," she said, low and through the thick scarf pulled up to cover her mouth, just as hushed as the rest of them, seeing how they were so close to their target. "Is Elfennol." She turned, squinted around the quiet stretch of trees between the battered little hunting shed only a furlong or so off and the impatient gathering of Wardens and Home Guard cadets hunkered behind her. She pointed a gloved hand. "There." Then turned and pointed again. "To there." She frowned back at Ellis. "They are..." She rolled her hand, searching for the word she needed. "Unwell?" She shook her head. "Not good done."

"Badly," Bethan piped in, muted but kind. "You mean the wards are done badly."

Bethan was another success story, though Ellis took no credit for her change of heart from the behavior she'd displayed when she'd confronted Milo on that bridge those years ago. That went to Andras somehow, and Zophia, Ellis reckoned, since Zophia was a likeable person to begin with, and was proving to be an excellent Warden besides.

"Badly," Zophia agreed with a grateful crinkle of eyes at Bethan before she turned back to Ellis. "Is a square." Her brow furrowed tight in clear disapproval. "Easy to find the... how you call... anchor?"

"Yes." Ellis nodded. "Anchor. I understand." He did, and he knew what Zophia was saying. Setting wards in a predictable pattern made it more likely someone could find the anchors and disable them before the person who'd cast them knew anyone had even come near. "Can you kill them without her knowing?"

"Is *Elfennol*," Zophia said, almost insulted, like Ellis should've known better than to even ask, and then she shrugged. "Is done."

Ellis grinned and pushed her toward Bethan. "You cover me, and Bethan will cover you." He blew into his hands to warm up his fingers, checked his rifle, then jerked his chin at the lieutenant. "All right, Yelton. She's clearly a sorcerer, so best let us take point, yeah?"

"Aye, mate." Yelton flashed a wry smirk and made a show of checking his rifle over. A thick hank of wavy auburn hair had worked its way from beneath his wool cap and fallen over his brow. He threw a grin at his cadets over his shoulder then shot Ellis a roguish look through his fringe. "Y'uns worry about the finessing bits." He winked with a cocky glint in his bright green eyes. "We'll see to the bits wot need a spot o' muscle."

Ellis merely rolled his eyes with a snort. Yelton had come to Wellech with his mam when he was ten, but he'd managed to hang on to both his South Werrdig accent and smartarse charm in the years since.

"Whatever makes you feel better," Ellis muttered with a smirk as Yelton quietly directed his cadets to surround the dilapidated little shed. Amused when he shouldn't be, considering the circumstances, Ellis huffed out a bracing breath. "Let's go."

They moved slowly, Ellis motioning for the Wardens behind him to keep silent and be careful of where they put their feet and how they stepped. The calf-deep snow had partially melted and then frozen over again; the skin of it was therefore brittle and potentially noisy. They were close enough to the strait to the east that Ellis could hear the far-off rush of the tide, but it wouldn't be enough to cover the crackle and crunch if they went thoughtlessly tromping through this intended ambush.

The trees here weren't sparse, but their trunks were all but bare and few of them were wide enough to provide much cover. So when the fog came out of nowhere and started to thicken, it was disappointing but not a complete surprise. They'd been spotted.

Ellis gave up all stealth and shouted, "She's doing a runner!" toward where Yelton was positioned, and took off toward the shed.

Zophia just said, "*Fin*," annoyed, and bloody damn, Ellis decided as she waved her hands in wide arcs, he was really starting to love it when she said that.

And for good reason—the mist thinned immediately. The sorcerer-spy was clearly visible as the last ragged whorls of the conjured haze sank to the ground as though weighted. Caught in midsprint, out in the open now and too close to Yelton, she was brought down by a simple trip and a subsequent rifle butt to the temple.

It was over so quickly, Home Guard and Wardens both just sort of stared at each other, wondering what to do with all the untapped adrenaline coursing through their veins. A silent, surprised moment later, Yelton slapped Zophia on the back hard enough Bethan had to steady her.

"There a pub 'round here, then?"

The Hawk and Dove sat high on the jut of a cliff overlooking the Hollywell Port Authority's piers on one side, and the long stretch of the Red Coral Strait on the other. Yelton assigned two of his cadets to secure the prisoner, and requested Zophia on the detail "in case of further magical shenanigans." Ellis allowed how that would be the smart thing to do, and though he could tell Zophia was disappointed she wouldn't be celebrating with the rest of them, she went without complaint.

"Oi, mate, you look like you just lost a sure bet instead of catching a spy." Yelton nudged in beside Ellis, gave him one of his wide, easy grins, and propped his elbows to the railing overlooking the strait. He made a show of looking down, as though trying to decide what Ellis was staring at. "'S freezing up here. And that's a thinking face, don't say it en't. G'wan, then." He pushed in close, the length of his arm warm against Ellis's, and dipped his head so he was looking at Ellis through his red fringe again, friendly and cautiously coy. "Give over."

Ellis knew what this was. Invitation, clearly. There'd been a few months back when they were boys it would be so easy to revisit, and Yelton had been all but telegraphing it with his sly looks and shifting eyebrows since they'd met up to start strategizing. And Ellis thought about it, honestly. Yelton had no magic and Ellis didn't Dream well enough for it to count; a simple conjugal contract between them wouldn't even have to go through the Sisters. Approval from the Wellech Council would do just fine, no fuss. Technically, Ellis could even approve it as Pennaeth, though it would also be just as technically improper, and he had no interest in stepping even a toe into Folant's footsteps when it came to abusing his office.

I could do, Ellis mused as he pulled his coat tighter against the steady winter wind and contemplated the churning dark water. A shifting tide of *He left me* rolled through him, capped with a silt-soupy froth of *Why shouldn't I?* and tugged toward the deeps by a rippling undertow of *It would serve him right*.

Lies, really, like the ones he told himself when he had too much time to think and the loneliness started to drag at him. *I'll always be the man who didn't deserve you but loved you 'til the end*, and though the "didn't deserve you" bit invariably made him clench his teeth, the rest of it was what Ellis hung on to. What he chose to believe with all his heart, even when it felt impossible. Ellis believed impossible things all the time. He still had the contract dissolution papers locked in his desk drawer, the envelope still sealed, because he'd had a mulish notion that if he never opened it, the contents would never be true. A more sensible man would've taken the papers for the answer they were intended to be, and done what had been asked of him.

Sensible had its place. Apparently, just not in Ellis's heart.

"I've just been thinking." Ellis pulled back from the railing, away from Yelton, and peered up instead at the sky just melting into the heady pastels and streaks of feathered cobalt of approaching twilight. "That mist she conjured. The fog."

It wasn't a new thing. A common tactic in battle since before recorded history. Given more respect and prominence in strategy once the tales of the Black Dog Corps became part of the common parlance of war. Even Ellis, in his limited experience, had seen it used before.

Except.

Combined with the sound of the tides churning in the strait, it had nagged at something as Ellis led the way back to the various horses and farm trucks they'd all used to get to the meeting place before the raid.

Images of Milo tearing off into the night, gunfire aimed at his back and fog rolling from his mouth. The burble of a stream against muddy banks. A glimpse at a half-burnt map with too-familiar landmarks and streaks of red possibility leaking from it in every direction.

He hadn't Dreamed much of Milo for months, though not for lack of trying. Glimpses here and there. Milo hunkered in a small room derelict enough to look abandoned, a blood-spotted bandage across his chest and fever blooming high on his cheeks. Milo sleeping against the concave bole of a thick, moldy oak. Milo hovering at the edge of a marketplace somewhere, jaw tight and fixed gaze tracking a woman haggling over what looked like a bolt of wool.

If the hints in the broadsheets were any indication, though, there'd been at least one other liberation of captured dragons before winter had set in across the continent. This time in Taraverde itself. The Confederation had started with, from all reports, twenty-seven dragons. Counting the ones set free from this last raid, they were down to eight, only six of which had been recently spotted in battle and confirmed alive and still active. The reports couldn't get over the audacity of whoever was doing the liberating. There were no accounts of any Black Dogs, but it didn't stop everyone Ellis knew from eagerly assuming Captain Ceri Priddy had answered the call of her country once again.

There was no denying she had, of course. But Ellis would bet blood that if it had to do with dragons, they could thank the Black Dog's son. And yet Ellis couldn't speak a word of it to anyone. Because Milo—*his* Milo—was a spy in a foreign land. Just like that woman in the woods. And Ellis couldn't pretend he didn't know what fate awaited her when Walsh and then Alton were through with her.

He huffed, shook it off. With a smile that wasn't real, he pushed his cup of cider at Yelton.

"I think I need to go see Walsh."

⚙

"They're coming for Kymbrygh. And they'll do it before Sowing." Walsh lifted her eyebrows, pausing with her jar halfway to her mouth. She stared at Ellis, narrow-eyed, before she lifted the jar the rest of the way and took a gulp of beer.

She'd already left her office on the Home Guard's base by the time Ellis had got back from Hollywell. He'd felt a little bad about pounding down her door and dragging her from her supper, apparently one of the few she'd managed to get home in time to have with her cariad since she'd transferred in from Werrdig. He'd done it anyway, and bullied her into the closest pub because, she'd snapped, "If you *will* insist, you're at least buying me a damned beer and some chips."

Come to think of it, it was more like she'd bullied him. Since it resulted in her sitting across from him in the otherwise empty pub and consenting to listen, he took it as a win.

She set her beer down. "They've *been* coming for Kymbrygh."

"No, they've been coming for Tirryderch. The rest of Kymbrygh was incidental, a bonus, and maybe leverage to take all of Preidyn. Or that's what we thought they were doing. And maybe it was, but it's changed."

"Tirryderch, last I checked, is part of Kymbrygh."

"Yes, of course it—" Ellis huffed. "No, you're not *listening*."

"You haven't said anything yet that I don't already know."

Ellis sucked in a deep breath, calmed himself, because she was right—he wasn't coming at this properly.

"All right." He leaned over the table, hands around the beer he hadn't otherwise touched yet. "We've all been assuming that Tirryderch is the goal because it would choke off the food supply, and that's what we would do. But Taraverde is doing countless things we'd never thought of before. Trying to take control of an entire continent. Using planes to bomb whole cities, and not because they're strategic sites necessary to their campaign, but for the shock of it."

"*We're* using planes, and we're proving much—"

"Using *dragons*."

It made her pause, thoughtful, before she shrugged concession and motioned Ellis to go on.

"The first dragon attacks sent us reeling. And in our shock, they managed to gain ground they shouldn't've, however temporarily." Ellis paused, mostly for effect, because this was important. "A full third each of the Whitpool and Tirryderch Home Guard have been stretched the length of Kymbrygh north to south, and are now patrolling Wellech's western border. Alton has pulled Whitpool's Wardens into his own troops and made them a bulwark between the border and the Whitpool base—which *just happens* to sit down the road from Old Forge. Now I don't know about you, but that tells me Alton had been expecting Taraverde to try using dragons against us. So why wasn't Preidyn?"

The *thud* he'd wanted that to hit with wasn't apparent in Walsh's demeanor. She was quiet for a while, blank-faced, watching Ellis across the table, clearly thinking. Ellis waited, patient on the outside, but jittering nearly out of his skin on the inside, until Walsh finally tipped her head with a purse of her lips.

"A country's intelligence," she said slowly, "is only as good as the boffins at the top who are meant to do something with it." She looked away. "You forget the Purity Party had very loud support in some corners of Parliament until very recently."

Ellis hadn't forgot. He'd just assumed it had been got past when the Queen's Constitutional Party managed to gather enough votes to purge a good portion of the MPs who'd shouted the loudest.

"And it must be said," Walsh went on, "that a nameless, faceless spy on the ground can sometimes be much more effective than any mastermind." She smirked when Ellis sat up straight. "Did you think his 'promotion' after the Green Coast War was a reward?" Her mouth went tight again. "It was punishment. Too many messages from Command not getting through. Too many flashy missions that couldn't be called off because of faulty communication." She shook her head with an admiring little chuckle. "He bloody invented the Black Dog Corps, and what's more, he was there on the ground with them. They may not have won the war all by themselves, but they bloody well had a large part in the winning of it. And some of those commanders who went ignored while the Black Dogs plowed through enemy country went on to become respected Members of Parliament."

Ellis almost couldn't fit it into the proper places in his head. Reprieve from an immediate answer came in the form of the pub's holder calling Walsh over to collect her chips.

When Walsh sat down again, digging right in, Ellis had to ask, "Are you telling me some of those MPs were allowing their country to potentially lose a war out of *spite*?"

"I'm telling you," Walsh said around a greasy chip smothered in gravy, melted cheese, and chunks of bacon, "that politics can be a ruddy great boil on the arse-end of any good government. And Alton didn't manage to lance this one in time to avoid a loss that shouldn't've been a loss at all." She shrugged, said, "We think he got the resulting infection in time, though," and went back to inhaling her chips.

Ellis was trying very hard not to reel. He shook it off, because it wasn't why he was here.

"We'll come back to that." Because boy, would they. He pushed his beer to the side and leaned in again. "I'm going to tell you what's going to happen, because there's a reason I'm here in Wellech and not off with the Royal Forces somewhere with a gun in my hand.

You know my mam Dreams." When Walsh merely nodded and kept eating, Ellis went on, "And you know my cariad is dragonkin."

Walsh stopped chewing and narrowed her eyes. "Your mam is under orders to relay any Dreams of consequence directly to my office."

Ellis blinked. Because that was news to him.

"Are you telling me my mam's a spy for the RIC too?"

Walsh stared, peered around to make sure no one was close enough to have heard, then rolled her eyes at Ellis. "D'you really think I'd tell you if she were?"

"You sort of just did." Again, Ellis had to push it aside, but bloody *damn* if he wasn't going to be taking that one up with Lilibet right after he was done with Walsh.

"*Has* she told you about a Dream?" Walsh wanted to know, harsh. "Has she been Dreaming of this dragonkin cariad and now—"

"*No.*" If only Lilibet *would*. Ellis shook his head, unwilling to say that he'd been the one Dreaming, though he reckoned that was going to have to come eventually. "*No*, bloody—"

"Then what's the point of even—?"

"The *point*," Ellis said through his teeth, "is that she Dreams for me. And she Dreamed that if Milo went off to do what he's doing for Alton, Wellech would need me here. And now I think I know why."

Walsh stared, still chewing, then rolled her eyes again. "Well, *get on*, then." Annoyed. Clearly assuming Ellis was wasting her time, and wanting him to get it over with.

"Because I know Milo." It came out fierce and angry. "And Milo wouldn't have volunteered unless Alton agreed to send him to find out what was happening with the dragons. And once Milo did find out, there was no way he wasn't going to do what he could to fix it. Except fixing it means taking away a weapon that Taraverde worked very hard to cultivate, and isn't easily replaced."

"Uh-huh." So far Walsh was unimpressed.

"So where," Ellis said slowly, "d'you think would be a good place to look for those replacements?"

Walsh paused with a chip dripping cheese and gravy into the basket. "Same place they got the last ones, I expect."

Ellis shook his head. "They'd already been messing with the migration path over there. Dragons aren't stupid. They know when there's a threat, and from the trouble Milo was having the past few years, enough had already veered off the central paths to be noticed before we had any clue full-out war was coming. Who knows how many have started to skip Colorat altogether, now that it's not a safe haven for them anymore?

"I had a sick redcrest cow that apparently wandered off that path, or more likely was set loose from captivity, and she'd managed to stumble all the way from Caeryngryf down to Silver Run and was well on her way to Corstir before Aleks finally managed to come get her. Thing is, I'm pretty sure she was following *me* for a while there, like a puppy that's got nowhere else to go, because the dragonkin she trusted betrayed her, the one who set her loose couldn't stay to help her, and she was lost and didn't know what else to do."

He wasn't pretty sure that was how it happened—he was proper certain. She'd come back a handful of times before winter hit. It had become a local joke after a while, but the first time she showed up, she'd swooped in over Corstir, settled in far too close to Ffrwythlon for the villagers' comfort, and wouldn't leave until the Wardens' office had got flooded with frantic messages and Ellis had gone to investigate. He probably shouldn't have been as pleased as he'd been. She'd scared half the village to drinking. But she'd also looked better, scales growing in, petrol pong intense enough to singe nose hairs. Glynn saying in a letter how the dragon was healing was one thing; seeing it was entirely another. And since all it had taken to get her to head back to Old Forge was Ellis telling her he was pleased she was feeling better but she should get back to home and kin, he was fairly confident in thinking she'd made the trip just to see him. Check up on him. And then had done it again. And again.

It was bizarre. It was, as far as Ellis knew, unprecedented. And it warmed him right through.

He huffed and asked, "How many more like her are out there, either too sick or too abused to even try to find their path again? Or avoiding it altogether because they know it's not safe anymore. Has anyone thought to ask Aleks how many breeds he's seeing that don't belong here on the western path? Because I don't think Kymbrygh's ever seen a redcrest before, and I know Milo was seeing other breeds that didn't belong as far back as two years ago."

He sat back and knocked his fist against the table. "They're coming for Kymbrygh. Tirryderch have got the food, Wellech've got the mines and livestock, but Whitpool have got dragons. *That's* what they really want now, because Milo's been taking all of theirs away, and they've yet been able to stop him."

Walsh was frowning down into her chip basket, gone still now, and pensive. Ellis had clearly hit *something* somewhere in all that ranting.

"They'd want to do it during Sowing," Walsh said slowly then shook her head. "No, it's as you say. Take it before, and then wait. Catch the clans on their way through, get as many healthy ones as they can before all that's left are the ones that can't make the trip."

"They all stop at Old Forge." Ellis drummed his fingers on his jar. "Reaping or Sowing, they all stop there. All of them."

Walsh swirled her droopy, gravy-soaked chip through congealing cheese but didn't eat it. "They can't get in through Tirryderch. And no one's ever going to take Whitpool from the sea."

Whitpool's shores were all towering sheer cliffs that sat atop what Ellis suspected was a not-so-secret force of military and former military spies from which had emerged the Black Dog Corps. Whether or not the enemy knew what Whitpool harbored beneath hire car drivers' caps and porters' smiling faces, the geography alone would make an attempt from the water foolhardy at best. From the air… possibly. But certainly not during Sowing when the skies over Whitpool were full of dragons. That would be just asking for midair collisions and a lot of dead pilots.

"Not even with dragons," Walsh mused. "*Especially* with dragons."

Ellis opened his mouth to ask why, but it clicked before he'd even taken a breath. Because that wasn't the way they'd done it in Taraverde or Colorat or anywhere else they'd tried to steal whole clans from and ultimately came away with fractions of them. They'd come for the dragonkin first, taken them away, and put their own in instead. And then it had been a matter of poisoning and manipulating and finally subjugating the dragons that both survived and displayed the reactions to the poison Taraverde had been after.

Dragons were territorial. A dragon that wasn't clan showing up and attacking a preserve wasn't going to make it out alive. Ellis had never seen an actual fight between dragons, but he'd seen them get annoyed enough with one another to snap and swipe, and even that did enough damage to keep Milo busy with poultices and patches for weeks after.

Moreover, their territorial nature applied to dragonkin as well. Milo was *clan* to the dragons at Old Forge, and now so was Aleks. So, for that matter, was Ellis, really, as long as he had the dragonstone. Ellis didn't know of any anecdotes involving dragonkin -vs- dragonkin, each attempting to influence their charges one against another, but if it had ever happened, he imagined it hadn't been pretty. A dragon swooping into Old Forge and going after other dragons—even the sick and hurt ones—wasn't going to end well for that dragon. And there was always the chance that it might switch loyalties to the dragonkin that ran the preserve. Because dragonkin were supposed to *care* for dragons, not use them, and, as Ellis had already pointed out, dragons weren't stupid.

"No. Not Whitpool." Ellis traced the routes in his head again, just to be sure. "We've just caught our second spy on Kymbrygh's east coast. And neither of them was even trying to get to Tirryderch. I'm thinking they were setting things up to try the Red Coral Strait."

And not because of the glimpse of the map he'd caught in a Dream, or because the southern end of the strait was plausibly accessible from the Surgebreaks, or even because the shore of the strait was where he'd been when it started to click into place in his head. The Red Coral Strait was the water corridor between Kymbrygh's east coast and Preidyn's west. Which could feasibly take anyone getting through it all the way up to Llundaintref. But Llundaintref, while unquestionably strategic, wasn't where they'd been trying to get since all this started. And if one managed to get control of Wellech, seize the roads and waterways and railroads, one could reasonably expect to have a much better prospect of taking all of Kymbrygh from the inside than it had been proving from the outside.

Walsh sipped her beer. "Too shallow. They'd never get the kinds of ships they'd need through it."

"All right. Point." Ellis thought about paddleboats trying to sneak their way into Wellech through the Chwaer Bach Estuary, and the just barely prevented carnage when only one of them made it. "Small merchant boats. They're up and down the strait a dozen times a day. Disguise one or twelve, load them up with soldiers instead of goods, slip around the Surreywitch Sound. Once you've got a good landing force entrenched, it'd be easy to take the ferries and bring in more, fan out all up the coast and just keep moving." Ellis set his teeth. "If they manage that, they'd have their pick of targets. All they'd have to do is come up the Aled through Hollywell, or try the Chwaer Bach again like they did at Riverfest. Or, they could just conjure one of those fogs laced with spells or that sleeping gas, like the one that sorcerer used at Old Forge—and try telling me *that* wasn't a test run to see how difficult an assault on Whitpool might be."

The more he thought about it, the more his heart pounded. Cennydd and his accomplice hadn't only been trying to steal a dragon—they'd been testing how easy it might be to go after Milo the same way the Elite Constabularies had gone after Aleks on his preserve in Colorat.

Ellis shook it away, teeth clenched. "No, they'll try to force an opening then overwhelm us with numbers. Offload assault troops up and down the coast in a burn-it-all approach. Go for the shock of it, try to take our heart before we've even started to fight back. That seems to be the way the Confederation are going anyway."

"Sowing's less than three months off. You're right—they'd want to hit us before that. They'd want to secure Wellech before they go for Whitpool, because they won't want to send dragonkin in until after they've got us down. If they've got Wellech, they might be able to take Tirryderch eventually, but I'm thinking they'd try to mow through us and then swarm in west to Whitpool. And then all they'd have to do is wait at Old Forge for a whole new crop of migrating dragons. Because, as far as the dragons know, Old Forge is still safe."

Walsh finally ate her chip. She chewed slowly, watching Ellis all the while, then said, "I like how you think you know more than the generals."

"I don't. I just know Kymbrygh. I know what it has to offer an enemy who thinks everything is theirs for the taking. And I know how I'd take it. Alton said he came to me because I know Wellech's weaknesses, which means I know Kymbrygh's weaknesses. This is the one that could break us."

"And you've brought it to me instead of Alton because…?"

"Because I've met you. And I know you get the job done."

"Or you know it's my arse if you're wrong."

"More like I think you'll make sure whatever needs to happen next happens fast." Ellis shrugged. "I'm not wrong. And you don't think I am." He peered across at Walsh with a half smirk. "It doesn't hurt that whatever does happen next will be coordinated through the Home Guard's Wellech office."

Walsh snorted. "And you want to make sure your Wardens aren't left out of it."

"I don't think that would be a worry with you. But I can't forget the lessons trying to work with Crilly taught me." Ellis picked up his jar, tipped it toward Walsh. "I'm a practical man, Colonel Walsh."

"You're a bloody amateur, Rhywun Ellis."

"Fair," Ellis agreed, because he absolutely was, but he also wasn't done yet. "The fog Cennydd and his accomplice used at Old Forge—that wasn't as thick as one would need, but it was widespread and only took the one sorcerer. Add in whatever gas was mixed in there and another sorcerer or two, and it would be possible for at least a small force to sneak up through the strait for a surprise assault on Wellech." He sat back with a shrug. "If I weren't a *bloody amateur*, I'd start keeping a very keen eye on the weather maps."

Chapter 21—Variation

: the compositional process of changing an aspect(s) of a musical work while retaining others

The problem with trying to rid a country of powerful mages was that it left the country without powerful mages. Granted the Confederation had more than its share of witches and sorcerers. But the number of mages who'd been expelled from their homeland before that homeland decided to just cut to the chase and start killing them outright was considerable. And a great many of those mages who'd survived and fled had since joined the armed forces of their adopted countries. Unfortunately, while all the expelling and adopting had been going on, Wellech had been run by a Pennaeth who'd done everything he could to make sure none of the adopting would be happening in his parish.

Now, Ellis remembered his chat with Howell very clearly. The outrage bubbling beneath Howell's calm narrative of powerful magic folk sent directly to the frontlines. The subtle anger in his tone when he spoke of the unfairness. Ellis also remembered the discussion in Nia's study and the conclusion of Tirryderch's Pennaeth that if her country wasn't going to look out for the best interests of her parish's magic folk, she'd do it herself.

And, morally, Ellis understood it. Supported it. Agreed with it.

Practically, though, he could absolutely appreciate the want for powerful magic on any frontline. Because damn him to the nether and back if he couldn't use some on his own right now.

"That's more than we were counting on," Ellis told Tilli, crouched behind the berm of the main coastal road, and watching too many soldiers dispatched from a small frigate and onto the rafts that would bring them to Kymbrygh soil. He winced at the thunderous volley of big guns from the ships still battling it out at the mouth of the strait, but didn't wait for his ears to stop ringing before he said, "We either need more ammunition or better marksman."

Tilli gave him a glare. "I'll just pull a few of each from out my arse, shall I?"

"That's the spirit."

It had taken a mere three weeks for Ellis's warning to be proven right. He hadn't been surprised to learn it hadn't really been news to

Alton, who'd already had an approach ready when Walsh brought it to him. The fact that the approach included a swift and orderly absorption of the Wardens into its own division of the Home Guard, on the other hand, was definitely surprising, but since Walsh had left Ellis in command of it, he took it in stride. He trusted Walsh, he more or less trusted Alton, and he couldn't deny there was a comfort in knowing there were people who knew more than he did telling him where he needed to be and what he needed to be doing. And also *listening* when he suggested a tweak to a plan based on his own knowledge of the geography, or a rearrangement of assignments to better utilize the talents or accommodate the weaknesses of Ellis's Wardens.

The Confederation had tried the assault-teams-disguised-as-merchants-cloaked-in-magical-fog tactic twice. The first time, Zophia had apparently been too subtle about dissipating the thick mist as it swarmed the piers of the Preidyn Ferry Harbor, because the small boats, clearly thinking themselves safely hidden inside it, merely withdrew as the haze did, then tried it again the next night. When it didn't work the second time either, they'd evidently got wise.

They were bolder this time. Actual gunships barreled at the Surreywitch patrols at dawn, harrying them, while rafts dropped one after the other into the strait, the too-numerous soldiers in them rowing like mad toward shore. Zophia had spent a good part of the night magicking any ammunition they'd put in front of her, so it was easy enough to wait until they were within range then bullseye the rafts, pepper them with enough holes they sank with little fanfare. The problem was, even with the tide in, the waters of the strait weren't that deep, and the current steered whoever was floating on it right to shore. And then the closest enemy ship turned its big guns toward the beach, laying down covering fire for the soldiers working their way to land. The blasts pocked wide strips of the shallow cliff holding up the road, gouging out new fissures big enough to house a dragon.

Ellis only hoped the road didn't collapse beneath the Wardens and cadets, all lined up behind it to defend their shores.

"Zophia!" Ellis stretched his neck so he could see her, crouching ten people down the line and blinking back at him, wide-eyed. Terrified. "Can you sink them?"

"I try." Her chin wobbled. "I *try*."

She looked awful. Exhausted. It hadn't merely been a matter of waving her hand and shooing away the fog the past two nights; she'd spent a lot of power and concentrated energy doing it. And then they'd gone and added the chore of spending more power and energy on ensuring the ammunition was more accurate. Ellis hadn't

The small ships abruptly turned to flee. They were cut off by the superior naval vessels they clearly hadn't been expecting. The soldiers still alive in the water saw their little fleet attempt to turn tail; some of them reversed direction and started back toward the boats, while the rest kept trying to gain the beach. The big guns had mostly taken over, pounding the enemy ships so steadily they couldn't have dropped more soldiers in the water even if they had them. The planes took up what slack was left, dropping bombs like a child sowing seeds into the wind, only these reaped fire and ruin in thunderous bursts that Ellis would swear were making his ears bleed. Three enemy ships were on fire just at the blurred stretch where sound turned to open sea.

It left the soldiers in the water to Wellech's frontline. Yelton kept shouting to "Hold your positions! *Hold your bloody positions!*" so Ellis relayed the order to his own line and kept shooting.

◉

It didn't hit him until later, much later, after the Home Guard took over dealing with the captured soldiers and left the dead to Ellis. Ellis felt a little bad about handing the duty to Petra. He did it anyway.

The residents had been evacuated days ago, the moment the first hint of fog had been spotted. Now Petra—still scowling at Ellis because he'd refused to allow her to enlist with either the Wardens or the Home Guard, since "If anything happens to me, Wellech still needs a Pennaeth, Petra, be reasonable!"—called the people back to help with the grim work of collecting identification from dead bodies. Salvaging guns and ammunition washed to shore. Digging a too-long trench in which to lay the bodies for as proper a burial as they could manage.

Still, there was nothing in Ellis but awe at the fact that all of it had actually happened. Gratitude that he and most of those on his side had lived through it. Fury that there'd been an attempt to invade his home. Pride that he'd been part of repelling it.

And it was odd, because he kept expecting to feel what he'd seen when he'd Dreamed of Milo flinging magic at a woman with a gun and turning her into a mangled mess of broken parts, and then standing there, staring.

Shock. Horror. Fear. Self-loathing.

Ellis wasn't feeling any of it.

Not until he caught a ride in the back of a Home Guard lorry from Hollywell to Reescartref, and watched, bewildered, the surreal illusion of "life as usual" going on around him. People collecting wash from lines; children clumping on the side of the road to yell and cheer at them as they passed. When he arrived at the Reescartref

Bridge to see his mam standing there, waiting for him, it crashed over him so fast and so hard he couldn't parse any of it. Only that it was awful and it *hurt* and it churned his guts into a roiling mess. He only just kept himself from stumbling from the bed of the lorry to kneel at Lilibet's feet on the boards of the bridge and howl.

Because *then* he felt it. *Then* he remembered every moment of it. Every magnified view through his sights of every eye he'd closed forever with the sweet pressure and deadly tug of his trigger. Every man and woman in the uniform of the Home Guard that had gone down because he'd been aiming elsewhere. Every cry of one of his Wardens when their cover proved just that much too sparse. Every gentle surge of pink foam over wet sand. Every order he'd given to target *that* group of living, breathing people—*that* specific man creeping too close, *that* particular woman who'd almost got her legs beneath her and was about to gain the beach—and the *satisfaction* he'd felt when his orders were followed.

Ellis managed not to let any of it out, only stood there and let his mam look at him, grateful she wasn't trying to touch him, because he didn't think he'd be able to keep it together if she did.

He only said, "We didn't lose any Wardens," thick and clotted in a throat gone full and tight. Because there was something in him that mourned the nine cadets Yelton had lost but was *glad* it had been them and not Ellis's own people.

Lilibet crimped a sad smile at him, like she knew. "Let's go home."

"Mam." Ellis stopped her. "I need you to call the Coven."

He needed more than that. He needed them to permit him to attend. He needed to be allowed to speak to them, plead with them, convince them. He needed Lilibet to Dream for him so he could find a way to make them listen to him.

Lilibet looked away, mouth tight. "You know what you ask."

No one who didn't have the kind of power or skill or credentials to call themselves a witch or sorcerer or mage was permitted to attend a formal Coven. No one who hadn't done their time as Newyddian and then sat the rites to become Arbenigwr was permitted to speak at one.

But that wasn't what Lilibet meant.

A good percentage of the Kymbrygh Coven were veterans. A bigger percentage of them had taken the places of those killed in the last war a generation before. All of them knew how few they were, how many just like them had died in the same way Ellis was prepared to ask them to do now.

He merely sucked in a tight breath, and said, "I'm sorry."

"Yes. I know." Lilibet shoved out a sharp, bitter noise that was nothing like the laugh she'd clearly intended. "I'll do what I can."

"I need more magic folk." Ellis paused, waiting for Dilys to say something, but when she didn't, when he didn't even hear the gap in static that signaled she'd toggled down to speak, he set his jaw, frustrated. "Dillie." He scrubbed at his eyes then his face, and thought *blight it all*. They were on a coded channel for a change. He could speak plainly. And he *needed* to. He set his teeth. "I can't keep overusing Zophia. Exhausting her two nights in a row made her near useless when they actually landed. She's strong, but she's not as strong as Milo, and not nearly so well trained. Mam's doing what she can with the folk who've volunteered, but they weren't that powerful to begin with and they're not prepared for actual war."

"None of us are," Dilys said, firm. "And it isn't as though we're hoarding all our folk. They can come and go as they like. We don't keep Tirryderch citizens prisoner."

The most annoying part about communicating via radio was that the person doing the talking had to stop and let go of the toggle before the other person could respond. Which meant Ellis couldn't interrupt.

"We can't be blamed," Dilys went on, "because we opened our doors when Wellech shut theirs. They're *our* citizens now, and you can't expect us not to protect them."

"That's a far cry from what you said last year." Ellis couldn't help how it snapped out of him. "They're not only Tirryderch citizens, Dillie, they're citizens of the United Preidynīg Isles. *United*. If Wellech falls, all of Kymbrygh follows, and if the Confederation have Kymbrygh, they have Preidyn. Why d'you think the Royal Forces are suddenly throwing everything they can around us? *They* know what the Confederation are after—are you going to tell me you don't? Because I know you're smarter than that. And I know Mastermind hasn't kept it to himself."

There was a huff from Dilys's end. "The Confederation don't know what they'd walk into in Whitpool. Half of *Whitpool* don't know what's waiting in Whitpool. They're never getting past the parish line."

"How lovely for Whitpool. But what will they have to mow down to *get* there?"

Silence. For quite a long time.

Then: "I can't make them help you, Ellis."

Ellis blew out a heavy breath. "I'm not asking you to. I'm only asking you to let them know they're needed. And that they can."

"They know that."

"Do they? And who's told them? Tirryderch's Pennaeth? Or its most influential witch? Because last I heard, Nia and Terrwyn were making it very clear that Tirryderch magic ought to stay in Tirryderch, and Steffan was very loudly backing them up."

"Let's not pretend that protecting our own is the same as dictating what they can and can't do."

"Wellech *is* your own, or is Tirryderch not a part of Kymbrygh?" There was only empty static for an answer. Ellis snorted, shook his head. "Right. Fine. You do what you think you have to, Wildfire. We'll just be here, putting ourselves between the wolves at our door and the rest of Kymbrygh. Maybe there'll be enough of us left by Sowing to make good sport when the dragons start coming for us."

There was a pause, a long one, before Dilys's voice came back, subdued and pained. "I'm *trying*, Ellis. I swear it, I am. I *have* been. They... I mean, they're a united front, the three of them, always have been, but it makes them..." A growl, a burst of static, then: "I'm not the one in charge."

"You're the one Nia will listen to."

"Bloody—" Dilys laughed. "Have you *met* my mam?"

"Oh, pull the other one, Dillie. You've had Terrwyn and Steffan eating out of your hand since the day you were born, and it's been plain for years that Nia's been grooming you for Pennaeth. So show her what kind of Pennaeth you'll be. *Make* her listen. Make all three of them understand that Pennaeth might not be waiting for you later if Tirryderch doesn't help us *now*."

A huff. "How much power d'you think I have against the three of them when every one of them still sees me as a three-year-old with scabbed knees and a ready tantrum?"

"Then you have to show them. Show them who you are now, and make them listen. Because if you can't, we're all done. And we can't be done, Dillie, d'you understand?" He paused, waiting, but when Dilys didn't answer, he pressed, "*Wildfire.* Do—you—under—*stand?*"

"Of *course* I understand, you great pillock." There was a bang from Dilys's end, muffled, then a sharp curse. "It's not... it's only... oh, blight it." A high-pitched oscillating whine nearly pricked holes in Ellis's eardrums. For a second Ellis thought Dilys had thrown her radio across the room like he'd been sort of wanting to do, but she came back, snapped, "If I pull this off, you will owe me *so big* I won't have to buy drinks in Wellech for the rest of my bloody *life!*"

This time, she *had* channeled off, Ellis could tell by the quality of the static. Didn't matter. Dilys might be a lot less serious than most people would prefer she was most of the time, but she was solid, she was smart, and she had very clear ideas of *just* and *fair* and *right*, and no qualms whatsoever about picking a fight and, more importantly, *winning* it.

Ellis couldn't remember, in all their lives, even when they were wee and wobbly, ever winning anything against Dilys—from archery tournaments to arguments to wrestling matches. And she was almost two years younger and probably half his size.

He also couldn't remember laughing so hard, being so *relieved*, in... well, probably ever.

The Dreams were getting... odd. Ellis had got used to clear pictures, actual scenes, which was unusual for Dreams in general, yes, but had become normal for those he had of Milo. Ellis had decided almost right away it must have something to do with the dragonstone, but the fact that everything was even more vivid and detailed when he Dreamed of Milo in the company of dragons had solidified the notion.

He didn't know what to think now.

Everything was murkier. Darker. Snatches of Milo playing in a smoky pub would segue without sense into Milo hitchhiking along a busy road then skulking in shadows somewhere dim and empty, red possibility striating out in confused webs in every direction. A bright, clear look at Milo casually strolling past an apparent checkpoint at dusk would abruptly become Milo ducking into an alley at midday, gaze wary and everywhere at once.

The things Ellis did see clearly only served to increase his unease. Because, though he didn't know the language, he was fairly certain the writing he was picking up on street signs and propaganda placards around Milo was Ostlich. Knowing Milo was in Colorat had been bad enough, but there'd been dragons freed from Taraverde, and now it looked like he was in Ostlich-Sztym. And Ellis had to think that going from a country that had been unwillingly occupied, then on to the one that occupied it, and *then* to one that had volunteered for occupation had to be an escalation in risk.

Once, only once, in all the Dreams he'd had over the long months, did he hear his own name from Milo's lips, see the soft look of melancholic tenderness that went with it. Ellis had no context for any of it—couldn't make out whether it was day or night for Milo; couldn't hear anything besides the low breath that carried his name on a despondent sigh. But he saw what Milo was looking at when he said it, a simple tarnished key held tight in dirty fingers, nails broken and ragged and knuckles dark with dried blood.

It probably shouldn't have heartened Ellis the way it did.

He had little time to dwell on it. The influx of Royal Forces troops was a relief, but also a logistical nightmare, because there was only so much room at the Home Guard's base to house them. And the fact that the base was up near Caeryngryf meant that if an invasion came by way of Hollywell, as everyone was sure it would, it would take too much time to transport the troops all the way south to defend.

Ellis volunteered the Croft as headquarters for the command staff then went to work on the rest of Wellech. Negotiating housing. Assigning tracts of land to be used for camps. Snagging an equally harried Walsh to insist that the bulk of the troops be stationed along the more vulnerable southern and eastern coasts. He'd been almost three-quarters of the way through his argument before he realized he hadn't needed to argue at all—Walsh had already made the arrangements. And she'd placed every witch and sorcerer at her disposal at strategic intervals up and down the coasts as well. Which was a relief, because Ellis had got so used to not having magical help, he'd forgot to include any in his diatribe.

The naval battles were constant, unrelenting. And getting closer. It was the rare day when Ellis couldn't hear the big guns in the distance, just out of sight from the beaches, or take a whiff of the chill late-winter air and not catch the sting of sulfur curling through it. They'd yet to get as close as they'd come when they'd tried to sneak up the strait, but they'd apparently called some of their northern fleet down from the Goshor and stationed them at the Surgebreaks. The intent behind it was clear.

All Wellech could do was watch the battles that skimmed the edges of the sound's waters, listen to the artillery boom and blast, and wait.

"That's all, as far as preparations go." Petra squinted down at the list in her hand, before her mouth quirked up, and she sent a sly glance at Ellis. "Ready for the list of complaints?"

They were at the Wardens' command post in Reescartref, having a cuppa after a grueling week, and trying to pretend everything was normal for five minutes while they went over the more mundane business of the day.

Ellis sighed. The list of complaints had grown exponentially since the Royal Forces had arrived.

He took a bracing sip from his mug. "Not really, but I reckon we'd best get it over with."

"Right." Petra was grinning now. "So, Cal over to Granstaf says you need to tell 'all these city folk' that cow-tipping isn't a real thing. He's getting tired of chasing off-duty soldiers from his fields in the middle of the night."

"Cow-tipping." Ellis set his mug down. Blinked. "Really?"

"Yup." Petra rattled her list at him. "I've already got a memo for you to send to Walsh."

Ellis snorted. "Yes. Grand." *Cow-tipping.* "And give me a copy of it. I'll personally hand it to one of the brass at the Croft to make sure the word gets 'round."

Petra made a note, still grinning, then said, "Lieutenant Edwards would like you to have a word with Folant."

"Oh, for—" Ellis pinched the bridge of his nose. "Why?"

"From what I can tell, for being Folant." Petra pursed her lips, clearly trying not to outright laugh, and raised an eyebrow. "Apparently, the soldiers bivouacked at the Grange have out of the blue begun asking for credit at the pubs and inns. When their lieutenant inquired as to why they were all suddenly poverty-stricken and imposing upon the good citizens of Wellech to fund their recreation, turns out Folant not only told them the good citizens of Wellech would happily do so, but he's also been—"

"He's been running nightly card games and taking them for everything down to the lint in their pockets. *Bloody*—" It wasn't funny. Ellis *should not* laugh. He threw his hands out. "What's he even doing there? I don't want him in any position to get information that might—"

"He's not." Petra shrugged. "He can't. Or at least no more than anyone else with eyes could get. And even if he could, he couldn't get it out to anyone who might matter. Walsh's people keep a proper eye on him, and they apparently check Oed Tyddyn every two days or so to make sure he hasn't got his hands on a radio or sommat." She gave Ellis a reassuring smile. "For what it's worth, I don't think he's up for trying anymore. I don't think he even understood what he might be leaving Wellech open to before. And now that he does…" She left it there, but she was looking at Ellis like she was waiting for something.

Ellis had no idea what. He huffed. "If you say so." Skeptical. He didn't trust Folant with so much as a 5p, but he trusted Petra's judgement when it came to pretty much every aspect of Wellech's wellbeing. He supposed he ought to trust her in this, though the words "trust" and "Folant" rather clashed in Ellis's head, but he had to admit he had a definite bias he had a hard time thinking past. He waved at Petra's list. "Fine, let's move on. Because, honestly, if that's the worst he gets up to before all this is done, we should count ourselves—"

"Rhywun Ellis! Rhywun Ellis!" Young Cled, one of the boys who'd been hanging about the soldiers just recently, eyeing their uniforms with clear envy, came skidding into the office. His bright gaze skimmed the room, then lit up even more when he spotted Ellis. He grinned. "Syr! Your dragon's back!"

The children had made a game out of spotting her last autumn, excited and gleeful as they watched her wing overhead, and trying to guess at where she might land. The adults had been much more sanguine about it, and though no one ever suggested Ellis should find a way to keep her from landing at all—because how could he, really?—they nonetheless never hesitated to alert their Pennaeth and First Warden that they expected him to do *something*. Luckily, she never stayed long enough for anyone to get truly antsy or to cause any more trouble than she'd done that first time.

At first, Ellis matched Cled's grin, pleased to hear the redcrest was back. A familiar warmth weltered through his chest, because though it was absurd and improbable, Ellis knew she was here to see him, to check up on him. It was almost an uncanny, improbable, secondhand connection to Milo. And the fact that she'd clearly made it through the winter was buoying.

But then Ellis realized what it all meant. And everything in him just sort of... froze.

He turned to Petra. "Go find a radio and get hold of Walsh." He stood, heart abruptly knocking against his ribs as he pulled Petra up with him. He all but shoved her away from the desk, past a still grinning Cled, and out the door. "Tell her the dragons are waking up."

◉

The surge, when it came a fortnight later, was brutal. Wellech wouldn't know it for days after, but the attack began with the airfields in Werrdig. Dragons, a ravager and a marauder, decimated nearly every plane that had been on the ground, and at least a handful of those that had made it into the air. The air support the Royal Forces—both naval and ground troops—expected never came.

It was inevitable that landing troops would eventually make it through. The Confederation forces had been somewhat depleted as the war had raged on, Eretia having turned several tides on the continent over the winter. And once Blodwyl got its feet back under it and retook what ground it had lost, its troops proved as ruthless and determined as any Confederation soldier on their most bloodthirsty day. But the Confederation had clearly decided Kymbrygh was worth consolidating most of what it had left in an all-out push. When the first Western Unified battleship went down off the waters of Surreywitch Sound, it rocked Wellech to the core.

"That's a blackwing marauder," Ellis said, hoarse, as he watched the too-familiar silver-white light sail from the deck of an enemy destroyer and splash the hull of a Royal Forces fast patrol boat. The light itself did no damage, but the dragon followed it, gliding across the battle lines to hover above the fringes of the Western Unified flotilla and spew jets of flame down in unrelenting swaths on the patrol boat. "I should've told Walsh about the lights."

He hadn't made the connection before. He didn't think he'd actually realized there might be one. But now that he'd seen how they were getting the dragons to attack exactly what they wanted attacked, Ellis remembered that ball of fizzy light that had stuck to

Milo's shield. And how the dragons had followed it when Milo sent it back at the witch who'd thrown it.

"They know." Yelton was stood beside him, looking just as sick as Ellis felt, and watching the pinprick of what had to be another dragon wing in over the sea from the southern horizon and toward the battle. "They've known since the first time." Yelton's jaw was so tight his red-stubbled chin quivered. "Doesn't mean they can do much about it."

They were difficult targets, dragons. Scale plating impenetrable to almost everything Ellis knew of. More maneuverable and reactive than airplanes. Built-in weapons. They didn't seem to have much problem dodging the missiles and heavy artillery aimed at them. Though the rockets launched from the decks of the Royal Forces ships did seem to at least stagger them off target when they managed to hit, it was *getting* a hit that seemed to be the first problem in defending against them. Ensuring the hit did damage looked like the second.

"They lose scales," Ellis said, seeing the redcrest in his mind's eye, the dragons he'd watched Milo set loose in a Dream. "The poison they feed them makes them lose scales." He turned to Yelton. "Vulnerabilities."

Yelton was still watching the battle, grim-faced, but he shrugged then nodded. "They probably know." He turned and jerked his chin at the cadet with the radio. "But we'll just make sure, aye?"

Ellis didn't know if the message ever got through, or if it did, if it made any kind of difference. Like every child of Kymbrygh, he'd learned about dragons in school. The different breeds he hadn't really remembered past the exams. The cautions against approaching one. The rarity of encountering an aggressive one. The damage it could do if provoked. How to avoid provoking.

None of it prepared him for the realization that he could do very little but watch as two dragons followed silver-white light toward the shores of Wellech.

Chapter 22—Presto

: a very fast tempo

If life were a play, or maybe a book, a novel, there would be a distinct villain, and a hero in counterpoint who'd been written into existence to thwart them. The villain would be casually evil, brazenly cruel, easy to spot by an obvious lack of a moral center, and their only goal would be something craven that good people could point to and confidently, unquestioningly judge as bad. The hero would be strong, and tall, and likely quite good-looking, always kind and always sure, their flaws small and common and forgivable, and their strengths—both physical and ethical—unquestioned.

If life were a play—or a novel—there would be a discernable plot. A beginning, a middle, and an end. An introduction, a conflict, and a resolution. The hero would grow as the story went on, learn important lessons about themselves and their world that would help them to address the conflict in the most noble way possible, probably find love along the way. And when it was all over, when the narrative was played out, when the story *ended*, the hero would go on to live the life that had been interrupted by the plot, and enjoy the love they'd earned.

Life was not a play. It was not a novel. There was no one clear beginning that could be recognized as a beginning except perhaps in hindsight. There was no discernable middle where one could judge the number of pages left and be confident the hardship was nearly done. There was no distinct end, only a continuation, a steady, sometimes reluctant journey onward into more unknowns—more beginnings unrecognized, more conflicts undeserved or maybe even deserved, more resolutions that too often resolved nothing at all.

Life was merely life. It moved analogous to the blue threads of time that only very few could See and none could wholly understand. It changed, it stayed stagnant; it gave, it took; it hosted conflicts with transcendent indifference, but it didn't actually create them, cause them. It simply was.

Once Upon a Time Ellis thought as he carefully placed the bomb in the crook of the lowest strut of the trestle, *Once Upon a Time* there was a man who realized that this was just how life was now.

Stretches of hollow-eyed, immediate existence between conflicts neverending. Learning how to prop himself just so against a sturdy vertical surface so he could sleep on his feet without falling over. Eating things he would've snubbed only a while ago but now merely shoveled it in because it was food, and his body needed it if he meant to keep it moving. Too-young faces around him that had aged decades in the space of weeks, days, sometimes hours. Firefights in the middle of streets he'd run along, blithe and happy, as a child; stumbled end to end, drunk and laughing with mates, as a teen; patrolled, brash and cocksure, as a man.

Once Upon a Time there was a man who always kept his gun clean and dry.

Once Upon a Time there was a man who always ensured it was loaded.

Once Upon a Time there was a man who always shot to kill.

He climbed up to the next sill, over one column, and placed the next bomb.

"Patrol," Bethan hissed from somewhere below, not even a vague figure in the dark, just a low voice nearly blending with the calm rush of the river.

Ellis stilled, hanging on to his unsteady perch, trying to fit himself to the too-geometrical shapes of columns and braces and struts, and thought about how war didn't end with an invasion repelled. War went on, war *was*, a life lived within it small and of little consequence unless the loss of it crafted it into something remarkable.

Memorials of war, as well as the dead made a part of it, had been a matter of course to Ellis. Sometimes ignored, sometimes contemplated. Names and dates and events dug into straight lines in marble, mapping out beginnings, alluding to middles, chiseling out endings, and demanding remembrance. *On this date, the armies of Blah and Blah met in battle. These are the lives that ended here, the names history has chosen to remember, these are their deeds, this is why it's important.* Ellis had never really considered the reality that words carved stark and tidy couldn't quite touch. Who'd been witness to this event and thought it demanded a record in history? Who'd watched the people around them fall and decided which among them would be a name in stone? Who'd been there and survived, observed an end, and made their history *the* history? Because history, after all, needed to be recorded, needed to *end*, before it could become historic.

And he'd never, not once, imagined he'd be the person witnessing history in the making. Marking the faces around him. Cataloguing events, words, actions and reactions, landscapes before a battle and landscapes after. Looking for *The End* written somehow into the fabric of his life, this war, woven through with the threads of red possibility that would disappear when it turned to reality.

A life could begin in the midst of war, it could end because of it, it could take on new meaning as a result of it, or it could lose what made it a life worth living. Time contracted to pinpoints within it while moments expanded toward infinity, and life became something easy to take, dear to hold, excruciating to endure, poignant to lose.

"They're gone," Bethan whispered. "Set the last two, and let's go."

Grim, Ellis pried his now-stiff fingers from their grip, moving quick but careful, doing everything by feel, because there was no moon, no stars. It was late spring in Wellech, which meant rain and mud and weeks without anything in the sky but clouds. Ellis couldn't see a bloody thing but the vague sparkle of the river beneath him.

"That's the last," he called down softly, hugging the nearest column as he began his cautious way down. "Get back to the radio."

He didn't look to see if Bethan obeyed, minding only his own movements for now, heeding only this moment and his place within it before moving on to the next. Because that was one of the first things he'd learnt about a war waged up-close: it was made of infinite moments, each spent one after the next by someone different, each moving on its own trajectory. And sometimes all those moments gathered like threads in a closing fist to become one moment shared, defining those who lived it together.

War didn't end with an invasion repelled, but Ellis supposed a life could begin with an invasion executed, because this new thing he was living was not his life. It was something new, something he didn't recognize, something built of brittle, too-brief-too-infinite moments, and all he was doing was moving from one to the next. The enemy surged, tried to move inland, and Ellis fisted the moments of his life in his hand and spent them on stopping it—one moment strategizing; one moment shouting an order; one moment watching it implemented; one moment taking away all possible remaining moments from someone else. And if he was lucky, Ellis came away from it with more moments to dole out, miserly, as it all began again.

"They're not getting past Gefēonde." Bethan was crouched on the high side of the watershed nearest where the Addfwyn doglegged into the Aled, neck bent and eyes faraway as she listened to the chatter through her headset. "The 142nd has them pinned to the beach, and Western Unified has regained control of the Blackson *and* the Goshor. Those Eretian troops aren't giving ground." She shook her head, still listening. "Nothing from Walsh yet, but three

Werrdig divisions got through to Caeryngryf, and it's holding strong." She gave Ellis something that might've been trying for a grin. "If we can get these bridges down and hold Torcalon..."

If, Ellis didn't say out loud. *If.*

Torcalon had seemed vast to him, once, the countryside between it and the Croft endless—fields and pastures; streams and pools; moors and bluffs; trees and trees and trees. Now it was only a few fingerlengths on a map, nothing at all between his home and those who meant to take it. Nothing at all but him, and those with him, and the men and women right now lining the banks of the Chwaer farther north, because if the enemy took the waterways, Wellech was done. And Wellech was bloody *lousy* with waterways.

The Confederation hadn't got through Wellech before Sowing. They'd come in through Hollywell, dragons leading the way, burning everything splashed by that silver-white light, but one dragon had been clipped on the wing early in the siege and gone down somewhere in the woods west of Granstaf. No one had seen it since. Everyone hoped it was dead. Ellis sort of hoped it had managed to limp to Whitpool.

Something young and optimistic in him had halfway expected an end then—*you didn't make it, it's too late, you're done here.* Except it hadn't ended. It just went on. Goals changed, timetables altered, strategies amended. Because there was always Reaping.

Bethan made herself more comfortable on the muddy ground, headset still in place, listening and digging in to wait for the signal to move.

They'd been separated from Yelton weeks ago. And then they'd been cut off from the RF lieutenant who'd made Ellis's ragtag assembly of Wardens and citizens with guns into a rearguard. Missions planned and sanctioned by people who knew better than Ellis, so he'd put up no fuss. That ended under heavy fire at the ferry port when the lieutenant ordered a retreat, and Ellis had decided they were *not* leaving all those ferries just sitting there, waiting to be used by the Confederation.

They'd lucked into Dyfan only a few days before. The lieutenant hadn't quite understood why having the head of the miners' union within reach was such a boon; Dyfan was not a young man, after all, more paunch now than pluck, and years in the mines had given him a distinct wheeze when he exerted himself. Perhaps the reports the lieutenant must've received afterward, detailing how every ferry in port had been reduced to kindling in the water, had clued him in. Because if you want a good, precise explosion—or a host of them— put a miner on it. And since the first thing Dyfan had done when the Confederation breached Wellech's beaches was to evacuate and hide every one of his demolitionists and squirrel away every last blasting cap and speck of gunpowder in various boltholes throughout the parish, Ellis had put Dyfan to immediate and violent use. Ellis might never know what the lieutenant thought of it all, because Ellis and the rest of his small band had been unable to get back across the lines in the aftermath of their first foray. And then, once Bethan got hold of someone in charge on the radio, they'd been ordered not to. Because even if the lieutenant hadn't recognized what Ellis was doing, Mastermind had.

They were M Company now. A band of guerillas. Officially unofficial, and answerable only to Walsh and Alton. *The M is for Miscreants*, Walsh had said wryly. Ellis liked to think of them as freedom fighters. Resistance. The enemy, he knew, thought of them as savages. With what he knew of the Confederation's tactics, Ellis thought that was proper hilarious. He also thought he was pretty much all right with it.

Demolitions, ambushes, theft, arson. Weaseling through back ways into enemy encampments or strongholds, and wreaking what havoc they were able. Wriggling through weak points in pickets, and stealing ammunition or just blowing it up, because this was their home, all of them, they'd lived here all their lives, they *knew* it, knew how to exploit it like the enemy never could. Blowing bridges, boobytrapping roadways, destroying railways, because if they couldn't get the enemy out of Hollywell, they could at least hold them there.

Bethan took off her headset and began packing up the radio. "Undeg says the way's clear. Just waiting on us now."

Undeg was one of the four who'd listened to Lilibet at the Coven and come forward to answer Wellech's call; she was also one of the few students Lilibet had grudgingly agreed had learned enough to be effective in battle without getting themselves killed five minutes in.

Ellis vaguely remembered Undeg and her brother Bowen spending summers at Rhediad Afon, like Milo used to do. Two near-identical faces among over a dozen eager young student sorcerers and witches, but that was about it. If he'd had impressions of them from whatever brief, distant encounters he might've had over the years, those impressions would've been *small* and *timid* and *quiet*. And he would've been very, very wrong.

"Let's move, then," Ellis said, and started leading the way back. They'd need every one of those five minutes to get clear.

"Syr, it's a matter of making the air pressure work for the detonation, enhancing the blast," Undeg had told Ellis, eager and bright-eyed, back before they'd got their first official order to keep doing what they'd been doing. "Making one stick of dynamite work like ten."

Dyfan had merely shrugged confirmation, his smirk small but definitely pleased.

It had been helpful, certainly. One stick of dynamite instead of ten meant bigger blasts with fewer materials, and fewer necessary raids to collect them. There were still places explosives were stored that Dyfan knew and the enemy hadn't yet discovered, but that couldn't last forever.

"And maybe even starting the spark," Bowen had put in, gaze keen on Dyfan, looking for permission, perhaps, and when he got a nod and another shrug, Bowen turned back to Ellis. "We haven't got that bit perfected yet." He wrinkled his nose, annoyed. "'Tisn't as though we can practice, yeah? But if we *can* do it, we could conserve the blasting caps and the timers."

They'd had plenty of practice since then. And that had been helpful too. M Company could travel lighter, move faster, hit more targets, do more damage.

The quiet whirr of a long-eared owl sounded out of the dark. Bethan pulled ahead of Ellis and quickened her pace toward it.

Bowen and Undeg were hunkered where Ellis had left them behind a ridge on the other side of the valley, facing each other with knees in the mud. Bowen's hands covered Undeg's, and Undeg's head was bowed, eyes shut, concentrating. Dyfan was keeping a close eye on them, and when both Bethan and Ellis had ducked down beside them, guns ready, Dyfan told Bowen, "Now."

Bowen gave Undeg's hands a firm squeeze; it wasn't even a second later that Tair Afon went up, the first explosion hitting Ellis right in the chest and rattling his teeth.

Ellis and Bethan immediately stood, heads poked just over the top of the ridge along with the barrels of their guns.

One second.

Two.

Voices shouting. Another explosion—bigger, louder, brighter. And then another, more distant, as the Crickway Bridge over the Chwaer went up.

Three seconds.

Two dark silhouettes against the bright strobe of the next bomb going off. Ellis targeted the figure on the left, knowing Bethan would take the one on the right. Two down.

Four seconds.

Five.

Four more silhouettes, running. A strut on the Twelve Furlong Bridge over the Aled gave with a grinding screech. Ellis kept shooting. Two more went down at the end of his sight.

Six seconds.

The stringers blew on the trestle of the Brunway over the

Addfwyn, the whole block giving way and crashing down through the braces. It was still falling when three explosions within milliseconds of each other took out the South Parish Bridge and every yard of roadway beneath it.

The valley of Tair Afon was little more than an overly large gorge—too rocky in its few flat places for planting, too wet in its lowlands for living, and hugging the western edge of Torcalon Wood so close it was doubtful one could dig anywhere furlongs out without hitting an impenetrable root system. It was, Ellis often mused, likely given a name on Wellech's map for the sole reason that it sat at the confluence of three rivers, and people needed to call it something. A travel artery more than anything else, it had no stations, no laybys, no people, only a wealth of choices by which one could pass over it. It was, however, practically made of bridges and trestles—waythroughs and fords and roadways and train tracks. And Confederation troops had gained control of it three days ago.

Ellis and his "miscreants" had tried to work their way up from Hollywell without *looking* like they were working their way up. Blowing tracks near Gwynedd one night, a small bridge east of Granstaf the next. Covering too much ground for sleep, but it was worth it for the lack of pattern and therefore the lack of foreknowledge on the parts of the Confederation troops getting more of a foothold around Hollywell every day. If Wellech could keep harrying the opposition, keep cutting off routes that would allow the enemy to expand its hold, Ellis could sleep later. Some day.

Ten seconds.

A siren began to warble. Someone was blowing a whistle. More backlit figures spilled out of tents along the banks of the three rivers, some of them too far out of range; Ellis pulled back to reload just as those he'd assigned to the Aled side opened fire. Three more explosions synced as one. The Brunway went down all at once, lashings listing over broken columns before pulling a ribbon of train tracks down into the river with a tortured shriek of twisted metal.

The orders were to sever transportation of any kind north and west. The Confederation's push west toward Tirryderch had given way almost immediately to a push north toward midparish and then would no doubt try for west to Whitpool, but that had been no surprise. Ellis wondered if the Confederation had given up on Tirryderch altogether—the naval reinforcements had ensured no one was getting in by sea, and the magical defenses on land were being discussed in international news with dry, informative language that still somehow leaned toward awe.

Ellis also wondered if the Confederation were finally regretting their self-inflicted lack of Dewin, because he knew he certainly was. What he wouldn't give to have Zophia and her broken Preidish with him here, but Walsh had commandeered her for one of the Royal Forces generals. Regrettable, but Ellis hadn't had much say in the matter. Or, well, any. Undeg and Bowen might be modestly powerful sorcerers, but Zophia was the next best thing to having Milo at his side, and bloody *damn*, but Ellis wanted Milo at his side right now. Ellis had barely even Dreamed of him lately. Then again, it was possible that was because he'd barely slept.

Fifteen seconds.

The night was near to daylight. The enemy camps, not nearly dug in yet, were chaos. The explosions were still coming, taking out every bridge and roadway and therefore any high ground Ellis's Wardens and ragtag magicals weren't already picking the stunned soldiers off from.

This, Ellis thought, vicious, *is what you get when you don't know the ground you're trying to take.*

To Dyfan, he only said, "You three start toward the rendezvous. I want to make those hills by sunup."

The Royal Forces had struck their lines along Wellech's southern tip from Gefēonde to Gwynedd, but that still left the Confederation troops too much leeway and too many resources, both held and potentially won. Cutting off the people of Granstaf and Hollywell, and anyone in between, was a harsh strategy, but even Ellis hadn't been able to come up with anything better if they meant to keep the enemy contained and keep the contingent on the eastern shore from making it through the Torcalon Wood.

And M Company was the only one—at least that Ellis knew of—between the two fronts. Which meant there was no one to ride to the rescue if this went wrong.

He waited until the last bomb went off. Until anyone in his gun's range was already dead. Until he was *sure* every easy way north or west was now smoking rubble.

Only when it was clear that there was nothing left to do but watch did Ellis give Bethan a nudge and tell her, "We're done here. Let's go."

His ears seemed stuffed with wool—he barely heard himself. His vision was spotty, bright green blobs in the shapes of burning bridges floating in front of his eyes, and blinking wasn't helping. He led the way cautiously, hoping he wasn't making more noise than what he could hear himself, though it did make him thankful for the mud for the first time since he'd surveyed the area with Dyfan when they'd been forming the plan. It had gone exactly as they'd hoped so far, though some small, optimistic part of Ellis that still insisted Wellech had a future was already calculating how much money and how much work was going to have to go into repairing the mess they'd just made when all this was—

Ellis stopped so short Bethan nearly walked up the back of him. He turned sharply, scanning the sky, but he still couldn't bloody *see*.

Bethan stopped beside him. "What's the m—?"

"I need you to run," Ellis said, low and firm, one hand gripping the rifle that was about to be useless, and the other settled over the stone in his pocket. The stone that had just flared so hot through his shirt it felt like it had burned a hole through his ribs. "Where'd it even come from?" he wondered. The Confederation had two in this region when they'd started their assault; one had gone down and the other had been sighted this morning over the Goshor. It wasn't unreasonable to assume a dragon could make that flight in the time given, but what about the dragonkin controlling it? "No way," Ellis muttered, because *no way* could anyone have got through all the roadblocks that had been thrown up all over Wellech, even if they'd managed to get through Caeryngryf, which he'd been assured no one could. Impossible.

To Bethan, he barked, "*Now*," and shoved her ahead of him, turning, saying, "Go, now, *go!*" just as the distinctive sound of a dragon's roar rattled the night.

That got Bethan moving.

"Head to the rendezvous!" Ellis shouted after her, watching only long enough to be sure Bethan kept going.

She moved slower than Ellis would like, but he didn't think the dragon would be sent after one retreating target. Not when there were a good fifteen other targets who'd thirty seconds ago thought having the high ground was a good idea. Targets *he'd* placed there.

He took off back toward the gorge, not even trying to be careful or quiet this time. The others down by the Aled side would have all started heading west to the rendezvous, *through* the flats and open spaces, betting on the Confederation soldiers being occupied with exploding roads and bridges for at least long enough that Ellis's people could climb the ridge and head toward cover. He hadn't even considered a dragon. There'd been no reason to.

He could hear the shouts now, down in the gorge where Ellis couldn't see. Close, though; close enough he could hear the sound of boots in mud, even through his still-clogged ears. "Andras, get *down!*" he heard someone shout—Tilli, he was sure of it—then a scream drowned out by the bellow of the dragon. Ellis was almost there. So close to the lip of the ridge he could see the orange flare when the dragon shot its flame. Hear the heavy flap of webbed wings. Smell petrol so thick in the air it burned his eyes and the back of his throat.

"Hang on!" He had no idea how to get his people out of what was happening. No idea what he was supposed to *do*. Except maybe get the dragon to focus on him long enough to give them a chance

before it crisped him. But he kept running anyway, yelling "Hey! *Hey!*" pouring his last breath into moving as fast as he could, then—
"Bloody..."
—coming up so short when he reached the edge of the dropoff he almost thought time stopped. He knew his breath did. Everything in him did. Except his heart—that he could hear thumping like a drumbeat in his ears.

All he saw at first was the top of the head. So close below he could see the pattern of the blue-gold scales struck iridescent in the shifting glow of the fires, and, well, that answered that question, Ellis thought numbly—the one up north was a marauder; the only dragons sometimes blue-scaled were... blunt-horned ravagers.

Because of *course* the Confederation would choose the breeds with the most vicious-sounding names to do their dirty work.

The air was hot, hardly even breathable. It *whooshed* in rhythmic beats against Ellis's face, pushing him back a step from the edge as the dragon rose. And *rose*.

Horns.

Brow ridge.

Eyes.

Eyes five times the size of a thresher's wheel. At least. Wider than the spread of Ellis's arms. A gold rich as the sun, slit-pupiled. Old. *Ancient*. Half-mad, maybe. Half something Ellis couldn't help thinking of as a peculiar rue. Misery. An uncanny sort of *asking* that made him think of the redcrest.

Clearly seeing Ellis. Focused on him. *Watching* him.

Huge. Bloody *immense*. Bigger than anything Ellis had seen before. Bigger than he'd thought anything could actually *be*. Or maybe that was just because it was so bloody *close*.

It hovered in front of him, rising slowly, rows of razor teeth twice the length of him *this close* to his face, venom dripping over them like drool. Smoke heaved from its nostrils in a noxious brume, twin dense puffs curling all around Ellis again and again in time to its wingbeats. It hung there, only for a moment, still watching, massive wings rhythmically thumping the air, pushing Ellis back and sucking him forth in a hot *swish* of wind wrought heavy with sulphur and the smell of burning. It resumed its ascent. Slower than Ellis would've thought possible for something its size. Deliberate. Almost meditative. He was face-to-neck with it now, could clearly see the thick iron collar, patches of missing scales around and beneath it, and a wide swath of raw, exposed hide down to midbreast, cragged with moss. The glow of its fire lit its throat, piping up then ebbing down, up then down, as though it wasn't sure if it should fry him or not.

The dragonstone had never been so hot, not even when he'd

been basically petting a razorback calf. Stunned, clumsy, he reached for it, closed his hand around it.

The dragon pulled back, still hovering right in front of Ellis, but its heat wasn't actually singeing his face now. Slowly, he drew the stone out of his pocket, held it palm-up in front of him like an offering, and said, "Tilli, Andras, get them all and go," shockingly calm and even.

Tilli and Andras moved immediately, thankfully without question or argument. Quickly they chivvied everyone into a wide berth and up the ridge.

Ellis merely stood there. Stone in his outstretched hand. Sweating in the heat the wings kept beating at him. Watching the dragon watching him. It was far enough back he could see both its eyes now. And yes, Ellis was sure there was something unutterably remorseful in there.

Whatever it was, it flickered, flared, when silver-white light skewed in from the ridge on the other side of the gorge on his flank, and slapped against the right side of Ellis's chest so fast and bright he thought it should've rocked him sideways. It didn't. It hit without force, without sound, swathing him from tip to toe. A shout in what Ellis was pretty sure was Verdish followed it from the southern end of the ridge opposite.

Ellis held his breath. Because he knew what this was. He'd seen it. Dreamed it. And he didn't have the ability to peel it off and throw it back like Milo had done. And while Ellis was glad he'd been the only one targeted, that the others were already well away and getting farther every second, he was also bloody *tamping* that it was going to end like this.

"Milo..." Ellis swallowed, throat raw, eyes burning. "My dragonkin would've helped you." Little more than a croak when it should've been a shout, a roar, because it was true and so real it had taken hold of Ellis's life and *shaken* it into this unrecognizable misshapen thing that was going to end here, like this.

Once Upon a Time there was a man who stood alone on a muddy ridge in the middle of the night and stared down the fiery throat of a creature the love of his life had left him to save.

"I only... Oh, blood and rot. *Milo*." Too small. Too... *something*.

Though fitting, Ellis decided, that his last thought, standing in front of a dragon and waiting for the fire to move up its throat, would be of Milo. Run off to rescue dragons in a foreign land while at least one he couldn't save, maybe didn't get a chance to, was manipulated into, *forced* into, roasting his cariad.

The perverse irony would almost be funny, if it weren't so terrifying.

Once Upon a Time there was a man who would've died laughing, if only he could breathe.

Except.

Except.

It didn't happen.

The dragon bellowed again—full of rage this time, and hot, so *hot*, all but shrouding Ellis where he stood in superheated air that made it impossible to breathe—then whipped its head to the side. The man kept yelling at it, clearly *ordering* it. It snarled, shot Ellis a look that Milo would probably be able to interpret but Ellis certainly couldn't, then it turned away. With a great, forceful shove of its wings, it lifted up then reeled, arcing away from the ridge with a cry that sounded less like a roar and more like a song. A sad one. A dirge.

Ellis only stood there. Frozen. Not quite believing.

He should be dead.

...Shouldn't he be dead?

His brain wasn't quite working. He was still muddling through the question when, halfway across the gorge, the dragon warbled something from high in its throat, wounded almost, and backwinged to an abrupt stop in midair. Hovering again, it twisted its head to one side then the other, searching, as though it heard something. It called again, that same unhappy song, and sailed upward, wings spread wide, circling slowly, until its head jerked, as though something only it could hear had answered.

The man kept yelling. Kept commanding. Kept pointing at Ellis.

With a cry that sounded anguished, the dragon whirled in a wide loop, plunged like an arrow to swoop just over the head of the man atop the ridge on the other side of the gorge, low enough the air thrashed into wind by its wings knocked him over. Still it didn't stop, it didn't turn, and it didn't attack Ellis like it was clearly being commanded to do. It circled back around and swept down yet deeper, spewing a jet of flame along the floor of the gorge.

Instant illumination. At least a dozen enemy soldiers were abruptly taken off guard, exposed, caught calf-deep in mud halfway across the bottom of the gorge. They yelled. Dodged back from the long line of fire the dragon laid down at their flank.

The dragon curled up and over, trilled out another song, or maybe it was the same, as it set its nose up and... away. Wings like sails unfurled, the great, steady *whoosh whoosh* of them coiling somehow louder than the sirens and the whistles and the shouting and the braces on bridges still collapsing as the fires raged on.

"Did... did that just...?" Ellis watched the huge bulk of the dragon become nothing more than a dark blot high up in a darker sky.

The man kept yelling. The dragon kept going.

And. What?

What?

Had Ellis just witnessed a dragon escaping its captor?

He didn't have time to ponder it. Not yet. The soldiers had only been diverted for a moment. They were once again making their way toward Ellis. Obviously set on pursuing the saboteurs. And Ellis hadn't even noticed them. Not until the dragon had called them to his attention.

And, seriously. *What?*

He was still lit up, it wasn't going away, and though he'd somehow just escaped certain death by dragon, that wasn't going to mean much once he was in range of those soldiers' guns. He might as well have a sign over his head.

There was still paralyzing disbelief sitting at the bottom of his veins. He was still heavy with shock. Sick with adrenaline gone stale and sour. His brain still wouldn't work. He couldn't think of anything to do.

So he turned and ran.

⁂

It took him hours to lose them. And he couldn't go anywhere near the rendezvous point until he did. The fact that he was bloody *glowing* didn't help. At all.

It went away gradually. Ellis didn't know if it was the magic wearing off or just that he'd finally put the proper amount of distance between himself and the one who'd cast it. But when dawn started to lighten the sky into a swirling murk of roseate sapphire, he was finally able to turn himself toward the hills southwest of Granstaf where the others were waiting for him.

They chattered at him. Glad he'd made it. Relieved he was safe. He didn't hear them. Someone pointed him at a bedroll, and he fell on it without a word. He was asleep with his face mashed against damp wool the second he hit it.

He Dreamed.

He wished he hadn't.

Chapter 23—Rubato

: a fluctuation of tempo within a musical phrase often against a rhythmically steady accompaniment

"We're losing here, Wildfire." Ellis jammed his hands between his knees so he wouldn't break another radio. Bethan had almost beat him about the head with the last one he'd mangled. "D'you understand what I'm saying? Tirryderch is running out of time to stop this before it gets to your borders."

"It's *been* at our borders, or have you forgot Ynys Dawel already?"

"I'll see your Ynys Dawel and raise you a Hollywell, a Granstaf, and everything on our southern tip. You don't want to play this game with me."

The Confederation hadn't gained more ground but they'd got more troops through, though they'd yet to land any cannons or large artillery. Still. No one was pretending anymore that Hollywell wasn't lost, and the lines holding Torcalon were suffering casualties every day. And Wellech hadn't been prepared for gas warfare. Anyone with even the slightest magical ability had been called in from every corner of Wellech—cadet or citizen; young or old—and formed into their own company to reinforce the Royal Forces' defenses against it. Still, the horrible deaths and debilitating injuries of those exposed were taking an alarming toll. Nonetheless, every able-bodied person in Wellech had taken up a weapon and joined a line somewhere by now.

But that marauder was still out there, and Desgaul had reported sightings of two bellwings over a Confederation flotilla massing on Blackfish Bay. Desgaul's navy had wasted no time engaging, rushing into service a small fleet of maiden dreadnoughts just launched from their cradles. Western Unified cruisers and gunships were so tight across the South Blackson there would be no breaking through by sea without using the bellwings. Thing was, from the sky it was almost a straight line from Blackfish Bay to Kymbrygh. And while enemy ships would have to make it around or through Preidyn's Lauxauhn Peninsula to engage, dragons wouldn't. If enemy dragonkin found a way through...

With the end of Sowing came an offer to the Western Unified Alliance direct from Taraverde's Premier: *Give up Preidyn, and you'll have your peace.* It told the world in no uncertain terms that this was definitely personal. And it no doubt made the other Alliance governments, those boffins Walsh had so little regard for, wonder if sacrificing the ally that had pushed hardest for this war against Taraverde might possibly be worth it. The fact that Taraverde had been pulling back from other theaters, ceding ground across the continent while focusing even harder on the Preidynīg Isles, only drove the point deeper.

Either way, a surge from the south was coming. Massive, Ellis could feel it. It was only a matter of time. And if the Confederation got hold of Kymbrygh, Western Unified would likely take it as their cue to accept Taraverde's offer. The Royal Forces had been fighting on too many foreign fronts, they were spread too thin across the continent, and the troops defending the islands weren't enough. There was no way Preidyn would survive long against the whole of the Confederation's war machine if she had no allies.

"I can't say... anything, really." Dilys had lowered her voice, just short of a whisper. "I *can't say*, Prince. D'you understand? Except Hammer's on the job, and daylight isn't far off."

Hammer. Walsh. Thank every goddess. Walsh and Dilys versus Nia, who would've had her own backup in Terrwyn and Steffan. And wouldn't Ellis have loved to be a fly on *that* wall.

"*How* far off?"

"Stop asking. Please, just trust me and *stop asking* or I'm going to have to cut you off."

Stop asking. Because even coded channels sometimes got broken. Which meant something was going on, Walsh had a plan, and Dilys knew about it. Was clearly taking heart from it.

Except.

"Except we need you *now.*" It shot out like gunfire, far too wrathful for someone who'd just got at least a tiny smidge of hope. "We can't lose, Wildfire, we *can't*, and we're running out of time—*I'm* running out of time. I have to get to him, and I can't do that 'til this is over, all right? So I need it to be *over*, I need—"

Ellis cut himself off, gripping his knees so he wouldn't crush any of the sensitive components of the radio. He shut his eyes, sucked in one long breath after another, while the radio squawked out Dilys's voice wanting to know "Running out of time for what? ...Who d'you have to get to? ...Prince? ...*Ellis?*"

When Ellis had gathered himself enough that he could breathe again, he toggled down, and said, "I think he was captured, Dillie. I think... I think they shot him full of holes and took him."

The silence this time was thick and choking, before Dilys said, "How would you know that?"

"Because I Dreamed it." Ellis shook his head. "He'd been shot before, I watched it happen, but this time it was—"

Horrible. Ruinous.

There'd been no sound. Only vision, sharp and clear. Like a picture show.

Milo at the feet of three dragons. Milo setting hands to chains and shattering them. Milo jerking back and clutching at a spot on the side of his neck, blood oozing from between his fingers. Milo stumbling back then shoving in again, determined, breaking another chain, and then the sickening jolt-lurch of another bullet hitting him, the chest this time, and then another, left arm, and then yet more, shooting his leg out from under him.

He'd flown back. Rolled ragdoll-limp. Stayed there. Unmoving. Facedown on the ground. Broken.

Ellis, helpless as ever, could only watch it happen and think *Your shield. Where was your bloody shield?!*

The dragons swooped back down into view, wheeling low over Milo. Slow, weak, he rolled until he was on his back, looking up, blood all over him. A small smile curved his mouth. He said something—*Go*—and a spray of blood shot out with it. He tried again, shouted, maybe—*Go!*—or tried to, and the dragons circled one more time before arcing back up and away. They were gone, escaped, by the time Milo let his eyes fall shut again. Everything was getting murky for Ellis, lines going blurred and dark, when the toe of a boot came into view, shoved at Milo's shoulder, kicked and pushed as though checking if he were alive.

Was he?

Because the worst part was that Ellis couldn't control what he was seeing. Couldn't somehow get closer to see if Milo's chest was still rising and falling. Couldn't hear what the people with the boots were saying. Had no idea what they might have in mind when someone snagged hold of one of Milo's arms and started dragging him away through the dirt like a sack of refuse. Could only see fine red threads snaking around Milo, shuddering, winding all over him, then unraveling, then winding again.

"He's too powerful for them to hold him for long," Dilys said when Ellis managed to shove the story out from between his teeth. "They wouldn't be able to hold me, and he's ten times stronger."

And save him, Ellis wanted to believe it so badly, but—"And how easy is it to use that power when you've been hurt?"

"He threw a shield at you from yards away with a hex burning through his back, and *then* he put out a swath of raging dragonfire while he was *this close* to being unconscious. He's *that strong*."

"Shot. He was *shot*. I saw at least three hit him before he went down. There was no shield. *No shield*. I don't even know if he's still alive. And if he is, how likely is it that he'd be able to magic his way out of *anything* if he was hurt enough he let them take him?"

And what if they found out he was Dewin? A Dewin, prisoner of people who'd gone to war over killing Dewin.

Silence. Because they both knew the answer. Until Dilys asked, "And what does Mastermind say?"

"Very little." Angry. Still furious, even though it had been weeks since Ellis'd had that conversation.

He'd wanted Alton to send him out *Now, I need to be on a ship tomorrow, I know where he was, I can find him, I can*—

Alton, of course, was having none of it. *We can barely get highly trained agents who know what they're doing across those lines. What exactly d'you think you could do?* and *Let the RIC handle it, Rhywun Ellis. It's what we do, after all.* And the worst, the lowest—*He wanted you in Wellech for a reason. Are you really going to invalidate everything he's fighting for?*

If he thought he might get through the heavily patrolled ports in Caeryngryf, Ellis still might've tried it.

"I haven't Dreamed of him since. Snatches here and there, and they have the same... feel to them, like I should be seeing him, but I never do. It's like I'm seeing where he is, but not *him*." It was windless by the end, too thin. Because it was always dark, always bleak, and with a feeling of *cold* that was impossible, Ellis didn't feel in Dreams, and he kept looking for the strands of red possibility, but they were never there. "I don't know what that means. I don't know if... I don't *know*." And he couldn't ask Lilibet. He couldn't ask anyone.

"He's alive." Dilys said it with steady conviction, as though no other conclusion were possible. "He's alive, and don't forget who else is out there. Mastermind might be a bit of a minger, but don't doubt for a second that he got a message out to the Bl—to *her* five seconds after he signed off with you."

It was the one hope Ellis had been hanging onto by fingernails already rough and ragged while he'd taken out his fears and anger on every single enemy Walsh had pointed him at. *For Milo*, Ellis thought as he set his bombs. *For Milo*, he snarled as he made himself a sniper's nest and started shooting. *For Milo*, he told himself as he fisted the dragonstone and shut his eyes, *hoping*, and tried to—

Ellis sat up straight, eyes popped wide. Blinked. Sucked in a sharp breath. Said, "Wildfire, I just thought of something, I have to go," and yanked the headset off hard enough he thought maybe he'd taken an earlobe with it. Didn't matter, wasn't important, wasn't *anything*, because he was bloody *asinine*, he was bloody *brilliant*, and he snapped, "Bethan! Get over here and get me Walsh on this thing!" so forcefully Bethan nearly fell on her face in the mud trying to comply.

It took seconds. I felt like hours. And when Bethan finally handed

Ellis back the headset, he hadn't even got it on all the way before he was asking Walsh, "Have you ever heard of a dragonstone?"

⬤

Alton was interested. Aleks was more than willing.

After Walsh got done shouting at Ellis for not telling her—

"I didn't know! I only made the connection when the one at Tair Afon didn't roast me!"

"Nearly *two bloody months* ago! No bloody *wonder* the codebreakers kept telling me the chatter on the Confederation end was insisting we had dragonkin!"

—and, well, she had a point there. But after she'd got done with that bit, she'd ordered Ellis "and the rest of your miscreants" to come out of the wilderness, find the 133rd at the Granstaf encampment, and report to Colonel Everleigh.

"She'll have your orders for you," Walsh had growled then gone off-channel.

By the time Ellis managed to slip M Company back through the lines, the weather had turned to high summer even if the calendar insisted spring was only a week gone. Ellis hadn't really realized exactly how unkempt they were all looking until he registered the stares they were getting from the soldiers once they'd exchanged passwords and been allowed in. They were given tents near the Home Guard units, provided with changes of clothes, and unsubtle directions to the showers. They fell upon the mess tent first.

Once Ellis gorged on food not much better than what they'd been hunting and scrounging themselves, and then made himself more presentable—with *hot* water, bless every goddess—he went to report to Everleigh. She did have orders. And quite a lot to say about *Wardens playing at soldier*, though she said it with a friendly smirk and an approving nod when Ellis briefed her on his last four months. She also had a message from Walsh.

Aleks only managed two more stones, because, and I quote: "Dragons is sometimes not nice." Also, it seems dragonkin themselves only ever get one, so he says we ought to be grateful we got any. Unless we can come up with more actual dragonkin, we'll have to make do.

It was somewhat disappointing. But it was also two more than they had now.

⬤

It was shocking to Ellis how quickly life in the trenches stopped shocking him. He'd thought he'd been thoroughly jaded when he'd first reported to Everleigh. It wasn't as though he'd been lounging on an estate somewhere all this time. And it wasn't like he hadn't seen a fair share of horrors in the past two years. Even inflicted a few.

This was different. This was becoming nothing more than the hand that fired the gun, the eye that sighted a target. There were no *people* in the trenches, only soldiers. And if the soldier next to you got their head blown off, all it meant was more targets for you, an immediate swarm of corpse flies, and maybe a decent pair of boots if they were your size and you didn't mind prying them off the feet of the person who'd handed you a cup of tea six hours ago.

Three days on the line, one day at camp, and then the cycle started all over again. Ellis didn't even know what day it was, what *month*, only that it seemed there really was such a thing as being too tired to sleep.

War's took my cariad far from me
Bones resting 'neath cairn stones 'crost the sea

It was lovely. A pleasing tenor, smooth and sonorous.

Still.

Ellis slitted open one eye, mouth pressed tight, and made himself as comfortable as he could against the tree, back pressed into rough bark, and roots poking into his tailbone and thigh. He only had a few hours until it was M Company's turn in the trenches on the western edge of Torcalon. And he *really* needed some sleep. He shut his eye again, trying not to huff out loud, and strove to catch hold of at least that blurry state of waking sleep he'd got so good at lately, but he couldn't seem to grab hold of it.

Eyes ne'r more rest upon Preidyn's green shores
Held safe in cool shadow 'neath
Dragons' wings the soul of my cariad soars

It was that *bloody* song. Ellis gritted his teeth, shut his eyes tighter.

He was no stranger to camp life. The 133rd's encampment was quite a lot bigger than what he was used to, more orderly and well regulated, but fundamentally the same. Separate tents were set up for things Ellis had at one time in his former life as a Warden on patrol assigned to individuals—food preparation, medical care, communications. But with the exception of having to get used to having a lot more people around, and not being in charge, it was really no different from any other camp Ellis had been part of since he'd been old enough to venture out with a gun in his hand.

Right down to the camp songs.

Rowdy ones to brighten moods. Dirty ones to lighten them. Old songs Ellis had been hearing all his life. New ones brought in by soldiers from all across Preidyn. Mingled now into Wellech's character the same way bonds morphed and melded among men and women who gathered face-to-face around a campfire at night then stood back-to-back when sunrise brought another battle.

Song was just inherent to campfire.

Rest in shadow
Cariad, sweet

Except this one was... irritating.

Beautiful, no doubt about that. Known and loved throughout Wellech, and apparently the rest of Preidyn, because the man—boy—singing it now was from Werrdig. Private Logan Malloch, Ellis thought, though he couldn't be entirely sure. There were three young men about the place that all had the same look to them—too young, too fair, too wide-eyed—and Ellis had a hard time remembering who was who. But the song emerged on a northern lilt so clear and pristine it was difficult to maintain annoyance for the one who was singing it.

Rest in shadow
'Neath their harbor we'll meet

Teeth clamped, Ellis adjusted himself against the tree's trunk again. Tried to stop hearing it. Tried even harder to stop letting his mind conjure a picture of Milo, alone on the field of a foreign country in the middle of the night, his violin tucked beneath his chin, and that same tune skirling from it as dragons blotted the sky all around him.

Green fields of Preidyn, succor me
Call my cariad home from—

The explosion came with no warning shriek, no distant sounds of propellers, no flash of light from the enemy lines. A violent burst of light and fire flared like the sun in the middle of the camp, only yards away from where Ellis slouched. The pull then *push* of it sucked his breath right out of his lungs, yanked him in then hurled him back, slamming into him with a brutal wall of fractured air that threw him away from the tree and onto his back in the dirt. It was so fast, so concussive, so world-filling, he didn't actually hear it.

Everything had gone abruptly white, utterly soundless, body-brain-heart wrought blank and numb. Ellis had an eternity that was probably less than a second to wonder if he'd just died before the pain hit him. His sight stuttered back, fuzzed and too bright, but none of it made sense, all of it gone to ruined disarray. Perception narrowed down to a ringing in his ears so high-pitched it crowded out everything else as his body reflexively scrambled and clawed and dragged him *away*.

Everyone was running. Where there'd been ordered yet mundane camp life two seconds ago, now it had all snarled into a knot of frantic confusion. The ground was a ragged crater. Fires burned. Everything was shaking.

There was gunfire in the trees now. Ellis could see the strobing flashes of it. Which meant the enemy had somehow got past the trenchlines. They hadn't been able to gain even a yard for months. And certainly not without the whole camp hearing it.

It made no sense.

Magic, he thought, trying to drag himself up but he couldn't gain his feet so only *push-push-pushed* back and back on heels and hands, dirt raining down, fire everywhere. Silence had arrived with whatever that bomb had been, and he didn't think it was just the concussion. They hadn't heard it coming. Not a whistle. Had to be magic.

Blinded for too long. Deaf except for the ringing until muffled rumbles and reports dug their way in then ruptured into reality like a train plowing through a snowdrift.

Everything came back. The camp was chaos. Names called. Orders shouted. People running. People dead.

Private Malloch with his sweet tenor and too-youthful face lay beside the fissure that used to be a campfire, the right half of him just gone, torn away but for the gory mess of what was left, glistening dark in the dirt. His face, untouched, was turned up to the sky, expression caught in surprise, eyes wide and shimmering gold with reflected fire.

Someone needed to close them.

Eyes ne'r more rest upon Preidyn's green shores

Someone needed to—

Ellis shook his head. Got to his feet. His throat burned. Everything felt like it was rocking, queering his balance. His gun's strap had been around his shoulder while he'd been dozing. It had been thrown with him, or at least he assumed the one by his feet was his. Disoriented, muzzy, he picked it up, hands moving automatically to check it over, found it working fine. Someone slammed into him, sent him reeling to the side. He almost tripped over Private Malloch. What was left of him.

Rest in shadow

A wave of nausea washed over him, but he couldn't think why. Everything felt distant. Nothing was making sense. Someone—Lieutenant Mason—was shouting something Ellis couldn't hear, but the body language was clear. Arms waving, hands beckoning then pointing. Urgent.

Go!

Ellis looked around. Spotted Tilli making her way toward him, skirting the edge of the crater where the bomb had hit. Andras was right behind her, one hand gripping Undeg's arm and the other his rifle. The rest of M Company came in a disheveled clump, pushing through the soldiers scrambling for their own companies in all directions and shouting commands.

There was still that surreality clinging to Ellis's edges. That sense of dream-walking that clouded his mind and made his body feel like it didn't belong to him. He moved anyway. Collected his company by eye, jerked his chin toward the frontline that had abruptly arrived at the camp's threshold, and started toward the sound of shooting.

So it was funny, he thought later, that he didn't hear the bullets that came for him.

A punch to the chest. That was what it felt like at first. It took his wind, heaved him back. Another. This one threw him down. He thought there were more. He felt the impact as he went down—*one, two, three*... Couldn't be sure.

The pain bloomed high and bright as he hit the ground again. Saw Private Malloch only yards away, still staring up into a sky going pastel with approaching dawn. Ellis could swear he saw Malloch's lips move, could swear he heard the fading resonance of that stupid song beneath the shouts and the booms and the boot-steps—

Rest in shadow
Cariad, sweet

—as his vision started to tunnel, black seeping in with the pain that was taking over everything.

Once Upon a Time there was a man who... something.
Rest in shadow, Private Malloch crooned.
Yes, Ellis thought, *all right*, and let his eyes fall shut.

It wasn't a Dream. Couldn't be, because Milo was looking at him, touching him, long fingers callus-rough and skimming Ellis's cheek, blue eyes overbright and desolate.

Ellis tried to say something—
How could you leave me like that?
You're not really here, are you?
Are you all right?
Tell me you're all right.
—couldn't.

"Don't." Milo's mouth turned up, not quite a smile, but trying. "It's all right. I know."

I don't think you do, Ellis thought, peevish and hurting and sad and angry and still so bloody in love he thought he might choke on it. But he only nodded, curled his fingers tighter around the dragonstone.

"I need you to be all right, Elly." Milo was so close now, leaning in, clutching with both hands, except it was wrong, fingers so crooked he couldn't get a proper hold. What was wrong with his fingers? "Please. *Please*, Elly. I don't know..." He bowed his head, eyes shut, jaw tight beneath his dark beard gone to unruly scruff.

He looked so gaunt. So ill. Pale to the point of near-translucence, full lips cracked and dry. His touch was like fire to Ellis's brow, then his hand, but... no, that was the dragonstone snugged in Ellis's fist, pulsing hot like a little coal that didn't burn.

"Cariad," Milo whispered, soft and distant, and, "Always," and then everything went gray and gauzy before Ellis could even gather the wind to protest.

✻

He knew it for a field hospital the second he opened his eyes. Dim light through tent canvas. Neat lines of cots, and moans in the dark, and white sheets, and the smell of ether. And he knew Milo wasn't really there. A dream. Not even a Dream, just a plain, old run-of-the-mill sleeping fantasy Ellis's brain had decided to have while he'd been busy dying.

Almost dying, apparently. He seemed to still be here, after all.

Still. The disappointment was crushing. "Milo," he said, soft and secret, trying to catch the dream again.

"Thank every goddess," someone breathed in the near-dark, and the hand that wasn't Milo's squeezed around Ellis's fist tighter. "Ellis, you soft-headed minger. What d'you think you're *doing*, getting shot? Your mam's going to proper *murder* you. Milo's going to have your stones, and not in a fun way, you absolute bloody *arse!*"

The corner of Ellis's mouth was turning up before he could help it. "Well, damn. I've gone to the nether, and here's one of its imps to greet me." He blinked hard, trying to bring Dilys into focus through the gloom.

She wasn't laughing. She wasn't even smiling. She was scowling. Fierce. She looked like she wanted to hit him but didn't dare.

"Don't joke about that," she snapped, quiet but plainly tamping. "You nearly—" She cut herself off, lips pressed tight, and took a long breath. Calmer, she said, "They took two bullets out of your chest, one from your thigh, and another two from your arm. You've been down for nearly a week."

Ellis frowned, shifting his glance down, but he couldn't tell the difference between the sheets and the bandages that must be there in the dim light of the tent. Musing, still fuzzy and very confused, he said, "I don't feel a thing."

"Well, I should hope not!" Dilys's sudden grin was a white scimitar-slash through the dark. "Not once Petra got through with Lieutenant Everleigh and then the colonel who runs the hospital." She snorted. "I don't know what kind of connections that woman has, but I'm told your Tomos showed up with a mule the next day, loaded down with catgut and gauze, among other things, and a crate of morphine pride of place."

Ellis grinned. No wonder he felt like he'd been at the bottom of an ale barrel for days. "I've always thought Petra would make a great Pennaeth."

Dilys's smile dimmed. "Well, let's not find out, yeah?"

"Eh, it's not as though... Wait." Ellis's thoughts were running slow as syrup. "Did you say I've been here a *week*?"

He hadn't moved—couldn't, really—but Dilys pressed gently on his shoulder anyway like she was trying to stop him from getting up. Ellis tried to bat her off, but he couldn't make his body cooperate.

"When did you get here?"

"I'm not officially here at all. Not yet. But the 2nd Tirryderch arrived outside Granstaf two days ago to provide magical aid to the 133rd." Dilys's mouth crimped tight. "Imagine my annoyance when I asked after you and heard you'd let yourself get shot. Lots."

"*Let* myself." Ellis rolled his eyes, since it seemed they were two of the few body parts willing to do what he wanted just now, but otherwise dismissed it. "Yes, fine, but *why* are you here? Why now? I thought—"

"I haven't the time to fill you in properly." She squeezed his hand, still holding the dragonstone. "But I'll tell you all about it when I get back. For now, just know that we've won the lost ground back. The 142nd is already advancing. The 133rd is following within the hour with the 2nd Tirryderch as outriders. And I'm taking M Company with me."

Ellis's stomach dropped. "To *where*?"

"*Damn* it." Dilys's hands went away. "My bloody *mouth*." She stood. "I'm sorry, Ellis. Truly. I shouldn't've... I just haven't the time." She took a step back.

"Dillie, I swear, if you don't—"

"I honestly can't, Ellis, I'm sorry, I really am." Still edging away. "This has been months in coming, and I swear you'll get the story straight from me as soon as I get back."

"Back from *where*?" It hurt—it hurt a lot, and oh, *there* was the pain he hadn't felt before—but Ellis managed to prop himself up on the elbow that wasn't a mess of bandages. "Is there a new offensive? Where's the front now? If we gained back all the lost ground, what are you—?"

"Ellis, I'm telling you, I can't—"

"Yes, fine, keep your bloody secrets if it makes you feel better. I'm only..." Ellis forced his brain into motion, because there was something... *something*... His fingers were nearly cramping around the stone. It was somehow wriggling through the larger pain flaring in sharp spikes and barbs all over him. "Are those dragons still out there?"

And yes. That was it. Because Ellis wasn't going to fool himself that he wasn't done, and fairly useless. At least for now. There was no effect he was going to be able to have on what came next, whatever it was that Dilys was here for, was leaving for, wouldn't tell him about. But it was big, Ellis could tell. Things were about to happen. And he was supposed to have been here for a reason.

Lilibet was his mam, she loved him, and she'd have done anything to keep him safe. But she wouldn't have lied about Dreams to do it. Dreams were sacred to someone like her. It wouldn't even have occurred to her. She'd convinced Milo that Ellis needed to be here, in Wellech, that his presence would somehow be necessary. She'd stood behind it firmly when Ellis had found out and shouted her down. Ellis needed to be in Wellech. *Wellech* needed Ellis in Wellech. And here Ellis was now, taken out of the equation entirely. There was nothing he could do from here.

Except maybe this one thing.

"The dragons. They're down to the two bellwings. Are they still in it?"

Dilys frowned, bemused. "Yeah? But Wellech have got the two stones now, and Tirryderch know our shields. Mine are almost as good as Milo's. So you mustn't worry about—"

"Oh, don't insult me, Dillie. Of *course* I'm going to bloody worry about you, I don't care *how* good you are at what you do. I only—" The hand Ellis needed was currently helping to prop him up. He let himself drop back to the thin mattress with a huff, then a wince because bloody *ow*, and uncurled his fist. "Here. Take this."

And this... *this* was going to hurt. Because Ellis had grown more and more sure as this war dragged on that it was the stone that somehow connected him to Milo and gave him the Dreams. Thing was, that connection had been... perhaps not lost entirely, but hampered at least, and made nearly useless. He couldn't even tell if Milo was still alive. But if it might keep *Dilys* alive...

Dilys came in slowly, gaze nailed to the stone atop Ellis's palm, mouth slightly open in what looked like awe. "He gave it to you."

"And if—" Ellis swallowed. His throat was all of a sudden bone-dry. "If it'll keep you safe, he'd flay me for not handing it over."

"But..." Dilys bit her lip. "I'm not clan. We don't even know if the other two will work."

"Maybe they won't." Everything was starting to drag for Ellis. The whole world was abruptly turning heavy. And painful. And damn it, he'd only been awake for barely five minutes! "But you're *my* clan. So maybe this one will."

Make sure whoever uses it actually loves them, Ellis had told Walsh, urgent. *They're smart, they can tell. Milo says they can See.*

No one had spotted the ravager from Tair Afon in Wellech again. And it hadn't shown up in any battle anywhere else since. It *had* to mean something.

He jerked his chin at his hand, because it was starting to shake and he didn't think he could hold it up much longer. "All you have to do is love them." It came out slurred as Dilys gently took the stone. Ellis let his arm drop, weighted like an anchor. "Love them like Milo does. And they'll know."

Dilys already did love them. Ellis didn't think Milo suspected, but Ellis had always known that Dilys secretly idolized Milo, which was the only reason she didn't perish from envy that he was dragonkin and she wasn't.

So when she leaned down, whispered, "Ta, love," and dropped a soft kiss to his brow, Ellis told himself a dragon *had* to love what Milo loved—why else would Ellis still be alive?—*had* to keep safe what Milo wanted safe, Dilys would be *fine*, and let the heavy blank dark pull him down.

The end had already begun by the time Dilys had shown up at Ellis's bedside.

It started with Preidyn's western ally Torope sneaking into the war—literally. *Now* Ellis knew why Tirryderch hadn't come when he'd begged Dilys. Their magical folk—every one of them but for Dilys and Terrwyn—had been scattered on daycruisers off the coasts of the western outer islands, conjuring cover over the Blackson, while Torope maneuvered its navy into position beneath it.

Torope waited until its navy more or less lined the ocean from Werrdig to Vistosa before it proffered a formal decree. And while Taraverde's ears were still ringing with the proclamation, Torope landed shock troops on the Surgebreaks. It was barely even a fight. Desgaul, already with a foothold in Blackfish Bay, swarmed northeast, chasing seven enemy troopships led by one of the bellwings. Three of the ships made it through the lines and headed straight for Surreywitch.

The dragon arrowed in over Gefēonde, silver-white light preceding it to mark the Royal Forces lines that had just pushed the Confederation back to the beaches. What happened next was already shifting into legend by the time Ellis heard it.

Dilys. Because of course it *would* be Dilys. Walking calmly through a path the soldiers of the 142nd opened for her. Stepping out into the open, nothing but a conjured shield between her and the bellwing swooping in over the carriers in the sound. The dragonstone held aloft in her hand.

Ellis wasn't sure he'd ever know what really happened on that beach, or what Dilys had actually done, because Ellis was still flat on his back, staring at the tent's canvas ceiling, and the story got wilder every time he heard it. And Dilys's account would top them all when he finally saw her again.

Some versions said the dragon landed in front of her and bowed like a royal subject. Some said it screamed as though struck, and wheeled off over the sound and out to sea.

Ellis assumed it had actually happened the same way it had with him—the dragon had acknowledged someone holding a dragonstone as clan and, given a choice between kin who'd betrayed it and clan that offered an alternative, chose the alternative. Because the same thing happened when the other bellwing came in over Silver Run and some soldier Ellis didn't know wielded one of the stones Aleks had sent.

No one knew yet where either dragon had gone. It didn't matter.

Once the last of the Confederation's most fearsome weapons had abandoned them, once they realized it was all or nothing, they dug into the narrow ground they'd managed to hold on the southern and eastern shores of Wellech. Except the absence of the dragons opened up the sky again, and Werrdig's Air Brigade took immediate advantage. The landscape of Wellech would never be the same, but the constant air raids did their part in finally forcing the Confederation to abandon what was left of Hollywell. They scattered for what little high ground they could find to the south of it. It left them pinned between the advancing Royal Forces and the coast.

The Battle of Torcalon heated up again, the Confederation well aware that winning Wellech meant winning Kymbrygh, and thus winning Preidyn and the war. So they stuck in like ticks and rained every last canister of gas they had across the lines. That's when the 153rd Kymbrygh showed up, apparently called back from somewhere near Colorat and arrived in through Caeryngryf only days before. As if the reinforcements weren't enough to gladden every heart in Wellech, the fact they came bearing crates of gasmasks— for soldier, Warden, and civilian alike—as well as a stockpile of heavy artillery, all but provoked parties in the streets.

And then things got ugly.

Western Unified troops Ellis hadn't even known existed had apparently been waiting on Preidyn's west coast. When Confederation carriers broke through the Southern Fleet's lines, battalions from Błodwyl, Macran, and Desgaul—along with a full division of Royal Forces marines—poured across the Red Coral Strait like locusts. The ferries, escorted across the strait by the Air Brigade, never stopped.

The entirety of Kymbrygh's east coast was a battlefield. Once again, Wellech's beaches turned red with blood. Enemy soldiers who'd tried and failed to install a network of trenches in the dense forest of Torcalon were abruptly finding themselves fighting on two fronts.

And then the 2nd Tirryderch swarmed in. The Confederation's sporadic magical assaults turned to defenses. Dozens of witches and sorcerers—taught in Tirryderch's best schools; initiated at Ynys Dawel; honed on the Blackson—bombarded the enemy lines with strikes both brutal and precise. Fog billowed out like a vanguard, catching the lethal gasses launched from the thick of the forest and blowing them back. Arrows fletched with hexes soared like flocks of ravens, following trails of magic around trunk and branch to pinpoint enemy targets wherever they hunkered. As though in homage—to the Black Dogs, to the Queen herself—three colossal birds made of mist gamboled overhead, razor-beaked and fire-eyed. Dreadful as dragons, they skimmed the tops of Torcalon's trees and screeched calls loud and piercing enough to wake the dead and terrify the living into wishing they were.

The Adar Rhiannon. Pulled from Kymbrygh myth just like the Black Dogs. Except with a bit of an in-joke twist to it. Because who else but those of Tirryderch—though Ellis knew, *knew* this one was down to Dilys—would fetch a pun into battle? More to the point— who else would make it *work*?

It was a matter of hours before the surrender came.

From there it was like a house of cards. One battalion after another folded, up and down the coast.

And while all that had been going on, divisions from Desgaul and Eretia took advantage of the near centralization of the Confederation's troops in Kymbrygh. Because, with a willingness to fight in the open like they'd never done before, the Black Dog Corp had charged their way into the center of continental warfare, and Western Unified was more than willing to let them open the way.

As though to make a point, the Black Dogs stormed the borders of Taraverde, and plowed corridors through whole battalions, raining the kind of destruction that couldn't be anything but purposeful and deliberately vicious. Ellis was left in no doubt at all that Ceri Priddy in particular was out for blood and on the hunt for her son. And determined to make anyone in her path pay.

If Preidyn had been stretched thin across the continent, the Confederation, no doubt thinking they sensed blood in the water, had allowed themselves to be stretched even thinner. Now they were caught in a scramble, companies pulling back from active battles and divisions diverting to try to intercept the Black Dogs.

It didn't work. The Black Dogs only got more spiteful.

They decimated whole swaths of Taraverde that had been untouchable until then, driving the enemy out of their trenches like swarms of rats, and picking them off as they came. No hidden spies this time, no stealth missions that could be written off to assumption and rumor. They fought in open battle, magical avatars as outriders, eyes like red coals and teeth like fangs, and the ones who commanded them no less fierce. They made no secret of where they were heading—their path never wavered from a straight line leading toward Taraverde's capitol.

The Premier wanted personal? Ceri Priddy would give him personal.

The way nearly cleared now, Western Unified redoubled their offensives in the central theater and advanced on Taraverde itself, driving in on the Black Dogs' wake. The distraction and sudden scramble of Taraverde's troops to its Premier's defense enabled Błodwyl, Nasbrun, and Esplad to swoop in from three fronts and finally break Ostlich-Sztym's lines.

Ellis heard it all from his hospital cot. Nurses' chatter. Staticky squawks from the radio. All of it somehow louder, seemingly more important, than the steady barrages he could hear coming from the east at all hours. A reality he was only hearing from a distance, while he ached and itched and tried not to whine too much when the pain flared. Because there were men and women out there dying with every boom and blast, and he *wasn't there.*

It was strange, he thought while he stared up at sunlight through canvas. Passing strange that even the words "truce" and "peace" and "over" only came to him from miles away, leaving him dull and numb while jubilation erupted around him. Whoops and cheers and hugs and kisses, songs of thanks swirling up to the goddesses like ash from an autumn bonfire.

He slept. He didn't Dream, but he dreamed.

Dead eyes glinting with fire. A song from a young man past singing, his pleasant tenor nonetheless fanning out and up on thermals born of dragonfire:

War's took my cariad far from me

Chapter 24—Recapitulation

: the third aspect of Classic sonata form; in this section, both themes of the exposition are restated in the home key (the second theme gives up its opposing key center)

Lilibet. Was *Tamping*.

"...last thing I *ever* do for that man, you see if it isn't."

She was talking about Alton. Snarling about Alton, really.

Sometime in the past few months—when Ellis had been out in the wilderness; when the danger to everyone in Wellech had ramped up—Alton had ordered Lilibet to take Bamps and retreat to the Kymbrygh MP's estate in Dinas Ganalog. *Your Dreams are too valuable to risk you*, he'd said. *Your country needs you safe and Dreaming*, he'd insisted.

"That bloody-minded, self-important, thoughtless *arse* is going to—"

"Mam." Ellis couldn't help the budding grin as he patted at Lilibet's hand—set atop his sternum. Healing charms were pulsing all through him, potent enough to hurt as they mended, and hot enough to make him sweat. "He told you as soon as he could. And you're here now."

"He could've told me a bloody *week* ago. Then p'raps *my son* wouldn't've been lying here *in pain* for all this time, while bloody *Mastermind* pried *just one more Dream* and then *just one more, I swear* from out my bloody skull!"

It wasn't funny. She was nearly gnashing her teeth—anger, worry, fright—as she bent over Ellis and *push-push-pushed* healing magic into him with her jaw set tight and wrathful tears shining in her dark eyes. It wasn't funny at all. Still, Ellis carefully kept his smile and made himself relax beneath her hands.

"He did what was necessary."

"He did exactly what Nia said he'd do. They all did."

"*We* all did." Ellis looked steadily at his mam, her hair a frazzled mess, her collar twisted, her fingers curved like rigid claws and yet still so gentle where they touched him. He'd never seen her so... undone. He kept his voice low and even. "Mam. I'm alive. I'm staying that way. All right?" He dipped his chin, trying to get her to look at him, but she wouldn't. "You Dreamed a long time ago that all this was coming."

She reared back as though struck, expression horrified, but she didn't move her hands and she didn't stop pushing charms into him. "I didn't Dream *this*. If I had, I'd've—"

"What? Sacrificed Wellech? Kymbrygh? Preidyn? Half the world?" He shook his head. "I admit I had more heroic things in mind when I found out about it." His smirk was a touch rueful. "Thought maybe I'd do something worth a good story, something they'd write songs about, y'know?"

"You *did* do—"

"I did no more than anyone else. Small things. The things I *could* do. Things that were necessary." Ellis angled a restrained shrug, probably too blasé for Lilibet's current mood, but he'd been thinking about this. "I wasn't meant to be the hero of this story. I don't know what you Dreamed, but I think for once you Dreamed wrongly. I didn't have to be here. Wellech was saved, but it wasn't—"

"Oh, *rot* to that! You pulled Wellech together. We couldn't've held them off half as well if you hadn't done. *Wellech Unedig, Kymbrygh Unedig, Preidyn Unedig.* You made that happen, Ellis. *You* did. You got rid of Crilly—d'you think *he* could've led the Home Guard through all this the way Walsh did? And all those bloody-minded raids, as though you were trying to out-do the Black Dog herself. If it weren't for your foolishness at Tair Afon, we'd've been done-for months ago. And that's not even counting pulling those dragonstones out your arse the way—"

"That's exactly what I mean, Mam. I'm not complaining, and I'm not selling myself short, but I'm also not fooling myself. I was only meant to hand others the things that would make them heroes. It was a part that needed playing, and I'm glad to have been able to play it. I just don't get songs written about me, that's all. 'S not so bad."

Once Upon a Time there was a man who knew lots of important people who did lots of important things.

He couldn't help the sudden laugh, surprised and pleased when it didn't make his chest feel like it was caving in. "Save me, I'm a minor character in my own bloody story."

Now *that* was funny.

Lilibet didn't seem to think so. She was glaring. "A story that was nearly a tragedy. I won't have you be so glib about it."

"But it *wasn't*, Mam. A tragedy, I mean. At least..." His smile dimmed, and he looked away. "At least not this part of it."

Lilibet was silent, ostensibly back to concentrating on what she was doing, but really watching Ellis. She pulled in a breath. Two.

"Alton thinks they've found him."

Ellis jolted so hard he nearly knocked his mam off her stool. "*What?*" He tried to sit up—she held him down. "*Milo?* Are you talking about Milo? They've found him? Is he...?" He couldn't make himself ask the question.

"Ellis Morgan, *lie down!*" Lilibet snapped, pushing at him and peering over her shoulder to see if any of the nurses were giving them the stink-eye. Skirmishes were still happening here and there, and wounded were still coming in. The cots here were nearly all occupied, and Lilibet had only been allowed in on special orders from Alton himself, provided she lend her healing talents to others besides her son. "I said they *think* they've found him. In Taraverde. I didn't want to say until I heard something more definite, but the raid on the prison camp has got Ceri written all over it, and yes, if it's him, he's alive. Only—" She cut herself off.

Ellis narrowed his eyes. "Only *what?*"

She pulled her hands away. Ellis felt the lack of heat immediately. He shivered a bit but didn't complain.

"*Only,*" Lilibet said slowly, "the young man they rescued is..." She pursed her lips, wrung her hands. Ellis was tempted to shake her before she finally shut her eyes, pushed out a long breath, as though bracing herself, and looked him in the eye. "You know that when a witch or sorcerer or mage is... hurt. It makes it difficult to use magic. It takes a lot of energy and a lot of concentration, and pain rather crowds that out." She tilted her head. "It's possible that's why your Dreams were so hard in coming, and then why they've stopped."

"I wasn't hurt when the dreams stopped."

"Ellis. Love." Lilibet's tone was cautious, her expression sympathetic. "I didn't mean you."

It was like a solid punch to the solar plexus. Ellis had to breathe through it for a moment before he could ask, "How bad?"

Lilibet's chin wobbled. Her eyes got bright again. It was a reminder that Ellis wasn't the only one who loved Milo.

"Bad." Too soft. Lilibet shook her head, set her jaw. "He'd been shot. Several times. He's..." She bit her lip. "He's lost a leg." She paused when Ellis sucked in a tight breath, then went on, "And apparently, when that wasn't enough to keep him down, they started breaking bones."

Ellis's gut roiled.

Unless, of course, you kept them in pain, but we wouldn't want to be cruel about—

Folant's voice. Telling Ellis over jars of elderflower ale how to keep a mage in a cell.

They'd known Milo was Dewin.

"I have to go." It was probably more forceful than Ellis's voice had been for weeks.

"Yes," Lilibet said, quiet. "I know."

It was definitely Milo. Confirmation came a few days later from Alton himself. He didn't even argue when Lilibet demanded he arrange passage for Ellis—*after* Lilibet was satisfied Ellis was healed well enough, and *Do not test me on this, Ellis Morgan!*

Three weeks Ellis stewed and fretted and haunted the communications tent until they booted him out. Three weeks he wished for that stone back so he could at least *try* to Dream, to see, to *know*.

Ceri was there, Ellis told himself. If nothing else, Milo had his mam. A woman who'd apparently torn through half of Taraverde to find him, Black Dogs carving a swath of unquestionably vengeful destruction behind her, and got him to a sanitorium in newly liberated Colorat. *Safe*.

It... wasn't enough.

It would have to be.

When the transport lorry finally arrived to let Ellis hitch a ride with soldiers set to ship out to various points from Caeryngryf, Ellis was not even a little surprised to see Dilys hop down from the bed of it and start toward him. She was trying to smile but it was grim.

She nodded to Lilibet, held her hand out to Ellis. When Ellis reached out, Dilys set the dragonstone gently on his open palm and said, "Ready?"

He was still in pain, though not nearly as bad. He probably always would be. He slid the stone into his pocket, *where it belonged*, and snagged up the cane one of the nurses had pushed on him; Lilibet couldn't stop frowning at it. With a nod, he adjusted the sling he wasn't allowed to discard for another fortnight. Didn't matter. He turned to his mam.

"Bring them home," was all she said.

Ellis gave her a nod, short and sharp, leaned in to crush her in a hasty one-armed hug, then turned to Dilys.

"Let's go."

The captain of the cutter was too young, if anyone wanted Ellis's opinion. But he didn't suppose he could complain much—with the good fortune of a brisk wind at their backs, the captain put the spinnaker to good use, and then they were flying across the Goshor. Kymbrygh was but a small shadow behind them. According to the petty officer assigned to the delivery of the stores they carried, they should make it around Preidyn and to a safe berth in the Gulf of White Sands by early next morning. From there it would be a three-day train ride through Alliance-occupied Taraverde, down through Ostlich-Sztym—also occupied—and then into liberated Colorat.

Ellis couldn't keep still. Dilys was ready to strangle him.

He decided to avoid her and spent his hours on deck, bundled in a thick coat and watching the sun spark on the water then burnish its frothed peaks into laced gold. He had to keep himself from chuckling too often—it always seemed that the larger, more dangerous-looking the person, the more time that person spent hanging over the side of the ship. Several times Ellis had received embarrassed glances as some soldier turned six different shades of green, fought with his or her stomach for a few useless moments before giving up, taking hold of the jackline and heaving. Ellis always tactfully looked away and mentally gave thanksgiving for growing up in a place lousy with rivers. And if he ever snickered into his sleeve, it was only because he was feeling cautiously giddy.

Alive. Hurt badly. Sick with fever now, last Ellis heard. But *alive*.

Only now did he realize he hadn't dared hope, not really, not so he'd admit it to himself. Perhaps he'd thought the grief would be easier to bear if it was expected, he really couldn't say for sure. But now hope flared bright and warm, and he willingly gave himself over to it.

Other than that, he thought of little besides the sensations pouring over his skin—the fine mist of briny spray, the cold wind howling at his ears, hair grown too long and shaggy whipping his cheeks. The constant aches—arm, leg, chest—sometimes clamored for attention, and more so when he'd accidentally bump against the railing. Ellis resolutely pushed it all away. Nothing but gratitude and good thoughts were allowed.

The sun finally fell, a last gush of brilliant gilt-cardinal across a stratum of cloud gone azure-gray, but Ellis barely marked the change. Only kept watch as the sea foamed against the hull and the wind buffeted, bringing him ever closer. Someone brought him a camp chair and someone else brought him food twice, but he had no idea what he'd eaten and neither did he care. Soldiers and sailors alike, spirits high with a war just won, tried to engage him in conversation, but he couldn't remember whether whatever he'd answered back had been polite or had made any sense at all. Their warm smiles and the occasional careful clasp of his shoulder told him they understood, at least, and that he wasn't making a name for people of Wellech or Kymbrygh in general as being dim-witted or rude.

The stars disappeared quickly, it seemed: one moment they were there, wheeling across the plum-dark sky, and the next they'd already given way to a burst of violets and corals. It was when the main sheets were reefed and the lines readied that Ellis realized they were reaching port. His heart picked up pace. *Injured*, his mind kept telling him, and then his heart would answer back: *Alive*.

The cutter churned to life with the routine of docking, all hands taking up their duties with assured efficiency, and those not involved in the mechanics of it all taking great pains to stay out of the way. Ellis watched it all with the same soft smile he'd been surprised to find on his face quite often over the past two days, though his patience was sorely tested with each passing minute. Finally, it was done. Ellis rushed off to hunt Dilys down, found her below deck in the middle of a card game—winning, of course—and hauled her up and out. It was the work of minutes to find their cabin, collect their scant things, and head back up to join the push toward the gangway.

One leg of the journey done, one to go.

If it hadn't been for Dilys, the train ride would've been unbearable.

The passing landscape was only interesting for a little while. Lush countryside only now going gold with autumn, seemingly limitless until the train rolled through a stretch broken by wavering lines of trenches like worm trails in churned mud. Cities with skylines of arches and spires and bell towers on one side, shelled-out hulls like broken teeth on the other.

Their Pennaeth would be busy for a while, Ellis supposed. Or whatever they called them here. If they were still alive.

It was funny, though. Two years ago, the job of Wellech's Pennaeth had been one of the most important things Ellis thought he would ever do. Yet he'd left it all behind—every survey that needed arranging; every assessment of damage; every estimate of repair. Every citizen who'd lost a loved one and deserved a personal condolence visit from their Pennaeth. Ellis hadn't even thought of any of it. He'd stopped in Reescartref long enough to tell Petra she was in charge, and he'd left.

Milo had called Ellis Wellech's favored son once or twice. Ellis wasn't feeling very favored. He was barely feeling like a son. He hadn't even asked after Folant. For all Ellis knew—

"Every goddess have mercy, have you *tried* these things?"

Nearly moaning, Dilys thrust some sort of puff pastry with sugar powder all over the top at Ellis's mouth, giving him no choice but to open up or have custard smeared all over his chin. Or, no, wait, it was jam.

Dilys didn't even wait for him to chew before gushing, "*Right?* Have you ever had anything like it?"

Ellis hadn't. And it really was quite good. Dilys stuffed him with three more before she decided it was time to see how uncomfortable the beds in the sleeping berths were, and chivvied Ellis along.

"I'm not six, Dillie, and you're not my mam."

"Uh-huh," was all Dilys said, then shoved him into his sleeping car and slid the door shut.

Ellis stood there for a moment, blinking at the door, before yelling, "I'm only doing it because the lounge car is closed for the night!"

"Uh-huh," came Dilys's muffled voice from across the corridor before Ellis heard the sound of her door sliding closed.

That was more or less the entire trip—Dilys stuffing Ellis full of every decadent tidbit on the dining car's menu; Dilys chattering at him; Dilys pushing him into his cabin for a kip; Dilys reading bits of the broadsheets at him as though he couldn't read them himself; Dilys demanding card games; Dilys annoying him; Dilys *distracting* him.

Ellis didn't think he'd ever loved her more.

He also didn't think he'd ever been more grateful for the end of a trip when the train finally rattled into Werszewa, Colorat's capitol city, and chugged to a slow stop when it reached the station. Three days on a train had not done good things for Ellis's still healing injuries. He was sore, he was cranky, and teeth-gnashingly impatient to see Milo.

"C'mon, then, y' great child." Dilys took charge of both their travel cases and led the way down the aisle toward the doors. "Smile pretty now. We're liberating heroes here."

Ellis rolled his eyes and followed, accidentally-on-purpose smacking the back of her heel with his cane. "Maybe *you* are."

Dilys grinned over her shoulder, eyes wide in feigned surprise. "I totally *am*, aren't I?" She waggled her eyebrows, sly. "I'll get Milo to make me dragonkin yet, see if I don't."

Ellis couldn't help grinning back.

Ceri was waiting for them on the platform when they finally disembarked. Brittle-looking and pale with exhaustion, and more hardworn than she'd been last time Ellis had seen her. Freshly scarred across her furrowed brow, a blotchy burn mark that smeared down one side of her throat, starting at her jawbone and disappearing beneath her collar. She didn't smile when she spotted them, but her shoulders relaxed a bit and she allowed Dilys to hug her.

"He's all right?" Ellis couldn't help blurting in place of a greeting. "We've only heard 'alive but injured' and not much more. How is he?"

"Well, *haia* to you too, Ellis." It was fond and accompanied by a wry smirk. Ceri gestured to a car waiting on the street. "I'll tell you on the way."

Werszewa had barely been touched. Banners hung from nearly every building, shouting out words Ellis couldn't read, but they were bright and gay, so he assumed they were celebrating Colorat's liberation. The sanitorium was on the outskirts of the city, set amid green lawns and gardens riotous with autumn-blooming flowers.

Two dragons circled overhead, gliding calm and slow in a sky like slate. The stone had been growing warmer in Ellis's pocket for the past five minutes. He'd had the romantic notion that it was because he was getting nearer to Milo, though he'd known the thought for absurd even as he'd thought it. Still. It was weirdly disappointing to have it proven otherwise.

He wondered absently what those dragons would do, now that Colorat's preserve had been proven unsafe for them and its dragonkin—its *true* dragonkin—had fled and made his way all the way to Whitpool. Reaping was almost upon them, after all. Did they sense Milo down there somehow? Was that why they were hovering about the city?

With everything that had gone on with kin and stones and Dreaming, Ellis wouldn't be surprised.

"I wasn't best pleased about moving him," Ceri said as she led them from the car and up the stairs of the long gray building. "But it's safer here just now than it is in Taraverde. It's where Alton wanted him until he's well enough to be moved to Llundaintref, and it's where they've been sending the brass, so." She shrugged as she gestured them through the double doors and into the sanitorium's lobby.

"But he *is* recovering." Ellis couldn't help the way it came out hard and demanding.

Ceri's attempt at a smile was nothing more than a crimp of lips. "As well as can be expected. Considering."

Considering.

Considering that they hadn't dragged him from that muddy field to save his life but to prolong his suffering. The prison surgeons had deigned to remove the bullets that had been pumped into him, but had done it without ether. Had taken his leg—mangled by a burst of machine gunfire, Ellis had *watched* it—at the knee the same way. Milo had been awake and aware through all of it. And they'd watched him, recorded it all in laboratory notes, as though Milo were some kind of experiment. They *had* known he was Dewin, just as Ellis had feared, because whatever glamour Milo had been using to hide the hole in his ear where his earring belonged had dropped when he'd gone down. So when he hadn't died of shock or blood loss, when he'd started to *recover*, they'd started methodically breaking the bones of his hands.

It was still too surreal for Ellis. Milo—*his* Milo—had been tortured. Had *actually* been tortured.

They waited for Ceri to check in with the attendant behind the lobby desk. Nervous, for some odd reason, Dilys and Ellis both. Dilys's short, sharp glances were speaking a language Ellis didn't understand, and frankly didn't have the patience or wits to try to interpret just now.

Finally, the attendant gave Ceri a smile and a nod and sent her on her way. Considerate, Ceri set a slower pace than she probably normally would have, making allowances for Ellis and his cane tapping on the marble floor as he and Dilys followed her to Milo's ward.

When they reached a door halfway down the corridor, Ceri turned with a smile that came nowhere near her eyes. "Dillie, darling, they have a lovely tearoom here, and you won't believe some of the pastries. Why don't you and I go and have a nibble? We'll bring a treat back for the boys."

Clearly surprised, Dilys opened her mouth, no doubt to object, but in a rare moment of tact, caught herself.

Ellis wanted to tell her it was *fine, don't leave, stay with me*, because this, this moment right here, this was all he'd been able to think about for bloody *weeks*, and now that he was here, he was somehow scared down to his boots. He hadn't seen Milo in nearly two years. People could change a lot in two years. And the things they'd both done, the things they'd seen, the things they'd been through...

How did one greet the love of one's life when the last real thing between them had been a broken contract?

Dilys cleared her throat, said, "Right," shooting glances between Ellis and Ceri as though looking for the right thing to say. Eventually, she seemed to give up, slumped her shoulders, and said, "That would be lovely," to Ceri, though she was clearly trying to telegraph something at Ellis with her eyebrows as Ceri led her away.

Ellis had no idea what.

"Right," he echoed, turning back to the door, and... staring, abruptly finding it difficult to swallow. He clutched the cane, shifted on his feet, wincing when he put his weight on his bad leg. Lifted his hand to knock. Dropped it. Shifted again. Winced again. Rolled his eyes at himself, and said, "Right," again, then, "This is ridiculous," and gave the door a brisk knock with his knuckles before pushing it open.

Thin was the first thing Ellis thought. *Far, far too thin*, and pale, and sunken-eyed, and someone must've given him a shave at some point, because his beard wasn't that lush, full black growth Ellis had last seen in Dreams, but a three-day or more scruff that only made him look more pallid. *Bandages* was the next thing. Everywhere. Old bruises gone yellow-green. A great scabbed-over gash from temple to cheekbone. An unbalanced dip of sheets, a blank spot on the bed where the bottom half of his left leg ought to be. And it was only now, seeing Milo's hands swathed in gauze and tape, that Ellis made the connection, remembered crooked fingers skimming his cheek when he thought he was dying.

I need you to be all right, Elly.

"It was you." Ellis took an unsteady step forward, pulled almost, like Milo was a magnet and Ellis a powerless iron filing. "You were there. It was real."

Milo hadn't said a word yet. Only sat propped in the bed, staring at Ellis, blue eyes too bright and brimful. His chin wobbled and he clenched his teeth. Said, "You came," all hoarse and cracked, and his eyes spilled over. "You're *here*."

And that... *that*...

It would be all right. Four words, that was all, but that was all Ellis needed. Milo was in there, *Ellis's* Milo, behind those hollow eyes and that face that had aged ten years in two.

There was no choice. Ellis *had* to cross the rest of the distance. *Had* to drop the damned cane because it was about to be very much in the way. *Had* to crawl onto the bed and slide up alongside Milo, pull him in as carefully as he could, and lay his head to Milo's shoulder.

"Of *course* I'm here, you nit." Ellis shut his eyes tight but the tears squeezed out the corners anyway. "You're my home. Where else would I be?"

◉

It wasn't quite *The End*, and it certainly wasn't *And They Lived Happily Ever After*. Real stories didn't work that way.

It was getting used to a Milo who was quiet, contemplative. A Milo with secrets behind his eyes. Ellis had been so used to Ceri's standoffish nature, her restrained reserve that, in retrospect, screamed *spy! spy! spy!* that it took him a while to recognize the resemblance to the way Milo was now. Understandable when it came to national secrets, but when it came to *How are you feeling today?* it was just... wrong.

It was watching Milo in pain and being unable to do anything about it besides be there while he gritted his teeth through it.

It was thanking every goddess for Dilys, who had an uncanny ability to be bright and amusing and irreverent, all at the same time, without once tripping over something that shouldn't be said.

"Will you get a peg leg, Milo?" Dilys's grin was wicked while Ellis only gaped at her, and Ceri looked ready to take Ellis's cane to Dilys's head. "Ellis has got all sorts of dodgy connections, y'know.

It'd be a doddle for him to scare you up a pirate ship, and he'd look proper stunning with an eyepatch."

Milo, head sunk deep in the fluffy cushion—not sanitorium-issue but a special purchase by Ceri, as was the thick down quilt—blinked up at the ceiling for a moment, during which Ellis all but writhed in discomfort, until Milo... snorted. He lifted his head, shot a grin at Dilys then Ellis, that pensive look that seemed like his new normal all at once gone.

"Don't think I don't know you're only angling for first mate." Milo relaxed back into the cushion, still smiling. "Pirate life isn't only rum and dirty pub songs, y'know."

"O' course not." Dilys poked Milo gently through the bulky quilt. "There's tropical holidays and buried treasure too."

It was eventually understanding that Dilys had become a buffer between Ellis and Milo, pushing into a stilted conversation and taking it over, smoothing over barbs Ellis didn't even know were hidden in what he thought were innocuous statements or questions. So when late autumn wandered in with cold winds and gray skies, when Dilys reluctantly made arrangements to go home, Ellis... panicked.

"You can't go, not yet!"

"Sure I can. Because I'm a grownup and you're not the boss of me."

"But!" Ellis took the bundle of clothes Dilys was packing out of her hands. "He's not recovered yet."

"He won't be well enough to move until after Highwinter. I can't stay here that long. I'm surprised you can."

Ellis wasn't, not really. Most of the problems with running Wellech had come from Folant. According to Petra's regular reports disguised as letters, that was no longer an issue. Folant had retreated to Oed Tyddyn and only emerged to occasionally ask Petra if she'd heard from Ellis, and if the parish's coffers could do with a boost. Ellis had honestly thought Folant had gambled away most of his wealth, but according to Petra he was being very generous with his purse when it came to rebuilding Wellech.

"Dilys." Ellis snapped Dilys's travel case shut. He only just kept himself from sitting on it to prevent her from continuing to pack it. "You don't understand. You're the only who can make him smile!"

Dilys gave Ellis a sad quirk of lips and a sigh. "Then p'raps I should've gone a fortnight ago," she said, and took her clothes back.

After Dilys had gone, it was caution and tension, because everything Ellis said or did seemed to be the wrong thing, seemed to make Milo frown or get that thoughtful look in his eyes. And it *wasn't bloody fair* that Dilys could make a joke about Milo missing an actual body part and get a real laugh as reward, and Ellis couldn't even comment on the weather without making Milo go quiet and introspective.

It was nurses treating Milo like he was a tantruming child when he cried out in pain the first time they bundled him into several blankets and set him in a bath chair. It was Milo all gray and sweat-wet with exhaustion when they maneuvered him back out and into bed after a ten-minute stroll up and down the ward.

"I'm not sure I'll ever be able to play again." Milo's voice was low, almost a whisper, but still loud in the silence that had fallen between them once the nurses had retreated. Ellis lay across from Milo on the bed now, Milo staring at his hand on the cushion between them, thick white gauze wrapped around his splinted fingers. "That probably shouldn't seem worse to me than missing a leg, but..." His mouth pressed tight, and he frowned, as though he didn't quite understand it.

Ellis didn't either, not really. "Why did you never tell me you play?" He kept his voice just as quiet, like the boys they'd once been exchanging secrets long into the night. Except this had never been one of them.

Milo blinked at Ellis, bemused. "What?"

"You never told me, Milo. It means something to you, you're good enough you've been playing for a long time, and yet I never knew. Why?"

It was odd that this of all things made Milo smile, soft and teasing, but it did. "If you didn't know I can play, how would you even know how good—?"

"*Not* the point." Ellis rolled his eyes, and the only thing that kept him from snapping it out—because it *bothered* him, bothered him a lot—was that smile, and the fact that Ellis had caused it. *Finally.* Somehow. "Now answer the bloody question."

Milo shrugged, blue eyes blinking slow and sleepy, and words coming softer around the edges now, though not quite slurred. "I didn't... *not* tell you. I expect I didn't think... It's only... I didn't realize you didn't know." He frowned. "I played mostly at school, when I felt... lonely. Melancholy, I suppose. And then I started to play for the dragons, because they like it, and giving them something makes me feel..." He turned his bandaged hand palm-up then palm-down on the cushion, squinting at it sadly. "I play when I want to feel *Seen*, feel... better. I expect I just never needed it when you were about."

...Oh.

"That—" Ellis had to swallow the knot abruptly clogging his throat, and take a deep breath so he wouldn't blub, and he didn't even know where the startling onslaught of emotion was coming from. Relief, maybe, because yes, *that* made sense, or pride over being the one who could give something like that to someone like

Milo, or maybe just plain old *love* that was so deep and so real it felt too big for Ellis's chest as it pushed against his ribs and made it hard to breathe. "I'm... thank you."

"For what?"

Ellis puffed out a wobbly laugh. "I've no idea."

That smile again, and Milo met Ellis's gaze, soft-eyed and fond. It lasted just long enough for Ellis to go all warm and sloppy inside before it slid away and was replaced by one of those thoughtful looks.

"Elly." Milo moved his hand, skimmed it carefully along the bed until it nudged against Ellis's breastbone. "I'm not... not the same."

"Neither am I." Ellis looked away. "The goddesses only know how my changes are going to eventually leap out and bite me on the arse. *I* haven't even had time to identify them yet, let alone figure them out."

True enough it made him pause. Because Ellis wasn't the man Milo had left in Tirryderch. And he didn't know if it was because he'd changed, or because he simply hadn't been who he'd always thought he was. He'd killed people. He'd barely even mourned the necessity of it. He'd pondered better and faster ways to do it. Catching a life in his sights and triggering its end had been all too easy for Ellis. And he still wasn't sorry.

There had to be something as broken about that as there was about Milo and his eyes that went distant with remembered horrors too often. There had to be something missing from Ellis, a space inside him just as blank as the space beneath Milo's knee.

It was part of the story of war, he supposed—ordinary people living inside extraordinary moments, doing things within them they'd never considered, and either coming out the other side to another moment, or lying beside a shattered campfire, eyes limned gold, and watching all remaining moments just... drift away.

Rest in shadow

"I'd like it if we could," Milo said, and there was that caution again. "Figure it out, you know?"

Ellis frowned. "I'm not sure I do."

"And I'm not sure I know what..." Milo let it trail off, mouth an unhappy line, then tried again. "Elly. D'you... d'you want to—? No, that's not..." He shoved out a breath, exasperated, apparently with himself. "You don't know what to say to me anymore."

Ellis couldn't really argue with that. Still, something in his chest went heavy, even as his eyebrows shot up. "What does that even—?"

"You extolled the virtues of pushing that bloody chair around the entire time we walked the corridor."

"What has that got...?" Ellis couldn't quite follow the hard turn the conversation had taken. "It was only that it made it easier to walk without the cane, that's all I was—"

"And before that it was a proper treatise on how much better the pears are here. And before *that* it was an in-depth discussion with my mam about where she bought my bloody *blanket*."

"So my small talk needs some work. What's that to do with anything?'

"Small talk." Milo's voice was still quiet, paradoxically intimate. He pulled in a long breath, bracing. "It's only... I didn't leave things... well. Between us."

Ellis narrowed his eyes. "Exactly what are you trying to say here, Milo? Because I'm *really* not following."

And if they were back to *I'm leaving you for your own good*, there was going to be a serious problem.

As though he'd read Ellis's mind, Milo said, "You're waiting for an end."

He was so... *calm* about it. A fear Ellis hadn't even known was there, that all at once swamped him now that it had been named, and Milo had just plucked it up and dangled it like bait on a lure.

Ellis couldn't help but take it. He set his teeth. "And is this an end?"

"I don't know." Still quiet, still calm. "This is not me leaving you."

"Again."

"...Again." It seemed as though Milo wanted to look away, but he didn't. The corner of his mouth twitched up, incongruous, in a shadow of a rueful smile. "Pretty sure you could outrun me now anyway if I tried." He waited, a glimmer close to hope in blue eyes watching Ellis for... something; when Ellis didn't give it to him, whatever it might've been, the smile faded. "No. I'm not leaving you. It's only that I can't See you right now, I can't See anything, and I need... I need to *know*."

Milo sighed, looked at his hand, eyebrows squinched and mouth turned down. "You go where you're needed. And there you stay. Your mam said that to me, back before..." He looked back up at Ellis, straightforward and open. "And it's true. It's who you are. Whatever your changes might be, that's not one of them. And I don't want that to be why you're... I mean—" He stopped. Huffed. "I want it to be all right that *I* need you. I want it to be all right that I want you to stay. For more than bloody *small talk*, and what time my next pill is due. So..." He looked down again, then, as though forcing himself, back at Ellis. "Is it? All right?"

And... oh. *Oh.*

Ellis hadn't understood. From the moment he'd arrived and seen *thin* and *broken* and *hurt*, for the first time ever, he'd thought Milo something fragile and altered and guarded. But it was only that Ellis had been looking and not *Seeing*, and he hadn't understood. Altered, yes. Guarded, absolutely. But fragile had never been it. Ellis just hadn't been looking at Milo's changes properly, had allowed old fear to blur his sight.

This wasn't Milo in Wellech overthinking what he wanted because he didn't believe what was good for him was good for Ellis. This wasn't Milo in Tirryderch stewing and fretting and trying to find a way to tell Ellis that he was leaving him but it didn't mean he didn't love him. This wasn't Milo saying *I'll always be the man who loved you 'til the end* and severing a contract to prove it.

Milo didn't think he was brave. That was the thing. The man who'd volunteered to walk into a country that was literally hunting people like him didn't think he was brave. Doing what one saw as one's duty didn't equal bravery to Milo; it merely equaled a job that needed doing despite one's fears. And in matters of emotion? Well. Ellis could see it, that shying away, that unwillingness to take a chance, because an emotional risk to Milo was so much more visceral than any other kind. Walking into machine gunfire was easier than laying his heart in an open palm, offering.

It wasn't cowardice, at least Ellis had never seen it that way; it was merely a man who'd been told from the time he was a boy that he must hide himself. That everything he was, everything he loved, depended on it. It was why, after all, Ellis had sent a contract offer—because he'd acknowledged the want rising between them that fortuitous night in Wellech, and he'd known Milo wouldn't. Milo was forthright and to-the-point in most everything, but he didn't take chances when it came to his heart. Ellis had known for a long time, before he'd even had cause to define its shapes, that it was because Milo didn't really know how.

At least, he hadn't before. Not when he'd left Ellis in Tirryderch.

This was, consequently, a change Ellis hadn't known how to see until just this second. Strength grown resolute; self-doubt turned to daring; a core of steel tempered by things Ellis would probably never know, and made adamant.

And there Ellis had been, walking on eggshells, chattering nonsense to fill up the quiet spaces, being *careful*, because yes, he hadn't known what to say, and all of it had made him so blind he hadn't even known to look. And all of Milo's cautious quiet had merely been a wounded soul waiting for Ellis to *See* the broken places, and decide if he might love them too.

A smile bloomed, profound relief and misery shattered aborning, and Ellis's eyes went hot. "Is this you asking for a cariad contract?"

The look on Milo's face wasn't the hope intertwined with despair it had been in Wellech when Ellis had asked that question.

This look was surprise, then resolve, and a quick, decisive "Yes." Firm.

That heaviness in Ellis's chest lifted, all at once. In its place, a soft burn ignited, glowing warm and soft as the heart of a dragonstone.

"Milo." Ellis dipped in close, dropped his voice even lower. "I never signed the dissolution paperwork." Stern. Serious. "In point of fact, I never even opened it, you massive *git*."

Milo pulled back, startled, frowning, until he caught Ellis's badly hidden smirk. The confusion cleared, and Milo tried to glare around a begrudging smile, said, "Oi!" and shoved at Ellis's chest. It only took a second for him to remember why he shouldn't—he barked out a sharp "*Ow*, bloody blighting—" and jerked his hand back, eyes shut tight and breath hissing out through a pained grimace. Ellis sat up with a dismayed yelp, but he cut it off when he realized Milo was *laughing* through all the hissing, bulky hand held protectively to his chest but shoulders shaking with mirth and not sobs.

"Get back down here, Elly." Milo's voice was rough and hoarse, but the laughter was still trying to dominate the involuntary injured gasping, so Ellis did. He lay back down, carefully, and waited for Milo to get his breath back enough to say, "I'm not through with you yet."

And all Ellis could say was, "Great goddesses, I hope not," thick and all at once so intensely grateful he had to sigh it out and shut his eyes tight.

Calm now, more comfortable in his skin than he'd been in two long years, Ellis pulled the stone from its home in his waistcoat pocket, and set it on the cushion between them.

"I'm still clan." He paused, remembering a sunny day and a razorback calf and Milo crowing out declarations that *still* made Ellis's stomach swoop. "It saved me, Milo. Twice. Your heart, entwined with theirs, and still loving me so hard that dragons could feel it. They say I'm yours, you stonking great numpty. And who wants to argue with dragons?"

Milo pulled in a shaky breath, stared at the stone, said, "Oh, *Elly*," subdued and windless, then looked at Ellis. "Only." Milo's gaze turned sad, and he blinked. "I lost the key." His mouth trembled, and his eyes filled. "They... they took it, and I don't—"

"Well, then." Ellis slid his hand into his trouser pocket, awkward with his still healing arm and the way he was twisted on the bed, and laid another key on the cushion beside the stone. "Good thing they're not as rare as dragonstones."

Milo's smile came back, softer now, warm but still rueful. "The Sisters." He shook his head. "They'll still never approve it."

Ellis rather thought they might do. He wasn't sure yet how things were going to work out when they got home, but if there was one good thing this war had done, it was to open some options for them.

Whether Milo recovered enough to run Old Forge again or not, Ellis didn't think Aleks would be going anywhere. Not if Glynn had anything to say about it. Ty Dreigiau was big enough for six families; there was no reason it couldn't house two dragonkin. And there was no reason Ellis couldn't make a home among clan for at least part of the year.

Wellech needed a Pennaeth, it was true, but it didn't necessarily need Ellis. He'd taken the position from his tad because he'd had to, not because it was something he'd aspired to. The only job Ellis had ever *really* wanted was Warden, and he could do that in any parish, provided he healed enough to one day sit a horse again.

Petra, on the other hand, was clearly better at being Pennaeth than Ellis had ever been, doing the job in his absence because she was good at it, because she loved it. And Ellis didn't think it would take much to get the council to change the bylaws by the time he got back. Not after he'd blatantly abandoned Wellech and left Petra to lead it through the aftermath of a war. It was past time for positions of power and responsibility to be earned rather than inherited anyway.

"Maybe they won't approve it." Ellis reached up to brush dark hair from Milo's brow. "But I remember an old rumor that my mam somehow twisted the collective arms of the Sisters so you could inherit. I don't know what she could possibly have on them that might bend them to her will, but it would be only fair that she do the same for me so I can have the love of my life for my cariad."

Milo chewed his lip, said, "Elly?" small and tentative.

Ellis slid his fingers down over Milo's fuzzy jaw, thinking distractedly that he was going to find out if he could scare up a razor in this place, give Milo a shave, do it right, with hot towels and everything.

"Yeah?"

"Only..." Milo twitched a self-conscious smile, there and gone, and swept the stone and the key off the cushion. "Only I've not had a proper snog in two years. D'you think you could—?"

He didn't get to finish. Ellis didn't let him.

Epilogue—Coda

: a concluding section appended to the end of a work

Life was not a play. It was not a novel. There was no one clear beginning that could be recognized as a beginning except perhaps in hindsight. There was no discernable middle where one could judge the number of pages left and be confident the hardship was nearly done. There was no distinct end, only a continuation, a steady, sometimes reluctant journey onward into more unknowns.

This, Ellis decided, standing on the edge of a clearing outside Werszewa, the collar of his coat held tight against the biting wind with one hand, and extra blankets in the other, this he was going to mark as a beginning. Milo didn't know it yet, sitting in the middle of a wide stretch of autumn-pale grass, grin on his face and eyes shining. Someday Ellis might tell him that he'd written *Once Upon a Time* across their pages as he watched a dragon glide into a soft landing, tuck its wings, and make its way toward Milo. Eager, though stepping more lightly than Ellis would've thought possible, as though it knew Milo needed the caution. Dipping its nose as it got near, smoke curling from its nostrils, thick limbs folding and great eyes closing as it carefully laid its immense body in the grass and rested its head on the ground beside Milo's bath chair.

Ellis couldn't tell what Milo was saying to it—the wind was too loud and Ellis was too far away, giving Milo privacy for this renewal between a creature that was clearly much more than what most people thought it was, and the man who saved its clan. But he could tell Milo was saying something, and he could tell Milo's voice pleased the dragon, because it purled out a song, smooth as a string beneath a bow. Its tail curled around the other side of the bath chair, protective almost, and it sighed when Milo laid his bandaged hand to the side of its snout, leaned in to rest his forehead next to it. A communion of sorts, the nuances of which Ellis could never hope to be privy to, but he didn't need to be.

Once Upon a Time he jotted in lines that were not chiseled flat and stark into marbled history but laid soft and malleable as a sonata within the liminal spaces between the beats of his heart.

Once Upon a Time there was a man whose story was jarred out of true by a torn and ruined page, moments splotched in blood-red ink, and eternities—

No. Ellis shook his head. No, that wasn't right. Too woebegone and bleak for this moment of brilliance. A note out of tune.

A life could begin in the midst of war, it could end because of it, it could take on new meaning as a result of it, or it could lose what made it a life worth living. Ellis had only been a small part of a larger story, when it came down to it, but this one that he was living right now, this story was his.

Theirs.

Ellis Morgan, Milo Priddy—they were not names carved in marble. And this was absolutely not *The End*. Nor was it quite *And They Lived Happily Ever After* because there was no such thing.

Once Upon a Time Ellis wrote on pages that were not ruined but only empty, waiting, a glissando echoing in pause before the symphonic swell carried on to the next movement.

Once Upon a Time there was a man who only wanted to live in the brilliance of his moments, and broke himself trying to save everything he loved.

Once Upon a Time there was a man who loved the other man, loved every broken piece of him, and decided that as long as he got to live in the brilliance with him, there were a lot more pages of their story that needed filling.

And They Lived...

Carole Cummings lives with her husband and family in Pennsylvania, USA, where she spends her time trying to find time to write. Recipient of various amateur and professional writing awards, several of her short stories have been translated into Spanish, German, Chinese and Polish.

Author of the Aisling and Wolf's-own series, Carole is currently in the process of developing several other works, including more short stories than anyone will ever want to read, and novels that turn into series when she's not looking. Carole is an avid reader of just about anything that's written well and has good characters. She is a lifelong writer of the 'movies' that run constantly in her head. Surprisingly, she does manage sleep in there somewhere, and though she is rumored to live on coffee and Pixy Stix™, no one has as yet suggested she might be more comfortable in a padded room.

...Well. Not to her face.

www.carolecummings.com

Independent Publishers Rock!

We appreciate your purchase of a Forest Path Book.

We do our best to cultivate distinctive and compelling stories for our readers.

If you enjoy our authors' efforts, kindly consider that a reader review can help spread the word.

To keep track of our latest releases, sales, & happenings, please join
Into the Forest
(the Forest Path Books reading group and newsletter)

https://forestpathbooks.com/into-the-forest

When you sign up for the newsletter, as our "Thank you!"
you'll receive a code for 15% off your first purchase at our store!

Forest Path Books
Independent Publishers of Divergent Speculative Fiction